THE PARALLEL APARTMENTS

by

BILL COTTER

MᶜSWEENEY'S

SAN FRANCISCO

www.mcsweeneys.net

Copyright © 2014 Bill Cotter

Cover illustration by Ron Regé, Jr.

McSweeney's and colophon are registered trademarks of McSweeney's,
a privately held company with wildly fluctuating resources.

ISBN: 978-1-938073-77-9

For Annie, whom I can't do without.

THE PARALLEL APARTMENTS

PART ONE

I

May 2004

Justine Moppett knew more or less why she didn't want to fuck Franklin. He scared her. He had many affairs. She didn't like him. And she had found him physically disgusting ever since the state of New York turned him loose from Sing Sing, in 1995, an event that ended not only Justine's own series of affairs (which began with one Henriette Desaulniers, a tidily self-scarified waitress from Chelsea), but the only years of occasional contentment that Justine had known, at least in New York.

And she did not want to fuck Franklin because she didn't want a baby. Why would she want a child if it might turn out the way she had? A cowardly runaway, a sexually imprecise mouse, a product of passive dysfunction, a suicide waiting to happen, a pharmacy employee? No. No children. And with only 99.98 percent effectiveness, *at best*, any form of birth control must be considered risky. One pregnancy per twenty thousand couplings was not assurance enough.

Conveniently, Justine rather preferred girls. Or, to be more precise yet less clear, she preferred non-men. She was still in love with her high-school guidance counselor, Gracie Yin, with whom she'd had no contact since Justine left Austin more than sixteen years ago. (In fact, she'd never had any meaningful contact with her at all; it had all been fantasy.)

Though she didn't like fucking Franklin, Justine stayed with him because it was easier than *not* staying. Justine wasn't going anywhere. She was a coward. Justine wanted to collage and be alone and watch *Law & Order* and experiment with the cognitive techniques for forgetting one's past that she read about on the internet but that never worked very well. Something really promising or ruinous or fetching or irresistible would have to happen to allow her to leave: Franklin going back to prison, her mother calling to apologize, a real shot at love, a Manhattan-sized comet exploding over Manhattan. The only real possibility among these was Franklin's recidivating.

Justine told herself she *had* to stay with Franklin. She told herself that Franklin had once saved her life. Whenever she grew ornery, Franklin would remind her that she owed him, that she had better let him fuck her now and then. And occasionally she did. She just made sure to douche with Krest Bitter Lemon Soda right after, and steal a few morning-after pills from her job at Midgie's Pharmacy, where she had started working within just a week of arriving in New York.

She had been seventeen, and freshly arrived in Port Authority, where she disembarked from a bus that smelled like the floor of a brothel, broke, alone, bleeding, wearing a torn, smelly, blood- and semen-striped blouse and Gracie Yin's underwear, with plans to become a hooker, which was the state of being the furthest removed from her sheltered Austin life, a life she would never, ever return to. In Austin, forty-eight hours earlier, she had witnessed something in her garage that she wished she had not. The hours leading up to that moment had begun, more or less, with a blow job—her sixteen-year-old Austin boyfriend, Troy, taking receipt, in his bedroom, while his profoundly deaf father sang sixties music in the den downstairs; the episode had ended two days later, also with a blow job—Franklin, thirty-four years old, under cover of a Hudson News kiosk in the world's largest bus terminal. After ejaculating in her mouth, Franklin, Justine's first and last customer, gave her ten dollars, took her by the hand, brought her upstairs to Forty-Second Street, hailed them a cab, lectured her on insisting on payment *before* performing the next time she fellated a stranger, and brought her home to his apartment in Hell's Kitchen, a not-unpleasant one-bedroom, where she spent the next half of her life tolerating a triple-bogey boyfriend, denying him a child, avoiding his rampant, bar-sinister penis, and growing to like him less and less, while at the same time he grew less and less likable, more aggressive, meaner, more controlling, more Franklin. This promenade was interrupted only once, very early on, by prison, where Franklin was placed after getting caught with his commodity in an underage throat at, where else, Port Authority.

One of Justine's only escapes from this existence was television. For instance, tonight's *Law & Order: SVU* marathon. It started at eight, in three hours. There sure as heck better be at least one episode Justine hadn't seen before. With luck, Franklin would find some reason to go out, leaving her alone with the remote, the refrigerator, and the thermostat, the last being the household contrivance over which Franklin held the most inflexible and fearsome dominion. Franklin—compact, neckless, insulated in pallid adult baby fat, coated with fur-like hair from collarbone to toe knuckles—was always hot. Justine—thin, unmeaty, paper-skinned, highly metabolic—was always cold.

The regular *L&O*s were great, even if they didn't bite quite like *SVU*, but *Criminal Intent*? A regularly scheduled letdown. Justine so loved Olivia Benson! She wished she was Olivia Benson. Liv would never have sucked off Franklin in a bus station when she was seventeen. Well, maybe, but she'd have arrested him right after, instead of moving in with him and spending the second half of her life trying to convince herself that the reason she wouldn't leave was her stick-to-itiveness, when it was really psychic intransigence borne of innate passivity. Only a few times in her life had Justine actually *acted*.

At the recommendation of their couples' counselor, Justine and Franklin went to see a sex therapist, Dr. Darling M'Nabb. The doctor insisted that Justine and Franklin go to the first of Darling M'Nabb's sexploration classes together. Dr. M'Nabb, whom Justine guessed to be about sixty, was in command of a huge, padded loft. She was built like Rosey Grier, and was wearing a tight, low-cut pink baby-doll tee emblazoned with glittery Pegacorns. Her entire face and neck were spackled with teriyaki-colored tanning makeup, yet her caulky décolletage she left unprimed: she looked as though she spent her spare time buried up to her neck in the Gobi.

Darling M'Nabb had her class pair off man-woman for digital prostate demystification. When Justine declined to participate, Franklin promptly partnered with the youngest-looking female in the class, Pilar, a thick-fingered but otherwise slender Cuban Chinese florist from Tenafly. Justine took her leave, descended from the West Village loft in a freight elevator through whose bars the chirps, shrieks, and moans of the prostate demysti-fiees three floors above reached her ears.

Of its own command the elevator skipped the ground floor and went straight to the basement. The door opened. In front of Justine was one of those old-fashioned soda vending machines whose access mechanism was not a trough into which an aluminum can is violently barfed, but rather a column of green-glass returnable bottles visible and identifiable only by their bottle caps, which all point at the consumer like vertical frigate cannon, and are accessible only by opening the long, slender glass jalousie door that protects them. Justine jammed a few quarters in, selected a Dr Pepper, seized it by the neck, and yanked it out like a baby tooth. She bought two more.

She never went back.

Franklin never missed a class. Over the following winter, spring, and summer, he went for special immersion retreats in the Berkshires, citrus buccal-stimulation delimited autoerotic asphyxia tutorials in Sedona, and warm river-stone gluteal hammerings in New Canaan. He would bring home sexual intelligence and vinyl tools and marital technics, none of which Justine would allow him to try out on her.

Late one night, some ten months into his erotic studies, Franklin, for the first time, came home with a third party.

Justine was sitting on the leather couch surrounded by mutilated books and magazines, spears of paper clippings, and a collection of glue sticks of varying adhesive powers. No *Law & Order*s were scheduled, but 4:15 a.m. was often rich in artistically inspiring programming, so Justine had the TV on mute, surfing between snippings, watching for arresting color schemes. She crossed her eyes and blurred her vision so that only abstract color and movement made it to her right brain. Ah, look there—a nice gazpacho red. What channel was this? Didn't matter. Justine knew exactly where a printed example of this color lay. She picked up a well-lanced copy of *Fútbol Mundial* and flipped to a page featuring some pencil-thighed drone from Arsenal. Justine snipped out a paramecium-shaped patch of his pepper-red jersey and stuck it down to her collage, a fantasia on *La poupée* featuring chimerical farm animals.

"Justine!"

Justine jumped, poking her thigh with the scissors.

"Ow."

"Look what I've got!"

It took Justine's eyes a moment to uncross and unblur, but when they did, she was not terribly surprised to see Franklin striding toward her, carrying, over one shoulder, bottom-first, a woman clad in grasshopper-green latex. "This is Epitymbria," said Franklin. "She's from Cyprus."

Franklin spanked the woman's bottom, eliciting a charming Mediterranean *ylp*, and set her gently on top of his ebony coffee table.

The coffee table, an inverted Malawian casket acquired at an open-air market in Queens, and its parallel companion, a huge, black-calfskin, bellows-like couch that farted out of an imperfect seam when sat upon, were two of the many objects that Franklin, immediately upon release from Ossining, had awarded himself for completing his sentence without getting raped or stompered or shivved or dropped in the hole. Franklin had behaved well in prison. Franklin had in fact cakewalked his stretch. To precise further, Franklin's sentence had been a lark, a goof, a success, an accelerated five-year undergraduate program in gaol arcana that graduated him, summa cum laude, in perfect preparation for his new life and fresh livelihood as a consultant. A prison consultant. Not just to meek, desk-jockey types convicted of bloodless financial enormities, but to any vulnerable convicts that would otherwise be Cheetos to the famished monsters who filled the modern-day American correctional facility. Franklin had finally settled on Bottom Bunk as a name for his sole-proprietorship—this after rejecting Stirmaster, Keeper of the Rosebud, Gang of One, and others.

Bottom Bunk had been good to him. It had bestowed his safe-deposit with Krugerrands, his spirit with identity, his desires with pussy, and his apartment with gravid black furniture. Franklin loved his couch. Franklin loved his coffee table. Franklin loved himself.

"Ouch," said Epitymbria, who had shifted her weight to one buttock and was massaging the other. "Mes fesses."

Justine did not look at Epitymbria sitting on the black coffee table rubbing her bottom, but the latex squeak provided the soundtrack to a vivid mental film. Justine loudly declared that since she was not interested in the second party, why would she be interested in a third?

"You don't even want to try?" Franklin said, obviously incredulous that someone would decline participation in one of the bedrock American dreams: the threesome.

"No, I do not."

"But look how great Epitymbria is."

"No."

Quamp, said the distorting latex. *Qut, quiwp.*

"Will you spot, then?"

"No." *Quub.*

"So I'll spot," said Franklin.

"No," Justine said, though with a bit less arms-crossed obstinance. Removing latex might be like peeling dried Elmer's from one's palm, an unbeatably satisfying diversion.

"Justine. Jesus. Will you at least audit?"

"I am going to see *The Philadelphia Story* before it leaves."

"Oh, I love Katharine, yes," said Epitymbria. "'I'm such an unholy mess of a girl.'"

Justine looked. Epitymbria looked back. Franklin seemed to vanish from the room. Epitymbria's chubby cheeks, dimpleless and perfectly smooth, were sirens for kisses. She wore a green latex trench coat and green latex mules and green latex kneepads. Shallow ligature marks, surely from a green latex rope, decorated her ankles. Her hair fell in a single thick dark wave, homogenous, a careless toss of black house paint, long enough that Justine could, if invited, hide beneath it and give herself up to the sirens.

"...oddamn movies, it's five o'clock in the a.m.," said Franklin, rematerializing. "Any idea what you'll miss at home? Justine? Huh?"

Epitymbria, her praline Cypriote cheeks howling for rough snogging, said: "'That's Miss Goddess to you.'"

"'Okay, Miss Goddess To Me,'" said Justine. Both women giggled in pleasant harmony at their recital.

"What's going on?"

Justine and Epitymbria were smiling like gassy infants. Justine covered her mouth with her scissor-holding hand, ashamed of her teeth, which had been interrupted in their orthodontia and remained gappy, not to mention a shade or two lighter where the braces had been, like dental tan lines. She noticed that Epitymbria's lower lashes brushed the tops of her cheeks, leaving rows of tiny mascara dots. Justine had never wanted to lick anything as much as she wanted to lick away those dotted lines. Maybe Justine *would* skip the movie.

But Franklin, possibly sensing the three's-a-crowd bazooka pointed at his head, quickly found a twenty, slapped it into Justine's hand, and led her to the door. "Have some Sour Patch Kids for all of us."

"Please put my collage things in my collage nook," said Justine, taking the twenty. If there was no one else in the theater, Justine would masturbate herself to stupefaction and sleep through the following showing.

"'Only in bed, Mother, and not always there,'" said Epitymbria.

When Justine arrived home, Epitymbria was gone. Long black hairs and shreds of green latex tinseled the living room. Franklin was lying in his raggedy yukata on the black leather couch. On the floor was a forty-quart pot filled with ice, in which Franklin had submerged one foot.

"What happened? What happened to your foot? Is Epitymbria okay?"

"Nothing; nothing; yes," said Franklin. "I had to give her your Hotel de Mallarde robe, though."

"Is—"

"Yes, she is."

The idea that Epitymbria had left naked but for Justine's white terry-cloth robe—complimentary raiment from a sexless and sleepless one-night stay at a boutique hotel some six months into Justine and Franklin's relationship—delighted Justine enough for Franklin to notice and misinterpret.

"Oh, you like that. Why didn't you just stay? Epitymbria knows a lot of tricks, lotta tricks."

"Then why aren't you with her? Have a baby with her. Then you'd have your stupid baby."

"Stupid baby."

"Yeah, an ankle-biter."

"Because I want one with you, Justine, damn you, you lezzy weirdo."

"I'm not a lezzy," said Justine, gently, recognizing in the hyper-Brooklynese way he pronounced *weirdo* the imminence of an ugly Franklin mood. "I'm just not sexual. Please let's not discuss the baby issue again."

"You brought it up!"

Justine smiled a little. She began to withdraw, which to her always felt like a tiny black hole opening up near her liver, slowly sucking her body into it. Lately, she'd found herself withdrawing more and more. Perhaps one day Justine would simply vanish, causing a sonic boom as all the surrounding air rushed in to fill the sudden vacuum. A smell of ozone, scraps of collage materials floating on the whorls of a violently stirred atmosphere.

Franklin grinned back brightly, looking a bit like an eight-year-old who had been given permission to discharge a pellet gun.

"That's a sex smile, I know one when I see one, my little Justine! How's about a little?"

"Mm, oh no, I'd rather not."

"I'll make it like it was, Justine. Like when we met. When I rescued you from your whoring debut—"

"I was not a whore," she said, prodding at the black hole near her liver. "And I didn't need rescuing."

She ducked into the bathroom to change into a nightgown so she could have a nap before work.

"—you and your outrageous green eyes and crazy bloody smile and third-world teeth. I made you love me then. I can do it again."

Justine went into the kitchen to satisfy a craving for sardines packed in olive oil.

Franklin then announced that he had just canceled on his current client, Mr. Nafarvedian, a once-respected bottled-water magnate who had just received forty-four years to life for buying and selling Eastern European children.

Justine stood in the kitchen doorway, ate sardines with her fingers, and watched Marla Mitz report the financial news on TV.

"Justine, you call in, too. Let's spend the day having sex."

She accidentally bit the inside of her lower lip.

"What?"

"I've got a new thing to try. Don't worry, Epitymbria didn't show me, and neither did Darling. I got it out of a *Cosmo* that was lying around the office. It's the shit. You'll like it—no straps or chants or shortening, I promise. And I'll do all the work."

Justine investigated her bit lip with her tongue. "I gotta go in. I have to inventory Tampax. It takes all day."

"I'll make you come."

Justine reddened. This was their sex. Franklin's assays, her dodges. His gambits, her retreats. His guilt trips, her guilt.

"No, it's too busy there, lotsa stuff coming up."

"Call Midgie," he said. "She'll let you off. And I'll get you off. Hahaha!"

"No, Franklin."

Franklin picked up the phone and dialed the number to Midgie's Pharmacy.

"Franklin, please don't do that."

"Hey, Midgie," said Franklin into the phone. "Look, Justine's sick. We're both sick. We're gonna feed each other pea soup and Nupe It and rest. No, she can't talk at the moment. She's on the commode. Yeah. No, that's Marla Mitz you hear. No, not here, on TV. Yeah. Really, Justine's laying cable. She'll be in tomorrow. She'll count cotton like a madwoman. Mm-hm. Bye, Midge."

"Franklin. Dammit."

He muted the TV. Carefully plucking his foot out of its ice bath, he limped up behind Justine, took her sardines away, then slid her ancient, gray cotton nightie up over her hips. He picked her up and laid her down on the black leather couch, which farted grandly. Franklin let his old robe fall. Naked, he stood next to her, closed his eyes, put his palms up out in front of him, and began to hum.

"You said no chanting."

He ignored her. He clenched his face into a constipated grimace. His erection grew.

"Put on a condom."

Franklin didn't protest. He reached into the pocket of his robe, pulled out a thirty-six-count family-pak of RootyRoot-brand lambskin condoms, tore one open, and rolled the stinky thing on.

"Put on another one."

Franklin rolled another one on, and then one more.

Justine turned to look at the TV. Even though not quite as spry as she used to be, Marla Mitz was still terribly attractive. She had always reminded Justine a little of Gracie Yin. More than a little. Something about her faintly yellowed canines.

A fantastic memory of Gracie quietly flared. High school. They ran into each other in the hall between classes. That's to say, they collided coming round a corner across from Mr. Chest's chemistry classroom. They wound up in each other's arms.

Justine noticed with surprise that she was modestly turned on. The black leather couch beneath her, usually tacky and cold, began to feel cozy.

Franklin got down on his knees, and, with his eyes still closed, spent several minutes arranging Justine in a way that made her feel like an ikebana project. For an instant she imagined Dr. M'Nabb at the end of the couch pumping her fists and weeping and waving a felt pennant: *Jusss… tine! Jusss… tine! Jusss… tine!*

Across the room Marla moved her mouth in silence. Justine watched. Marla's mouth formed lazy O's, gibbous moons, invitational puckers. Justine imagined kissing her, her tongue slipping through the tough curved glass of the television and between Marla-Gracie's lips.

Justine bit into her own cut lip. It tingled and bled. Franklin got on top of her and went to work in a complicated, bebop-like rhythm. He said he'd read about the present variant in *Cosmo*, but Justine was sure Darling had taught him this oddball syncopation. Justine didn't care. She began to buck back. Why had she been unconscious for so long? This was just fine. This was nice. Franklin had, after all, rescued her. She owed Franklin this at least once in a while. This was as good as love.

Justine held her breath as the first spinal chill of an orgasm sparkled and then dissipated. She stared unblinking at Marla, who had now fully transformed into Justine's old guidance counselor, her tie loose between her breasts and accidentally twisted a half turn so the label (Burberry) was visible, silently licking her lips and puckering in a silly, slatternly way. *Your PSATs are a little low at least you have an interest in art under my guidance-counselor-newscaster's desk I'm wearing brown suede kitten heels a half size too big come fuck me.*

Franklin worked steadily, occasionally pushing a thumb under Justine's rib. Marla-Gracie winked into three dimensions. She thrust her hand out of the TV and offered it to Justine. But she couldn't reach.

"Come closer," said Justine, without taking a breath.

Marla-Gracie came closer. Justine's eyes watered and her throat swelled and her lungs idled, waiting for the orgasm, waiting for the kiss. Justine closed her eyes. She stuck out her tongue as far as she could, and Marla-Gracie sucked it in.

Justine's ears popped, her heart forced blood through the constricting arteries in her thighs, she opened her eyes to look in Marla-Gracie's beautiful black eyes while they both came together.

But she wasn't there.

Buildings instead, woolly smoke from one of them drifting blackly to the left.

Franklin stopped moving. Justine bucked against him furiously, holding her breath an instant longer than she thought she could, sucking in air with a hollow shudder that burned her throat and dried her teeth, but it was too late. She trembled and buzzed from the missed orgasm. Franklin thrust one last time, came, withdrew, and sat at the end of the couch.

They watched the smoke and agonies and news crawls for the rest of 2001 like everyone else.

In spite of the condoms, Justine became pregnant. The pregnancy ended with the birth of their daughter, Valeria. Valeria lived for thirty-nine hours and two minutes, every instant of which she spent in miniature critical-care agony, until the late afternoon of June 8, 2002, when she smiled, once, and died.

On April 14, 2004, Justine became pregnant again.

She and Franklin were standing at either end of the woodblock island in the middle of their kitchen, exchanging humid sighs, pinched looks, and half sentences. Justine was sawing away at the tough end of an asparagus spear with a dull knife. Franklin was laboring over their taxes, belching now and again, the residua from a Whole Foods breakfast of three shots of wheatgrass juice chased immediately with a triple dulce de leche macchiato. This had sent him to the men's room first, and then to the drugstore for Kaopectate.

Franklin hulked over Schedule E, dabbing an inappropriate shade of Wite-Out over his mistakes.

Justine gave up on the asparagus and began to saw at a handsome red bell pepper.

"Won't cut," said Franklin, looking up. "That's because you didn't grow up with the right tools in the house. You didn't even have sharp knives. Know why? It's because there weren't any men around. Men like to have tools and sharp knives. I mean, I know you had razor blades, duh-right, but not paring, boning, slitting, cleaving, slicing, shaving knives. *Stabbers*."

Justine scarcely ever thought about the old cuts on her arms and legs and stomach. But now all the knife-chatter in the room awakened them all at once. They seemed to hiss with the exotic pain that the original slices had produced.

"Aah," said Justine.

"What?"

"Nothing." Justine sawed; finally the bell pepper gave. Inside was another, much smaller, green, and rather deformed pepper, growing parasitically from a rib. Shiny, translucent, fetal. She wondered if maybe there was another pepper inside the little one, and then another, like matryoshkas.

"That's what a pure matriarchy is good for. Dull tools." Franklin chuckled and belched. "Wait. My mistake. Wasn't your grandfather around for a while? Like just before you blew town to come to New York to whore and go to collage-college? Charlotte's husband? What was his name?"

Justine had not heard her mother's name spoken aloud in years. In Franklin's Brooklynese, "Charlotte" sounded like a sexual slur. And the mention of Justine's grandfather...

"Lou. I don't want to talk about them."

Justine tore out the tiny deformed pepper.

"That blade'll barely cut water for chrissake, Justine. I'm not hungry anyway. Definitely not for what you're making. Hah, just kidding, looks great."

Justine took a good whack at the little pepper. Instead of dividing, it shot out from under the blade, sailed out of the kitchen, and landed on the black leather couch.

"Please go get that; it might stain."

Justine went to find the pepper, but it had disappeared.

"I can't find it."

"Jesus, Justine."

"Jesus yourself, Franklin."

"The wit! Wooo! Did you get that from Lou or Charlotte?"

"Why do you care about my stupid family all of a sudden?"

"Because I was thinking about family in general, know why? Because of these documents here before me. We're not Married Filing Jointly and I can't claim Head of Household and I can't designate you a dependent and I can't designate a child who would now be nearly two, because she is dead. And plenty of other IRS reminders of family."

"It wasn't my fault," said Justine, though of course it had been.

"Yeah? It wasn't *me* that spent all their free time down at Ground Zero sucking in carcinogens and babycides."

"I was—"

"Helping. I know. Like letting a little kid help you make breakfast. They put up with you for a while, but you were in the way, Justine. Did you know I couldn't claim Valeria as a dependent in 2002? *She didn't live long enough.* It would've taken a couple grand at least off of my AGI."

"I knew you blamed me."

"Maybe that's why a destitute twenty-year-old widow would adopt a one-year-old. For tax purposes. Isn't that how old you were when your 'mama' adopted you?"

"Charlotte was twelve when she had my mother, and—"

"Twelve. Talk about precocious."

"—almost thirteen, for your information, and Livia adopted me when I was thirteen months."

"And Lou? I bet he was nine. Mannish boy. That's Texas for ya. Yee haw. Don't mess wuh Texas. Were they cousins? Brother and sister? Luke and Leia?"

Justine tore the wrap off two veal cutlets. She broke a couple of eggs into a metal bowl, and then into another poured some basil-garlic bread crumbs. "Fourteen. And they were in love."

"I bet they sent Lou to an oil patch and Charlotte to some Panhandle gulag."

Justine slapped a breaded veal cutlet into a cold skillet. "How did you know about the home?"

"I read minds," said Franklin, who leaned on the woodblock with his chin in his hand, no longer interested in taxes at all. "Besides, what else would happen to a pregnant junior-high-schooler during the Cold War? Where's Livia now? How could your grandparents and your mother all have pissed you off so much? What the fuck happened? Some kind of talk-show family horror? Oprah, Jerry, Geraldo?"

Justine turned red.

"Look. You never blush. Only when…"

"I know. But that's not why."

"…there's fucking on your mind!"

Justine threw the other cutlet into the skillet. She turned the dial for the burner, but the automatic pilot light just clicked and clicked, refusing to ignite the gas. The rubbery musk of liberated methane swirled around them.

"Fuck you, Franklin."

"C'mon, what happened? You caught your mother doing it with a cowpoke? A Mescan? A Neegrah?"

Justine grew cerise. Her cheeks hurt. She ripped out a kitchen drawer to look for a box of matches. She found one. It was empty. She threw it at Franklin.

"There's a lighter in there," said Franklin, who didn't even blink when the matchbox hit him on a pinkie knuckle and bounced into the bowl with the beaten egg. "God, I love it when you throw. Turns me o-o-o-on."

Justine found a tiny pink Bic lighter, tried it twenty or thirty times without success, and tossed it back into the drawer.

"I'm the only thing on fire in here," he said, licking a finger and touching his forearm. "Sssssssssssss."

"Don't, Franklin," said Justine, breathing in deep the local combustible vapors. "I don't want to do anything."

"Why?" said Franklin. "Perhaps you need psychoanalysis. Mein little Chustine. I heff unt larch Vienna sossitch for you." He pushed aside his tax forms. "I vant to place it into yorn schnitzel."

"Quit."

Franklin giggled. He feinted, as though he was going to chase Justine around the island. She jumped to her left. He started to chase her for real.

"C'mon, little dogie. Lemme git some. Yee haw."

"Franklin, quit."

He stopped and reached across the island as quick as a bantamweight and hooked two fingers between the buttons of her blouse. She slapped at his hand until he let go, but not before he'd torn three buttons off and dislocated her bra, exposing a nipple.

"Damn you."

"You know that's what I love about you. Those flat titties and big black nips. Like charcoal briquettes. Lemme squirt fluid on 'em and light 'em up. Rowr."

He swept the bread crumbs, egg yolks, vegetables, knife, antidiarrheals, and tax forms off the woodblock. He climbed on top. Justine slipped on the yolks and fell hard. Franklin reached down and grabbed her blouse again. It came off completely when she began to scurry on her hands and knees toward the living room.

Franklin came after her. He chased her into the bedroom. He cornered her in the bathroom, picked her up, and tossed her over his shoulder. For a pasty little man, he was strong, with hairy forearms like stone beneath the half inch of soft, indoor, fluorescence-baked baby fat.

"Done snared me a one," he said. "Gon' have me a lil' poke!"

Justine grabbed a rusting can of Barbasol off of the sink and hit him on the back of the head. A little dollop of shaving cream escaped and stuck to her wrist.

"Ow. You bitch. Yow."

He squeezed her. He exhaled his playfulness. He carried her into the living room. She hit him with the Barbasol over and over. He pitched her onto the old black leather couch and got on top of her. He pinned her hands against the arm of the couch.

"Off."

"No."

"Yes."

"What if I do things against your will?"

"Stop, Franklin, please."

"Guess how many men in the joint are there for spousal rape?" said Franklin, right into Justine's nostrils. "None."

Franklin, both hands busy holding her down, had nothing but his teeth with which to remove her bra. He bit right through the little bow at the cross-your-heart juncture.

"There they are!" He licked at her nipples with his Kaopectate-dried tongue, a horrible gray lizard convulsing on her chest.

"Off me, you bastard."

They both stopped struggling. Justine stared fiercely at her endless boyfriend. Now was when he grew either genuinely angry or pathetically skunkish. He chose the latter.

"Justine, please? I'm suffering here. It's been ages. I'm like teak down there. Please? It'll be good. I'm so turned on I promise it'll be over in a second. Pleasepleasepleeee…"

"No."

And, as if she'd consented, he reached down and pulled up her skirt. With her just-freed hand she covered her vagina. He stuck two fingers in her mouth. He tasted of bile and clay. The backs of her thighs were slick: egg. She was sweaty from fighting. The leather couch was still subtly tacky from the Armor All she had once used to clean it, after Valeria died.

Outside, it began to hail. Little white stones bounced off the window. They reminded Justine of Boggle cubes. Franklin stopped for an instant to see what the noise was. Then he looked at Justine with an expression of open desperation. Justine had never been able to ignore open desperation.

"Condoms," she said.

"Justine, c'mon. Let's bareback. Let's make another baby. C'mon."

"No. Put on your lambskins or get off me."

"They're not convenient and they're probably expired. C'mon, it'll be quick."

"Get off."

"No."

He reached down and violently pulled her hand away from her vagina, and, using his penis like a lobster fork, he managed to sneak it inside her panties and, ultimately, force his way inside her.

"Stop it! I do not want a baby! Ever, ever!"

She kicked him in the ass over and over with the heels of her Keds. He bucked and ground hard for a few seconds, and came. She felt no flood of pinguid warmth; Franklin had never been a copious producer.

"I hate you."

"I hate you."

"Get off."

"I love you. Let me get hard again, one more choadload."

"Take that thing out."

Franklin put his head on her shoulder. He soon fell asleep. Justine listened to Franklin's breathing and the *tikitiktiki* of Boggle cubes. His heart bumped against her collarbone. His respiration caught and stopped, as though he were breathing in and out a strand of yarn interrupted here and there with little knots. And his heartbeat—fast and regular, but each one followed by a tiny hiccup of arrhythmia. Justine wondered which of them would die first.

The following morning Justine went in for her shift at Midgie's. Next to the cabinet where the amber safety-cap twelve-dram pill bottles were kept was an unlabeled, unlocked drawer in which Midgie stored the morning-afters. Justine immediately dry-swallowed three and stole three dozen more. Each night, just before bed, she took another.

A few weeks later, while taking the trash out at work, a sudden nausea overtook her. The nauseas visited regularly for a full week until the day her period came, an atypically light spotting that stopped after a day. Her scalp hurt. Had she not been through this before, she would've thought she was merely dying. She wondered, with unexpected detachment, whether taking too much morning-after, rather than acting as a surety, simply canceled itself out. And, if not, why and how *she* had to be one of the small percentage for whom the pills did not work.

Later, Justine locked herself in the pharmacy's unisex employee bathroom, glanced once at the OSHA poster tacked up over the hand-soap squirter, sat down on the toilet, urinated onto an e.p.t. wand she'd stolen a few moments before, and waited with her thumbs pressed into her eyeballs for what surely must have been the required nine minutes. She opened her eyes, noted the inevitable, terrible smalt blue at the tip of the wand, considered having a good cry right there but decided to wait to go to the Ninth Avenue Dunkin' Donuts, where she did her best crying. She dropped the wand into the trash, where it landed prominently on a hillock of wadded brown paper towels, flushed, left the bathroom, returned to her register station, snuck some mifepristone into her red canvas Midgie's Pharmacy apron pocket, and left the store without a word to old Midgie, who had been busy all day crawling along the baseboards spraying ant trails with Pif Paf, and who wouldn't have paid Justine any attention anyway.

Justine had had several purgative, renewing wailings at this particular D&D over the last decade and more, and, for whatever reason, nobody ever bothered her. Nobody ever asked her what for. Most New Yorkers knew, somehow, when to leave somebody alone. It was a most valuable privacy.

Justine got in line for her ice coffee. Ahead of her, a homeless woman whom Justine had seen in here several times lately leaned over the glass doughnut case and pointed at the least appetizing thing in there: some kind of jellied cruller. The woman was wearing a heavy white canvas cloth with a hole cut out of the middle for her head, in the poncho style. What the original function of the cloth might have been was not immediately evident. A deaccessioned jib, maybe, or a shred of an infield tarp. Except for her height—at least six foot two—she looked like ten thousand other homeless women who'd gotten three dollars together and needed something better than the goddam mini-cans of water-packed tuna fish New Yorkers had recently taken to giving out instead of cash.

"No, not the cruller, thank you," said the woman. "Please give me two dozen doughnut holes. Plus I'd like a house-shaped box to carry them around in."

A Texan. A Hill Country Texan at that. But Justine had no energy to contemplate the dialectology of the homeless; she needed her damn ice coffee and her crying corner.

After doctoring her coffee with Splenda and sugar and milk, Justine squeaked a straw into the lid, sat down in her spot, and waited for the spigots to turn.

Her cries always began with a holding of the breath. Then a purpling of the face, a pulling-back of the lips, a baring of the gums, and an attenuating of the neck sinews. A squeak pitched at G-flat. Then: snot, drool, tears milky with salt, followed by a long, steadily amplifying *gnnn*, which, at the instant it began to tremolo, dropped two octaves, doubled in volume, transformed into a short, syrupy growl, and ended with a whistling gasp that dwindled to silence. Repeat.

After her third cry cycle, Justine looked around for more napkins; she had cashiered the chrome napkin holder before her.

She sensed behind her a large, canvas-draped presence.

"Here, baby," said the presence. Her pleasant warble reminded Justine of her grandfather.

Justine shook her head, shedding the memory like a wet dog twists to dry. Justine turned around.

The homeless woman looked like a witch in a German fable. The witch's hand emerged from a narrow opening in the stained canvas poncho, holding a thick stack of napkins.

"Thank you," said Justine, taking the offering. It seemed that the witch took advantage of proximity to brush Justine's hand with her own. It was limp, damp, and permanently soiled, like a root. She stared carefully at Justine through large, red-framed glasses that might as well have come right off of Sally Jessy Raphael's face. Her teeth shone, white and even—not something often seen among the homeless. Her nose was turned up, red and round, like a little Christmas bulb.

The witch leaned forward and stared into Justine's eyes with the curiosity and investment of an ocular surgeon. Then the witch jumped, turned away, and threw her head back with enough force to flip her long, ashen braids against her back.

"Oh Christ, the green there," she said to the ceiling.

The afternoon's lone employee, Meenakshi, paid as much attention to this outburst as she had ever paid to Justine's concussive bawls; *viz.*, little. This Dunkin' Donuts might as well have been the world's Parnassus for the public-outburst-prone.

The witch whipped back around, sending the braids into brief orbits.

"Hole?" Her doughnut carton emerged from the same opening the napkins had come from. There were seven left, all plain.

"That's okay."

"Why are you crying?"

"I'm... tired."

"How long have you been tired in New York?"

The witch stared, smiling, beseeching. Perfect white squares. Oh: dentures.

"Since, well, I guess 1988."

"Oh, poor thing, you came right to New York after you left, didn't you?"

Bullwhip hair. Watery, malarial eyes.

"Uh, do you live here?" said Justine, only subconsciously apprehending the witch's remark. "In New Y—"

"Are you married now?" said the witch, putting her doughnut house on the counter next to Justine's ice coffee, and throwing the wings of her poncho over her shoulders like a magician. Or a superhero. Or a vampire.

She sat down on a pink stool, put her elbows on the counter, then rested her enormous head in one of her roots.

Justine looked over at Meenakshi, who was leaning over the sink trying to bite off a piece of powdered-sugar doughnut without dusting her lipstick, a magnetic sienna Justine committed to memory in order to reproduce in magazine parings an abstract collage that would hopefully guide Justine into deciding what to do with this pregnancy. Abort the fetus now, or allow it to self-destruct after delivery, be it three days or seventeen years? *Do it now,* said the sword-wielding Justine; *Just let it do it to itself,* said the opposing Justine, crouched behind a poison sumac with her thumbs jammed into her ears. Justine sighed with such hot volume that condensation formed on the lid of her coffee.

"So," said the witch, like she was Justine's best friend, greedily begging for the sopping details of a one-night stand. "What's he like? Are you happy? Does he tell you how wonderful you are every day? Children?"

She reached out and touched Justine's hair, which was slick and matted from the sweat she invariably squeezed out of the pores along her hairline whenever she cried hard.

"You should have him brush your hair," the witch continued. "Prestige Mélange, I love that brand, it's good to cry now and then, you cry a lot, I've seen you cry, I know your cry, I've known it."

Justine stared back.

"I worry, you know," continued the witch. "Oh, daily, I think, What have I done? Why did I? I have no excuse, I offer none, I blamed him, but *I* did it; I didn't act quickly enough, that was what I did... didn't do. I know you hate me, and you should, you should. Darn it, we could have made it, too. We could've stole off in the night, together, I mean really together, as one, and gone to Phoenix. Or Richmond. Richmond was a good, pretty town then, 1971, or that's what people said. Could've gone there. As one."

Justine did not like being accosted by anyone, especially the occasional chatty homeless person who appeared to have modest gifts of historical clairvoyance and who could focus like a ruby laser on their particular vision. Justine reached into her apron—had she been wearing this the whole time?—for a dollar and slid it across the pink Formica under a root. The witch disappeared the note like a conjure.

"Thankyougodblesshaveanincredibleday."

The witch selected a hole, opened her mouth grotesquely, and tossed it in. Her lips snapped closed over it like the shutter on a large-format camera.

"But after all that, I really worried when you disappeared. I didn't expect it. I saw it on the news, your picture, in color. Yearbook picture, I know—I dropped into the school library later on to verify. Justine, so youthful, you look exactly the same now—"

"How do you know my name?" said Justine, exhausted, done from a dehydrating cry, not ready for whatever was now happening. The witch talked and talked.

"—a baby. I was so alone, before you. Who could I talk to? Not Quentinforce."

"Who are you?"

A vagal nausea, different from morning sickness, that she hadn't experienced since Austin began to rise like a moon in her gut.

"The only comfort Quentinforce ever offered me was when on our first anniversary he bought me my own bed. When you came to be with us I was never lonely. Even after they stole you—even if I didn't see you more than once every couple of years afterward—I would never be lonely again. I let you be, you know, when you were growing up. I knew that was best for both of us. I didn't seek you out; as long as you were near, in the city limits, I was all right."

Justine turned to make sure Meenakshi was still here. Yes; she had finished her doughnut, her twenty-dollar lipstick undusted.

"What's happening?" said Justine, unsure if she was addressing the witch or herself.

"Sometimes we would meet, by accident... you don't remember, I'm sure. I saw you a few times at Fiesta Mart, the one off Thirty-Eighth? At least three times. Isn't that funny? Once in the makeup aisle, you tried on blue mascara, bought that and a bottle of Dr Pepper and a Skor bar, you dropped your receipt outside and the wind blew it almost to I-35 but I caught it, I still have it. You paid with your ATM card 5545 1000 0678 3401 expiration 10/90 and once I saw you walking down South First with a boy, a little sweet thing, he loved you and I wonder how he is, is it him you married? and another time I saw you in a drugstore, working, you were working so hard behind the register, selling film and Brach's and Cogentin and Haldol, those're what I bought, do you remember? and once and I'll never forget this I saw you at St. David's emergency room, me I was there after Mrs. Cracy from Progress House dropped me off for not taking my pills and for getting loopy and falling off a bus-stop kiosk and cutting myself and you were there with a nice policewoman, Officer Prado, do you remember her? Big, big, big and strong, enough to carry you all by herself, you didn't have on any shoes and there must've been a hundred beach towels wrapped around your arm but there was so much blood soaked all the way through I thought you were holding a dead baby, I've never seen so much blood, before you got through the swinging doors you looked at me once, during an ad for Squirt gum—remember that stuff?—it was on the waiting-room TV, oh, I bet you weren't paying attention to TV at the time, hahaha, and I remember thinking the gum goo was the same green as your eyes, a green there's no name for except maybe in a dictionary but I wouldn't be able to find it, oh, they're just as mysterious and beautiful now as they were then."

The witch leaned within five inches of Justine's face and looked into one eye, then the other, then back again.

"And my pain disappeared," said the witch. "I told a nurse I was your mother and I asked if you were okay and she said you were going to be all right, and I was going to go inside to visit with you, but Officer Prado wouldn't allow that, she was just coming out from behind the swinging emergency-room doors, her black uniform shiny from blood, I decided I didn't need stitches for my little scratch, so I left, a man was already there with his dirty yellow bucket on wheels mopping up all the drops and smears of you on the floor, there were footprints in it, oh, I was sad all the way home to Progress House. Look, here's my little scar."

The witch extended her right arm. It was bare, smooth, hairless, and sunburned to a color that reminded Justine of canyon walls. On her bicep near the crook was a white, raised and rippled scar in the shape of a fishhook. It even appeared to have a tiny snell.

"J," said the witch, smiling, her dentures stuck loosely to scurvied gums. "Isn't that something. So can I see yours?"

The nausea rose. Justine did remember. Not this witch, but the emergency room. She hadn't meant to cut herself that badly, but they didn't buy that, and as soon as she was stitched up they trundled her off to Austin State Hospital, where she stayed for months and months, till Christmas, 1987. Justine laughed.

"Ha ha, yes, isn't that amazing," said the witch, laughing along with her.

"You're scaring me."

"But then, one day, a few months later I remember, April 5, 1988, you left and I was alone. I know I deserved it. I left you once. Then you left me. It was my punishment. I hated myself so much. Then when they came out with the internet I found out you were in New York—"

"How?"

"Oh, I don't know, I just asked a man at the library how to find you, and, like magic, there you were, a picture and everything, right on the screen, something about space, it said you lived here. So I left Austin to find you, baby Justine, to ask you back, to explain and apologize, to beg, but I couldn't find you, the internet doesn't tell you everything, so long outside in this moody steam-grate city. But then one day I heard you."

Justine looked over at Meenakshi, but she seemed not all interested in, or even aware of, the accostment in her shop.

"And now," said the witch, "we're together again."

She leaned over and hugged Justine so quickly Justine didn't have time to even blink: her bare cornea touched the dirty white canvas shoulder of the witch's poncho.

"Oh dear," the witch said, in a way that seemed systemically familiar. "I so want us to be one."

Justine slipped away, and backed slowly toward the restroom, blinking.

"Justine, oh, forgive me. It wasn't my fault. It was my husband. He took you and threw you back like small-fry. But I got away, and he's still in Austin, we'll never see him again."

Justine ran into the restroom and locked herself in a stall. She hung her apron on the unsure-looking hook on the door, lined the toilet seat with toilet paper, sat down delicately, and waited for the danger of this frightening woman and her distressing monologue to leave. Justine tried to pee, with no result—she had done all her peeing on the e.p.t. strip a couple hours ago. Presently, the witch's shoes, grimy, cracked Air Jordans with zip-cord laces, appeared underneath the stall's door.

"Justine?"

Justine raised her feet so the witch couldn't see them under the door.

"Quiet in there," said the witch. "Trouble tinkling? Let me turn on the water."

The Air Jordans turned and went to the bank of sinks. The sound of running water, the velvety, aerated water peculiar to public restrooms. She returned.

"Justine, I know this is a terrible surprise, I'm so sorry. It was quite a shock to me, too, when I came here, to the doughnut-hole shop one day, weeks ago, April 15, actually, and there behind me while I'm in line, the cry. The crying. Unique. Like a thumbprint. Unchanged, except deeper, more mature, womanly. But the same cry, terrible and magnificent, as when you were my baby. My cry. Our cry, Justine."

Graffiti shallowly lacerated the liver-colored metal cube. One, scratched in an arrow-pierced heart, read: *its not the fall that kills you its the sudden stop.* Justine giggled.

"You're laughing again," said the witch quietly. "I'd never heard you laugh till today."

"Shouldn't have given me away!" shouted Justine.

A long silence. The water *thhhh*ed.

"Oh, Justine, I didn't. Don't you see? Thanks to my husband, *they took you back.*"

Justine suddenly missed Franklin. She missed Valeria. She missed Troy, and she missed Gracie. She missed Texas. Austin. She missed her grandmother. More than anything, she missed Dot.

Justine studied the graffiti. She took out her keys, located a couple of barren square inches of wall, above and to the left of the big transparent plastic toilet-paper wheel, and scratched *are you for eighty six?* into the gizzardy paint. Not very original—she'd read the numeric rebus in the *Voice* months ago and it was only today imbued with meaning.

The witch tapped on the door again.

"Dear?"

Justine reached into her apron pockets and felt around for the pills she'd stolen from Midgie.

She stopped.

"What," said Justine, her hand still dunked in the pocket of her apron, "do you mean 'back'?"

"What do you mean, baby Justine?"

"You said 'back.' What do you mean they took me *back*? And who's 'they'? And don't call me baby Justine."

From the witch there was no sound. Her feet did not move.

Justine did not want to call her 'Mother,' so she said:

"Hey."

Then Justine peed mightily. She must have some beta bladder, a reserve of tinkle ready for expulsion in times of shock and indecision.

"Hey," Justine said again.

The feet moved away. They stepped into a little puddle on the tile, then disappeared out the door.

"Hey. Wait."

Justine tried to stop in midstream, but she'd never been able to do that, even though Franklin had always urged her to practice whenever she found herself sitting on the toilet—he'd assured her she would gain superb vaginal control and consequently improve both their sex lives and thus their stability as a couple.

At last she finished. She grabbed her apron, yanked open the metal door, and ran back into the coffee shop.

Through the big picture window Justine saw the witch on the street between two parked cars, waiting to jaywalk. Justine ran outside.

"Wait."

The witch started to run across the street. She moved like Big Bird. When a large white Toyota delivery truck with the single word FISH crudely stenciled on one side raced by, her canvas poncho flew up over her head. She put her roots out in front of her and continued her way across the street, a huge trick-or-treating kid lost under an eyeless sheet. A tired-looking black limousine skidded to a davening halt a foot away from her. She made it to the other side, but tripped on the curb and ran into a *New York Post* box. Her poncho came off from over her head.

"Hey!" Justine shouted across the street, now perilous with hurtling traffic. The witch did not seem to hear; she turned and began to trudge down Ninth Avenue.

"Momma!"

The witch stopped. A rock-star tour bus, black and mirrored, came between them, groaning, laboring down the street, as though filled with slag iron. When it finally passed, Justine and the witch were staring at each other through a great purple billow of bus exhaust.

"No," said the witch, loud without shouting, bright and clear as tearing foil, "*I* adopted *you*. Your mother, Livia, gave you to me. A year later, my husband gave you *back* to Livia. Back. He said I was bananas and took you away, and sent me to a jail-hospital. I thought you always knew."

The traffic thickened and sped.

The witch made a strange, dark face, like a hole in a tree.

"You never knew I even existed," said the witch, touching her face with her roots.

"Why?" Justine mouthed the word.

The witch smiled, her eyes lit like skyscraper windows.

"Let's steal away," she said. "Just us."

A light changed. Traffic began to gush between them. Justine could no longer see the witch. When the grinding, sawing conveyor belt of Ninth Avenue again came to a stop, the witch was gone.

Justine walked quickly toward home, holding her apron shut with one hand. She reached their apartment building, ran up the stairs to the fourth floor, stopped in front of their door, held her breath, wiped away her tears, and listened. Then she quietly let herself in.

"Franklin?"

On the little table in the hall the little craquelure bowl, into which Franklin emptied his pockets when he got home, was empty.

Justine stripped on the way to the bathroom. She showered, scrubbing and rasping. She *erased*. As she dried herself off she stuffed a couple of Macy's bags with panties and nightgowns and a whole bathroom-closet shelf of cosmetics and hair clamps and materia medica. As she dressed, she called Middling Car Rentals on Tenth and Thirty-Ninth and reserved a Chevy Meagre. Her voice was calm but colored with a fauvist palette of rage, dolor, and conviction; her throat, wrecked from crying, felt like it was coated in iron filings.

"And how long will you need the car, ma'am?"

"I don't know."

There would be no more Franklin. There would be no more New York. There would be Austin.

Justine had always loved the way the entire building trembled when she slammed her apartment's heavy oaken door.

II

May 2004

Livia Durant locked the door to her house, an old, drafty bungalow on Forty-Fourth Street in Austin, climbed into her Nissan pickup, and drove the half block to her mother's house.

She parked in Charlotte's gravel driveway and turned off the engine. She stared at the dashboard clock, only the second hand of which worked. She held her breath for 120 seconds. This always calmed her nerves, especially when she went to Charlotte's, which was at least once a day, more on weekends. But this time she hadn't seen her mother in a few days—Livia had been in Marfa on a mini-vacation with Archibold Bamberger, her boyfriend of sixteen years, and had gotten home late last night. While in Marfa, she had not thought often of her mother, who had begun in the last several weeks to behave oddly, more so than usual. She smoked more, kept and slept strange hours, grew contrary over small things. She took cabs late at night—Livia'd heard them honk and wait, engines idling, dispatch radios sputtering, until the familiar slam of her mother's front door. Livia's vacation to Marfa had been less about spending time with Archibold than it had been about not spending time with her mother.

Livia felt guilty when she and Archibold got home. So when Charlotte called her at work this morning to ask if she'd leave early to take her mother—who, since retiring from bank-tellering the year before, had refused to drive—to a doctor's appointment, Livia leaped at the chance to assuage the guilt, which had been sharp enough to prevent her from concentrating on debt-collecting anyway.

...four, three, two, one. She let her breath out, and went into the unlocked house that Charlotte had lived in since 1951.

"Hello, Mother," said Livia as she came into the kitchen, a little blue from breath-holding.

Charlotte Durant, Livia's mother, who was sitting at her kitchen table smoking Belairs and fashioning inch-high, red, white, and blue garden gnomes out of clay, jumped.

"Me," said Charlotte, touching her neck under her chin as she always did when startled. "Why, Liv, you frightened me. What are you doing here in the middle of the day?"

"Mother. Dr. Gonzales. Remember?"

"Oh yes. Did you lock the doors to your vehicle? What if a Reviewer sneaks in the backseat and garrotes you with concertina wire?"

"The Reviewers don't attack people, just things. And concertina wire... oh, never mind."

The Reviewers, a group of unidentified Austin fundamentalists who broke into houses and businesses to destroy things like sex dolls and bongs and *Necronomicon*s and anything else they found that ran counter to their ideas of morality, had so far not hurt anyone.

"How do you know they won't start breaking into cars to garrote immoral people?"

"Are you calling me immoral?" said Livia.

"No, I'm not calling you immoral. I just know the Reviewers are a bad gang, capable of anything, like the Blips and the Cruds."

"You mean... oh, never mind."

"So. Is your car locked?"

"Yes, it's locked," said Livia. "*Your* front door was unlocked, though, just now. You've been doing that a lot lately."

"Yes. Well. Bring your mother a bicarb and a Tuborg."

"I will bring you ice water. Why are you so red-faced and contrary?

And you're... aggressive. You are not an aggressive human being."

Charlotte smiled but did not answer. She turned to the big picture window that looked out over her backyard, a monkey-grass-smothered eighth-acre staked with half a dozen unoccupied birdhouses on twenty-foot poles.

Livia found a butter knife, opened the freezer, and began to chip away at the massif of ice that filled the interior. She vaguely recalled that someone had once euthanized a hamster doomed by intractable wet tail in this freezer. Justine, probably. Conducting a mercy killing in the same chamber that housed the Tater Tots was the sort of revolting act her daughter had often felt called on to perform. Probably still did; not the kind of thing a person outgrows.

"There's a corner of a chicken pot pie poking out of the ice here," said Livia, shaking her head to fling off the memory of Justine. "I can't imagine what else there is inside this floe. Maybe it's time you defrost."

Livia swept a small accumulation of ice chips into a glass. Some of the chips missed the mark and landed on the linoleum, skidding this way and that.

"When my gnomes are done, we can go."

"I've never seen you play with Play-Doh before."

"It is not Play-Doh, which is a child's sculpting medium. This is Fimo clay, a substance for adults, which I acquired at the Kaplan estate sale this morning, along with a spokeshave and a wedding gown."

"Mother, are you going to tell me why we're going to the doctor?"

A snuffling pug-type dog raced into the kitchen and endeavored to eat the ice chips on the floor. Unable to gain a purchase on any of the pieces with his inefficient mouth, he simply selected a single chip, nosed it into a corner, and went to work licking it away.

"Dartmouth, go," said Charlotte, gently punting the pug dog back toward the living room.

Dartmouth came to rest at the kitchen doorjamb, which he reflexively marked with a jet of tinkle. All vertical surfaces in Charlotte's house Dartmouth had at one time marked with like jets, creating a kind of house-wide urinary bathtub ring.

"I have no idea," said Charlotte, scratching at her chin with a pinkie, a gesture Livia knew meant her mother was concealing something. "That's what I'm going to ask Dr. Gonzales."

Livia put the glass of ice water in front of her mother, stepped back, and regarded her with severity.

"What I mean is, what are your symptoms?"

Her mother slid an ancient, blackened aluminum baking sheet ranked with imperfectly constructed garden gnomes across the table toward Livia.

"Please place my gnomes in the oven at 275 degrees and set the timer for fifteen minutes."

"These aren't ready to go into the oven yet, Mother. You need to anchor the heads to the bodies with toothpicks, or the heads will roll off your gnomes and into the bowels of your oven."

"How did you become such an expert, Miss Fimo USA? Please do as I ask."

Livia did. "Now, are you going to tell me what your symptoms are?"

Charlotte waved her hand in front of her nose and returned to survey her birdless backyard.

"If you can't confide in me after fifty-three years," said Livia, "then I guess you can take a taxicab. I'm sure you have the number memorized."

Charlotte stood up and pointed at her daughter.

"What exactly do you mean by that? *Livia?*"

Livia took a step back. Her mother stared into Livia's eyes, something she did not often do. Charlotte pointed right at her daughter's nose with a smoldering Belair between her fingers, something else she didn't often do. And she called her Livia, perhaps the rarest of all three rarities. Her mother liked to observe and report on backyard flittings; she liked to host short, low-census parties; she liked to rationalize, to pooh-pooh, to change subjects. But she had never liked to confront, argue, curse, duel. And she did not often exhibit a flush in her neck and cheeks that looked, the more Livia thought about it, flagrantly sexual, and a little bit murderous. In fact, it may have been the first time she'd ever seen her mother like this, since at least the late 1980s, when Lou, the only person Livia had ever heard her mother declare romantic love for, was last in evidence. There's no way her mother was in love with anyone, though. Livia would know.

At the thought of Lou, Livia shuddered, a flag surprised by a sudden, wild gust.

"What?" said Charlotte, evidently noticing the shudder.

"What?" said Livia, pretending not to have shuddered.

"Your flip tone is not appreciated, and as for your taxicab remark, I do not know what you are talking about."

Charlotte sat back down. It seemed to Livia that her mother did so slowly, charily, arthritically, yet also with menace, like a bloodthirsty but aging queen. A queen well practiced in—but not perfect at—lying.

A small bird, bluish-black and oily, glided to a perch atop Charlotte's tallest bird feeder, a tin replica of the Château Frontenac that her grand-daughter Justine had brought her from Quebec, where Justine had gone in junior high school with her French class. Justine hadn't brought anything back for Livia.

The birdhouse was one of the only things of Justine's that had remained on the property since Justine had threatened suicide and then run away to New York at age seventeen, and it was the object that most sharply reminded Livia of her uncontrollable, unknowable daughter.

There were many times Livia'd wanted to cut the birdhouse down or uproot it or bump it with the mower or pay Duck Baby, their now-and-then handyman, to haul it off, but she never had.

The bird immediately got all of Charlotte's attention.

"Oh," said Charlotte. "A juvenile grackle."

The oven timer. The grackle heard it, too, and flew off, a plum-black wash, calling its crisp, electrical gurgle.

"Good *night*," said Charlotte touching her temple. "My gnomes have scared off Justine's boat-tail."

The mention of Justine swung in the air between them, a hanged man on a windy day.

"There are one hundred octillion grackles in this neighborhood, Mother. One of them will happen upon the damn Château again very soon."

Charlotte stubbed out her Belair, dumped the ice water into the sink, got a Tuborg from the refrigerator, refilled the glass with it, and disappeared down the hall. She returned with some Alka-Seltzer in a long glass bottle sealed with a screw-top lid. She opened it and plopped two tablets into her beer. They did not fizz, but rather disintegrated and sank to the bottom as pharmaceutical silt.

"Gas?" said Livia. "One of your symptoms is gas? Why couldn't you just have said, 'Livie, darling, one of my symptoms is gas.' Instead you conduct a charade. Where did you find those, anyway? They're bound to be expired.

They don't even make glass bottles anymore."

"Alka-Seltzer does not expire," Charlotte said casually. "They were in an old suitcase of things I found in the shed."

Livia was not prescient. She prided herself on having no preternatural gifts. She did not see ghosts or dream of plane crashes or have a feeling she was going to get a full house. She knew astrology and numerology were for paranoiacs and Eastern cultures. She had never awoken from a night's sleep feeling she'd been borrowed from the planet Earth by curious alien beings with probes. She knew that luck was a form of the future and therefore unknowable, even with crystal balls and Aleister Crowley tarot cards. She left such things to Archibold.

But Livia began to feel a foreign stirring. She had caught a whiff of the spoor of a future of… what? *Disorder* was the word that came to mind. *Disintegration. Disease.* Pleasant nouns prefixed with *dis*.

"I've asked you not to go into the shed. There are nails and glass shards and explosive solvents in there. And brown recluse spiders. No suitcases."

"I shall go anywhere on my premises that I damn well care to go."

"What's gotten into you? Why are you being so fierce?"

"The suitcase was hidden behind piles of old linoleum squares much the same character and color as the linoleum upon which you now dawdle."

"What…," said Livia, but she didn't know what the right question was. *Who? When? Why?*

"Oh, just some old stuff of Lou's."

The preternatural stirring she'd felt a moment earlier graduated to a tremble.

"Daddy's stuff?" Livia said, keeping her voice as even as possible. "In the shed?"

"I brought it inside."

"I didn't know there was anything of his here."

"Me neither," said Charlotte. "I just stumbled across it while I was looking for my crème brûlée torch."

"God*dammit*, Mother, what's happening? Torches, Justine, doctors, Daddy? I command you to sit down and explain every single one of your maddening utterances over the last thirty minutes."

Livia turned her mother by the shoulders so they faced each other, which was how Livia established communication when she felt that Charlotte, or anyone, was being unreasonable or balky. Whenever she faced her thus, Livia couldn't help thinking how much it was like looking into a mirror in a room lit with black light—Charlotte was duskier and subtler, but they had the same round faces, long noses, brown-black eyes set far apart. Livia was taller, more voluptuous, and generally larger in all dimensions, but they both walked with the same chaise-longue leisure, they both sat Indian-style no matter the seat, and they both could arch a single eyebrow in a way that made people want to apologize. Charlotte's thick, gray hair was cut shoulder length and tied back, whereas Livia's was long and wavy and the color of vine charcoal. But when they were younger, they had both been cloaked in the same heavy, coffee-black tapestries. Charlotte was only thirteen when she had Livia, and they had been routinely mistaken for sisters—occasionally twins—ever since. Sometimes even now.

They had certainly grown up more as sisters than as mother-daughter. Charlotte's mother, Mère Durant, had been the acting mother to both Charlotte and Livia. Charlotte had never shown any especially motherly tendencies toward Livia; their relationship had nearly always been one of competitive sisterliness.

But, in the late summer of 1969, after Burt, Livia's newlywed husband, died in boot camp after being bitten by a big spider hiding in a bunch of bananas, Charlotte, seemingly overnight, became a protective mother, and Livia, then eighteen, became a daughter needing shelter and maternal attention. The sisterliness vanished. Then, two days after Burt's death, Mère died of a heart attack while bowling. That was the story; the truth may have been that she died of grief—Mère had loved Burt, even though she had pretended otherwise.

Time had diminished and blurred the edges of the memories of 1969, but the mention of Lou and Justine, just now, brought that summer back in sharp resolve.

Charlotte pushed off one tennis shoe and began to massage her big toe.

"I didn't know we had anything of Daddy's here," said Livia. "You got rid of everything when he left in 1988. I mean everything."

Her mother's expression, a composition of tiny, shallow dimples around her mouth and hairline, Livia recognized as her nonverbal *Well, I thought I had.* That had been the third time he had broken Charlotte's heart, and the last. Charlotte evacuated the house of his presence, leaving nothing, nothing.

Livia had looked, too. She'd always hoped to come across something, a letter, a comb, a deck of cards, the wool army blanket he used while he and his friend Dot were living in the house in 1988. But she'd never found anything. In fact, all she had was one of his teeth. She kept it in a taped-shut matchbox in her purse. Everything else Charlotte had thrown in the front yard for Duck Baby to haul away. It could be argued that all that was really left was the house itself, where Lou had spent exactly one night, on a divan in 1969, and, nearly two decades later, several months on a cot in the garage. That visit ended when Dot died and Lou and Justine disappeared, all on the same day: April 4, 1988. Neither Lou nor Justine had been heard from since.

Evidence of Justine, on the other hand, was, in spite of Livia's efforts, everywhere on the property. After Justine had written her a horrible letter and threatened suicide and run off to New York, Livia had thrown out everything of hers she could find, but there were still unmovable indexes: POW! scratched with a glasscutter into the concrete of the garage floor, poster-tack punctures in closet doors, a collage of Brooke Shields faces pasted to the inside of Charlotte's bedside table drawer that Livia'd come across once while searching for triple-A batteries, pen marks on the doorjamb in the utility room that chronicled Justine's height until age eight and that Livia'd tried to remove with a rotary sander but which creepily reappeared the following day, a yellow spray-paint silhouette of a pogo stick on the shed, the faint chrome glint, noticeable only when sitting in the living room in the wicker chair on late sunny afternoons, of a buffalo nickel Justine had hammered down into a gap in the floorboards when she was nine. And, of course, the Château Frontenac.

"I don't know," said Charlotte. "He must have hidden it back there. It has since been simply overlooked."

Charlotte put her Tretorn tennis shoe back on, lit a cigarette, and daintily, consummately Charlotte-like, sipped her beer.

"Is he visiting?" asked Livia as evenly as she was able.

"Not that I am aware of."

"I assume that's it?"

Livia nodded to an old, typewriter-sized wort-green American Tourister covered in greasy dirt and spiderwebs that she'd just noticed sitting in the corner of the living room by Charlotte's pinochle table.

"That is it."

"I don't remember ever seeing that before."

"And yet there you have it."

"What's in it?"

Charlotte finished her beer without a word.

"You opened a time capsule and the only thing you found of any interest was a tube of expired Alka-Seltzer."

"A comb. A pair of green platform shoes for a large-footed woman; I imagine they were the property of that friend of Lou's, Dot."

"That's it?"

"That is it," said Charlotte, stubbing out her one-third-smoked cigarette. "Oh, and some old leather books. Two, both the same."

For the first time in years, maybe even her entire life, Livia thought she might faint. She sat down. She had forgotten about those diaries.

"Have you read—"

"Unlike most doctors," said Charlotte, standing up, "Dr. Gonzales sees his patients precisely on time. If one is tardy, one must reschedule, even if one has just swallowed a bottle of ant poison. It is now 2:36, and we must detour around Forty-Fifth due to construction. So. Are you or are you not going to take me?"

Dartmouth raced into the room and marked the suitcase with a jet of tinkle.

"Okay. Come on." Livia stood carefully. "No smoking in my Nissan."

Charlotte locked the front door on their way out. Livia had lived two doors down from her mother for years but never had she owned her own key. Her mother had never offered and Livia had never asked. This sort of non-exchange was a feature of their relationship (and, in general terms, was a family dynamic—if Mère or Justine were here, they could non-exchange just as expertly), and the longer a non-exchange lasted, the more keen and envenomed it became. The non-nonissue of the key had survived for so long because it was not that important: Livia hardly needed one. Since Charlotte had retired from the bank she never left home. Even before retirement, they had worked roughly the same hours, at the same bank (Livia, collections; Charlotte, teller), so if Livia really did need to go to her mother's during the workday, she just took the elevator down from the collections offices to the lobby and asked her mother for the key.

At the moment, though, Livia had never wished so earnestly for her own key. If she had one, the minute Dr. Gonzales called her mother into the exam room, Livia would bolt home and rifle the suitcase, subtracting from it anything that might really, really complicate their lives. Most specifically, those diaries. Dot Disfarmer's journals, a brace of masty leather-bound octavos filled with illegibly minuscule cursive. Dot, the woman who'd known Lou better than anyone. Dot, in whom Lou had probably confided all his secrets, including the darkest non-exchange the Durant family had known.

Dr. Gonzales, who was eighty-six years old and had been a doctor since graduating from Universidad Autónoma de Guadalajara in 1944, shared his office with two other physicans: Dr. Rosental, a fiftyish neuropsychiatrist who collected sand from the beaches of the world, and Dr. Barney, a pediatrician who had gotten her medical degree at nineteen and still lived with her parents in Westlake.

Unlike Dr. Rosental's and Dr. Barney's shares of the waiting room, which were cheerily carpeted, strewn with invulnerable toys, and furnished with cushiony love seats and low, shin-killer tables stacked with antiquarian *Redbook*s, *Cryptotaxidermy Worlds*, and *National Review*s going thirty-deep, Dr. Gonzales's waiting area was floored in antiseptic gray linoleum, furnished only with benches constructed of the same material bedpans were fashioned from, and entirely undisrupted by toys or magazines. It contained not a single manipulable entity with which one might pass the time.

The doctors shared a receptionist, Alva Giddings. She had worked for Dr. Gonzales for as long as Livia could remember. In 1966, during the summer before Livia's sophomore year at Austin High, Burt Moppett, her classmate and, later, husband—for three days—had been spending his lunch break from a shift as a university-sidewalk-weed-plucker by napping on a divan in the lobby of a dorm on the Drag, when Charles Whitman started to shoot people from the top of the UT Tower.

Two years later, just after she and Burt had started dating, he told her he remembered waking up to see people racing urgently, but in eerie silence, through the dorm lobby.

"When I think of people running scared," he'd said, pulling Livia closer as they sat in the car on Friday night watching Olivia Hussey enchant the drive-in, "I always think of it coupled with screaming. Don't you, my little October pumpkin?"

Bubbly goose bumps crept up Livia's neck at the word *coupled.*

"I do, darling, I sure do," she'd responded, stroking his ear as he yawned and stretched in preparation for a catnap. They'd both seen *Romeo and Juliet* twice and were just here to mess around and give Burt a chance to catch up on his sleep. Burt especially loved sleeping on the bench seats of cars.

"But it was all quiet. I went outside and stood next to a telephone pole on the sidewalk, looking to figure why all the automobiles were stopped smack in the middle of the street and folks were crouching behind mailboxes and pickemup trucks and it was a hot afternoon, and real quiet except for faraway shouts and faraway sireens and itsy-bitsy pops."

Burt had seen a man in an undershirt across the street pointing to the top of the Tower. A tiny puff of smoke appeared there. An instant later, a head-high chunk of the phone pole near Burt exploded. A substantial splinter, half a yard long and glazed with creosote, speared him laterally through the meat of the tip of his chin, where it lodged, hat-pin-style.

The man in the undershirt hoisted Burt over a shoulder and hauled him dazed and bleeding to Dr. Gonzales's office, a block and a half away. But Dr. Gonzales had gone to Brackenridge Hospital to help the other victims; the only one left at the office was Alva, the receptionist.

Alva ordered the man in the undershirt to lay Burt down on the bench in the waiting room. She emerged from her reception booth with an old-fashioned leather doctor's kit, put her white leather nurse's-shoe-shod foot against Burt's jaw, pulled on the splinter with one hand, was defeated, and so used both, with success. Burt squeaked and fainted. Alva cleaned him up, sutured the entrance and exit wounds, and left him resting on probably—surely—the same bench on which Livia and Charlotte were now sitting.

With a fingernail Livia picked at a flaky bit of the bedpan-bench between her legs and thought of Burt: *He bled here. At least he was lying down. Burt loved to be prone.*

Over Alva's window hung an analog clock calibrated in military time. Livia practiced holding her breath. Given her mother's recent spleen, which promised a future of patience-testing, Livia decided it was time to move her nerve-calming, breath-holding exercises to 130 seconds.

From the other side of the room came the communicable hacking and barking of ill children, the *schk* of magazine pages being turned, and the occasional thump of a toy's durability being tested by one of the barking children. During the brief intervals of silence, all that could be heard was ambient music, tuned to a tiresome KUT program of the sort where the DJ, in order to demonstrate his diverse musical acumen, might play a forty-minute timpani soundscape immediately followed by Dessert Helmet covering Hootie, or maybe the Niagara Chickenshits playing their notorious live version of "It's Damp" (the one with the Tek-9 tragedy uncensored), segued inharmoniously into any one of the many upsetting ballads Livia couldn't help but associate with the last, hopeless moments of a junior-high-school dance. Livia hated the unpredictability of such programming. She liked her radio to reliably stick to a genre. Psychedelic rock, for instance.

Alva glanced up once and stared at Livia. Livia stared back. She suppressed an urge to stick out her tongue. Alva continued to stare until Livia cowed and looked down at her fingers, which had started to tremble. Her mother's fingers, crossed tightly in her lap, as was her habit when she wan't permitted to keep them busy operating cigarettes, were perfectly still, though stained red and blue from the Fimo.

By 16:35 the waiting room was mostly empty and had grown quiet. Livia had lost two more stare-downs with Alva. At nine seconds before 17:00, Alva slid her window to the side with a sandy crunch and shouted, "Durant, Charlotte Gue."

Charlotte, who seldom moved at a pace quicker than could be described as purposeful, leaped.

The door to Dr. Gonzales's office opened, and Charlotte disappeared into it as though swept in on a simoom. The door swung shut. Livia found herself alone with Alva and the depressing chirr of Gene Pitney.

A new song took over. It was familiar, too—three-chord rhythm guitar, tinny drums, thwippy bass line—but Livia couldn't quite place it. Maybe the vocals would help.

Like ye jar of fireflies...

Livia jumped up. She ran to Alva's window and tapped urgently. Oh, what a look Alva did beam. But she slid her window aside.

"Miss Alva, would you turn up that song?"

Livia hadn't heard that voice in decades, and never had she noticed the plangent boyishness in it.

...love trapped inside of me...

How often she and Archibold had spent a day searching record shops and junk stores and yard sales looking for records by Burt's band, Ye Moppe Hedds, but never finding anything, even an old 45, its label nearly rubbed away and the grooves worn matte by time and tonearm needles.

Alva stood, steadied herself with a complicated walker whose legs were coated in several generations of medical warnings—biohazard trefoils, CAUSES DROWSINESSes, photoluminescent quarantine stickers—made her way to the back of the office, and turned the radio off.

It didn't really matter. Livia'd heard enough. The entire song came back to her as though she were watching Burt right this minute, his chin decorated with absolutely the sexiest scar in the history of such things, onstage at Wolford's, singing and strumming the guitar he'd bought new at Sears, the nightclub stuffed with screaming, sweat-drenched women. Livia, deep in her memory, barely noticed the appearance of Dr. Gonzales, his shrunken, white-coated figure ushering Charlotte out of his office and into the waiting room. Livia barely noticed Charlotte's blood-test-bandaged arm, her plastic bag of drug samples, her flushed, happy, guilty, *erotic* radiance.

III

In the lobby of the Frito Motel, just off of I-35 in Austin, Justine waited impatiently, all her weight borne by her left leg, behind a man and a tall teenage boy pokily registering for their stay. The two were evidently digging the check-in experience.

Her whole drive down, Justine had been anticipating this very moment, when she would be given a key to a room in which she could live until every credit dollar and every real dollar had been spent. She would rest. Reset. She would research. She would decide whether to keep the baby. She would hunt down and confront her awful family and wring some truth from them. She would find Gracie Yin, seduce her, and then move to Houston with her to make art and have sex and be in love and work in a pharmacy. Or maybe waitress, where the real money was, until the collage commissions from her elegantly simple website started pouring in.

But the moment was a disappointment. Austin seemed like a city now, stormy traffic, cloverleaf interchanges, strip development stretching so far out that the neighboring towns had been annexed and were now more like suburbs, and an architecturally brisk skyline visible at ten miles. She did not feel welcome. The homesickness burn that had grown itchier as she drove south remained, unscratched, somewhere in her large intestine, even though she was "home." Plus, she was lame: the rental car's pedals had seemed like they did not care to leave New York and were fighting back, so hard were they to depress. Her accelerator foot buzzed, the attached ankle and calf shuddered, her knee creaked as though the cartilage had turned to oak. Justine had had to stop dozens of times to massage and baby her right side.

Judging by his rosy, whiskerless cheeks, the younger man in line must have been at the junior-high-school end of adolescence. He was about seven feet tall. He kept bumping his head on the security camera over the check-in desk.

"Pelletier," said the older man, who lisped slightly and wore old-fashioned wire-rimmed glasses encumbered with heavy bifocal lenses. "We have a reservation. We're here for the Ninth Annual Symposium on Cults and Extreme Clubs."

"Of course," said the clerk, a young woman whose perfectly radial blond bangs complemented the many ounces of gold jewelry that encircled her neck and appendages. "I'm Amy, your Frito front-desk specialist team player. 'Kay. Member, leader, or scholar?"

She adjusted her monitor with both hands; it creaked and she jangled.

"Uh, scholars?"

"Okay... sorry, but only cult leaders get a 10 percent price break on the room. Scholars, historians, gawkers, cult members, and the deprogrammed pay full price."

"What about friends and families of victims?"

"There's a schedule of CultAnon meetings taped to the waffle machine, there behind you."

"Yeah, well, Jimbo here," said Mr. Pelletier, indicating his son with a gesture similar to a game-show hostess calling attention to a shiny Frigidaire, "his sixth-grade teacher was Manfred Truwt."

The clerk looked up at him and smiled. "Hello," she said, waving.

"'Lo," Jimbo said, waving back.

"Pretty exciting," she said, blushing lightly and touching her bangs, perhaps checking them for radial symmetry. "Was Manfred weird? Like did he mesmerize you and the other kids with unignorable charisma and get you to do his yard work?"

Jimbo mumbled and turned a color akin to salsa.

"Jimbo's shy," said Mr. Pelletier. "Look, which way's Palmer Auditorium?"

"See that highway?" said Amy, pointing out of the tinted windows of the lobby at a roaring overpass not thirty feet away. "I-35. Go south— thataway—and then..."

Amy incanted directions that included roads Justine was familiar with. It soothed her to hear their names, even though there was nothing comforting about the memories of events to which the streets themselves once bore witness.

"...but you'll have to pay for parking, in cash, so be ready. Okay, let's get you situated. That'll be $32.99 a night."

Thirty-two ninety-nine, thought Justine. That's twenty bucks less than they told me on the phone.

The clerk gave each of the Pelletiers a key and a smile.

"Again, I'm Amy, if you need anything."

"And you've got our reservation for January, right?" said Mr. Pelletier. "Two thousand five? We'll be here for the serial-killer convention, too."

"*True crime* convention," Amy politely corrected. "Not just serial killers this time. There'll be experts on spree rapists, kids who kill, black widows, internet scammers; there'll be capital-punishment seminars, DNA-exonerated prisoners, weapon-mongers, life-size famous-assassination installations, a scholar on Scary-Clown Syndrome, loads of crime skits, an Are You a Sociopath? booth, and also Sanazaro Ballopio, the president of the political wing of the Reviewers, will be there. Do you know who they are? They invade people's homes to destroy immoral objects."

"I know who they are."

"Right! Plus that guy will be there, the one who wrote *Bad or Batty*, you know, about criminality being nature or nurture. And plenty of TBAs. Okay then, looks like your reservations are confirmed."

Amy watched Jimbo as he left with his father.

"Uh, yes," said Justine, hopping up to the registration desk. "I have a reservation."

"Name?"

"Justine Moppett. I think the rate I was quoted was too h—"

"Here we go. Miss Moppett. Welcome to the Frito. Your reservation is for four nights? That'll be $52.99 per night plus—"

"Fifty-two ninety-nine?" said Justine, who hated to quibble; she usually just caved quietly when overcharged or otherwise ripped off. "I think I heard you tell those guys $32.99."

"Yes, but you have the Room," said Amy, glancing out of the heavily tinted window into the parking lot, where Jimbo and his dad were taking a cauldron out of the trunk of a hail-damaged Lexus. "The Room is $52.99."

"'The Room'?" said Justine. "It sounded like you said that with capitals. Did a rock-and-roll star stay there?"

"Don't you know? The Room is where there was a murder once, a really nauseating and out-of-control mass murder," said Amy. "They wrote a book about it. People rent the Room just because of that, you know, true-crime people? So it costs more. The new clerk we have working here, Angel, who gave the Room to you when you made your reservation a couple of days ago must not have known."

"And," continued Amy, "it looks like Mr. Huppholtz, the manager, is going to raise the rate *again* when you check out. The Room is a very desirable room. Fifty-two ninety-nine is a bargain. You lucked out."

"Gross," said Justine, thinking she'd have to stop by the library or a bookshop later to brush up on mass-killer profiling so she wouldn't get caught unawares in a Dan's Hamburgers or someplace when a maniac came in and took down all the diners with automatic-weapon-fire. "I would like another room, please. A $32.99 room. Like the Pelletiers."

"I'm so sorry, we're booked," said Amy. "Probably no more rooms in the whole city, with the Symposium and the Sackbut Six reunion concert at the Erwin Center tonight. Like I was saying, you were very lucky to get a room at all. There must have been a cancellation, since you got it on such short notice."

The phone rang. Amy answered it instantly.

"Frito."

Justine hopped over to look at the sightseeing-brochure rack and piles of free weeklies while Amy embarked on what sounded like a non-business-related conversation, with tears and accusatory shrieks. On the cover of the *Chronicle* was something about the many icy swimming holes around town. Justine flipped the pages till she arrived at *News of the Weird*, a compelling feuilleton reporting just what it announced it would.

Amy slammed down the receiver, which promptly rang again and which Amy answered with a colorful oath.

"Oh. I am so sorry. I thought you were someone else, Oh my god, sorry..."

One *Weird* item featured an awful man, an attorney named Peter Bradley, who'd donated a kidney to a friend, but when Peter got stabbed in his remaining kidney by a madman a few weeks later, he sued to get his original kidney back. He succeeded, and was alive and prospering. The man he'd donated to died. People were so awful. Justine would never Indian-give an organ. But, she admitted to herself, she might not part with one in the first place. Except Gracie. She'd give Gracie both kidneys and an ear and her Islets of Langerhans if she needed them. Maybe more.

"Miss? Miss Moppett?" called Amy. "Are you going to keep your room? Because I have a customer on the phone here who wants it if you don't."

"I'd like to keep it, please."

The Room didn't seem all that special. Not twenty-extra-dollars special. There wasn't a diorama or framed crime-scene photos or even a copy of the book about the murder next to the faux-morocco Gideon in the bedside-table drawer. There was certainly no evidence of a crime. No holes in the walls. No disorder. No spatter. No creepy vibe. Justine was sure that there had been a lot of true-crime thrill-seekers disappointed with the Room. But maybe if she ripped up the carpet she'd find a rust-colored stain. Justine wondered if she could get some Luminol on eBay. Probably not. It was surely a controlled substance, available only to those with a license and a good reason to need it.

Justine tossed her Macy's bags on the bed, checked the number of channels the TV got (twenty-seven), hop-limped next door to a diner, where she remembered once having been served a plate of huevos rancheros in which she discovered the spring from a clothespin. She had not complained and had overtipped.

Justine poked at a plate of migas, and tried not to get caught looking at her waitress as she and her rope-muscled calves darted around the diner. Her face was decorated with a vivid port-wine stain that Justine found beautiful, wondering if by some chance it also tasted of tawny port, or something even better.

Back at the Frito, Justine fetched ice and a couple of Dr Peppers from the machines outside the lobby, went into her Room, poured the ice into the sink, stuck the cans in, and lay on the bed. She kicked off her shoes and turned on the TV to see if a *Law & Order* could be found. No, nothing. And no TV-channel schedule channel, either. Patience; an episode would be on in the next two hours, she was sure. She tuned in to TNT, turned the sound down low, shut her eyes, and decided to get the day's panic attack over with. She summoned it.

But the panic did not come.

Justine analyzed:

1. She had a car. She couldn't rightly return the Chevy Meagre to Middling Car Rentals in New York. She could just leave it in an H-E-B grocery store parking lot and call Middling to tell them where it was and that she wouldn't be able to return it. What could they do? Charge her extra? Fine. Maybe she'd just extend her rental indefinitely. At $48.99 a week, Justine had enough credit to rent a car, and the Room, for *six months*.

2. She was not in a relationship. She was single, like people sometimes were on TV. People in such a state seemed to enjoy no end of fun and sex and restaurants, and appeared to have more money.

3. She had RU-486. And abortion, for the moment, was, she was pretty sure, legal in Texas. And if it wasn't, she did not care.

4. No one knew where she was. No one except Amy downstairs. And it wasn't like she was alone in Pampa or Lahore or the Kuiper Belt; she was free in a city she knew well. Or *had* known—Austin seemed a hell of lot bigger and meaner than it had been in 1988.

Conclusion: the panic hadn't come, because there was nothing to panic about.

In the criminal justice system, sexually based offenses

Justine opened her eyes.

are considered especially heinous. In New York City

She turned up the sound, chose the iciest Dr Pepper, and eased back into bed, trembling with sudden excitement and optimism. Ah, there, on TV, a tiny foot poking out of a trash bag. At the commercial break she tapped out a particolored sparkler of an orgasm, the last shivers of which dissipated just as *SVU* returned to find Olivia Benson in morbid trialogue with Stabler and Dr. Melinda Warner, the show's brilliant medical examiner.

"I can start again," Justine told Olivia.

Right after you settle all of your family accounts, Olivia seemed to scold. *Including your own little inner family.*

"I will."

You're going to keep her, right? Start your new life as two?

"I don't know."

Those pills could kill you both, the brilliant Dr. Warner seemed to say.

"Yeah, I know."

And you're no good to us dead, said Stabler.

"Huh?"

We need you here at the precinct, said all three at once.

"Me? Why?"

Just come with us.

The elite SVU force all call her Justine except for the Captain, who calls her Just, and Fin, who calls her Baby, and Justine wears tight dresses and fuzzy tops and vintage Tiffany earrings with little golden clapperless bells, and she mans a big desk, sips tarry black precinct coffee from an ILOVEAUSTEX coffee mug, and reads stacks of *New York Post*s, *Austin American-Statesman*s, *Der Spiegel*s, *Le Monde*s, *Village Voice*s, etc., because her job is to hunt for signs of child abuse and sexual crime in the funnies. She is good at her job. She saves lives every day. She's saved at least a dozen in the past week. In the last panel of Monday's *Curtis*, little brother Barry gets chased into a garage by a stereo salesman bent on abduction and ritual trepanning but Justine is able to get a SWAT team to the garage before Tuesday's installment; Larry Lockhorn, disguised as a perverted Santa, turns up in *For Better or For Worse* with unspeakable conduct on his mind, but Justine clips him out and pastes him into *Mark Trail*, where he drowns in a trout stream; *Cathy* appears manacled upside down to a stone wall in a secret dungeon in the *Wizard of Id*, but is freed when Dr. Huang awakens the king's buried abuse; a new child, Kevin, turns up in *Family Circus* without explanation, and Justine, on a hunch, sends Munch to Bil Keane's house, where he finds all the *Peanuts* on choke chains in little basement corrals, living on doodlebugs and belt leather. Schroeder is found dead; Justine and the rest of the SVU crew must submit to Huang for grief counseling. Huang makes a sudden pass at Justine; she submits. But before he can lift her elite SVU skirt and take her, Justine wakes up in a sweat, humping the Frito bedspread, which indeed appears Huang-shaped in the blue glow of the TV.

Justine fetched a Dr Pepper floating in the tepid sink-water. She pulled up her nightgown and used the hem to swab her forehead and underarms. She examined herself in the mirror. Her belly did not appear to have swelled. It was only forty-three days, after all. She shouldn't be showing yet... should she? Justine couldn't remember. After Valeria's death, her mind had shed every baby-book fact there was to know.

She leaned as far over as possible to sniff at her nethers. Not unlike mutton bouillon, the aroma. She hadn't stopped to bathe on her whole trip (except once, arguably, when she stopped at a Chevron someplace in Virginia to rasp Doritos residue off her hands with dry paper towels), so Justine took a long soak, eroding to slivers two credit-card-sized bars of Frito Motel deluxe marionberry-verbena soap.

She got out, refilled the tub, this time with scalding water, squeezed a one-ounce bottle of Frito Motel deluxe shampoo into it, then submerged her clothes, including her faded and flaking Frank Frazetta warrior T-shirt. She stirred and agitated the laundry with a Dr Pepper can for a few minutes, squeezed and wrung them, three-rinsed, then draped them over the balcony railing. The direct sun dried everything in less than fifteen minutes. The warrior was hot as burned toast. The heat of it reminded her of the day she bought it, when the decal was brand-new and still hot from the T-shirt shop's mangle.

She'd bought the shirt in 1990, shortly after a public, hissing argument with Franklin at Mulda's Eatery about the nature of the perfect fleur-de-lis-shaped scar on their waitress's belly, which was audaciously visible between the belt of her jeans and the knot of her Hee-Haw country-girl red-gingham tied-up halter top.

"Brand," Franklin had whispered to Justine while the waitress was busy marrying bottles of ketchup at a vacant table, her scar plainly visible, high-lighted by the raking light of a warm, sunny fall afternoon.

"I think it's a bunch of little cuts."

"It's a brand," he said again, a bit distantly, as he was obviously in deep study of every aspect of the waitress's body. "French brand."

"Little cuts she did herself," said Justine. "In the mirror, I bet. Maybe she's from Quebec, or New Orleans."

Franklin flared his nostrils just enough to indicate incredulous distaste. "God."

The waitress came over and refilled their ice teas, leaning over enough so that both Franklin and Justine got a look at the fleur-de-lis scar with almost peep-show intimacy.

"Okay, maybe it is a scar from cuts," said Franklin after the waitress left. "She wouldn't've done that to herself, though."

"Wasn't an accident."

"The cutter nonpareil issues her verdict."

"Shut up, Franklin. Why do you make me out to be wrong about every single thing?"

"She had a pro do it. A scarifier. Besides, she doesn't have cuts all over the rest of her."

"You don't know that."

"Why would anyone disfigure their bod like that? A lacy, meaningless tramp stamp, or Star-Belly Sneetches–style nipple stars, mayb—"

Justine stood up.

"Sit."

Justine walked over to the waitress, who was sitting at her ketchup-bottle table. Dozens of ketchup-bottle towers, each with one bottle inverted and standing lip to lip on another, stood before her like bloody chess pieces.

"Did you cut your fleur-de-lis yourself?"

Justine had not initiated many conversations in her life.

The waitress smiled.

"Yes. X-ACTO."

"It's pretty."

She stood up.

"Yeah. See, sixty-two slits."

"Wow. You're a really good artist."

She looked at Justine's arms.

"You, too," the waitress said, in a timbre that was all at once decorous and dallying and art-critical. "Action painting."

The waitress bent over to get a better look, but accidentally bumped the table with her bottom. All the ketchup towers wobbled perilously, and one of them uncoupled, sending both of its bottles clatter-clinking to the table.

"Oh," said the waitress.

"Oh," said Justine.

"Got it," said the waitress. She picked up the bottles and reintegrated them as a tower.

Justine blushed—awesome, prickling hives—then hugged herself, squeaked, "Bye," and went back to Franklin, who was standing next to their table throwing five-dollar bills at the dirty plates.

"Why would you embarrass me like that?" said Franklin, when they were on the street watching for cabs. "I swear you were hitting on that girl."

"No, I was not."

"Were. I thought you were going to mate. I mean, if you were inviting her into a just-the-three-of-us pah-tay, I'm all for it, but we both know you'd never— *Cab!*"

Franklin stepped onto Avenue A and waved with possessive vigor at a dented green gypsy cab. When it stopped, he got in by himself and slammed the door before Justine could follow. He rolled down the window.

"Maybe you two can go shopping for box cutters and mercurochrome together, Justine, huh, fuck me Jesus. Oh, by the way? You've got ketchup on your blouse or your top or whatever you call that."

"Drive," said Franklin, slapping the dirty Plexiglas behind the cabbie's head.

Within the soft hug of a warm cloud of cab exhaust, Justine examined her smutchy blouse. A fair amount of ketchup, enough for a child's hamburger, had found safe harbor between the third and fourth buttons.

Women do not walk nine semi-sketchy crosstown blocks bedaubed with vegetable gore. She briefly considered taking her blouse off, but remembered that neither do women walk the same dubious route with the boobs out, no matter how well brassiered. So Justine folded her shirttails up over the offense and headed west.

A souvenir shop soon appeared. Justine peeked inside. It was more like a slogan shop: personalized keychains swung from tippy, spinning racks, clever bumper stickers and anarchist patches and gender-identity buttons all but blacked out two walls, and from the open ceiling beams toon-illustrated nylon fanny packs swung like emergency oxygen masks on a depressurized airliner. Piled high on rough plywood tables were hundreds and hundreds of dirty, dusty photo albums. Tacked on the back wall were plain T-shirts in scores of sizes, styles, and colors.

Justine went in. She opened up a random album, denominated #9 KiTTEN'S. Another album: #103 BEER. And another: #30 FUNNY. And #336 BUBiES. #1061 LiTTLE KiTTEN'S. #57 BEViS 'N' BUTTHEAD.

In #590 DEATH Justine found a heavy metal–style picture of a muscled and freshly bloodied man in an Ostrogothic helmet holding a huge dripping sword and standing atop a low peak composed of variously diced and headless ex-warriors. A voluptuous red-haired vixen strapped into a suede war bikini clutched his thigh. A mustardy après-massacre fog wisped around them.

"Sir?" said Justine to the proprietor, who was busy eating a falafel while working a massive, creepy mangle that reminded her of a Stephen King story. "I would like this on that white V-neck. Medium size."

"No," he said, shaking his head and chewing. "Frazetta, best on baby-doll. Cuff sleeves, yellow color. See? Very chic."

"Okay."

Wearing her soft, snug new shirt, mangle-warm, Justine walked back to Mulda's, nearly drugged with adulterous ambition, and strode inside. The waitress had just left for the day.

Three weeks later, Franklin pled guilty to sexual contact with a minor, earning five hard years. The same day, Justine returned to Mulda's, wearing her Frank Frazetta T-shirt, found the waitress, Henriette, and told her that she needed her. Their affair began shortly after, and lasted until their four-month anniversary, when Henriette posted on the bathroom mirror a note saying she was going back to her husband in Neptune, New Jersey. Justine had not known she was married.

From the balcony railing Justine collected her Frank Frazetta shirt and a still-roasting pair of blue cotton-rayon sweatpants whose legs were enlivened by vertical racing stripes. The garment had been semi-stylish for about thirty minutes in 1990, and was now, she felt, fashionably inoffensive.

She looked at herself in the bathroom mirror, and was not totally displeased. She removed her clothes and laid them at the end of the bed. It would be her library outfit.

The next day, on the second floor of the main branch of the Austin Public Library, at Eighth and Guadalupe, Justine signed the waiting list for the public internet, then sat down at a long table, the other end of which was occupied by a skinny Hispanic girl partly hidden behind a yard-high Machu Picchu of dozens of dark red *Who's Who*s.

"Mary Martin?" sotto-voced the commandant of the internet terminals, a woman who reminded Justine of Susan B. Anthony as she had appeared on those old quarter-sized silver dollars, her sharp, pissed profile here renewed in three dimensions. "Your turn."

The Mary Martin girl jumped up and sprinted to a terminal just being vacated by a towering Eastern Orthodox monk, his camouflage hi-top sneakers visible under his cassock as he walked toward the stairs. Less than ten seconds later, the girl sprinted back to Justine's table.

"No one writes to me," she said, falling into her chair and flipping open another *Who's Who*.

"Justine Moppett," whispered commandant Anthony. "Term. 5."

Justine sat down in front of the antique Dell computer. Google returned 650 results for "Quentinforce," all pointing to the graduate program in literary criticism at the University of Texas.

Justine took the opportunity to google "The Banana Splits," in whose otherwise-intolerable oeuvre was an episode quickened with the brief appearance of a fetching go-go girl who had once made an impression on Justine. But Google found nothing.

Justine sat down on the linoleum outside of Bass Lecture Hall and listened to the rumble of obsequious group chuckles that slipped under the door. Watchless as she was, Justine had no good guess as to the time, and even less of an idea how much longer Professor Quentinforce "Q" Johnsonson, PhD's lecture on semiotics in *Dr. Who* fan fiction was scheduled to last. At least she'd brought a bag of Andy Capp's Hot Fries to cure the munchies and pass the time.

She crunched. She wiped her orange fingers on her sweatpants. Her right leg was still sore and gimpy from her drive, but Justine felt strong, fearless. Even though the decal on her shirt was wearing away (the warrior's codpiece and one of the vixen's bare feet had disappeared), the indomitability it represented was still powerfully comforting.

"Screw *him*," said Justine to the unpeopled hallway. She stuck a Hot

Fry between her lips and took a long, cigarette-style drag, and was about to exhale like Katharine Hepburn when her upper respiratory tract decided instead to reject the suspiration and cough dramatically.

The doors flew open and students spewed into the corridor as though Bass Hall had been under several atmospheres of pressure. After the room and hallway finally achieved equilibrium and the last of the students floated away, Justine held her breath to stifle the coda of her orange coughing opus, and peeked inside the deep, steep lecture hall.

A man whom Justine presumed to be Professor Johnsonson sat erect on a tall chair of the sort usually seen clustered around tiny circular tables in sports bars. Next to him was an identical chair, occupied by an old and worn Bit-O-Honey-colored leather satchel.

The professor descended from the chair like an eight-year-old climbing down from a jungle gym. When he alighted on the proscenium, he took his satchel, adjusted a pair of nearly invisible glasses, and then paused, motionless, between the two chairs, which he matched in height.

Justine could no longer hold it; she became a blare of coughs.

"Euk," said the professor, jumping back like a challenged hamster.

"Sorry," Justine managed to say after a moment. "Professor Quentinforce Johnsonson? Hak."

"I am. And you are?"

"Justine Moppett. Husk."

"Hm," he said, producing a black comb that he used to expertly restore perfection to a shiny, three-inch pompadour that had become briefly mussed in the excitement. "Moppett."

"Yeah. I'm…"

"You and I are not acquainted," he said, holding his glasses a foot in front of his face and pinkering through them.

"Well, yes, we are," said Justine, all at once frightened and uncertain; lighter by the weight of why confronting this terrifying fifty-six-inch over-degreed Wayne Newton was so urgent. Now she thought her shirt-warrior's lacunae were flags of her own weakness. She grew nauseated, aquiver with vertigo.

"Educate."

"You mean…," said Justine, sitting down quickly.

"Me."

"I'm…"

"An alumna come to exact some form of vengeance."

"…your…"

"A fanatic, with Uniball and my novel *The Ant Mill*, suggestively spread open to its title, begging for my valuable inscription."

"No, a…"

"An abductee who has succeeded with the aid of an emery board in severing her bonds and escaping her captor, the dean of engineering, in room 217."

"Not…"

"A stalker, convinced of our mated souls, with an invitation to a candlelit double suicide."

"That's not…"

"An heretofore vagrant pupil, here to gruntle."

"Your ex-…"

"A darkling mirage, courtesy of this morning's tipple of Laphroaig."

"…child…"

"A sadistic doula of the earth, here to midwife me into hell."

"I'm just here…"

"A sightseeing Midwestern dotard, separated from her bus."

"More like…"

"An overgrown limbus puerorum, forever knocking about the University of Texas in blinkered rapture."

"Warmer…"

"A tousled medium with a nagging missive from my tetchy ex-wife."

"That last…"

"Another hypomanic independent researchess with a silly postulate on my Nixon-era activities."

"Yes," said Justine, loud. "That's really close."

"Then I recommend you march over to the Ransom Center and entreat the library lady to show you the well-thumbed transcript of my statements to the S—"

"No, not those activities."

Professor Johnsonson shifted his satchel from one short arm to the other, then stuck his hand into his narrow-waled sport-coat pocket, leaving his thumb out and hooked over the seam, a little pink sea horse hung up on a corduroy fence.

"Then, my lovely scholar, which? I have many secrets, you see, and they will be as such until I'm slabbed and bloodless and the rare-book vultures have started nipping at my archives. Of which this institution and its vampiric acquisitions board will receive not a fragment."

Justine did not miss the punch on the first syllable of *fragment* that signaled the mercy stroke of the conversation.

The professor began to climb the stairs at the other end of the amphitheater.

"Sir, I met your wife, in New York."

The professor stopped. He did not look at Justine. He resumed climbing.

"She told me some stuff," said Justine. "Kind of crazy things—she was pretty bananas—so I came here to ask you if what she told me is true."

He reached the top of the stairs.

"Did you," said Justine, "in 1971, *really* return your adopted baby daughter to her birth mother, like a record with a scratch on it?"

He stopped again. He cleared his throat.

"I am impervious to blackmail, you depressive Patty Hearst."

"Blackmail?" said Justine. "I just want to find myself."

"Then I urge you to consult a guru, a member of the ill-bathed residuum who specializes in such searches. There are many, many gurus here in our little town."

"You're mean. I hate you. I'm glad you're not my dad."

Justine held her breath. She began to turn purple.

The professor took off his glasses and squinted through them as before.

Justine bared her gums, and the cords in her neck contracted.

Holding his glasses before him, the professor started to walk toward Justine along the shallow curve of the top tier of amphitheater seats.

Squeak, G-flat.

"Pity me," said the professor, beginning to hurry.

Began the milky tears, the drool, the amplifying juggernaut whine.

"Stop."

The professor was now running toward Justine.

"Please, mercy, I had to give you back, now stop that pother!"

A security guard stuck his head into the lecture room.

"Vanish, Pinkerton!" shouted the professor. The security guard retracted his head.

Justine's wail dropped two octaves, causing objects in the lecture hall to vibrate. The professor reached her.

"Please," he said dropping his satchel and collapsing into genuflection. "Gahhhd. I had no choiii-oi-oi-oi-oi-oiiice uhhuhhu huh hoo hoo, hoooooo..."

Justine paused in her crying, deferring to Professor Quentinforce Johnsonson's own powerful bawl.

"Quit that," said Justine, wiping her face with the short sleeves of her T-shirt.

"Hoo. Hooo."

"Look, I quit crying, now you quit."

Professor Johnsonson quieted down. He walked on his knees over to a red-velvet-covered seat and wiped his face on it.

"Good," said Justine, strengthening, recovering from her second substantive wailing jag in a week. "Now. Did you adopt me? From...?"

"Ooo. Yes. Livia. My Livia. Livia Durant."

"Livia was my real mother?"

"Mhm."

"Then you gave me back to her? After a year? Why?"

"My wife. Betsey. She was—is—was—insane."

This was new; a man, on the floor, cried-out, spilling. Justine liked this. She put her hands on her hips.

"I know that."

The professor took a breath and sat on the steps. He removed his glasses.

"Livia was my student once, back when I taught summer school. It was awful, teaching reflexively dim, ungraduable seniors, but Livia—she was Livia Durant then—I felt for her. She was special, an electric intelligence. I saw it at once.

"She passed my classes effortlessly, and Austin High School awarded her a diploma. This was 1969. I then urged her to continue her summer studies, assuring her that if she did I would save a place for her in one of my classes, which I as a rule opened only to juniors and seniors—I had never before known a qualified sophomore, let alone a freshman.

"I began to go to her house, where she lived with her rock-and-roll-singing boyfriend, a Belton or Burpon or some such bisyllabic vocable—your real father, I presume?—to advise her on the Quellenforschung of allusions to masturbation in *Ulysses*. Livia seemed terribly proud of her boyfriend. They were in puppy-lovey bliss.

"Our studies went well, but there was something more between us. We discussed philosophy, linguistics, logic; Suarez, Chomsky, Gödel. We discussed family, her fatherless upbringing, my insane, barren wife. Even though we never discussed it, I know she sensed it, too, the something-more. Then, in late summer, she married that crooning poetaster. A few days later, he died while in basic training to perform some patriotic function in one of our proud nation's many obscure Oriental to-dos. The deceased, however, had of course found a moment before his tour of duty to deploy within his new bride that portion of genetic material necessary for the manufacture of yourself. After the funeral, Livia, then surnamed Moppett and freshly primigravida, abandoned her little house on Threepenny Street, and returned to bondage under her mother. I did not see her, Livia, that is, until the following summer—a summer through which I persisted in the daydream that the death of her husband would cause her to run to me—when she appeared at our house with you, a month old, in her arms.

"Betsey, who was just beginning to slough reason but had not yet bid fare-thee-well to the daylights, answered the door. Livia, her mother, you. You were gaunt and jaundiced and might have been a mere corpse if not for the ineluctable anima in those absurd green eyes, which, I see, adulthood has not occulted. Livia's mother, er—"

"Charlotte."

"—yes, Charlotte, who bore an almost sibling resemblance to her daughter, seemed ghostily absent, as though in shock from bastinado and no longer responsive. Livia was not crying—in fact was radiantly happy— but she appeared as though she had been crying for weeks; she was puffy and florid, with tiny flakes drying in the corners of her eyes. I wanted to cast Betsey aside, strike you from her arms, and take Livia away with me, to Turin or Singapore. But instead, Betsey invited everyone inside, arranged a theater in the round on the floor of the living room, placed you in the center, and said, *Livia, tell us about your baby*.

"Livia said to Betsey: 'I can't afford to keep her. She reminds me not of my husband, Burt, but of his death. And I can't afford a baby. Professor Johnsonson, when he was tutoring me in the *Baiae*, told me of your trouble getting pregnant and desire for a baby, so I thought you would like her. She's nice.'

"'Then let it be done,' Betsey said.

"Livia, for one, left our house without a child, universally relieved. Charlotte, for two, seemed—and there is no better word or I would use it here for I so loathe the watery ubiquity of its only contender—brokenhearted. For three, I was happy to have at least some reminder of Livia, videlicet, you, since I could not have the woman herself. Betsey, for four, was soon the happiest I'd ever seen her, a happiness so psychologically plump there seemed no room for other dispositions, especially—as became clearer and clearer—sanity. She was devoted to you, dear—is it still Justine?"

"Yes."

"Possessively devoted. And five: you were simply... present. There on the floor of the living room, wrapped in some form of absorbent textile. Inert you were, odorless, scarcely an interruption of space-time. Except those eyes.

"Our agreement—Livia's and mine—was one of extrajudicial secrecy: there would be no papers. Neither family would contact any member of the other. And you, when you grew cognizant, would not be notified of your change of status.

"At first I argued for a name change—'Justine' I thought tired and was at any rate already signally monopolized by the shuffling secretariat. I championed 'Porcia'—you had a little mark on your thigh. I wonder, do you still?"

Justine, already disturbed by the professor's remembering her as a baby, felt like she'd been mashed by a perv in a movie theater at his mentioning the little eye-shaped strawberry mark on her inner thigh, which at sixteen she had sliced transversely after watching a week's worth of Luis Buñuel films on a rented VCR.

"That's... gone," she said.

"Oh. Well, 'Justine' won out."

"I know that."

"Of course you do. So. At the time I was laboring over *The Circumcision of Leopold Bloom*, my second important work, in which I, er, dissect the state of the great man's, er, Irish heritage. It was the work most hated by my critics, and thus the one of which I'm most proud. This period was one that could stand no noisome intrusion. But you, as I said, were as quiet as a noble gas, but also kept Betsey busy. It was, in spite of the burden of the manuscript, and Betsey's eccentricities, a sweet, rewarding era."

Now the professor turned around. He put his glasses back on.

"Then," he said, looking at Justine as if he were trying to find something of Livia in her, "a few days later, somehow, your insubstantial corpus became the channel for what seemed the sum anguish of a gulag. Why, I wonder, did you begin to cry so... sensationally? Do you know, young lady? *Do you?*"

"No," said Justine, a little frightened of the tiny fellow.

"Cotton earplugs first, then, when those failed, waxed cotton, then, like Goscinny and Uderzo's Romans, parsley sprigs, then small clots of dental wax, then dedicated cylinders of expanding memory foam, but no earthly matter that would fit in my ear would also damp the power of your blarting wail. I moved to a hotel until funds ran out, then to the couch of a tolerant friend, then, when the friend's tolerance evaporated, leaving a precipitate of black ire, to the backseat of the Dart, which I would drive two blocks to a parking lot on Neches where on dry, cool nights your noisy woe could still find me; then, defeated, back home to you and Betsey. In that short period, your crying had gained a bel, and was even more urgent. Why during this period Betsey was not at all perturbed by your moist theater, I have never understood. But she seemed to love you all the more.

"A student of a sympathetic colleague in the architecture department contrived a helmet of sorts, an inverted fishbowl with two holes in the top which, after goggling and snorkeling me, he placed over my head, sealed around my neck with a flexible oiled gasket, and then filled with water. It almost completely blocked out sound. It was uncomfortable at first, but once I'd gotten the goggles correctly aligned and had greased my exposed skin with petroleum jelly, I could wear it for hours upon hours, typing, reading, meditating in submarine tranquility. I was even able to enjoy you, dear, for a few moments at a time. Your tiny mouth stretched apart in almost mute appall, white seedling teeth, perceptibly larger every day, and your eyes, even through the sea tint of my glass—as I called my fishbowl—a mineral yet vital green growing more and more... *more* as the weeks passed.

"Soon I was able to wear my glass... er, 24-7, as they say, removing it only to shave and change the water, which over time would flocculate with atomized Vaseline and moorless gleet; or to replace my snorkel, through which I had taught myself to eat soups and cognate liquid sustenance, and in which a horrid plaque would accrete; or to scratch the occasional itch, a priority emergency that twice required me to break my glass with a chasing hammer. Apart from these pit stops, life resumed its normal, productive hubbub. I was able to make short assays into the world, for newspapers and the like; I could dreamlessly sleep for half a day; I could play squash and euchre at the Burnet Club; I could teach by penning my lectures and delivering them through my oracle, Denise Rodrigg, a graduate student and violist with a tremendous speaking voice and a presence like a small, voluptuous sun. I could even make love to Betsey, loop-the-loop Betsey, with you in a tiny wicker bassinet in the corner of our bedroom, constantly awail with some private dread."

Justine tried to imagine being Betsey, gazing at the professor and his wet pompadour waving like a sea-vent creature through three inches of water and glass, thrusting and gyrating, an epically colicky infant a yard or two away, screaming. Listening.

"But Betsey repelled most of my stabs at ardor. Her love—and there was much of it to be sure—she shared with, and spared for, you alone. You and she were *never* plural, never separated. You rode on her hip, suckled at her teat (which, miraculously, responded by producing milk), regurgitated on her shoulder, dozed in her lap, cruised at her knees, clutched at her hair and collarbone and spectacles, and, while arching and purpling across her naked knees you screamed at her face. She drank in your screams. She lived off of you.

"When autumn was nearly over, Betsey had taken to indoor nudism— both of you now in the altogether—carrying you around the house, never allowing you to yourself, embracing you against her breast as though catheterizing your screams directly into her heart. When she went out, which was seldom, she covered you both in a blanket with two holes cut in the center for your heads. Come winter, she stopped leaving the house altogether, and I was forced to do the shopping, collect medications, and walk to campus to accomplish those occasional tasks even the abundantly able Denise was not qualified to do. By issue of pure necessity I found myself less and less domiciled in my water-world, and thus more and more unshielded from the sounds of your obscure ague, and the ballooning scope of Betsey's insanity, her immaculate postpartum depression.

"By springtime 1971, Betsey had begun to mimic you; she would 'sing' along, harmonizing in sevenths. The cantata was perverse, and, in a way, beautiful—the way that some beauty can craze or revolt or destroy. And it was powerful enough that my glass became vincible and porous."

"Your fishbowl leaked?"

"No, it still functioned perfectly. It was I who compromised the arrangement. Your and Betsey's choral venom found the base of my spinal column like roaches find orts, traveled up it, circumvented my inner ear, and went straight to the pain centers of my brain. I was forced, again, to move out. I asked Denise if I could stay with her. She said yes, as she was in love with me. But that need not concern us here. To resume: I filed for divorce. I also filed—and this may surprise you—for custody. As intolerable as you were, you were a small being, helpless, insensible, and, as I was soon to learn, in danger. I did also impose on a colleague, a teacher of psychiatry who owed me a favor, to find a nurse with experience in lunacy who could take care of Betsey. And, hopefully, you."

"You have a lot of colleagues."

"Fools, clods, dilettantes, each; naked, delicate egos, all. At any rate, in the early summer, the solstice, as Denise was in the backyard of her little bungalow, raising a cone of power with two of her hairy-ankled lesbian crones and could tolerate not the taint of male animus in their magical space, I returned to my house to pour boiling vinegar down the fire-ant hills, as it was something Betsey could never do herself.

"When I arrived at the house there was absolute silence. Usually the two of you could be heard some distance away. Indeed, the neighbors on either side, and one across the street, had all placed their houses on the market. With no little apprehension, I opened the front door. The odor that emerged was faintly ptomaine, like tinned milk spilled and forgotten. Then your wail arose, coming from the back bedroom. I was never so glad to hear it.

"But my relief quickly resigned when I noticed that Betsey was not singing along with you. And I realized your wail was of a different timbre; a longing cry, a tired cry. It was the cry of... a baby. Not a suffering, racked prodigy, but an ordinary, tiresome baby, perhaps in need of diaper renewal. For the first time in my life, an atavism of paternity took me.

"There was Betsey, on the made bed, leaning against the headboard, legs spread, knees up, naked. An edged knife, the heavy bone-cleaving sort favored by cinema madmen, lay on the bed at her elbow. You were between her legs. She was forcing you, your foot, *into* her. Carnation dots of blood peppered the goose-down duvet. Whose blood? I don't know.

"'Quentinforce,' she said, breathless with mania, 'we, Justine and I, will be together forever.'

"I was transfixed. Betsey then forced your tiny leg——you were under-sized, just as you appear to have remained—up to the knee into her vagina; she stopped, screamed. She picked up the cleaver, raised it. A fool, I flew across the room, jumped onto the bed, and reached for the instrument with my bare hand."

Without looking at Justine the professor raised the palm of his left hand to display a thirty-five-year-old scarred gash. Three of the fingers of that hand were limp, atrophied, like rotten asparagus spears.

"But it was sufficient. A brief tussle and the cleaver was out of her reach, and I plucked you from her vagina and made for the hills. Betsey was soon after installed in the state hospital, and Denise agreed to quarter you and me for the time being."

The security guard who had poked his head in earlier repoked.

"Y'all settled down in here?" he said.

"We are settled, my tutelary friend," said the professor.

The security guard retracted his head, and let the door fall shut again.

"Justine, dear," said the professor, "are you all right?"

"Fine."

"Well. You were not injured. Soon after the incident, you ceased crying. You slept hard, snored delicately. I slept on a Murphy bed in your room, as this brief period, in addition to being a formative time for you, was also the start of Denise's and my denouement, a steep and rapid plunge that met its end with a great splatter of mutual repulsion."

The professor thrust his limp hand into a coat pocket and came up with a pale blue handkerchief pinched gently between his thumb and uninjured forefinger. He transferred it to his other hand and began to wipe at his spectacles while they were still on.

"To be specific: you'd been with us for some weeks when one late after-noon Denise raised from nothing a moderate-to-strong temper tantrum regarding the recent overcrowding in her small rented house, and you and I were bounced. Not knowing what else to do, having never confronted a related scenario in life or literature, I fetched from the carport a child's wagon, and we proceeded on a nice walk. We went to the park, to the ceme-tery, to Dirty's for a hamburger—I fed you bits of melted cheese from my cheeseburger; you were particularly fond of cheese. I wonder, are you still?"

Justine said nothing.

"I suppose cheese isn't good for a baby," said the professor. "Nothing is, it seems."

"I love cheese," said Justine.

The professor put his handkerchief in his pocket.

"We made a daily habit of our strolls. Every day a different route and pace and pause. Saturdays, Sundays, too.

"One day we became lost, deep in the absurd intrication of cow paths just north of our university. But happily lost: I saw no reason to be on any schedule at that time. And you seemed content, humming and waving and grasping at weeds and uttering a pleasantly squeaky babel. Then, as we were about to cross a street, a van, of the sort a wealthier hippie might own, stopped near us. Your grandmother Charlotte—hardly a fringe citizen, you'll agree—emerged. Livia was in the passenger seat. She remained in the van."

The doors to the lecture hall opened. Three or four students with ceramic-gray laptops and book-strained backpacks began descending the stairs.

"I don't know how it happened, but…"

A girl wearing a dirty red-and-blue rugby shirt that was surely recently worn in an actual rugby game threw open the lecture-hall door and strode directly up to Quentinforce Johnsonson, PhD.

"Professor," she said, "this syllabus is bullshit."

"That syllabus, Miss Jenkins," said the professor, looking up at the girl, who was at least six-one, "is in fact compressed wood pulp, size, and kaolin, bedaubed with ink in patterns that form sentences in the American variant of the English language, and excludes bullshit altogether, which I leave to my students to manufacture."

Justine imagined the professor looking up at Betsey like he was looking up at Miss Jenkins.

"No," said Miss Jenkins, "I mean, I said, *What the fuck?* when you handed this out and I asked somebody old and they said this is a mimeograph. It smells and it's kind of damp when you get it. It's faint. It's bullshit."

Justine noticed that the girl smelled of moist soil, dark and just dug. The smell of grade-school summers and fireflies. Justine wanted a cheeseburger.

"Mimeography is a perfectly satisfactory method of graphic repro-duction. Sit."

Miss Jenkins went to sit.

"I have another lecture," said Dr. Quentinforce Johnsonson.

"Oh," said Justine. "Okay."

"In conclusion: I don't know how it happened. It just seemed... correct. As if it were the best, and only, thing to do: inevitable and immutable as a tide."

"You gave me back. To my mother and grandmother. On a street corner."

"Yes." More students came in. The professor ignored them. "At that moment, Livia's feelings were difficult to guess. But Charlotte, she was euphoric. She held you tightly but tenderly. She apologized to you over and over. She helped you up into the van. She was tearfully triumphant. She did not want the wagon. This was 16 July 1971."

The security guard came in carrying an old-fashioned overhead projector, a long, thick power cord trailing behind him. A small student wearing a Joy Division T-shirt followed the guard, pretending for the benefit of a girl swaddled from neck to Nikes in burnt orange that he was going to stomp on the cord.

"I didn't hear anything of you, or Livia or Charlotte, until 1988, when they said on the news that you'd disappeared. There was a photo of you, perhaps from a yearbook. By then I also had not heard from Betsey since 1980, when our lawyers had gone to depose her at ASH as part of our divorce proceedings, a juridical buggering lasting seven years. Beg pardon."

Justine watched the students compress themselves into the neat rows of the amphitheater like atoms of carbon. She felt a sudden lust for college, a kind of anti-nostalgia for the idea of elective learning, which she'd never had a chance to try. The only formal class she'd ever taken (apart from Darling M'Nabb's) was a pastel-drawing class in Brooklyn, which she'd quit in blanching embarrassment after two sessions when she realized she'd brought *oil* pastels—basically crayons, in both cost and substance—when the medium that was being taught was soft pastels, which cost, by volume, approximately forty times as much. Nothing had since convinced her more that her artistic calling lay in the discipline of collage.

But real college, like the professor's class, not a $225 two-subway-and-two-bus-rides-away class in coloring, seemed pleasant, doable. Hot, even. Why Justine felt this way, after being told by a professor of such a class that as a child she'd come *this close* to having her limbs segregated from her torso by a madwoman intent on the piecemeal stuffing of as much of Justine as she could into her womb, she did not know.

The faint odor of mimeography chemistry.

"The fire ants were bad in 1971," said the professor. "They were bad again in 1988. And they're bad now. Be careful, my dear Justine."

The professor picked up his satchel, and, taking each step with caution and concentration, holding out his dead hand for balance, descended into the pit of the hall to the stage.

IV

In 1968, as a junior in high school, Livia had known four things about Burt Moppett: that he was the guy who'd nearly been a mass-killing victim when he was fifteen; that he was dreamy without seeming to realize it (which just made him all the dreamier); that he led a local band, Ye Moppe Hedds, that was based on the 13th Floor Elevators formula, a sound at odds with the prevailing Austin scene; and, last, that she was secretly falling in love with him.

Livia had never gone to hear Burt and Ye Moppe Hedds, partly because her slowly fermenting crush on Burt had lately grown intoxicating, rendering her shier than ever, and partly because she was too young to get into the bars and roadhouses he played in. Her sort-of best friend, Brenda Lathers, whom Livia tutored in math and civics (and who, in a recent poll conducted by a private group at Austin High in order to subvert school spirit and to amuse themselves, had been voted Most Likely to Choke on a Large Dick), had seen them twice now, and told Livia that she intended to become not just Ye Moppe Hedds' most zealous groupie but Burt Moppett's personal aide-de-camp and concubine. In contrast to Livia, the richer Brenda's crush, the more proactive Brenda became.

Livia, with uncharacteristically little compunction, began to realize that the social dynamic at work might allow her to exploit her friend, Burt-wise. Livia began tutoring Brenda more and more. For free. Livia was smart enough—possibly the smartest person in the whole school—that she could have tutored anybody in anything, for money. But the potential payoff—Burt—was worth some free lessons on checks and balances and the volume of a sphere.

"Anything he wants, Livie," Brenda had said one afternoon in the school cafeteria while they observed Burt, who was napping across four cafeteria chairs a few tables over. "Anything. I'll get it. I'll do it."

A nearby group of gangly junior-varsity basketball players was practicing trajectories on Burt with balls of compressed hamburger bun. Since Burt, when planning his nap, had apparently pushed in his four chairs first and then gained them by crawling under the table, he was almost completely bunkered and practically inaccessible to bun wads. On top of the lunch tables a small bunch of bananas, a pile of weathered schoolbooks, and a couple of sleeveless 45s waited for him to wake.

"I wish they'd leave him alone," said Brenda, trying to peel open a half-pint carton of chocolate milk. "He rehearses and composes all night and he's sleepy."

"That's the wrong side," said Livia. "Open the carton on the side with the arrows. Okay, now, back to question number six: the quadratic formula is an example this type of—"

"Come hear them with me Tuesday, Liv. At Wolford's. You know, he wrote a song about me, called 'Brenda,' and he's going to sing it for the first time. It might even be on the record. You knew that International Artists Records wants to maybe sign him?"

"No fooling?"

"But when you hear him sing and play electric guitar, and see how groovy he is, don't you fall for him, Livia Durant, because he's mine. You're allowed to be a frantic groupie, though. You won't be able to help it, anyway."

Brenda had delaminated both gables of the tiny carton, but a tougher sub-integument kept the carton firmly sealed and the milk from Brenda.

"He looks pretty goofy," said Livia, working to convince Brenda of her own indifference regarding Burt. To add to this charade, Livia yawned and took the chocolate milk carton away from Brenda to give it a try herself. "And he's got those holes in his face."

"They look like big dimples when he's onstage in the dark," said Brenda, going through her purse for something. "Come with me. You'll see."

Brenda took the carton back and tried to stab it with a bobby pin.

The ballplayers meanwhile had discovered that a bun wad carefully aimed and thrown hard, with a low, flat trajectory, could possibly travel *under* the table and peg Burt in the temple, but no one had yet succeeded, even though Bo Fettle, a mean, eczematic country boy whose eyes were cyclopially close together, had come very close.

"How do you get in?" said Livia. "We're not old enough."

"Quit that, Bo, you jackass!" shouted Brenda.

Bo skyhooked a hamburger patty, which slapped meatily on the linoleum behind Livia.

"I can get us in," said Brenda. "Through the back where they take the trash out. I know the fry cook. I won't tell you how."

Livia yawned again and said: "I just remembered—I can't go. I have to take my granny Mère bowling. It's her night at Saengerrunde."

That Livia was due to chauffeur Mère was true, but that it would stop her from going was utterly false.

"Oh."

Bo and the junior-varsity bench got up, crept up to Burt, and yanked out all four of his chairs at once. Burt spun and landed on the floor. Then they tipped the table so Burt's property slid off and joined their owner.

A varsity team would have stayed to mock and prod the fallen schoolmate, but the JVs, probably still unsure about just what they could get away with, ran off giggling.

Burt Moppett slowly sat up and touched his scalp gingerly, checking for blood or knots. He gathered up his books and records, stood, looked at his naked wrist as though it wore a watch, then picked up his bunch of bananas and examined them for bruises and rents.

"Burt!"

Brenda waved to him and smiled with unconscious venery. He came over.

"You girls know what time it is?"

He towered. Maybe it was his enviable height the mostly shorter ballplayers had been attacking. Burt had one ordinary hand, and one large, knotty, coral-like fretting hand, with which he picked up the impervious milk carton. He tore it open with his teeth, which were small and white behind the curtain of the forty or so long black whiskers that constituted his moustache.

"Fifth period's almost done," said Brenda.

"Are you coming to see us next week, my greatest fan?" he said, handing the milk back to Brenda. "We're playing at Wolford's. Your song's ready."

"Mmm. Maybe."

From under the rich, clover-honey blond bangs of her pageboy, Brenda watched Burt.

"You're Libby, right?" said Burt, who Livia noticed was deliberately not looking at the pillowy contours of her yellow blouse, an article, chosen for this hoped-for occasion, whose buttons were spaced such that if Livia effected a specific posture, the hems would part, allowing a glimpse of brassiere. Livia effected the posture.

"Hi. Right."

"Yeah," said Burt, peeling a banana. "I think I know your momma. From Braunschweiger's S&L, right? I drop by there to trade in dollar bills for small change for work. I work at Centennial Liquors by UT after school. She's really pretty."

"Oh. Thanks. Yeah."

Livia, in order to give Burt a chance at a full assessment of herself, turned her attention toward Brenda for a moment. Then she looked up at him, catching him mid-ogle. It was as polite and gentlemanly as an ogle could get.

Burt smiled. A tiny fragment of brown milk-carton cardboard was stuck between his two front teeth. His chin-holes curtsied pleasantly.

"You look a lot like your mom," he said. He nibbled on his banana lengthwise, like corn on the cob.

To drag Burt's attention back to herself, Brenda sat up and thrust out her own unignorable bosom, which Burt did not ignore. A bell rang.

"Right on. I'll see you next week. My greatest fan. Fans, I should say."

Brenda poured the rest of the chocolate milk into her mouth and briefly swished it around before noisily swallowing.

"I guess I'll try to make it," said Livia, yawning like a sinkhole. "I'll tell Mère Durant I can't take her bowling."

Brenda said nothing. She wadded up the carton, tossed it onto the table, picked up her books, and disappeared down a hallway lined with trophy cases.

After school, Livia went home.

Charlotte and Mère Durant were teamed up against their friends, Nance and Bull Wheeler, at Charlotte's pinochle table.

Pretty much everyone knew the Wheelers in one way or another. Nance was well known for her philanthropic work, and for being a good friend of Ladybird's, and Bull one knew either from a card game, an air show, a polling station, Longhorns baseball, a fistfight, or as dean of UT Law, one of the grandest seats of civic power one can hold without being publicly elected, at least in Austin. Nance and Bull had nine children. Livia suspected that her mother had possibly slept with Bull, mainly because he was the only person Charlotte acted indifferent toward. Livia also suspected that Nance knew this.

"Mère," said Livia.

"Not now. I'm at labor."

"Can I skip taking you to bowling on Tuesday?"

The Wheelers looked up at Livia. Then at Charlotte, and finally at Mère Durant.

"Pooh," said Mère, slapping a jack of spades onto the table.

"You will take your grandmother bowling," said Charlotte. "She hasn't missed a league night in... how long?"

Bull picked up the jack of spades and held it close to his face, as if to authenticate it. "This is a goddam jack of spades, Nance."

"Put it down, it's not your turn," said Nance.

"But I have to go to Brenda's," said Livia. "She's learning cotangent."

"Go, then, teach your sister, so that she may one day sunder the masculine grip on the sciences," said Mère, who, given her magnanimity, must have been winning. "Your mother will take me to Saengerrunde."

"Will I?" said Charlotte.

"You will. You will regard it as a penalty for playing that jack."

"Thank you, Mère," said Livia, who turned to head into the kitchen to make a pimiento cheese sandwich. She stopped and turned back around. "Oh, Mother? I forgot to tell you—my friend at school, Burt? Burt Moppett? He said to say hi."

Now everyone turned to regard Livia.

"Who?" said Charlotte.

"Ooh, a boyfriend?" said Nance, who was deeply fascinated by relationships, especially the extreme details in the history of Charlotte's and Lou's.

"What man is not a vicious clown, show him to me!" shouted Mère, waggling a queen of diamonds at Livia.

Mère often claimed she'd never met a man she liked, or trusted, except for her husband, Big Red, who had deserted her by falling into a tower silo and drowning in sorghum only four months after Charlotte was born. Charlotte and Mère had lived together alone until Lou came along and got Charlotte pregnant at twelve. Later that year Charlotte had Livia, and the three of them—grandmother, daughter, granddaughter—moved to Austin to live in their matriarchal outpost, governed by Mère and as such impermeable to males, especially Lou, whom she pronounced a demon and public enemy number one. Charlotte had told Livia in private, more than once, that Lou was the only man she'd ever loved.

"To encumber and flee is the duty of the male," said Mère, her upper lip sweating tiny dots of outrage.

"Burt Moppett," said Livia. "He has a group. He comes into the bank after school?"

"Is he sweet to you always?" said Nance, ignoring pinochle for the moment.

"Nance," said Bull, throwing up his hands, "leave the young lady alone, pick up your cards, and continue to play pinochle."

"Hmm," said Charlotte, scratching her chin lightly with the tip of her little finger. "Not sure..."

"Chin scars," said Livia.

"Oh, sure," said Charlotte. "I know who you mean. Polite. Nice boy. Sugar, bring me a Coors."

"Durant women will forever bludgeon ourselves with the hardened members of absent men," said Mère, waving her arms, which exposed her cards. "All but my dear old Big Red."

"I might be home kind of late," said Livia, bringing Charlotte an olive can of Coors.

"Will you be tutoring your friend Burt Moffett, too?" said Charlotte, obviously trying to get a look at Mère's cards as she waved them around.

"Ooh!" said Nance. She was ignoring pinochle, and following the conversation with raccoon-like focus.

Mère stood up. "How can we be both sun and shadow to the patriarchy?"

"Moppett," said Livia, ignoring Mère. "No, just me and Brenda."

Livia smiled and nudged her mother. They sometimes told each other about crushes and encounters. Charlotte blushed and fanned herself in a Southern-belle kind of way. Mère paced in tight circles, pulling on the chain of her reading glasses so it bit into the skin on the back of her neck.

Mère pointed at Livia, apparently trying to produce lightning with her fingertip.

"There is no tutoring to be done, siren, I know, I see. Go to your Burt-man. Go. He shall be to you as Belial was to her."

"Thanks Momma, thanks Mère, bye," said Livia, deciding she'd skip the cheese sandwich and go right to her room to plan an outfit that would make Burt fall in love with her instead of Brenda.

On Tuesday after school, Brenda and Livia raced home to the Lathers' house, locked themselves in Brenda's room, a converted garage separate from the house, cued up a well-worn 13th Floor Elevators record, turned it up loud, and began experimenting with Burt-transfixing ensembles. Brenda was meticulous and thorough: it took her three hours to decide on a pair of panties, an unremarkable knicker-fabric garment as loose and pretty as a diaper, which she claimed was an ideal mix of utility, facility, comfort, and did not say, *Rip us off her body she'll screw anything*, a message she was sure would repel an artistic gentleman like Burt Moppett.

"I have lots of *those* kinds of panties," said Brenda, removing her diaper-panty for final ironing and perfuming. "I'll save the yank-em-offs for next year's freshman football squad."

Livia had brought her outfit along in a grocery bag, planning to wait till Brenda was fully dolled, powdered, and painted before she put on her own. Livia had been successful the past few days in keeping up the appearance of a friend and collaborator rather than a rival and backstabber, but when her turn came to squeeze into her own outfit, she was sure Brenda would catch on. She wanted Brenda to see, and not to see, how sexy she could be.

"The main thing is the bed, Liv," Brenda said, explaining what to expect at the show, while wiggling out of a heavily reinforced beige brassiere that was designed to remold the breasts into mortar rounds. "Really, what do you think of when you think of a bed?"

Brenda told Livia that while performing Burt liked to lie fully clothed on a king-size bed that he would share with as many and whichever female groupies cared to be there, a number limited only by space and the groupies' mutual tolerance; usually four.

"Uh, sleep?" said Livia, lying back on Brenda's bed, watching her snap, with one hand and no mirror, a drum-tight bra that looked to be made of snowy billiard-table felt. Brenda, by admission and repute, had had a great deal of sex in this bed, and in lots of others besides. Livia could understand this: Brenda had a nifty figure, looked a good bit like Ann-Margret, and could, without notice, for anyone she chose, unfetter a smile that seemed to welcome, promise, and forbid all at once.

"Sex."

Brenda popped out of her felt bra and tossed it over her shoulder, found another of the same color but silken, lacy, and roomier, and strapped herself in.

I have the better bosom, thought Livia, who was wearing a featureless underwire from Bealls. *And* the better pubic area. Brenda's seemed a tad balding, its sparse hairs sallying too far into space.

"Sex. Yeah. Hey, shouldn't we get going?"

"Eeeeee!" screeched Brenda, ripping off the latest experiment in bosom support. After a moment she pulled on a black T-shirt. "Who needs a bra in bed? Hey, get dressed, we're late."

It took Livia all of ten minutes to dress in a yellow miniskirt and sleeveless white blouse (a composition whose assembly required a day's hooky and a secret Saturday drive to Neiman's in Dallas in Charlotte's car), brush her hair some more, lay on some blush and lipstick, curl her eyelashes, and slip on a pair of wedgy orange platforms that caused her calves to subtly tumesce and cleave in a way that unhinged her granny and clabbered her mother's usually sweet camaraderie.

"Say, you look great," said Brenda, when Livia finally turned to pose.

"Thank you."

Brenda smiled.

The smile said: I see what kind of friend you are. I've had friends like you. If there was time I'd change into an outfit that would make you look like Pig Pen. Later, after the show, I will squash you.

They didn't get to the Ye Moppe Hedds show until an hour after it started. Brenda had to "talk" privately with Krug, the fry cook, before he'd let them sneak through.

Inside, Wolford's proved so dark and crowded that they got separated almost immediately. Livia soon found herself crushed against a sticky wall near the back of the club, a not-cold can of Pearl beer pinned between her collarbone and the adze-like scapula of a tall, oily man in a leather vest. As uncomfortable as she was, she was happy to be able to watch Burt Moppett without worrying how far along Brenda was in her seduction.

Onstage Burt was lying in a big bed, as described. An adjustable microphone stuck out of the headboard. A large mirror suspended at an angle over the stage gave the audience a bird's-eye view of the goings-on in the bed, and Burt a view of his adoring duchy. Burt was performing "Ye Cube of Happy Sugar," a ballad Livia recognized from Brenda's rendition. Four groupies, two lying on either side of him, leisurely undulated to the fuzzy rhythm. The crowd rocked from side to side.

Jerry, the organist, Gary, the bass player, and Larry, the drummer, did not have beds but rather stood or sat in the proximate shadows, artfully backing up Burt's charisma without intruding on it. Livia could just make out their nodding, backlit heads.

Burt ended the song by holding a single chord for several minutes, until it finally vanished. The club grew quiet and still, so that only the *yng* of the bartender's cash register and the occasional smoker's cough could be heard. Burt gazed dreamily into the mirror at his flock. He looked like he might close his eyes and fall asleep.

One of his bedmates appeared to be genuinely asleep; her face was slack, and one of her sandal-shod feet twitched in a decidedly narcoleptic way.

Burt began to monkey with a couple of knobs on his guitar, and then strummed one quiet chord. Gradually, he turned up the volume and treble. Soon, the cash-register sounds and the smoker's coughs were swallowed up by the amplifying chord. Burt worked another knob until Wolford's vibrated and shuddered like the *Saturn V* escaping Earth.

The groupies began to undulate again, a little faster this time, except for the sleeper, who simply threw a leg over Burt's thighs, an arm over his belly, and buried her face in his rib cage under his strumming arm.

Burt held the one chord for several minutes, decorating it with the fuzz-tone pedal clamped to the feet-end of the bed, which he manipulated with his toes. Jerry laid a lonesome, trippy melody over the noise.

Burt began to sing.

Water and holes like ye kitchen sponge
Is my love of you today.
Plastic circles in ye Spirograph game
Are my thoughts of you today.
Ye tortoise in ye rocketship
A microbe on ye paper clip
Are things only you can say
How much they weigh. Today.

Brenda's song? God, please, no. Not a song with a declaration of love in it. Livia thought she might cry.

Majestic goose, she paddles in ye water
For only you today.
Rods of metal I join without ye solder
For only you today.
From you I hear "Why why why?"
Because I have no choice, aye
I love only you this way
Like ye dormouse loves his cheese. Today.

Burt's hypnotic croon soon made Livia forget about crying, about Brenda. The wandering sustain of his guitar made her forget she was flattened against a treacly wall. The way he was able to dance just ever so slightly while lying down made Livia forget about her mother, her grandmother, the treacheries of high school. Livia wished more than anything that she was a groupie, onstage and in bed, right now, while he played the love ballad.

She closed her eyes. Goose bumps metastasized over her entire body, reaching even the backs of her thighs and the soles of her feet.

Like ye chocolate milk in ye carton jail
My love cannot run free today
Like ye jar of fireflies or skeeters or snails
My love cannot fly today
Unless you are mine, and wish to be
Ye Moppe Hedds' hedd groupee
To free ye love trapped inside of me
Like ye scofflaw in ye penitentiaree

Brenda. Brenda's song. Livia was surprised by the speed and force with which the dejection and crestfall flattened her goose bumps and took her over: the familiar inflation just under the breastbone, tears like hot glycerine, and a feeling of dizzy buoyance, as from a pause in gravity. She pressed her face into the back of the sharp-scapulaed man's leather vest and drowned it in waves of sobs. He seemed not to mind.

A squeal poked through the din. A commotion near a bank of speakers by the bar. In the dark, Livia could detect only bobbing heads of hair. A shiny, ginger-blond hairdo soon distinguished itself by its steady advance toward the stage.

Brenda climbed onstage and yanked a groupie off the bed, then another. Brenda directed both groupies off the stage and into the crowd. She went around to the other side to pull off a third groupie, but this one simply jumped off the bed and helpfully ran away.

It seemed to Livia that Burt didn't even notice that there were contentions all around him; he continued to sing and play without missing a note.

O like ye jam and Skippy all mixed up
Be ye insides of my lunch sandwich today,
Or ye scary Boo! to cure ye hiccup
Be a Curad on my heart today.
Ye fair maiden riding the Lassie dog
Ye yellow shirt shining in ye lunchroom fog
Save me from ye lesser maidens today.

And help keep them away from me. Today.

"Did he say *yellow?*" Livia, screamed into the ear of the man whose leather vest she'd just glazed with heartbreak. His mouth formed the continuum of shapes of the word *what?* and Livia mouthed *never mind,* to which he answered with another *what?*

Brenda grabbed the sleeping groupie's long braid with one hand and her jute-macramé belt by the other, and pulled. The sleeper woke up. She grabbed Burt's belt and hooked her leg in the crook of his knee. Brenda karate-chopped the groupie's thigh and wrung her braid like a wet towel. The groupie wasn't able to defend herself without letting go of Burt, but she showed no sign of loosening her grip. The madding saloon rocked and thundered.

Brenda let go of the groupie's braid; her head recoiled and bumped Burt in the rib cage, causing him to hit a rotten, un-balladlike note. He opened his eyes and glanced up at Brenda for a second, the first time he'd shown any indication that he was aware there were other people onstage with him. He closed his eyes again, and began his refrain.

Night and charcoal and certain stones, yeah yeah yeah
Ye brunette head is blacker than, woah woaaahh.
Racetracks and noodles and ye sacred banana, yeah oh yeah
Ye figure is way curvier than, woah yeah woaaahh...

Livia screamed into her leathered barroom confrere's ear: "Did he say *brunette?*"

This time, he smiled brilliantly and mouthed, *Yes.*

She put her arms high in the air, squeezed past him, and began to make her way, fan by fan, to the stage. The going seemed to get easier as she got closer, as if the crowd were parting for her, as if she were a bride on her way to the altar. As if they knew it was her immutable destiny to be onstage, in bed, with Burt Moppett.

Brenda continued to hammer and chop at the groupie barnacled to Burt. Brenda stopped, stepped back, and put her hands on her hips. Her black T-shirt was soaked through with sweat, reflecting the stage lights like a wet sea lion in the sun. After a moment Brenda approached the groupie and jammed her clawed fingertips into the girl's armpits.

The groupie shrieked and rolled up into a ball to protect her ticklish areas. Like lightning Brenda grabbed her by the head with both hands and pulled her off the bed before she could recover enough to regain a purchase on Burt. Brenda dragged her to the edge of the stage. Just as she pushed the tenacious groupie off, Livia started to climb up on the other side. When Brenda first saw her, she smiled and clapped, and went over to help her up.

Burt sang.

Ye magical lamp rubbed on one side
has lots of little pillows
and chairs and Jeannie from TV inside.
Trapped be she, until Master the lamp uncorks,
Trapped be me, until ye set me free,
Like ye tiny finch-bird in ye finch-bird egg,
Like ye catfish in ye bubble bath, you see,
Is helpless and lost without ye, dear Libby.

Brenda stopped smiling.

Livia darted over and jumped into bed with Burt, who paused for an instant to give her a wee buss on the apple of her cheek. Livia looked up in the mirror at the spasming crowd.

Brenda stared at Burt and her friend. She stared and stared and stared. Burt patted the mattress, inviting her to lie next to him on the other side. She did not move. She stared.

The crowd, smelling blood, screamed like the bleachers at a circus maximus. Burt began his refrain.

Brenda approached the bed. And, with the kind of superhuman ease that sometimes allows a panicked mother to lift up a crashed car under which her child or corgi is pinned, Brenda flipped the bed so Burt and Livia and the mattress and covers wound up all over the stage. Burt's guitar went arcing into the drum kit, causing a couple of the speakers to feed back. Brenda began to attack anything within reach. She caught Gary by the shirt, took his bass away and threw it at Jerry, who, along with his organ, collapsed. Something in the ceiling popped, raining down sparks. The lights went out. The pitch of the crowd changed to one of disappointment, quickly transforming into one of we-want-our-money-back indignance, then of confusion, then panic.

Brenda screeched, long and loud, momentarily defeating the roar of the powerful ruck. Then, a crash.

The only thing that could make that kind of racket was a Marshall stack falling over and landing on a drum kit.

Burt, who had crawled under the mattress, found Livia's hand and pulled her with him into the perfect darkness.

"Hi!" shouted Burt.

"Hi!" shouted Livia.

The pops and clangs of what sounded like a can-and-bottle fight began to escalate. Something big shattered, certainly the mirror above them. They lifted an edge of their mattress harbor to see spears of silvered glass falling, knifing, slicing, sticking into the black plywood floor around them. Brenda could be heard huffing and growling somewhere in the black bar.

Without another word, Burt and Livia listened to the wails of the police and fire engines, the shouting and threats of the cops and bartenders, the insults and protests of the arrestees, the honking and screeching of tires out on the street, the *chnk* of the electricity going back on, the gravelly scrape of glass and wet trash being swept up, the lock and bolt of a strong door, and, finally, perfect silence. Rain.

"Do you think we're alone?" said Burt. His breath smelled like teaberry gum under the tent of the mattress.

"It seems like it. I don't want to look, though."

"Me either," he said. "I'm comfortable under here with you."

The rain came down harder.

"I wonder what happened to Brenda," said Livia, whose own breath she noticed smelled like antique salad. "She was pretty mad."

"Yeah. She's bananas."

"I don't think we're friends anymore."

"Yeah."

"Yeah."

Burt sighed. He gave Livia's hand the merest squeeze.

"My mom says hi."

"I love you, Libby."

* * *

A week after Livia had spent the night with Burt under the mattress at Wolford's, she brought him to the house to meet Mère and Charlotte. Charlotte gave him a warm hug, a magnificently gooey smile, and a kiss on the cheek, delighting Livia, mortifying Burt, and repelling Mère, who refused to acknowledge the lovefest in her living room, and instead selected a folding pinochle chair, placed it in a corner, her back to the living room, sat down, and remained facing the corner until he left. That evening, Mère and Charlotte had an argument at the pinochle table over Burt. Mère and Charlotte quit speaking.

"Mère," Livia'd said about a week following, "are you mad at me, too?"

Mère was sitting on the divan squeezing Elmer's into a seam of one of her bowling shoes.

"Are you going to take me to the Dart Bowl or do you have to go see an evil man play rock music again tonight?"

"See, you are mad."

"You labor in confusion. I am just worried. It's your mother I'm mad at."

Some glue spilled onto the carpet.

"May God herself fell this devil man Elmer," said Mère under her breath.

Livia sat on the floor.

"Give me the glue, Mère."

She did. Livia carefully filled the splitting seams of her grandmother's shoes. Mère leaned back on the divan.

"Mère. I love Burt Moppett and we're getting married."

Mère did not move.

"You and your mother," she said. "You and your mother."

Charlotte came in. She was smiling wildly. She had her hands clasped in front of her bright red face.

"So?" she said. "Have you two been talking about anything in particular?"

"I told her, Mother," said Livia. "Can't you tell?"

Mère was still leaning back on the divan, looking deceased, as she was wont to do when visited by odious surprises.

"Mère," said Charlotte, taking her mother's hands and massaging the thin bones. "Burt's a very nice boy. I see him every day at the bank. Polite, intelligent, respectful. And you know he was nearly murdered. By Charles Whitman."

Mère, now revenant, sighed.

"Burt's good to me, Mère," said Livia, massaging her grandmother's other hand. "I know I've only known him a couple of weeks, but I feel like I've always known him. He opens doors for me. And for everyone else, too. And he has a good job at Centennial. He's in charge of vodka and cocktail mixes, and in a few months will get promoted to airplane nips manager."

Livia left out a lot of things she liked about Burt. She also didn't mention that he had just volunteered and would be on his way to Fort Campbell soon—Mère would hardly approve of that. Mère was a member of the Texas Socialist Party—the original one—and did not exactly adore her country or believe in its leaders. She would regard going to war as an act not of courage and patriotism but of cowardice and mental density.

Mère opened her mouth and rolled her eyes back into her head.

"He will lash you to a wheel and force his member into you and then leave for Houston or Baltimore with your money as your body teems with demons."

"Dammit, Mère," said Charlotte, who had far less patience with her mother than Livia had for either of them. "You sound like the Pentecostals. Quit it. Can't you at least have a little compassion? He was nearly murdered by a madman. Now, that's a man you should be worked up over, Charles Whitman. Not Burt Moppett, who proposed on his knees to your granddaughter, because he loves her."

Charlotte stood up. She looked at her mother and pointed at her daughter.

"Be happy for her."

"Livia," said Mère, "tell your mother I don't care to partner with her anymore."

"Livia," said Charlotte, "you tell your Mère that she can't quit, because she's fired."

They were halfway home from Dr. Gonzales's when Livia's woolgathering evaporated.

She was stopped on East Forty-Fifth Street behind a large orange machine whose apparent function was to rhythmically cloud the air with poisonous farts of violet smoke while poking holes in the asphalt with a ten-foot pneumatic bodkin.

"What is that thing?" shouted Charlotte over the noise of the machine. "Get away from it."

"I can't, Mother. We're stuck here until it moves."

"Why did you come this way? I told you to take Thirty-Eighth."

"Wasn't thinking."

"Weren't listening."

"Sorry."

"Ask that man to let you through."

A small, weary-looking, grandfatherly fellow wearing a fluorescent orange vest and a hard hat with a RECUERDO 107.1 FM sticker on it brandished a dusty STOP sign at them.

"No. I'm not going to bother him. He's busy and hot."

"Then just drive on the sidewalk. Those pedestrians will let you through."

"What's wrong with you, Mother? Have you been taking loony pills? Is that what Dr. Gonzales's diagnosis was? That you're nuts and it's giving you gas and a rosy glow? What's your hurry, anyway?"

Charlotte ignored her daughter. Charlotte got out of the car.

"Mother!" said Livia, as Charlotte slammed the door. "What are you doing? Stop it. A serial killer will snatch you off the street and chop you up and store your organs in a freezer."

Of course it was not a serial killer that worried Livia, but the diaries.

Livia could not easily get out of the car on the driver's side without breaking her ankle on some roadwork swarf, so she tried to climb over to get out on the passenger side, and had gotten halfway over the gearshift when she realized by the panicked shouting of the road construction man that the truck was still in gear.

She was able to the stop the truck before anyone got awled, but by then Charlotte had disappeared down a side street guarded on both corners by dense, blooming magnolias.

A moment ago, she and her mother had been the same distance from the diaries. Charlotte could cover the twelve blocks to her house in ten minutes. If she had to, Livia would knock her mother down to get them.

V

April Carole stood at the threshold of her efficiency on East Fifty-First Street, watching her friend Ryan pack the last of her belongings into baby-formula boxes salvaged from behind Fiesta Mart and tote them down to his F-350 pickup, in which he was about to make the last of six back-and-forth trips from here to April's new place at the Parallel Apartments over on Airport Boulevard.

"Don't forget my meds in the bathroom cabinet," she said.

"Already packed," he said. "Why do you take that stuff? You don't seem like you need it anymore."

"If you saw what I was like without them, you'd wonder why I wasn't on them."

"All that mental-illness stuff can be controlled by determination and sheer will. And exercise."

"You just called me weak, passive, and fat."

"I'm just saying that discipline can save you about a hundred bucks a month on crazy pills."

"That's the same old AA bullshit. Why don't you quit *them*? You drink every day, anyway."

Ryan did not respond.

April stared at Ryan, a classical composer and Liszt scholar, as he crawled around on his hands and knees picking up objects here and there. Guitar picks, transistors, coins, knobs unmoored from the many pieces of recording equipment that April owned or rented and that were now safely at the new efficiency, waiting to be wired together, powered up, and made ready to record the most sublime and charismatic undiscovered mezzo-soprano in the city, April Carole.

This was not her sentiment, but her father's. Her mother, Blaise, had no opinion of April's voice. Or anything, for that matter, at least since Bryce, her daughter and April's twin sister, had been beaten to death in a part of Houston Bryce should not have been loitering in, buying items she should not have been buying. Bryce left a two-year-old child, Harry, a blond whirl-wind of obscure paternal provenance, who had been far more attached to April than he had been to his mother. April wanted him. So did Blaise. Her mother won, in court.

"Tough, your mother, a toughie," Archie Carole had said to his daughter after he'd picked her up from Travis County Corrections, where she'd spent two nights for throwing a quarter at the judge after his decision to award Harry to April's parents instead of her. "*Tough.*"

"I thought you were on my side, Daddy."

"I am, and I'm on your mother's side, too," he said as he fiddled with the reliably fallible air conditioner in the 1972 Coupe de Ville he'd bought with an unexpected oil-lease dividend before he got married.

"Harry's mine!"

"You're lucky you didn't hit that judge."

"If one more person says that, I'll…"

"You could've put his eye out."

"Please take me to my apartment. And tell your wife I never want to see her again."

"Your mother lost a daughter, dammit, April, remember that," said Mr. Carole. "So did *I*."

April had hated Bryce. They were identical twins but didn't really look all that much alike. Bryce's blond hair was several shades more honied than

April's, Bryce's eyes were greener, Bryce's ears didn't stick out like side-views, Bryce's feet were two sizes smaller and two letters narrower, and her shape was not teratologically asymmetrical—Bryce was all airy wiggle, while April was a blackthorn cudgel. Bryce, in April's opinion, was prettier, smarter, sexier, and more talented (oboe)—all the things at issue in sibling rivalries of any intensity, anywhere, anytime. The girls grew up screaming at each other, lying to each other, hitting each other with closed fists. April focused this violence on Bryce only; Bryce, however, expanded her crimes to her parents, friends, eventually strangers, and, ultimately, Harry. CPS took the child away and gave him to her parents. After Bryce was killed and April took her parents to court, the judge suggested that since April and Bryce had been twins, there was every likelihood that April would adopt a similar attitude toward the child. It was seconds after this that a shiny 1988 quarter dollar sailed three inches from Judge Polemp's head and silently struck the blackish-red drapery that seemed to backdrop every goddam judge's bench in the land. He found her in contempt of court, an edict that sent her to jail, where they kept her meds from her until they let her out two days later.

"Looks like your wife lost two daughters," said April, noticing on the sidewalk a chain of little children holding each other by the hand, all bell-wethered by a slender East Indian woman holding a leash attached to the lead child. If April was allowed to take one, she would bring home the tiniest of all: a roundish, red-haired little girl wearing a light-blue frock over which was draped a red superhero's cape. She—Montserrat, April would name her—was last in line, and seemed to have no interest in holding hands, and so was quite rogue, jumping and stomping and wandering, pulling behind her on a string a kind of miniature sulky filled with leaves and trash and a headless, Burtless Ernie. She turned and looked at April as they drove by. *Maybe I'll come back here one day and take you for myself, Montserrat. How hard could that be?*

"I'm sad to hear you say that," said Archie Carole.

"Maybe I'll just come get Harry and move away."

"Stop it, now."

"I want Bryce's Mini Cooper. You guys owe me."

BILL COTTER

* * *

April didn't really consider stealing Harry. In truth she wanted not a child but a *baby*. She doubted she could bring herself to actually steal an infant, but still she made regular visits to mommy-baby gatherings around town, like BabyStock at Central Market once a month. She also visited maternity rooms around town. They seemed impossibly secure. The obvious solution was to have one of her own. The endeavor might even be fun.

The few carefully timed attempts to fertilize her eggs with the sperm of sympathetic and willing friends were unsuccessful. Before long, April was beginning to grow desperate. Desperate enough to start having sex with strangers, sometimes as many as four in a single day.

Soon her life was occupied by temp jobs, fertility sorcery, screwing, and scales, the latter two producing enough racket that her neighbors and landlady eventually harassed April into moving out of the Fifty-First Street apartment. Ryan was the noisiest lover so far. He was also the first of her friends she had sex with. April had since slept with him occasionally, but that was about to cease. That was going to be hard on Ryan: he was in love with April to roughly the same degree that she was not in love with him. He expressed his love by performing chores and duties for April, which routinely included vanishment whenever April brought home a new conquest. And April expressed her non-love by asking him to do more and more chores.

"April, what's this?" said Ryan, handing her a tiny whitish object he found in the grotty shag-pile carpeting.

"Wow," she said, "haven't seen one of these in a lo-o-o-ng time. It's a good-luck charm. A piece of carved ivory. It came with more eggs just like it in a little ivory basket, but I have no idea where they are. They were in a plastic Easter egg I found tucked between two bricks lining the walk in the backyard at home when I was nine. It was December. No one even remembered putting it out there."

April placed the egg in her mouth, and with her tongue tucked it up between her gum and cheek, where it found a natural cranny. She would swallow it the next time she was with a man—tonight, actually—right at the moment he ejaculated. April was cautiously excited. She had been turning more and more to occult rituals. The tiny egg seemed to be a gift from the gods, or whatever was in charge.

"Is that everything?" she said, testing the egg's security with her tongue. "Good work, man. Thanks."

Ryan stood stiffly; he had been crawling around a long time.

"We still gotta clean this place and spackle divots and repaint."

"I don't care about the damn security deposit."

"I do," he said. Ryan often took upon himself the neglects of others. "I'll take care of it when you're on your date. You do have one tonight, right?"

"Depends on whether you set up the futon at the new place. I don't like fucking on the floor."

April also didn't like talking to Ryan about her other dates. It made her feel guilty for excluding him. But the fact was she didn't want to waste time sleeping with him. He was a proven failure. She'd rather take a chance with attractive, brown-haired, green-eyed, boyish strangers who blushed visibly in dark Sixth Street bars when she explained her plans.

"I set it up, sheets and everything," said Ryan, a micaceous glint— hope?—in his eye. "Ready for immediate use." It was an imperfect glint, though, dulled at the edges, as if it knew Ryan had Buckley's chances of ever being with April again.

"C'mon," she said, looking away from the glint. "Grab my cat—she's behind the toilet—and let's go. I never wanna see this place again."

She had found tonight's date, Christian, on Craigslist the week before. Pretty damn cute, and a freshman at UT, so she could probably count on some vigor. She demanded that Christian spend the week leading up to the encounter acquiring a clean and current bill of health. She demanded this of all her dates.

Christian would be arriving at April's new apartment at 10 p.m., while Ryan was still back at the old place, probably plucking tacks and nails out of the walls and razor-scraping the scum out of the tub and cleansing everything with C.C.R. and painting the walls with enough coats of an eggshell white so brilliantly opaque that everything the walls and ceiling had ever been witness to would be suffocated and forever sealed away. That's what April was imagining, anyway, as she surveyed her new apartment's freshly painted walls. One was already marred by a gouge, a dingy avulsion of sheetrock, probably from moving the futon. How much crap she'd moved over here! The most important thing, excepting her cat, was the delicate, nineteenth-century bassinet she'd found at the Marburger Farm Antique

Show. It was filled with CDs at the moment, but soon it would function, goddammit, as intended. April's desire for a child hurt like a cramp. But it seemed possible that the new digs, along with the little egg in her cheek, a fresh outlook, and a conquest of above-average cuteness just might do the trick. And, most important, she was ovulating.

A knock. April opened the door. Christian? Yes. Come in. Would you like a beer? Yes. Good, here. Thank you. Can I see your papers?

Christian, dressed in a tight black suit and tie that matched his slick-backed hair, and shod in brown spectators that matched the frames of his glasses, stood uncomfortably among the brutalist city of unpacked boxes, sipping the longneck of Mutter's Crystal Lager.

It was April's M.O. to get her conquest drinking, play Scrabble on the futon with him till he was amply besotted, then sweep the board from between them, land a wet kiss on his neck, and get to work. It was usually all over in three minutes, the conquest already at the gates of profound postcoital catalepsy. April would lie back with a pillow under her bottom, holding her vagina shut so that nothing could leak out before it had a chance to accost her egg. If there even was one at all.

She allowed Christian to stay all night, though she had to throw him out by nine the next morning, as Ryan was due over with the vacuum and an assortment of cleansers and the last of the last of the last of the objects April could not throw away. But she was too late: Ryan knocked on the door at 9:00, while April was still under the blankets with Christian, both in the altogether, if you didn't count the pair of waist-high tights they were sharing, each with a leg holstered into the legs of the tights, like someone with both hands jammed into a single glove. Christian had proved himself capable of multiple rebounds, and, as a reward, had been given the okay to engage in this particular kink.

April freed herself, tiptoed to the door, and opened it a crack.

"Go away!" she hissed at Ryan.

"Jesus, dude's still there? Or do you have a new guy in there? A morning roll?"

"Asshole."

"You said for me to come at nine!"

"Come back in an hour."

"Rehearsal."

"Just leave the shit outside and don't come back."

"Wait, April, sorry, I'll come back at ten, promise, I can skip rehearsal, no biggie. Need anything? Maybe some—"

"No." said April.

"Sure? Anything?"

"Nuh-uh," said April. "Well... wait."

"Yeah?"

"I want you to go to my parents' house in Bee Caves—you remember where, right?—and ask my mother where my little ivory eggs and basket are. I bet she's got them. Bring 'em here."

"Jeez, I haven't seen your folks since you snapped them off last year. I bet they hate me."

"I doubt it. They always considered you a stabilizing influence on me."

"You're kidding, of course."

"No. Now move. I'll make sure Christian's gone by the time you get back."

"Can we sleep together again one day? I've been reading up on how to increase my virility."

"God, Ryan. You can be so pathetic."

"Sorry."

"And do not tell them anything about me!"

Ryan returned later, bearing the little basket of eleven ivory eggs.

VI

January 1988

Justine lay on the floor in the den in front of a hissing gas heater, playing with a puppy, a Christmas present from Livia. Livia and Charlotte were out driving around, hoping to find someplace open that sold canned black-eyed peas. In the months since Livia had begun dating Archibold Bamberger, he had convinced her that luck was a real thing, evident in every single action from the motions of quarks to the licking of stamps; that it was sometimes predictable yet never innocent, and could be influenced by the simplest things, like not picking up heads-up pennies off the ground or kissing something red if you saw an ambulance or forgetting to have black-eyed peas and bacon green beans on New Year's Day—especially New Year's 1988, which he said was pregnant with bon chance.

The idea of getting green-bean strands and bacon flecks stuck in her new braces annoyed Justine as much as they made her teeth hurt. She had not wanted braces, reasonably citing cost, pain, risk, and vanity, but Livia had insisted, and Justine had been in an orthodontic throe for three months now, almost all of that time spent in Austin State Hospital, where she had been sentenced for a pseudo-suicide attempt the day she got her braces. Her teeth appeared not to have moved at all, yet hurt as if they had been twisted in their sockets like little Christmas bulbs. Justine suspected that the puppy, a pug named Dartmouth, had been a kind of peace pipe, to be regarded as the end of the braces discussion.

With the aid of a long plastic back scratcher, one end of which was an injection-molded hand in the posture of a claw, Justine tried to keep Dartmouth from getting close enough to get drool or other oral canine colloids on her new sweater.

Livia and Charlotte had been gone a long time. Justine expected them to barge in the front door at any moment.

Instead, a big, soft *knock-knock*, as though issued by someone outfitted in a furry panda suit, came at the door.

At the noise Dartmouth positively blurred with locomotive excitement, flinging slobber around the den, some of which landed in the open gas flames of the space heater and burst into terrible novae of steam. Dartmouth hadn't gotten the hang of barking, so he redirected all the energy that an ordinary puppy would have expended on barking into snuffling and tinkling and flinging slobber.

Justine, on the other hand, did not move. Ever since she'd been discharged from ASH two weeks before, she had answered neither door nor phone. Well, why would she? There was no boyfriend: Dick had dumped her before she'd been committed. The same day, in fact. So who would call? Shrinks? Right. Who would come by? Gracie Yin? Right.

The somebody knocked again.

She'd missed nearly eleven weeks of school and the only person to have called was Troy Bugler, a skinny philatelist and schoolmate not at all bashful about communicating his desire for Justine. So far he'd been pervious to rebuke, but just barely.

Another knock. Today was the last day of Christmas vacation. Tomorrow, school. No way was she going to spend even a single instant of her last few hours of freedom in dialogue with who-knows-who. New Year's Day should be spent alone, in private dread. So she continued to ignore the presence on the other side of the front door.

Some shifting outside. A sigh.

Maybe it was Duck Baby, the man who came by a few times a year to do yard work, usually when he needed money to gamble. Charlotte would give Duck Baby ten dollars and then Duck Baby would "mow" the lawn by running around and stepping on weeds until they were no longer erect. Then he would run away. During the night, the weeds would recover and by morning would be fully upright.

But it was winter. Even Duck Baby would be challenged to find something in the barren yard to step on.

Another furry knock, more timid.

"Who is it!"

"Ah, it's ah, is Charlotte at home in there?"

A man's voice.

"She's out."

Justine rolled onto her stomach and looked at the stiff, lacy yellow valances that covered the three eye-level rectangular windows in the front door. There appeared to be the shadows of two heads against the curtains.

The big furry knock at the door again.

"Hello, how 'bout Livia?" said the man. "Is...?"

Another voice, quiet, a woman's, apparently directed at the man, said: "I need to sit down, baby."

"Just a minute," said the man. "We'll sit you down in a minute."

Justine stood up. Dartmouth was an unstoppable williwaw of incontinent excitement. She opened the door. A small woman, and a large man holding her around the waist with one hand. In his other he held a small, well-traveled green American Tourister.

The man, fifty or so, was covered with a black-and-red-checked-lumberjack-style wool jacket. He was freshly shaved, but didn't look as though he shaved regularly—his skin was reddish, and textured a little like a neglected football, except where his whiskers would be: there his skin was papery and shark-belly pale. His eyes were green, similar in hue to Justine's, but not as luminous; his were more like the muddy antifreeze she sometimes saw puddled along curbs during cold spells. His hair was slicked back and his hairline curved along the same contours as James Garner's. He was tall and solid. He was handsome. An ineffable feature of his posture suggested that he fell down a lot, or walked into doors, or backed into tables, upsetting all the bottles and glasses and vases of bluebonnets thereon. He wore huge woolen mittens; Tribbles, almost.

The woman, in maybe her early seventies, was leaning on the man and holding his arm. She seemed frail, but frail in the way that a Panhandle dustbowl farmwoman who'd pulled a lot of carrot and made her own bobwire but had come down with pneumonia might seem frail.

Her big brown eyes were surrounded by lashes as thick and black as threads of melted pitch. Her gray hair was shiny and full, like the hair of middle-aged models in the AARP magazines that were the only things to read in Justine's shrink's waiting room. The woman's thin body shivered, visibly, even though she was wrapped up in an oversized white down jacket, weathered and grimy, lacerated with L-shaped slits, bleeding feathers. She wore white cigarette pants that looked to be made of oil-smeared typing paper, and gecko-green slingback platform shoes that revealed deep and wrinkly toe cleavage.

"Hello," said the man. "I'm Lou Borger. I'm, ah, related."

Justine looked beyond them. There were no cars parked on the street that she hadn't seen before.

"Hi."

Dartmouth slalomed the six legs.

"Oh, and who are you?" said the woman in a cracked, quiet voice that made Justine think of the neighbor's big live oak that lightning had splintered the summer before.

"That's Dartmouth," said Justine. "He won't hurt you. Anyway, we don't think he will. He's new."

The man looked at Justine. She couldn't decide if his expression was sad, or nostalgic, or defeated, or one of relief, or some combination. Or maybe it was just his regular look, the one he wore whether he was knocking on people's doors or watching *Hollywood Squares* or what—after all, she'd never seen him before. Justine wondered what he thought of *her* expression.

The woman slowly bent down, still holding on to the man's arm.

"Hi, darling," she said, allowing Dartmouth to sop her wrinkly, blotchy hand. "I'm Dot. Call me Dotty. Or Dot. All my best puppy dogs do."

Justine watched Lou Borger watch Dotty pet Dartmouth. Dot slowly stood back up.

"Can I sit down, baby?"

"Okay," said Justine, though it was unclear whether the woman had addressed her or Lou. "But Livia and Charlotte aren't here."

"That's fine," said Lou. "Okay if we wait?"

Lou led Dot over to the divan. She let go of his arm and allowed herself to fall into a sitting position. Lou put down the green suitcase, sat down beside her, and put his arm around her. Dartmouth sat on Dot's platform-shod feet. Lou continued to look at her with the same unclassifiable expression. No one said anything. The gas heater faintly *ushed*.

"Happy New Year," said Lou.

Usssh.

"Mm," said Dot. "Tired. Long day."

"You're Livia's dad, right?" said Justine.

"That's right. I sure am. I sure am. You're Livia's daughter?"

"Adoptive. I guess that makes you my adoptive granddad."

"Adoptive, huh," said Lou, who plucked off one of his large, silly woolen mittens and shook Justine's hand—her whole hand, thumb and all. "Well, hi."

His palm was so rough and hard but his grasp so gentle that Justine felt as though her hand were sheltered in a warm little cavern. "Livia never told you about... getting me?"

"She did indeed. I posted you a letter now and then. I guess you never received them."

"No. Figures she'd wouldn't tell me she talked to you."

"Well, it was some time ago, years and years. We have not been in touch since."

Lou let go of her hand and looked down at the yard of carpet separating them. Justine's hand seemed to ice over after its withdrawal from the warm cavern. She shivered. Her interior sine wave of despair peaked for a moment.

"And are you my adoptive great-grandmother?"

Dot looked at Justine for a moment, then at Lou. She slapped Lou on the arm, then opened her mouth and shut her eyes and tom-tomed her kneecaps until she burst in a fit of crackly laughter that sent Dartmouth whistling down the hall, helplessly decanting tinkle and foams.

"Oh, me," said Dot, wheezing and gasping. "My. No. True, Lou acts like a child and thinks I am his mother, but I am not."

"Oh. Sorry."

"The Disfarmer women do age young, but we live forever. I am forty-six, born on the day the Brits raided the Lofoten Islands."

"Sorry."

"You're awful pretty," said Dot. "You have pretty eyes. I wish I had shoes that green color."

Dot bent over to admire her extraordinary platforms.

Justine looked around furiously for Dartmouth, who would have been a perfect barrier against the embarrassing compliment. But Dartmouth was still in hiding. Instead, Justine studied Dot's legs, specifically the six inches of flesh between the green straps of her shoes and the cuffs of her pants. Her skin was smooth and faintly coppery. On the calf of her right leg, just peeking out from under the cuff, was the edge of a bruise, fresh and angry.

Dot leaned over and pulled on the cuff. The bruise disappeared.

"Cool shoes," said Justine. "So what are you guys doing here?"

"Dot's here to see a fellah, so we just dropped by for a little visit," said Lou, looking over his shoulder out the picture window.

"You don't live in Austin, do you?"

"Nuuuu," said Dot. "New Orleans."

Justine had always wanted to go and become a genius waitress and learn how to make perfumes like Priscilla in *Jitterbug Perfume*, or go to the movies all the time like Binx in *The Moviegoer*, or sell Lucky Dogs in the French Quarter and then commit suicide and get a posthumous Pulitzer Prize, like John Kennedy Toole.

Someday, that is. First, she was going to go live in New York. The instant that Principal Yarn handed over her high-school diploma she would be on her way north. She would become a pioneer in two-point perspective collage, with works for view at MoMA and for sale at Gagosian.

"You ought come visit sometime," said Dot. "We just live a little ways from the Quarters. Part of town called the Bywater."

"Lot of artists in the French Quarter, right?"

Dot shut her eyes and appeared to quit breathing. Lou leaned over her.

"Dotty, let's put you down for a rest," he said. Addressing Justine: "Can my mommy stretch out and nap right here?"

Justine smiled. It hurt a bit, so long had it been since she'd last stretched her face like that. "Okay."

Lou took off Dot's shoes and put her feet up on the bolster. He and Justine covered her with an afghan that had lain over the back of the divan for so long the sun had bleached the exposed part from blue to light gray. Lou tucked the green suitcase between the end of the divan and the side table.

Dartmouth's tiny cortex had apparently given him the all-clear: he rock-
eted back into the room and went straight for the divan. He tried to bound
onto it, but misjudged by several inches and instead reflected off the bolster
and back onto the floor, where he whirled in damp confusion until Dot
reached down, picked him up, and placed him next to her on the divan.

"Justine," said Lou, looking down at his knuckles. "Got any Coca-Cola?"

Justine sat Lou down in Charlotte's birdwatching spot at the kitchen table
by the picture window. In the refrigerator Justine found an eighth-full two-
liter bottle of Coke she knew to be intolerably flat, but since she did not
want to disappoint her adoptive granddaddy she put it on the table anyway
and found a plastic cup in the dishwasher that might or might not have been
clean and gave that to him, too.

"That might be a little old. We have beer instead if you want."

"I quit drinking," said Lou, who appeared to be counting the bird feeders
in the backyard. "Last time I was in Austin, as a matter of fact. Some seventeen, eighteen years ago."

"Oh. We have faucet water. It's cold if I get it from the bathroom sink.
Or I can make Swiss Miss if you want."

Lou looked at Justine for an instant. His unplaceable expression had not
departed; Justine figured it must be his regular face. It was probably hard
for him to make friends. Justine felt glad for him that he had Dot, whoever
she was. She didn't seem like a girlfriend, but maybe she was.

"This Coke'll be just fine," said Lou.

"I gotta go do some stuff. In my room. Charlotte and Livia'll be back
soon. They just went out for black-eyed peas."

"Okay, then," said Lou, opening the bottle, which issued no compressed
gas; it even seemed to suck a little air back in.

"It's pretty flat," said Justine.

"I don't mind one bit."

Lou smiled. It was the saddest smile Justine had ever seen.

Justine went upstairs to her room. She lit her own gas heater with a barbecue
match and lay down on her bed. She kicked off her shoes and let her feet

dangle over the end, where the heater would toast them. She shut her eyes, breathed in the smell of schoolroom paste that always activated when the room was warming up, and tried to remember Chewbacca.

Justine had had images in her head of what Lou must look like ever since she was six, when she had first heard his name mentioned. It had been while Livia and Charlotte were arguing over some point in their common personal histories one Saturday in late fall.

"Who'sLouWho'sLouWho'sLouWho'sLouWho'sLouWho'sLou?" Justine had said while lying in the middle of the kitchen floor dressed in a Little Orphan Annie costume, its curly red wig component wadded up and stuffed under the smock component in order to create a bosom component, which Justine felt essential for her interpretation of the character.

"He is your granddad and a common roughneck," said Charlotte. "And we do not talk about him."

"You're talking about him," said Justine. "My real granddad?"

"No, you're adopted, remember?" said Livia.

"No duh."

"Get off the floor this instant and put on your shoes and wig. We have to go in exactly one minute."

"I'm wearing my wig!" Justine squealed.

Still stretched out flat on the kitchen floor, Justine began to rotate herself using her bottom as an axis.

"What does he look like?"

"Justine," said Charlotte, "please get off the floor now or your understudy will have to take your place because you'll be in your room at home in a state of disapprobation."

Justine accelerated her rotation. She did not take Charlotte's threats seriously, as they were rarely carried out.

"What's my understudy?"

"Justine, dammit!" shouted Livia, nearly tripping over Justine's feet.

"What does Lou look like? Is he old?"

"He looks like Chewy."

"Ew."

"Who," said Charlotte, "is Chewy?"

"From a movie, Mother. Never mind."

"A movie. Well, remind me not to go see that one."

And ever since then, when the very rare subject of Lou came up, Justine had imagined him as a yeti-man who pumped gas into Charlotte's X-wing fighter, taking her MasterCard and running it through his credit-card knucklebuster while she checked her lipstick in the rearview.

But now, presented with the genuine Lou Borger, that image dissipated. The real Lou didn't look much like Chewbacca at all. Well, a tiny bit.

Justine turned on her little black-and-white. Football, football, football. She turned it off. There was nothing to do except homework, which was to read *The Once and Future King* and write a paper on it for Mrs. DeBrackton, something that she had decided even before Christmas vacation she would not do. This wouldn't be a problem, either—mental illness, for all its unpleasantness, worked great as an excuse for not doing stuff.

So she lay back on the bed and began to play her favorite (nonsexual) daydream, which was that Livia would get into a car crash and die instantly. Justine didn't necessarily want Livia to suffer, and she didn't like to think of her as a wadded corpse on an enameled-metal morgue table, or even as a name die-sunk into a gravestone; Justine just wanted her out of the picture. Livia was mean and moody and had always seemed to dislike Justine for no really good reason. Charlotte was much nicer, always sweetly apologizing for nothing, and much more like the mothers engineered for TV. Livia, on the other hand, fit tidily into the TV mold for stepmothers and foster-mothers: razor-eyed, taut-browed, suspicious and lording. Livia and Charlotte got along most of the time, but when they did fight, it was over something having to do with Justine.

For variety, Justine adjusted today's car-crash scenario in her head: Livia had Charlotte with her this time. Justine didn't want anything to happen to Charlotte, so Justine had her forget her checkbook in H.E.B. and have to go back for it; meanwhile, Livia, who is idling in the fire lane by the front doors, waiting for her mother, is blindsided by an old man in a green pickup truck who's just had a convulsion and accidentally stomped on his accelerator. The old man finishes his convulsion and is fine, but Livia is dead from blunt force trauma to the head, even though there is no blood and she never knew what hit her. Charlotte emerges from H.E.B. with her checkbook, screams and faints, but is secretly relieved that Livia's dead. Justine and Charlotte grow closer, and on the hottest nights they turn on the powerful upstairs air conditioner and sit in the hallway under blankets, drinking beer and talking shit about Livia.

"Why was she so mean, Charl?" Justine would say, opening a can of Falstaff and handing it to her beautiful grandmother.

"Darling, so many reasons."

"I'm glad she didn't suffer."

"Fatherlessness is one reason."

"I'm fatherless, and I'm not mean."

"You're just darling."

And they'd be finished with their first beers and well into their second.

"Charl, I want to be a collage artist."

"You may be whatever you wish."

"I want to go to New York and enroll in art school."

"Your mother wouldn't have wanted you to go to New York."

"Livia's not my mother and besides, she's dead."

"You are so right. I hope you go to art school in New York City."

Third, fourth beers. Cuddling together under the blankets, the thermostat down to sixty.

"I love you Charl."

"From now on, darling, call me Mother."

"I'll never be depressed or cut myself or try to commit suicide again, I promise, and I'll take my pills. Except Cogentin and Prolixin."

"That's just wonderful. Let us finish the Falstaff beer, and then will you show me some collage basics?"

"I love you, Mommy."

Justine woke up freezing; the gas heater had gone off. She sat up and looked out the window.

Livia's car sat in the driveway. It did not appear to have been stove in by a convulsing man in a runaway green pickup. It looked the same as always.

Voices downstairs. Calm. Charlotte, Livia, Lou.

In the kitchen Justine encountered Lou still sitting where she'd left him, and still wearing the same expression. He had drunk all the flat Coke and had somehow managed to squeeze the white plastic cap inside the bottle. Charlotte was leaning against the kitchen counter with a Belair in one hand and a Tuborg in the other, taking delicate pulls on each. Livia stood in the kitchen doorway, arms tightly crossed under her breasts, wearing an expression of tense uncertainty. Dot was visible through the kitchen doorway, still lying on the divan in exactly the same position, with Dartmouth stretched out alongside her; both were asleep.

Justine went over and pulled on the refrigerator door Charlotte was leaning on.

"Oh, Justine," said Charlotte, stepping aside. "This is Lou, Livia's fa—"

"I know, I let him in. He told me."

Justine found a Tuborg, opened it, and then shut the refrigerator with her bottom.

"Justine," said Charlotte, her voice uncharacteristically firm, "you may not have that Tuborg. Give it to Lou before it gets flat."

"Lou doesn't drink," said Justine, consuming a third of it. "You have it."

Charlotte took the beer from Justine with her cigarette hand.

"So," said Livia, still squeezing herself, "what else did you two visit about besides sobriety?"

If one of Justine's high-school friends had uttered that question in that tone, it would have implied this addendum: *You better not be talking about me.*

Lou chuckled politely. "Art."

"I'm going to visit them in New Orleans," said Justine.

"That right."

"That's right."

"And, Lou, when will you be on your way back to the Crescent City?" said Charlotte, who took another sip of her first beer and then another. Then it was gone. She had a sip of Justine's beer. Charlotte rarely finished a beer or a cigarette; such practices she considered vulgar. When she did finish one, it meant she was brooding or furious or in some way out of kilter.

"Mother, Lou has said he's here to take his friend to a doctor." Livia's tone, punching the *doc* in *doctor*, suggested that she thought Charlotte should allow them to stay as long as they wanted.

"That has been mentioned," said Charlotte. *No way*, she meant, thought Justine. Justine thought Charlotte was being a little harsh, and for a change felt some defensive sympathy for Livia, who seemed as infantile and destabilized as Justine had ever seen her.

"So what's wrong with Dot?" Justine said quietly.

The kitchen was as cold as the upstairs, and the beer had made her shiver for a moment, but the forge-red complexion of the conversation was making Justine perspire with curiosity.

"Dot's sick, darling," said Lou, looking down into his Coke bottle. "We're here to see a specialist."

"She just appears sleepy to me," said Charlotte. "And she has infected our new puppy with languor."

Charlotte extinguished her cigarette with a quick jet of tap water, then put the butt in a trash can under the sink. She usually let the door under the sink shut gently, but this time she let it slam.

Then Justine caught Livia looking at her in a way she'd never seen. Eyes slightly narrowed and her mouth open, not to speak, but as if to draw words back in that she wished she hadn't uttered. Normally when Livia gave her a look of any kind, Justine would be quick to comment, rebut, or rebel, but this one was freighted with something she could not name, and never knew Livia carried. It frightened Justine at first, but then she noticed that Charlotte and Lou, in turn, received the same look.

Charlotte wore no occult look. She just seemed put out, which was, for Charlotte, a guise for ire. After all, a stranger had annexed her puppy and passed out on her divan; her petulance was understandable. Still, Justine seldom saw her this nettled.

Lou's expression had lightened a little, but he did not look directly at anyone except to glance out into the living room at Dot every few minutes, leaning forward to see around Livia's body, which was blocking the doorway.

The first chance she got, Justine was going to corner Lou alone and ask him what was happening. Some kind of horrible family secret? And what does Dot have? It looked like AIDS, that big blotchy, bruisy red patch. There'd been this skinny guy at ASH with AIDS, Charlie. His blotches had been similar. They'd finally taken him to a hospice, where he lasted about four days, finally dying alone, without any family, only some grouchy hospice cat in his bony lap. Lou, Justine was sure, would tell her the truth.

"Your companion, Dot," said Charlotte finally, "may stay on my divan until her appointment. And you, Lou, may stay on Livia's purple-heart-awarded dead-war-hero husband, Burt Cornelio Moppett's, army cot, in the garage."

"Mother——" said Livia.

"Now I am going to take a short nap and then bake a ham and warm up black-eyed peas and everyone shall have a large helping, as we are each going to need it."

And with that atypically bold and revealing discharge, Charlotte walked into the living room, lifted a snurfle-squeaking Dartmouth off of Dot, who made no sound, and took him upstairs. She went into her room at the end of the hall and shut the door firmly. Not a slam but not a click, either.

Usually the sudden absence of such an electromagnetic being as Charlotte Durant affected a room like a pulled tooth affected a person's skull; a drafty, saline, confusing vacancy. But this time, with Lou and Livia still there, the emotional potency vibrated almost as much as it had before Charlotte left. Nothing was said.

On the divan Dot groaned and laughed in her sleep.

"When does she see her doctor?" said Livia, stuttering slightly, her arms crossed concretely, as though girding herself.

"I reckon soon, but he's a busy man. Famous. Folks come from all over."

"So you might be here awhile."

"I just don't know," he said. "I just don't know."

I just don't know, he said one more time, mostly to himself.

"The garage," said Livia. "You might as well be outside, it's so chilly in there." After a pause, she said: "We can't have that."

"Why, I don't mind a bit," said Lou, who appeared to mean it. "I'll be out from underfoot, there."

Justine and Livia had shared a room until Justine turned twelve, when Livia moved into Charlotte's room with her. The rearrangement had come about following a terrific three-way fight that was officially about thermostat settings but was really about the small house's sudden invasion by Justine's olid and huffy puberty. The solution pleased no one: Livia, having lived with Charlotte more as sister than daughter since 1951, welcomed this reversion even less than she had welcomed Justine's admission to the family in 1971; Charlotte, a turbulent sleeper who occasionally rose to her feet while still in deep REM to wander around the house naked talking to herself and sometimes placing phone calls, was furious to have to share her room with the nosiest of all three Durants, the one who would likely follow Charlotte around during a somnambulism and listen for secrets to be divulged; and Justine, who thought she'd wanted the room to herself, after the reformation found herself not in liberty but relegated to a kind of Durant-family purdah.

This view changed to one of appreciation and relief when the world of masturbation, and the household privacy its success and piquancy depended on, was revealed to her one afternoon while watching the *Banana Splits*, the episode where Fleegle opens a barber shop. It was not the skit that got her attention, though, but the following production of the show's theme, "The Tra La La Song"; more specifically, a riveting go-go dancer wearing a print minidress and ankle-boot platforms, and whose shimmies, hair-tosses, and shapely legs drew Justine first to the edge of her bed, then to the floor, then six inches from the screen, watching for glimpses of the sixties siren, who appeared for only an instant at a time, such was the editing style of the period. The segment was over in two minutes, and the orgasm, which Justine achieved on all fours hunched over a Dressy Bessy hand mirror angled so that her manipulations were visible, was over in less than a minute. As the years went by, she never took for granted the luxury of having her own room in a two-bedroom, three-person house.

And so it came as a surprise not only to Livia but to Justine herself when Justine said, "You can have my room, Lou. If you want."

"Justine—" said Livia, her confusion and unsureness growing even less subtle, but now glazed with a strange, slumber-party anticipation. It was foreign, this composite look in her mother. It worried Justine. She couldn't recall the last time she'd worried about her. After all, Justine regularly extinguished her in daydreams, and in waking life regarded her as some immortal Jurassic prototurtle so tough as to have practically no natural enemies and which could fell a cycad with a single beak-snap. Justine did not want to worry about her mother. She was now realizing how long she'd taken for granted just how valuable it had been to not have to worry about her.

"I wouldn't mind the garage," Justine said, imagining the thrill of masturbating under the muffle of a dozen blankets. "For a change."

No one said anything.

"Thank you, darling," said Lou, "but I'll be just fine out there."

For the first time, the three people in the room seemed to share what felt to Justine to be the same emotion: relief. Lou smiled. So did Livia. Justine tried not to, but she couldn't help herself.

* * *

Lou set up Burt Moppett's old fold-up canvas army cot right in the middle of the garage, over the grease stains. Justine trawled the house for blankets and came up with a half dozen of variable insulating properties. Lou kept his shaving things on a low shelf next to the breaker box, and a change of clothes hanging from a higher shelf occupied largely by clay pots, dusty books of S&H green stamps Charlotte had filled but never cashed, and a third-full bottle of Smirnoff that had been there for years and years and that Charlotte, during particularly trying times, would visit to fashion herself dirty martinis. The bottle's level had fallen roughly a half inch per year for a decade, until Justine turned sixteen and became weird, at which time the level fell three inches in a few months.

Just before Lou settled in, Justine removed the bottle and dumped it out in the alley.

Dot lived on the divan under old, soft sheets, surrounded by little boxes of animal crackers, her little green suitcase, paperback biographies Justine brought her from the school library, and a TV-dinner tray piled with makeup, rubbing alcohol, a matching pair of old leather books in Baggies, witch hazel, pills and vitamins and vials of strange elixirs Lou would make in the kitchen while hulking over a double boiler and squinting at a xeroxed, staple-bound pamphlet of recipes entitled *Draughts*, which he'd gotten from Dot's specialist, an individual he and Dot referred to only as Sherpa. Dot often had Dartmouth on her lap, at least until Charlotte came home from her bank-teller shift at Braunschweiger's Savings and Loan downtown, and took him away.

Charlotte, when she was not at work at the bank, spent much of her life daintily smoking and sipping beer at her kitchen table, a vantage which offered the most panoptic view of the surrounding property: the backyard, the garage door, the utility closet, the upstairs hallway, the bathroom door clear at the other end of the house, and the whole of the living room, including Dot on her divan. The door that permitted this view had probably been open since 1951. The day Dot and Lou arrived, Charlotte closed it.

Justine, who as a rule holed herself up in her room as much as possible, found herself more and more in the company of Dot, saying hello when she cut through the living room on her way out, stopping for a minute to sit on the end of the divan, fetching Lou out of the garage for her, running little errands for both of them.

One Wednesday Lou asked Justine if she would run them out to Sherpa's office.

"Long drive, short appointment," said Lou.

"Sure."

The "office" was a house way south of Slaughter Lane, deep among unmanageable cedar and juniper, neighborless, completely invisible from the road, even in winter.

Justine parked at the end of the long dirt-and-flint driveway.

"Back soon."

A trail that started where the driveway left off was so steep that Lou had to carry Dot.

While listening to the car radio and peeling off her nail polish as Dot and Lou were inside consulting with Sherpa, Justine saw a big tarantula crawl down the trail.

"I saw my first tarantula," Justine said, when Lou and Dot got back to the car. "Big."

"In the middle of winter?" said Lou, absently. He was arranging Dot in the front seat, making sure the seat belt went over the partly sunbleached-blue-to-gray afghan that she had become attached to and which Charlotte had told her to keep. His manner with Dot was firm but gentle, intimate but bedside, competent but hesitant and thumby. It reminded Justine that even though they'd been staying at the Durant's for more than two weeks now, no one really knew Lou and Dot's relationship. His pertinence in her life, hers in his. They seemed like siblings more than anything else, but that was the only impossible relationship—someone surely would've referred to Dot as a great-aunt at some point. Whatever its nature, the relationship had clearly been in place a long time.

"It's pretty warm for mid-January," said Justine. "Maybe she got barn sour in her burrow and decided to go for a walk."

Dot had her eyes closed and did not say anything. Justine was paralyzed for an instant. *Had she died?*

"Mm," said Lou, shutting Dot's door and climbing in the backseat. Dot emerged from her transitive state to say:

"What seventeen-year-old uses the term *barn sour*?"

"I read it in a book last week," said Justine, her cheeks numb. "I wanted to fit it into a sentence as soon as I could."

"That Sherpa fellah's barn sour," said Dot. "He could use a walk in the sun."

"Tarantulas are scary," said Lou, "and they do bite hard enough for a man to wail from, but they won't hurt you in the long run. Anyone want to stop and eat?"

"Dan's," said Justine.

"Wendy's," said Dot. "Frosty and french fries."

"Okay," said Lou, sounding beaten and exhausted.

"How about both?" said Justine, starting the car. "I'm rich. Somebody bought one of my collages at Flightpath Coffee. Thirty-five bucks."

"Good for you, darling," said Lou.

"Good for you, darling," said Dot. "Don't run over your spider."

No one mentioned what had gone on inside the Sherpa's house.

Justine began to take them regularly to their late-afternoon thrice-weekly appointments at Sherpa's. Justine was never asked inside, and frankly was happy to sit in the car and listen to KVET. Afterward, they would drive through Wendy's, then go right over to Dan's and get a booth, where Lou would order three hamburgers and a Coke and Justine would order one hamburger and a Dr Pepper, and Dot, wrapped in her afghan, would devour her Frosty and fries.

Justine would then take everyone home. Lou would nap for a while in the garage, and Dot would read, do puzzles, and sleep, often in strange positions, laughing and cursing and gesturing. Justine would go to her room and masturbate with what she was certain was illegal lechery and élan to fantastically invented scenarios involving her guidance counselor, Gracie Yin, which always ended with excellent, whipping orgasms that quickly withered to shame and guilt, mitigable only with homework and macaroni and cheese and later a visit with Dot, if she was awake. Around midnight, she'd go back to her room again, masturbate some more, despair, listen for Charlotte to stir and creep around the house while it was quiet. Finally, around two in the morning, when she heard Lou opening and closing the side door to the garage and starting the washing machine, Justine would fall asleep.

* * *

One afternoon in the beginning of February, Archibold Bamberger, Livia's boyfriend, was at the house baking Shrinky Dinks with odd symbols on them and placing them atop doorjambs around the house, muttering convocations over each one. As he went about his enterprise, Justine followed him around, complaining about how broke she was. The two of them lowered their muttering and complaints to whispers when in the living room, so as not to disturb Dot.

Archibold's silhouette recalled that of the Liberty Bell. Always sitting daintily on top of his head was a large straw sun hat, the beaded hatband of which read I ♥ COBLYNAUS. From under the sun hat his long, stout, brown-gray macrame ponytail ran down his back. All of Archibold's shirts were soiled along the spine where the ponytail lay, an effect most obvious in the oversnug white T-shirt in which he was presently encased.

While he consecrated a Shrinky Dink to the bathroom doorjamb, Justine recognized with no little appall that several long locks of Livia's distinctly black hair were interlacing his fuscous do. It had never been easy, or desirable, for Justine to picture any of her relatives in sexual activity, but seeing her adoptive mother's dismembered waves enshrined in another person's ponytail was somehow way more disturbing than picturing her bouncing around on some faceless lover, her big boobs flippery-floppering about.

Archibold turned, lifting the ponytail into orbit.

"I think I can get you a job," he said.

"Really? How?"

"I'm a magazine and newspaper deliveryman. I deliver to bookstores and newsstands and grocery stores all over town. And in one of those places I know a lady looking for a smart girl."

"Is it Crammed Shelf?" said Justine, excited; she'd always wanted to work in the city's largest and hippest bookstore.

"I do deliver there, it's true," said Archibold, with what seemed like a little pride, "but that's not where."

The next day a certain Fanny Kimball, the manager of DeLeon Drugs on DeLeon street, called and offered Justine an after-school position.

"Archibold Bamberger indicated you were looking for a job," said Fanny. "Well, I need a self-motivated person whose only flaw is perfectionism and whose only reason for speaking is to agree with me, to manage our famously comprehensive magazine and newspaper arena, as good as or better than Crammed Shelf's. Make your own hours. Can't pay you no minimum wage, though, so you can just forget about that. But you can keep the unsold magazines, minus the covers, that's what we send back for credit. And you can buy candy at 10 percent over wholesale and sell it to your friends at school. Plus you'll see Archibold when he delivers. So there're perks. Whaddaya say?"

"Okay."

Fanny paid $1.97 an hour, in cash, on Mondays. Justine put in more than thirty hours every week, about half of those on weekends. It was nice to see Archibold, who came by almost every day with papers and new issues of magazines. Sometimes they went to lunch together across the street at the Circle-Star Steakhouse, a greasy spoon that opened in 1912 and that might not have been cleaned since, such was the connatural sticky, smoky, deep-fried disposition of the place. They would order chicken-frieds and talk about magazines, the occult, and, occasionally, the bearing of the odd family unit that comprised the population of Justine's house.

"I think," Justine said one afternoon between chews of a steak so tough she'd had to pick it up from the plate with her bare hands and tear a piece off with her teeth, "my grandmother might be warming up to Lou. I wonder what went wrong in the first place."

Archibold looked at Justine, open, wide-eyed, flushed at the temples, as if he might start crying.

"I wonder," he said finally, looking down and digging the biscuit out of the loch of cream gravy on his plate, which he'd surrounded with saltines.

Justine sensed prevarication, but said nothing. She didn't really want to know. Probably irreconcilable differences, a term she'd learned from *L.A. Law* last week. But it didn't matter; Charlotte and Lou seemed on the verge of reconciling. Justine wondered if they'd fall in love again.

Now Justine thought *she* might cry.

"I'm buying," said Archibold, putting an end to the threat of waterworks.

"Thanks, Archibold."

"You're one of my favorite entities, Justine," he said, leaning over and tapping out a rhythm on her head with his fingers. "You and your mother."

That was one thing they never talked about: Livia.

. . .

Fanny kept her word about the back issues, so Justine was soon nose deep in collage materials. Fanny also kept her word about the flexible hours, so Justine was still able to run Dot and Lou around town. She did not, however, keep her word about the cheap candy.

"Changed my mind. Instead, I will give you one cent for every person you persuade to buy a candy bar here."

"Okay. Thanks, Fanny."

"You're welcome. You can start by making that little boyfriend of yours eat my candy."

"Troy?" said Justine, blushing. She didn't realize anybody knew she had a boyfriend. She wasn't sure if he even *was* a boyfriend. They hung around each other a lot, but he didn't turn up in any of her fantasies. She was quite faithful to Gracie there.

"The one that looks like Eddie from *The Courtship of Eddie's Father.*"

"I guess. I don't know him too well yet, but I think Troy only likes savory snacks. I'll try, though."

"Good girl."

On Valentine's Day, Justine came home from a two-hour shift at DeLeon, where she'd been made to paint the employee bathroom Pacification Pink in order to keep the pharmacy employees calm while doing their business, to find Lou, Livia, Charlotte, and Archibold sitting around Charlotte's bird-watching table in the kitchen, playing cards. She had never seen all of them together in the same room before.

"Hi," said Justine.

"Hi, darling," said Charlotte, reaching behind her to give Justine's arm a friendly squeeze. "Liv, greet your child."

Justine expected a grumpy and brief *hi* from her quasi-mother, but instead both she and Archibold put down their cards and turned and smiled at Justine.

"Hi, Justine."

"Hi, Livia."

"Hi, Archibold."

"'Lo, guv."

Everyone took simultaneous pulls on their beverages: beers for Charlotte and Livia and Coke for Lou. Archibold consumed about two fingers of a cloudy, bluish fluid in an Erlenmeyer flask personalized with a masking-tape label reading ARCHIBOLD'S DON'T TOUCH in green ballpoint.

"What're you playing?"

"Pinochle."

Everyone seemed mellow, as though it had just been mutually agreed upon that the indiscussably uncomfortable living situation could be tolerated if cards were played and social beverages were drunk.

"Lou, we gotta go pretty soon," said Justine.

"Mm," said Lou, frowning at his cards. "I believe plans've changed."

"Really? What're we doing now?"

"Better check with Dot on that."

"Arch, we need to go soon, too," said Livia, patting her boyfriend lightly on the arm.

"Mm?" said Archibold.

"I want to go over to the used-record store, that new place out on Montopolis, to look for Ye Moppe Hedds records. We've never been there."

Archibold responded by pouring a drop of Livia's Tuborg into Charlotte's ashtray and watching it intently for a moment.

"Growrl," he said finally.

"Bad luck, Arch?" said Livia, tugging on his ponytail.

She smiled at him, and then glanced over at Lou, who was still in a pinochle fugue. Justine observed her watch Lou, all the while absently milking Archibold's ponytail.

Eventually Archibold plucked his macrame pride out of Livia's hand and said, "Moocow dry."

Livia jumped. She began to titter. A blush, starting at her forehead, fell like a madder veil over her face. Justine saw her adoptive mother as she might have been at Justine's age, in high school, when she was gaga over the legendarily perfect Burt Moppett. A moment of pity for Livia transfixed Justine, and she caught herself staring at her precisely as Livia had been looking at Lou. *Pity is the most poisonous form of contempt.* Some shrink had once cut Justine down after she told him how on the way to therapy she'd begun to cry at the sight of a dramatically deformed teenaged girl on the bus. *You have no idea what that girl thinks and feels.*

Lou finally extracted a card from his crooked fan and placed it on the table. Immediately Charlotte trumped him.

"Dammit."

Lou began to fiddle with a dirty bandage on one forearm.

"What happened, Lou?" said Justine.

"Aw, nothing, just a little old cut I got on the job."

Justine had no idea what Lou did at the Registry, a job he'd recently taken. Now Lou was gone from nine to four most days. Justine could not imagine working at the Registry. She'd rather work in a pumice mine.

Justine went into the living room. Dot was sitting up on the divan, reading one of her old leather books, Dartmouth in her lap, endeavoring to lick the volume's gilt spine. The books had been intriguing from the first day Justine'd seen them, no titles or authors on the spines or covers, well read and a bit scuffed but tidy and sturdy, like books in an eighteenth-century scholar's working library. They looked Oxfordy, Cantabrigian; weathered but succulent, seductive but forbidding; rare. Maybe they *were* rare, worth thousands. First editions of some kind.

Dot produced from somewhere a small fountain pen with a tiny, needle-like nib, and began to write on the page she'd been reading.

"Are you about ready?" said Justine, sitting down next to Dot, sneaking a glance at the open page. It was covered with the tiniest cursive she'd ever seen, one large paragraph of which was preceded by today's date in a barely larger hand. A diary. "Lou's caught up in one of Charlotte's pinochle massacres."

"It doesn't look like we're going today, baby."

"Really? How come?"

Dot put down her book. Was the other one already full? Or waiting to be filled? How long had she been keeping them?

"I'm a little better today."

"Really? So that guy Sherpa's treatments are working?"

Justine reached over and scratched Dartmouth's hamlike sides while Dot scratched under his collar. Dartmouth, always in spectacular appreciation of the wonder and glory of life, seemed to have transcended to an even sublimer plane of being.

Justine noticed Dot had painted her nails green. On a paper towel on the floor was constructed a neat pyramid of cotton balls tinted kelly, like old, grass-stained golf balls.

"I believe so."

"You look pretty excellent."

"Bless your heart."

"So what does he do?"

"Sherpa? Well, he hasn't really done—"

A moderately unrestrained group chuckle from the kitchen.

"—a whole lot except give Lou recipes for potions to make me, and sometimes Lou brings him dried herbs or some such that Sherpa brews into hot teas. He never says much. The real treatment—it's just one appointment, five hours or so—doesn't start until around early April, once I've been 'prepared,' as he puts it."

"I was a little worried you were seeing a quack, but I didn't want to be nosy."

They scratched and scratched Dartmouth's brisket.

Justine continued: "I'm still a little worried about that."

"Dammit," Lou said from the kitchen. Everyone in there laughed, quite unfettered, quite ignoring the yeti of awkwardness that had been wandering around the house ever since Lou and Dot came.

"You can be as nosy as you want," said Dot, adjusting her pillow. It was smeared with iridescent green eyeshadow.

"What is it that he's..."

trying

"...going to fix, anyway?"

Justine could not look at Dot. She concentrated hard on scratching Dartmouth between each of his ribs, feeling for muscle, for meat, tissue, the pulses of living. While scratching a spot between Dartmouth's fifth and sixth left-hand ribs, about a third of the way down, Dartmouth decided he needed to be in the kitchen, and thus explosively embarked Dot's lap. Justine now had nothing to scratch, nothing to deflect her question, whose intrusiveness grew and grew as the instants that Dot did not answer passed. So Justine yawned.

"It's a disease that's getting more and more common," said Dot. "AIDS. It's not contagious, except through sex or shared needles..."

"I know," said Justine. "We learned about it in health class."

"*I* got it from *sex*."

In the kitchen, one, then another bottle cap *chk-tk*ed on the linoleum floor. *From Lou?*

"It wasn't from Lou," said Dot, with timing so precise it was as if she had read Justine's mind. "Most certainly not. We've fucked—pardon me—but that was many years ago, and we gave up trying pretty quick. Our styles did not complement."

Justine scratched and kneaded her palms.

"Was it a heroin addict?" she said finally, her voice sand-dry. "Or a gay guy?"

"Could've been either. I've had a lot of... lovers."

"Wow."

"Dammit," said Lou from the kitchen.

"Has he told you much about me?" said Dot.

"Lou?"

"Lou."

"Well, we're pretty much all together at the same times, you know, us three, so nothing you haven't already heard."

"You knew I was—*am*, for life, I guess, like an Episcopalian—a hooker?"

Justine hadn't known. *Wow.*

"So that's how you got it?"

"Yep."

"So Sherpa's gonna cure you."

"He might yet."

"Good," said Justine, though she wondered why she'd never heard of somebody who had found a cure for the most incurable disease since leprosy.

Dartmouth appeared in the kitchen doorway.

"Come," said Dot, and Dartmouth cameth.

"How many... lovers do you think you had?"

Justine shivered at the shape of the word in her own mouth.

"Two thousand six hundred and sixty."

"Whoa. Serious? All different people? You kept track?"

Dot picked up one of her books and gave it an I've-got-a-secret waggle.

"You don't mind me asking you all this?"

"Long as I get to ask you some stuff."

"Blistering barnacles," said Archibold. "Crikey, what a bloomer."

"What did he say?" said Dot, looking in the direction of the kitchen.

"It's from *Tintin*."

"What's a *Tintin*?"

"Comic book. My boyfriend reads them."

"Oh," said Dot, looking at her three books. "I used to enjoy *Wonder Girl*. She was foxy. Who's your boyfriend?"

Justine thanked god for returning Dartmouth, whom she began to scratch and scratch and scratch.

"Troy."

"Fellah at the drugstore?"

"From school. We've been friends a long time, but going out for only about three weeks."

"Have you had him over?"

"He's kind of a secret."

"You like him okay?"

"I guess. He's kinda gay."

"Bi?"

"I mean, I don't mean he's really gay, he's just a dork."

"Barbershop quartets were all that was gay when I was a girl. And songbirds and maybe fawns bounding through meadows. So did you let him fuck you?"

Dot had a wee glint in one eye. Justine shivered again, the word *lovers* coming back, crowding her mouth like cocktail cherries.

"No... not yet."

"Virgin?"

"No," said Justine, exploding into a hot blush.

"Him?"

"Troy? Yeah. He's dying to not be, though. He pleads and cries and bribes. He's very simple."

Ask me something else

"And yourself? Who did the popping?"

Justine spent an instant creating a story about a graund and gentle knight who died tragically, but abandoned it.

"Dick."

"Dick. You say that like he's a dick."

"He is."

Dick also had breasts, womanly breasts, that he hated and that Justine had always been careful to be neutral about. They'd had sex a few times, always at night, always in the interior black of his Dad's Bronco, Dick always naked from the waist down only.

One late-fall night, near one in the morning, at the foot of Enchanted Rock, both of them abrim with an hallucinogenic zuppa of shrooms and sun-dried jimson-root (recipe and ingredients sponsored by Mac, Dick's older brother), Dick let Justine take off his shirt and suck his shameful mammaries. The experience was mutually painful, on several levels. Justine had had orthodontia installed for the first time that very morning, reducing her mouth to a kind of achy oral mulch, and Dick's nipples turned out to be highly quick, especially to metallic nibbling. After some shrieking and bloodshed, they gave up. She told him that she loved his breasts; that she loved *him*, and he cried. Instead of going home, where they were expected, they fell asleep. When she woke the next morning, Dick was not in the Bronco. She found him sitting naked on a nearby cedar stump, a filet knife gripped loosely in one hand, wild hatred rimming his big black pupils.

"Fuck off," he had said when Justine approached him. But Justine did not fuck off. She tried to take his knife away, first with pleas and commands, then with force, but Dick ran away, screaming, "Fuck you!," hacking twigs off of arid scrub oaks. Justine ran after him, but tripped, and Dick disappeared. Justine left the Bronco unlocked and walked home. She was received there by two furious and worried generations of Durants and remanded to her room. Later that night, she cut herself.

"You're a pro," Dot said, holding Justine's arms, wrists up, in her hands. "A lefty, huh?"

"Yeah." Justine was proud of her arms. "Been at it for years." From shoulders to palms, Justine's arms were crisscrossed with scars of all character. The cuts were noticeably denser and deeper on her right arm.

"What about this?" said Dot, indicating with her thumb one end of a much thicker, newer scar that ran like a Nazca line from the base of her thumb to the calluses of her elbow and which was lined on both sides with small perpendicular scars, like dashes.

"I'd always used single-edge razor blades, the kind you get at the hardware store," said Justine. "But I was out of those, and so I bought a pack of double-edged blades from 7-Eleven on the walk home, you know the kind that have a weird-shaped cutout like a candlestick in the middle, for old-fashioned shaving razors?"

"Old Lou still uses one of those."

"They're a *lot* sharper. I cut deeper than I meant to. It slipped right through cables and tubes. My ring finger and middle finger don't work very well. See? It's why I got committed."

"Two, four six, eight, mm, mm, mm... ah, fifty-four stitches."

"Fifty-two. This one and that one were already there."

"That's a better number, anyway. Jokerless deck."

"Tons of blood. Charlotte had to pull up the carpet and throw out the mattress. Livia told me Charlotte was in a quandary over that—she didn't know how to throw them out without the whole world knowing. She couldn't just leave the blood-soaked stuff on the curb and wait for Big Trash Day. Finally she had her lawnmower man, Duck Baby, come by with his pickup, after dark, and haul it all off. That was the worst part of the episode, upsetting Charlotte like that."

"You just don't think of that sort of thing when you feel rotten," said Dot. "Disregard is an insidious effect of the disease of depression."

"I still feel awful. And just a few days ago she nearly had a heart attack when she found some leftover blood on a fan blade. As a granny, she was upset, but as a housekeeper, appalled."

"Lucky you didn't die, young lady."

"I knew how to do a tourniquet. It was in a Webelos book I found in the library a long time ago. But I've been telling anyone who asks that it was a real suicide attempt. People scoff at cries for help. They condescend. And I've been cutting myself for so long, there's no way anyone really believes it when I tell them it was real."

"It wasn't, though, was it?" said Dot. "Maybe they pick up on that."

"I don't know. It sure looks bad. And even though I keep it covered, I still like it when people want to see. It looks like the real thing. And that at least gets me a little respect. Or at least it kills off some of the contempt."

"Like doing time. That gets respect. But you'll get addicted to respect, and really shuffle off one day if you're not careful."

"I don't know. It doesn't buy me that much, anyway."

Justine thought of Clarissa Speen.

"So what happened to Dick?"

"He didn't do anything to himself. I saw him a few days ago in the guidance office. We have the same guidance counselor. It was like nothing had ever happened between us. We chatted about stupid stuff. He talked about how hot our guidance counselor is. I could tell he had his smasher bra on under his shirt."

"So was he any good?"

"You mean…"

"In the sack."

Justine had no idea.

"He seemed to like it."

"Blow him?"

"Yeah. He really wanted me to."

"I can't believe it."

"It's true."

"I know, I'm just playing. What's it like blowing a man with all that metal in your mouth?"

"I never did it before I had braces, so it's all I know."

"There was this girl I knew, Clancy, in New Orleans, found a dentist to pull out all her front teeth, top and bottom, so she could give a good blow job. You can guess how she paid the dentist, who afterward declared the procedure a great success. Soon she was the costliest suck in town."

Justine tried to imagine this and could not.

"Wow."

"Plus, her lisp she'd had all her life? Cleared right up."

"I don't think I'm very good at it. I can't concentrate. I lose track of what I'm doing. It's like something is missing, you know what I mean?"

"Oh yes," said Dot. "I do."

"It felt like something that's always been missing, though. Even when I was little."

Dot nodded, barely.

"When I was little I used to like to lick mirrors. Or anything reflective I could see myself in. It gave me great feelings—sexy feelings, if you know what I mean, like it made me feel grown-up like Charlotte, who was the coolest and most beautiful thing in the world, and like Livia, who was the sexiest."

"She's still an erotic presence."

"Yeah, well, she's a cold bitchrocket now. And all my sexy feelings, the good, warm ones that had nothing at all to do with body parts, disappeared when I was, like, eleven."

"Period?"

"Period, yep, and period. Now I don't care that much about having…
fucking Dick. Except for sucking his boobs, *that* was pretty great. Apart
from that, I'm kinda asexual now. Like an echinoderm."

"What the hell is an echinoderm?" said Dot, placing her hand on her
chest. "No, don't tell me. I don't want to know. But look. No one's asexual.
Especially somebody with eyes like you have. Those are *bedroom* eyes, young
lady. You just haven't found what you like yet."

Gracie Yin.

"Blow jobs, however," said Dot, "will grow on you. So to speak. Everyone
likes blow jobs."

"I don't think I really like Troy. I mean, he's great and everything, and
he's a pretty good friend, but…"

Dot patted Justine in the center of her long scar.

"I know, darling," she said. "Really, though, that's a perfect situation.
For *you*. Practice on him. When you're ready, of course. Fuck him with your
eyes shut and just think about what *you* like, what makes your tonsils buzz
like sour apples. Then shuck him."

"Whatch'all doing in there?" called Lou from the kitchen.

Justine froze.

"Justine, whatever she tells you," said Lou, "is a fiction. Don't listen to
a word she says."

"Play, Lou," Charlotte grumbled, to which Lou responded by giggling
happily. He had clearly trumped somebody, finally.

"So you tried…," said Dot, leaning in to Justine, quieter now.

Justine tried to thaw. What if they *had* heard?

As though she'd read Justine's mind, Dot said: "I promise they can't hear
us. Now, you were saying?"

"I tried imagining things," whispered Justine, almost into Dot's ear,
"but nothing really comes up, you know."

"When do you do this?"

"Well, you know…"

"When you're sorting oysters?"

Justine paused for a moment to analyze and decrypt the euphemism.

"Ohmygod."

Dot cackled.

"Sorry, child. That was crude. Go on."

"Um, yeah…" She could not think of a euphemism, though she was sure she knew one or two. "When I'm… The finger. Ing."

"*Diddle* is a useful all-around term."

"I close my eyes, and there are these heads. Without faces. And bodies. Not dead bodies, just people, naked, but… blank. I can't tell what's where. Where my mouth is, and what it's kissing, or licking, or what it is that's in it, is it a, you know, penis, and if it is, whose, and then I think even maybe it's *mine*. And I can't even tell what or even *where* my, um, vagina…"

"*Cock* and *pussy* are current."

"…pussy is, I can't really see it, or if it's even *mine* or not. It's weird. I get lost in it, all this flesh. I try to put Troy's face, or Rogers's—another guy at school—but they disappear. There's just black hair and pink bodies. I can't tell sometimes if my fingers are my own, or someone else's, or even fingers at all. Then I think maybe I'm just watching someone else, or other people, but they're darkened or blurry or I can only hear them. It's scary and makes me feel pervy. And it makes me feel crazy, too, like I should be back in ASH. Sometimes it makes diddling not fun, even though I do it, like, ten times a day. And I feel so ashamed and guilty when I… orgasm."

"*Come* is universal, though spelling is at issue."

"I cannot believe I'm saying all this. Never told any of this stuff even to a shrink."

"What do you think about that?" said Dot.

"I don't know. What do you think about what I said? Is there something wrong with me?"

"Sounds like you're not getting enough."

"Do you think I should let Troy have me?"

"I think you should order him to. And I think you should tell him exactly what you want. Even if you can't name what that is. Just grab his hand or cock or ass or nose and *put* it where you want. Fill the holes that demand filling, boss him around. Bite if you want. Use tools, bad words, stuff from the pantry. *Use.* Don't worry what he thinks. He's a virgin; he'll be a spent casing in ninety seconds no matter what *you* do. And guilt is good when it comes to sex, so welcome that."

Justine was coal under a bellows. She wanted to go get Troy right now.

"I don't think Livia would think you're a very good influence."

"Surely not. But I'm not advising you to charge the boy for your services."

Dot smiled, and looked down at Dartmouth. She grabbed a handful of his loose skin and gave it a squeeze.

"So, uh," said Justine, "what did you used to charge?"

"When I was fourteen, anything I wanted. I got a hundred dollars once. For a *kiss*. This was 1955, let me remind you."

"Fuck," said Justine. She wanted to say it again.

"Granted it wasn't just a peck, a kissing-booth smack. The man, a certain now-dead poker player, Sandy Cagh Whipple, down from the Jacksboro Highway, fresh off a win, had a tongue like an electric pork tenderloin. He took twenty minutes, came three times, and left nary a square inch of my upper GI unmapped. 'Druther of fucked him for twenty bucks."

"That's what a... that's what sex cost?"

"Back then that was high. Nowadays they charge a hundred or more for a straight fuck, I've heard. Other stuff a lot more."

What other stuff?!

"So," said Justine, smiling, trying to produce a saucy glint in her eye, "did you have a pimp?"

Dot seemed to flatten and recede, as though her body remembered all at once how ill and helpless it was.

"Not until I was around thirty. Then a man took me over. Barkeep in Texas City."

"What did you do?"

"I hated him, that's what."

"No, I mean..."

"I know what you mean. I had to give him pussy for free, whenever he wanted it, and he kept everything I earned."

"Everything? How did you live?"

"He bought everything he thought I needed. Pills, panties, bus fare, beans and rice, beauty parlor, booze. But no cash. And nothing that could be turned into cash."

"Szplug!" shouted Archibold from the kitchen.

"This all just started one day?" said Justine.

"Mmm. He thought I owed him for something. He threatened me. He threatened to hurt Lou, too, if I didn't stroll for him."

"So—"

"So why didn't we just leave? We did, but separately. We had a little fight, next thing I know he's gone. I left right after. It was a good bit later that Lou came down and found me in New Orleans. We were free of Kelly Miller, and I was doing fair, but Lou was in a bad way."

"Do you think the bartender is still after you?"

"Kelly? I don't think he'd go looking, but if he came across me, I'd be in trouble. I'll tell you this, I'll never go anywhere near Texas City ever again. Even Austin feels too close."

"I hope you... I hope he... I wish he got AIDS, not you."

"You and me both."

"Maybe he did."

A loud slap from the kitchen.

"Lou," Charlotte said, "please do not throw your cards down. It's childish."

"Dammit," said Lou. "I hate pinochle."

"It's because you aren't any good at it," said Livia, giggling. "You only like what you're good at."

"I'm good at checkers and I can't tolerate checkers."

"Checkers is the chess of the unpunished," said Archibold.

"What does that mean, Archibold?" said Lou, his voice rising. "You employ English words and English syntax, yet you cannot communicate. I sure hope my daughter can sort out your knotty babble."

"Dishes, wishes, Corningware lies," said Archibold.

"Rhubarbrhubarbrhubarb," said Lou.

"Don't excite him, Arch," said Livia. "He's very exciting."

An uncomfortable instant of silence, then Livia added: "Excita*bull*, I mean."

"Nothing knotty about that," said Charlotte.

"Homophone," said Archibold.

"Or that," said Charlotte. "Deal, Lou."

"What the hell's going on?"

"Archie, let's go record shopping, c'mon," said Livia.

"Couple more hands."

Justine and Dot scritched and scratched Dartmouth and listened to the *ftch* of cards and *kck* of bottles on Formica brighten the next room.

In the window through the yellowing curtains the sun fell behind the magnolias toward February the fifteenth.

VII

February 2004

Upon Campbell Brodsky's death, at age fifty-five, in late August of 2002, he left an estate worth nearly half a million dollars to his wife, Brenda Lathers Brodsky, who quickly liquidated the house and moved into a room in a rented duplex, where she began to accumulate rare sixties and seventies rock posters at approximately the same rate as an undiagnosed cancer spread through her body. Upon her death, less than a year later, she bequeathed her estate of $443,990.59, in cash, to her only child, Marcia Brodsky, twenty-six.

Marcia's mourning comprised forty parts shame, thirty parts guilt, ten parts therapy, five parts crying, four parts extra sleep, and one part shoe-amassing. The shame derived from the stellar credit-card debt she'd accumulated, the guilt over not using the inheritance to pay it off, the therapy to deal with the guilt and shame, the crying a response to therapy, sleep the only escape, and shoe-shopping the best of the worst of it all.

In late February, at Last Call, the Neiman Marcus outlet store on South Lamar, Marcia was hit with an idea, a way to emerge from this orphan dark, a way to escape guilt and shame and all else attendant to lugubriosity.

The idea had come quickly. The idea had come with a magnificent sneeze.

Marcia had just slipped on a powder-blue suede Blahnik with a fake-rubidium heel that had been marked down from $850 to $399 to $199 to $89 to $39 minus 50 percent, when she happened to glance up at the window display, which featured two mannequins, a woman and a man, each half dressed, trying on each other's shoes. Though the female mannequin was provocatively—almost obscenely—posed, it was not lifelike at all. It did not radiate; it was just a bronze-washed bone-hard injection-molded ball-joint doll arranged like a preteen in a Balthus painting.

The male mannequin, though, was different. He seemed real. As though he could move on his own. Walk. Hug. Do things. Many things. Special things.

And so Marcia Brodsky sneezed. A certain kind of long-forgotten sneeze. Then again. And again, again, all of them face-clenching sinus-reamers, right there in the 6½–7½ aisle. It had been quite a while since she'd sneezed like that. It was a naughty sneeze, the rare kind of sneeze she sneezed only when she'd just been awakened from psychosexual dormancy by a sudden and powerful erotic notion.

Her first such sneeze had been in seventh grade, in the school library, when she observed the outrageously adorable Ty Fishflag deposit an armful of *Goosebumps*es in the book return slot. Her second had been that night, in bed, thinking about Ty. The sneezes, a quick series of keen, wet barks, woke her father—not easily done, as Campbell Brodsky was given to profound sleep. Thereafter Marcia sneezed so often and with such lustihead that she was sure that everyone, from her classmates to her teachers to her father and mother, must know that she was not just another mild junior-high-school shadow with cedar fever but a hair-trigger freshet of inappropriate passion.

The phenomenon disappeared as quickly as it had come, shortly after she saw Ty and the new girl from Australia, Jessamine, slow-dancing to "Stairway to Heaven" at the last school dance of the year. The sneezes resumed, for one glorious day, when she happened upon an old ten-gallon fish tank while going through a closet of her junior-high-school junk during the Christmas break of her sophomore year at Vanderbilt. It wasn't the tank that got her started, though; it was what was inside: a small black compressor that, when plugged in and properly installed, was designed to oxygenate the water in the fish tank by means of a steady stream of air bubbles; this selfsame box, when plugged in and properly manipulated, would quietly buzz in such a way as to create thumping orgasms.

The naughty sneezes stopped on the last day of vacation, when she came downstairs from a particularly fruitful session with the compressor, only to find that her father had passed away while peacefully napping in front of an Oilers game. Ever since, naughty sneezes were rare, and when they did happen they were rather dry and atonic.

But not this one. Marcia glanced at the mannequin again and expelled another shuddering yawp. She kicked off the Blahniks, picked them up by their Mary Jane buckles, dropped them into a box, and jogged toward the checkout counter, one eye on the mannequin. "Set me free," she mouthed in his direction.

Freedom to Marcia meant finally discharging the roughly $425,000 in credit-card debt that had been swelling without apparent upper limit ever since she'd received her first card, a Visa with a $20,000 limit, when she was a freshman at Vanderbilt. She never told her father, a tax accountant, how quickly she cashiered those first five digits of credit on shoes, penny stocks, and quarter horses. She never told her mother how copiously the new credit offers came in; how stupefyingly high the interests rates could leap when she missed a payment; how chilly was the atmosphere of serious debt. Mercifully, both Campbell and Brenda went to their graves never knowing the shame of a financially irresponsible child.

"And would you like to use your Neiman's card today?" asked the dramatically fashionable and attractive Neiman's salesgirl.

"Not today," said Marcia, sliding her pair of Blahniks across the counter, excited and happy for the first time since... well, when? A long time. "I'll pay cash."

She had maxed out her Neiman's card in 2001. She owed them nearly four thousand bucks, nine hundred over the measly limit. A pittance, compared to her general debt, virtually all of which was carried, unsecured, by MasterCard, Visa, Discover, and American Express. She even had a couple of JCB cards, a Russky Standart, and an LG from Korea. Every single card was completely full and floating helplessly in a shoreless ocean of its own interest, penalties, and fees.

"I have ninety-one credit cards," Marcia told the salesgirl, with not a little pride. "All maxed."

"Wow," she said, attractively impressed.

She was more attractive than Marcia, and Marcia was pretty attractive. Marcia was attractive enough that she had far more gay male friends than straight women friends. This was a reliable formula. The higher the gay-male:straight-woman-friend ratio, the more attractive you were. To everyone. At least this was what Casey, her best male friend, had once told her.

"Believe you me," Casey had said, "Aishwarya Rai has no straight women friends. Stalkers, sure, but zero friends."

"That's stupid," Marcia had said.

"There are lots of stupid, true things, Marcia. This is one of them. Let me give you some money."

"No."

"For god's sake, why?"

Casey had a lot of money. Before Marcia's inheritance Casey had offered—many times—to pay some or all of Marcia's debt. But Marcia was determined to honor her father's memory and financial probity, and to make his benefi-cent spirit proud by paying off her debt, on her own, even if it took her entire life, even if it meant assuming even more debt. Which was part of her fantastic new idea.

"I want to do it on my own, no free rides."

"Whatever," said Casey. "But why all the ethical wind now? Too bad there weren't any ethics blowing around back in your Faro parlor days."

Almost all of Marcia's debt had come from cash advances and convenience checks that she used to start small businesses or invest in stocks or schemes; the fervidity with which she invested was in stride with the anxiety investing provoked. Not all of these commercial assays had been wholly legitimate, and none had been profitable. Marcia had asserted and fully believed that her Faro parlor was entirely legal, and she could not be convinced other-wise, until her game, run after-hours in the woodworking studio at Austin Community College, was raided by Travis County constables, who placed her in jail. The following morning she was released on her own attractive cognizance. Later, in place of ten days in Del Valle Corrections, she paid a breathtaking fine using a virgin WaMu Visa that she found clipped to the passenger's-side visor of her old Toyota Cressida, a twenty-five-thousand-dollar card she had completely forgotten about.

"My intentions were always honorable," Marcia would say to Casey when-ever the subject came up.

"I still think you should just rent the goods," Casey would respond.

"Jesus, Casey. You can be awful sometimes. And *that's* illegal, goods-renting, in case you forgot, Mister Moral Compass."

"You could pay off quite a bit, quickly, if you put together a really good personal website. Especially if I was your McDaddy. Might pay it all. Less than a year. We could get fifteen hundred a day, easy."

"It's 'Mac Daddy,' Casey."

Even though she knew Casey had never been serious about her becoming a hooker to pay her credit-card bills, Marcia *had* thought about it. She was very attractive, after all. Her shoulders were naturally set back, causing her enviably shapely bosom to thrust just a little, making her attractive in even the schoolmarmiest outfits, and causing people to want her to shed her clothes and give them sex.

But she would never have sex again, either for love or money or fun, at least any of the variants where pregnancy was a risk. And pregnancy *was* a risk, since Marcia was unable to provide her uterus any harbor from the fertile rains of the many men she would like to fuck: she was either fatally allergic to or repulsed by not just latex but lambskin, nonoxynol-9, neem oil, and the alloys composing IUDs, and thus would be forced to screw in the untrammeled way impelled by evolution and intended by God; a way she could not enjoy for its possible conclusion.

Because, if she did have a child, and if Marcia orphaned it by dying in one fashion or another, her child would inherit all of her debt—not to mention her genetic wont to accumulate it—and the child's life would be ruined. That's how it worked. So, no sex. It was one of the hardest parts of her oath. Because Marcia liked sex a lot. The straight kind. The straightforward kind. A needy penis in a needy vagina, a practice in vigor and endurance, uninterrupted by kissing and sucking and all that other moist ancillary theater. Blow jobs she especially hated. They felt gross and gobbly, like she was bingeing on gristle in the dark. She wasn't any good at the business, anyway. Her gag reflex was abnormally shallow, and there was nothing fun about throwing up naked. Cunnilingus wasn't fun, because nobody she'd ever slept with had executed it correctly, no matter their level of enthusiasm, and it frustrated her to the point of tears trying to explain or pantomime or guide or demonstrate the process to even the most enthusiastic of students.

Schmidt, her sheepdog, was the only being that seemed to understand the oral laps and rhythm-shifts necessary for Marcia to reach orgasm. Thank goodness for Schmidt. Yes, thank goodness. But even he wasn't really very satisfying, and would sometimes gnaw. Plus, to get him going, Marcia had to paint her nether parts with bacon grease. Marcia ate a lot of bacon. This, collocated with her aversion to dishwashing, meant there was always a pan in the sink with lots of bacon grease inside.

Marcia had told Casey about Schmidt. Marcia had regretted doing so. Casey had a bit of a cruel streak, and it was this bestial tidbit that most vividly sparked it. But Marcia never did, and never would, tell Casey that she and Schmidt had taken Schmidt's fore-actions to the next level. Marcia quite liked being on her knees, and even though this was the female posture Schmidt would by nature become most rutty about, and the position that held the most promise for them as a couple, it never quite worked out: Schmidt was insubstantial; Schmidt was as quick to finish as he was to start; Schmidt's toenails would leave long, welting scratches on Marcia's rib cage; and bacon grease, though superb as cunnilingual bait, was inadequate as a lubricant. Plus, like some real couples, they fought afterward. For the several hours following an engagement, Schmidt and Marcia pretended to ignore each other around the house, but would express remote petulance by slamming cabinets or tipping over water dishes or playing XBox really loud or chewing through spendy purse straps. The day they both contracted outstanding infections of great medical rarity was the day their affair ended. Schmidt, limited by his canine sense of cause and effect, understandably took the breakup much harder than Marcia, and grew depressed.

"Twenty-one eleven," said the Last Call Neiman Marcus salesgirl.

Marcia reached into her large purse and removed a hundred-dollar bill, one of more than four thousand she had in there, all so crisp that she had to be careful two didn't stick together. She slid the banknote across the glass counter.

"Out of one hundred," said the salesgirl, Jilliette, according to her name tag.

Marcia no longer had a checking account, as credit-card companies, when owed, are permitted by law to evacuate them. This fact had come as a surprise to Marcia when one day, while at a drive-through teller to withdraw a little cash for things that credit cards could not buy, her Bank of America business checking account, supposedly fat with six thousand dollars recently cash-advanced from a Chase MasterCard, reported her balance as zero. It turned out that Bank of America had taken all the money to pay down the nine Visas they had issued her over the years. It was the first time she'd ever heard the word *garnish* outside of a culinary context.

So Marcia did not put a cent of her parents' bestowal into a bank account. When Casey had, with dramatic protests, cashed her probate check and given her all of it in hundreds, she immediately put the banded wads in her largest purse, the one made of recycled seatbelts.

"Thank you, Casey," she'd said, hugging him hard in a personal banker's windowless office at the Wells Fargo on Airport Boulevard.

"Don't forget about Uncle Sam," said Casey.

"I won't!"

"You can't pay with credit anymore, you know that, right? Because you have none?"

"Leave me alone," said Marcia, unhugging Casey.

One of the smartest things she'd ever done was to always pay her income tax—when there was any income—with credit cards. Better to owe Discover than the IRS, she reasoned. Even Casey had concurred.

"I know, Casey, jeez. But I'm not going to pay any taxes on money I haven't made yet."

"And how are you going to make it this time?"

"I don't know. I'll know when I know."

The shopgirl counted back Marcia's change. Marcia took the opportunity to steal a look at the salesgirl in the reflection of the counter. God, she was looking back.

"Those are great shoes," Jilliette said.

"Lucky."

"Yeah. They'll look great on you."

She was smiling warmly. Marcia wondered if she had a boyfriend. Surprisingly often, very attractive people did not have mates. Marcia didn't, a case in point. And if the salesgirl didn't, maybe she could be the first customer for Marcia's new venture.

"I hope you'll come back and see us."

The two woman traded attractive smiles. Then Marcia leaned over and said quietly: "I bet you have a shitload of boyfriends."

She shook her head. "No... none."

"I might be able to set you up, if you want. Do you have a business card?"

She did. It read, Jilliette Baylor, Client Satisfaction Specialist. When the time came for Marcia to hire Casey as business manager and client-drummer-upper for her new startup, now nearly fully formed in her head, she would have him cold-call Jilliette Baylor. She might not like the idea at first, but she'd call back. She would.

"So that's a pretty awesome window," said Marcia, dropping the business card into a purse pocket not crowded with cash. "Bet you did that."

Jilliette smiled and flushed just the slightest bit.

"That man mannequin," said Marcia. "I swear I'd date him."

"God. Tell me about it."

A fifties-something woman armored in shoulder-padded blue silk and swinging bangles of hammered gold appeared. She could not have been from anywhere except Dallas, perhaps banished to Austin as a penance for some anchor-store botching.

"Jilliette, darling," she said, "Nan looks like a Weimar Republic hooker. I would like you to make her decent. Please spray more Fake Bake on the backs of her knees and please have her sitting on her bottom rather than presenting it to our window shoppers like a doe in estrus."

"Yes, Billie."

"And put some Ray-Bans on Rance. He watches me."

Billie jangled off toward Intimates, a couple of times glancing over her shoulder at the male mannequin.

"Rance," said Marcia.

"Rance," said Jilliette. "I thought about stealing him. Just for a night."

Marcia nodded and smiled. A year, and her debt would be gone. A year at most. Guaranteed.

Marcia spent the next week researching, calculating, imagining. Finally, when she felt confident she was on to something big, she quit her waitressing job, a position her dad would have insisted she keep, despite her sudden wealth.

"I'm going into business for myself again," she told Brown, her boss.

"Not that bauxite mine you were jawing about."

"Nope, no half-assed investments this time. I'm gonna have my own cash-only home-based LLC. I got a DBA this morning, and a state-sales-tax certificate is in the works. And the whole idea's pretty much totally legal, I'm pretty sure."

"Sounds foolproof."

"Shut up. The important thing is that I'm my own boss again and the Monstrum can't get me."

The Monstrum was the drooling, leash-straining, long-jawed credit-card industry.

"Your job'll be here waiting for you in two weeks, when you go under. Unless you're in jail, of course."

"Shut up again. You're mean."

"Tell Casey yet?"

"About my idea? No. I'm on my way to."

"Bet he'll be meaner than me."

Casey *had* been pretty mean upon first hearing Marcia's idea.

"That's silly and perverted and probably breaks about two hundred state laws. And I won't be able to stay friends with you."

Marcia ignored him. She'd expected this, and had spent the day preparing to dissert on the matter.

She found the website and handed him the laptop.

"Look for yourself."

Casey accepted the computer and immediately began to *hmm* and *yeah right* and *oh that's obviously Photoshopped*. Soon, though, he grew quiet, except for an *oh* or *ow* or *ew* or *my*.

"See? What do you think about *that*? I've already decided to call him Rance."

"You're clearly insane."

"Come *onnn*, Case," said Marcia, groaning at the ceiling and raking her cheeks with her nails. "Support me. Encourage me. Believe in me for once."

Marcia snatched her computer away from Casey. She loaded up a DVD and dropped the computer back into his lap.

"Watch *this*."

A clean, white laboratory. On a large white plastic table is laid out what appears to be a somewhat waxen, anatomically correct doppelgänger of a naked, mid-career Jan Michael Vincent. From stage right a lab technician wearing a clear vinyl clean-room suit over a slingshot bikini emerges. She lifts Jan Michael's head and peels back a flap of scalp, revealing a series of rheostatic dials. The technician twists a dial and stands back. She produces a remote control equipped with a small joystick, presses a button, and Jan Michael's penis slowly, awesomely, tumesces. The tech presses another button, which appears to adjust the curvature of the top half of the organ.

Then, a sexy male voice-over. It explains that this model's penis has an arc range of 0 to >1.5ϖ radians.

"The spectacular organ," continues the voice-over, "also has controls that will adjust its helicity, arc length, tone, attitude, locus of projection, and numerous glans:shaft ratios, and let us not forget glist quotient, relative animus, and decency."

The hour-long video demonstrated many more of the robot's features, to some of which the lab tech, now divorced from her lab-coat swimwear, provided riveting accompaniment.

"It does have some curious appointments," said Casey, his voice cracking.

"*Rance*. And among Rance's curious appointments is a skeleton made of vulcanized xanthan-gum foam force-formed over Buckyball-fiber rebar. Top-secret, patent pending, light, resilient, indestructible. Better than the human bone."

"If I were shopping around for such a thing, I would question its hygiene and septicity."

Marcia was prepared for that.

"He cleans himself and replaces his own replipenis and replirectum and repligullet, though every twenty-five events we have to give him a full gasoline-and-Vulpex wipe-down and run him over to Darque Tan for an ultraviolet bactericidal. Kills everything, including feline HIV."

"That's a relief."

"And every five hundred encounters we're supposed to send him back for deep cleansing, but the manual says we can just strap him to the top of the car and run him through the OttoSqueej behind the Mobil station half a dozen times. That's what the manufacturer does. No wax, though."

"I bet this thing would break down in the middle of a ride, like a Jaguar."

"*He*. Gives you a boner, though, I bet."

"Is this all about your own sexual needs?" said Casey, picking up a 2,625-page file on Rance's technical specifications that Marcia had spent seven ink cartridges and all of Saturday printing out. "If it is, you are going way too far."

"This is about honoring Daddy's memory."

"I'll bet you're thinking, *Oh dear, that didn't come out right.*"

She blushed attractively, a sunny carmine.

"I just want to pay my debt honestly. And then get rich."

"I think it's about sex. I know you don't want to get pregnant, but there are much cheaper ways to get that deep lovin' feelin' without worries. For instance, tube-tying."

"I couldn't handle the pain."

"And persons with strap-ons. And castrati. I know some. They're very focused and obedient."

"It's not about sex. I'm not interested in sex."

"You've gotta be tired of Schmidt."

"You're a jerk sometimes, you know that?"

"Schmidt doesn't have everything," said Casey. "Does he."

"Why can't you be my friend and say, 'Go for it, Marsh'?"

"Look. I don't blame you. *I'd* take old Rance for a ride."

"You can," said Marcia, jumping up. "As much as you want. Free. Anytime, Casey. Just be my friend and support me."

Casey appeared to consider the offer of carte-blanche quasi-sex.

"You'll never earn enough."

"Yeah? Look."

Marcia opened an Excel file populated by dollar signs and large integers. "My plan has no holes. Well, two." She chuckled at her own joke. After a moment, Casey chuckled, too.

"Come on, Casey. What the hell else have you got to do?"

It was true. Ever since Casey had retired from Dell, at twenty-nine, just before the entire computer industry began to darken with conflict and antitrust and halving salaries, he'd been terrifically bored. He couldn't find anything that thawed the daily, hourly, freezing ennui. Gambling and collecting contemporary art quickly grew old. He couldn't get the hang of alcoholism. Men were dull or cheesy or dim or Republican or smelled. Making things out of clay was messy, and he hated the feeling of slip. Hot-air ballooning was cliquey. Pornography brought him down. Bookbinding was suited only to compulsive simpletons. Stocks were fun until he realized it was gambling. Bicycling hurt. And after he spent forty thousand dollars for a black-market flowering *Pennantia baylisiana*, then promptly parboiled it with water from a hose that had been lying under an August sun all day, he struck gardening from his list of possible avocations.

"Think of it as a job offer," said Marcia, leading Casey into the unoccupied back bedroom of her rented Windsor Park bungalow, where she imagined the boudoir eventually to be. "Manager, aide-de-camp, adman efforts to be remunerated at 20 percent commission on sales."

"Sales," said Casey, looking around the room and then sitting on the only softish object therein: a naked twin bed.

"Services. Whatever. Your job will be to find people who need servicing."

Marcia sat down on the bed next to her friend. They began to bounce in sync. The bed squawked and *ptoing*ed.

"This bed feels like it's full of elbows."

"We'd need a really big, really special one," said Marcia. "A honeymoon-suite bed. And blackout curtains. And flattering, incandescent lighting. Did you know that most people like the lights on? Read that in *Stuff*."

"You read that crap?"

"Came in the mail, free, one day. It's funny."

"Personally, I like the lights off. The human fundament is a terrible place, to be neither seen nor heard."

"And we'll need a mirror on the ceiling."

"Your landlady'll never let you remodel."

"Are you kidding? She hasn't been inside this house even once in the five years I've been here. She drives down the alley on Sundays to make sure there's no ivy climbing the shutters. That's all she cares about. Ivy."

"She clearly cares not for leaky roofs," said Casey, looking up at the tobacco-spit-colored tidemarks staining the drop ceiling. "This is going to cost a fortune. This entire part of the house will have to be glass-bead blasted and rebuilt."

"After we get Rance, we'll have about thirty grand left for everything else. It'll be more than enough."

"Thirty? You mean you're going to get Advanced Rance? What's wrong with Classic? Only a tiny fraction of users will be able to appreciate a love doll that can rim itself. And you'd save fifteen thousand dollars. With which you can buy inch-thick hotel curtains and your eight-hundred-square-foot ceiling mirror."

"We need Advanced Rance. He doesn't just auto-rim, he can interpret dreams, shudder, and cry 'Don't stop' in hundreds of languages and dialects, including Nuxalk and Oxyrynchene. And he does *tons* of other incredible shit. *Casey*."

"Fifteen thousand doesn't sound like much, comparatively, but..."

"I'm getting the best."

"I just have to repeat, one more time, what I always say when you embark on a new commercial journey, *just* so I don't feel guilty for not saying it the only time you might be listening..."

"W—"

"Cash. Flow. Cash. Flow. Cash. Flow."

"Don't yell. Your breath smells like Tostitos and preservatives."

"Marcia, have you learned nothing from your past business fuckups?"

"I learned that the most successful startups have everything they need from the very beginning so they'll have low overhead. A really attractive older guy at S.C.O.R.E. told me that. I can't even think of any overhead we'd have. Light bulbs. Accoutrements. Maybe carpet shampooing or replacement every now and then. You saw my spreadsheet."

"Exactly my point. You'll hardly have any overhead, so save the cash you'd spend on it for unknowns. Liability insurance will probably eat it all up, anyway, if you can find somebody to insure you. What if his dick breaks or flags or pumps out molecular acid instead of a body-temperature, semen-flavored rice-starch suspension of customizable viscosity?"

"Comprehensive indemnity is available through a few select insurers. But look. Rance will not shoot anything he has not been instructed to shoot. If he does, HoBots LLC flies out a technician and a team of attorneys that same day. If we ever have to send Rance back to the factory, they FedEx SameDay you a replacement. For free, if it's within the first ten years."

Casey let out a great sigh, which turned into a great growl of reluctant submission.

"If I give in, promise me you'll (1) Accept only cash payment, (2) install a James Bond–quality security system, (3) keep my name out of it."

"Fine. We can just get a normal security system, though."

"Are you kidding? Look, one of your main enemies, besides God and the police, will be the Reviewers."

"What? The Disney movie?"

"No, the gang! The fundamentalists! Don't you read the papers? Watch TV?"

Marcia did not read the paper, and she did not watch TV. Marcia plotted.

"Rance can take care of himself. He's bulletproof and fire-resistant."

"Rance is not invincible. The Reviewers are."

"They'll never find out—I'll be careful."

"Get good security. As a favor to me."

"Fine."

"So I'll take the fucking job."

Casey and Marcia bounced on the edge of the elbowy mattress for a few minutes. Marcia wanted to shriek with excitement, but she knew better than to do that. Casey would seize the moment and use it against her later when he wanted to make some point or other.

"Good. Your first assignment is to design business cards and check ad rates for the back page of the *Chronicle*."

"What's your job, then?"

"Accounting. Tech support. And customer service."

"Customer service is Rance's job."

"You know what I mean."

"Well, let's go see him, then."

Marcia sat next to Rance, who was stretched out on one of the twin beds of her and Casey's room at the Tropicana in Las Vegas. Marguerite La Pucelle, the salesperson-in-chief at HoBots LLC and Rance's custodian during the transaction, sat at the end of the other bed.

Marcia opened her purse to pay Marguerite La Pucelle—$385,000 in cash.

"Nice to see you again," said Marcia, scrabbling around for the banded stacks of hundred-dollar bills.

"Yes, yes, you, too. Ah, a great deal of American dollars to carry on an aeroplane, yes?"

"I don't trust banks," said Marcia, glancing at Rance's long eyelashes. She sneezed.

"À tes souhaits. You are certain you don't wish to play with Nicaise first? Before you pay? How do you say, test drive?" said Marguerite. "I do recommend. Sometimes there is no... chemistry. You see?"

"I'm sure he'll be fine," said Marcia, finding the last five grand and putting it on the bedside table. "We've decided to call him Rance."

"Rance. Very sexy."

Marcia wasn't sure if Marguerite was making fun of her.

"Do you want to count it?"

Marguerite smiled, shook her head, and began to place the stacks of cash into a classily scuffed Murakami Vuitton.

"Perhaps your companion would like to give Rance an... interview."

Casey, who was sitting in a chair scrutinizing a laminated card that listed the available TV channels, seemed not to have heard.

"Casey?" said Marcia. "Last chance. Then he goes into the crate."

"Gnth."

"That's a no," said Marcia, addressing Marguerite.

"You are sure?" said Marguerite. "He's a *virrrr*-gin!"

"Nuhuh."

"That is understandable. You'll both feel much more comfortable when you get him into your own *bou... doir*," said Marguerite, tapping Marcia on one kneecap, and then the other, with two ten-thousand-dollar bundles of cash, in time with the last two syllables of her assurance. Then, turning to Rance, who was dressed in a snug squash-player's outfit, she said: "And au revoir to *you*, mon cher."

She leaned over and landed a shade-more-than-platonic peck on the bridge of his nose.

"Oh my god," said Rance. "Kiss me again. And again."

An extraordinary tongue snaked out between Rance's lips and licked the bridge of his nose where Marguerite had kissed him.

"Nevermore," said Marguerite, shaking her finger at him.

Rance began to whimper. In his shorts a convulsing bulge appeared. The swelling replipenis, having nowhere else to unfurl, forced itself out through the left-hand pocket, turning the lining inside out and threatening to split the seam.

"My goodness," said Casey and Marcia.

Marguerite took off one of Rance's white Sauconys and extracted a bit of metal shaped like a grenade pin out of the sole of Rance's foot. Rance immediately deactivated.

"I will pack him for you," said Marguerite, handing the little brass key to Marcia. "When the Federal Express drops him off, there will be two crates: Rand himself—"

"Rance."

"—and a smaller crate holding the compressors, the equalizers, a remote, er, 'kill-switch,' a very special saline for his eyeballs—after rolling back into his head in ecstasy many, many times, the eyeballs, they dry out and sometimes get stuck, leaving him with a look, a stare, like... zombie? No good."

"No good," said Casey. Marcia double-barrel sneezed.

"Also in the crates? You will find manuals, tuning forks, Allen wrenches, spare ears—many virgins bite them off, they lose control, so splendid are the petits-morts of their first session."

"Session? That makes him sound a bit like a shrink."

"No, that is our Dr. Vassbender, MD, PhD, still in development. He is not allowed to sleep with his patients, so, yes, a conundrum. But, so. That is neither here nor is it neither there. My point is, when the Federal Express delivers your crates? Take names and photographs. With time stamps."

"I guess you've had trouble with deliveries," said Casey.

"Bah," she said, erasing with a wild swipe of her hand the entire subject of the failings of parcel couriers. "Please give me that crowbar."

In truth, Marcia *was* looking forward to sex with Rance. It was her job as CEO of the Dollhaus to try him out and tune up any vibrations, tics, ratchetings, or other sour notes that might stall the erotic journey of a paying customer. If Rance was as fun as he was supposed to be, she might even double the price. Or triple. Or nonuple. One client a day and she'd be out of debt and even modestly wealthy before she turned thirty. Then she'd really get busy, opening Dollhauses all over the country and the world.

And if he wasn't so great... she could return his ass within sixty days for a refund. Minus a 32 percent restocking fee, but that would still leave her with a lower-six-digit pile of cash to launch venture 93, nascently a corpse-flower nursery out in Llano. A lotta dough in corpse flowers, Marcia had heard.

In the exciting days before and the sleepless forty-eight hours since their Vegas trip, Marcia had hired a decorator, found a general contractor, commissioned a glazier capable of silvering very large panes for use as ceiling mirrors, queried a soundproofing company specializing in RWAR acoustic-decoupling technology, scheduled an appointment with a local Lloyd's of London agent, discussed architectural foundation requirements with a commercial bondage-and-discipline consulting firm, hired a wheel-chair-ramp builder, compared security companies, and bartered from her old web-sharp high-school classmate Keerthy Anand the construction of a tony website in exchange for three prime-time hours with Rance.

"Can he brush my hair?" asked Keerthy. "I like sex and then hair-brushing."

"I think so," said Marcia. "I know he can do Topsy Tails."

Keerthy squealed in assent.

Marcia hung up the phone and fell back onto the elbow-bed, exhausted. The phone immediately rang again.

"Hi, is he there yet?"

"No, he's not," said Marcia. "I told you I'd call you."

"FedEx tracking says he's on vehicle for delivery," said Casey.

"It's 6 p.m.," said Marcia, so tired she slurred her words. "He won't be here till tomorrow. I'm asleep. You go to sleep."

She hung up just as the doorbell rang. In an instant, Marcia was in a state of raunchy wakefulness. She raced to the front door, snatching her Nikon hanging by its strap from a doorknob.

On her flagstone walkway Marcia found a team of three scrawny FedEx deliverymen sitting on a wooden crate about the size of an adolescent's coffin. All of its huge red arrows denominated THIS END UP were pointing to the left. A smaller, more cubic crate sat in Marcia's flowerbed of zinnias.

Marcia signed the dumb FedEx Etch A Sketch thing.

"Can you help me bring h— them inside?"

"No," they said.

"Hmm, well, stay put for a sec, gotta get a picture, you know, routine, for insurance and whatever."

"No," they said, and ran off in different directions.

Marcia was not going to call Casey. She wanted Rance for herself, privately, for a night. A secret.

Marcia stepped into the yard to examine the crates. She worked her fingers under one end of the big one, and lifted. Rance was five-eleven and weighed 110 pounds; the crating added at least 30 more. She could move that much weight if she was at the Hyde Park Gym working the leg-press machine, but in a state of sexual perturbation and confronted with a handle-less casket, she was quite helpless. Marguerite had said they'd experimented with different body weights: any heavier, and test subjects complained that Rance reminded them of a corpse (though Marguerite admitted this could have been a selling point in more instances than one might expect); any lighter and the recoil from Rance's enthusiastic pelvic plunging action tended to shatter verisimilitude.

"Our next model, ʊ10,000, will be equipped with internal ballast sponges, which one may fill, you see, with water, or with helium, depending on one's needs," Marguerite had said.

Ballast or no, there was zero chance Marcia was going to get Rance inside on her own.

She looked up to see a strange vehicle idling at the curb.

"A hand?" said the vehicle's captain.

It was a man about her age she saw almost every day pedaling down the street on a tricked-out homemade recumbent tricycle. A thoroughly chromed work of art, a gold springer fork and a pair of bullet lights and a big high-back sissy bar backrest illuminated with a sexy painting of Julie from *The Love Boat*. A silly bike helmet resembling a dinner roll, four orange safety pennants sticking out of the sissy bar on long poles, and a small basket housing a yipping dog, were all that spoiled the overall lowride effect.

"Yeah. What's your name?"

"Porifiro. And that's Tom Mix," he said, pointing to the dog.

Porifiro couldn't have weighed much more than Rance, but nevertheless he hoisted the crate onto his shoulder as though it were filled with balloons, and carried it inside.

"Just put it down by the bed, please. How can I thank you? Diet Sprite? Bacon? A hundred dollars?"

"No, thanks."

"Want me to take pictures of you on your trike?"

"Okay."

Against the setting sun, Marcia shot a roll of real 35 mm pictures, not stupid digitals, and promised she'd mail them in a few days.

"Let me have your hand, please," said Porifiro. He produced a pen from somewhere and inked his address in Marcia's palm. "Say, would you always wave to me and Tom Mix?" he added, undoing a bike lock that looked like a link of battleship chain.

"Promise," she said, just before a great sneeze knocked her into the grass. For four days Marcia did not answer her texts or phone or email or door or Casey's shouts of "Pygmalion!" from the front yard. Schmidt, who in the past had spent not a whole lot of time outside, found himself living under a vast pecan tree in the backyard while fearless possums stole his Snausages at night and craven squirrels dropped pecans on his head all day. In retribution for all facets of this outrage, Schmidt gnawed at the corners of the house, rounding them off to a height of five feet, his maximum reach.

O, how his life had changed since his mistress spurned him so!

VIII

March 1988

It was unseasonably hot and humid. When Justine got home from school, temperatures had hit the upper nineties and the front door had swollen shut. Justine had to shoulder it open. Inside, bugs had been coaxed from their wintering and were colonizing the living-room windows. Her own room reeked of paste and printer's ink, a sheen of condensation had treacherized the toilet seat, Dartmouth's water dish had been taken away and replaced with a casserole dish filled to the rim with water and ice cubes. The dust in the air illuminated by the afternoon sun was motionless, fixed, like a galaxy. Dot's blankets were on the floor, her TV tray crowded with Coke cans and beer bottles. Dot herself was stretched out on the divan. Her sweat-heavy green satin nightgown stuck close to her body and was bunched up mid-thigh, exposing the scab-colored sarcomae that randomly patched her legs and which looked, to Justine's eye, impatient. *Ready.*

"Dot?"

Dot didn't move.

"*Dot.*"

Dot opened her eyes.

"I'm up."

Justine ran over and turned on the air conditioner, which groaned like a trash compactor and expectorated trillions of mold spores into the room.

"I think we should go to a regular doctor."

"Bring me a Coke, would you, darling?"

"Okay, but let's go to St. David's. I have Troy's Aspen today."

"I'm fine. Just hot."

"I mean, I want you to give up on this Sherpa guy and see a regular doctor. I finally decided Sherpa's a quack. Let's go now."

"You haven't even met him."

"He makes you drink disgusting teas all day. How is that helping?"

"I told you, we've been to regular hospitals. Good ones, Mass General, Johns Hopkins, Cedars-Sinai, lots of other places. Money's gone, baby, all our savings, everything we could get from beneficent programs, generous doctors, test studies. The only treatment costs more than most anybody can afford. We hitched here from Baylor in Dallas. The last trucker dropped us off nearly a mile away from here, and Lou carried me all the way to your front door. Did you know that? No place else to go. He was terrified of coming here, afraid you'd hate him, afraid of Charlotte and Livia."

"I love Lou," said Justine, not wanting to know why Lou thought so much fear and hatred was due him. She never wanted to know. She loved him just like he was. "And everybody's getting along fine. And I love you, too."

"And I'm glad we came. But understand, Sherpa's what we got left—he's the last chance, and cheap enough so Lou can afford him with his Registry job."

"Let me just run you over to St. David's so they can give you some fluids at least, and maybe talk to somebody. They can't refuse an emergency."

"Just go get me that Coke. Get one from the bottom shelf, now. Things're colder, you know, on the bottom shelf."

"When is Sherpa going to do the final treatment? Why isn't he ready yet?"

"He says if he does it prematurely, then it'll ruin everything and I'll die. And there has to be a trial run with a surrogate first, anyway, which he wants me to audit so I can see what my own treatment will be like. The right time has something to do with the weather, barometric pressure. He won't know when until that day, and he'll call us. Kind of like a liver transplant."

"Or like a Soviet execution. He's a quack. I think he's just getting as much of your money as he can before you..."

"He's not a quack. It's just nontraditional medicine."

"He's a nut. A quack."

The air conditioner roared. The den was growing cold.

"You need to let this go now, Justine. I appreciate your candor and your position, but I'm doing this. A lot of sacrifices have been made."

"What if I called an ambulance?"

"I wouldn't forgive you for it."

At 6:15 a.m. on the following Sunday, the phone rang. Justine ignored it, and it stopped ringing. Then, from Charlotte's room across the hall:

"Justine. Phone."

It was Fanny. She'd had a dream where she'd been working at the store and Doc Severinsen came in.

"I often dream about men of entertainment," Fanny told Justine over the phone, her breathing rapid and shallow, as if she were having an asthma attack in the Arctic. "The big names, you know, Lee Marvin, Jerry Lewis, John Denver, Charlie Pride. Last night it was Doc. He comes into the drugstore to drop off eight rolls of film to be developed. I say, 'Hi, Doc,' he says 'Hi,' and tells me he wants duplicates and another roll of film. So I set him up. He smiles at me, a handsome old smile, but then his eyes get big and they turn into gumballs, one yellow and one blue, and somehow in my dream I knew he could read my mind."

Fanny paused. Justine heard her drinking something, a cartoonlike *glgglg*, rising in pitch as whatever she was drinking drained out of its decanter.

"Then he reaches up with a weird long finger and pushes in his yellow gumball eye like a doorbell, and the blue gumball eye explodes. Me, I wake up on the floor, the night table tipped over, cigarette butts and pills and cough syrup and flashlight batteries and Jolts everywhere, and I guess somehow falling off the bed I break off my Swee'Pea nightlight and get little shards of night-lightbulb stuck in my ass."

"Oh my god. Are you okay?"

"Fine," said Fanny, calming down. "So guess what?"

"What?"

"I ain't opening the shop. Closed today."

"Really?" said Justine.

"A day off. Unpaid, sorry."

"What about Mr. Krupp? He picks up his insulin today."

"Al Krupp can kiss my peppered ass, then drive himself over to People's Pharmacy. But look. I want you to run over there and put a sign on the door that says we're closed and why."

"Like, CLOSED DUE TO ILLNESS or something?"

"No, like CLOSED SO DOC SEVERINSEN CAN'T COME IN TO READ THE PHARMACIST'S MIND."

"Serious?"

"Know how to spell 'Severinsen'?"

"I think so."

"Okay, so run down there and put up that sign."

Justine lay back down, a little disappointed she wasn't going in to work. She needed to save money in order to take Dot and Lou to Wendy's or wherever, or just to have it if they needed it. Justine also needed money for the costlier varieties of cold-pressed watercolor paper, the preferred support of the collagist.

The phone rang again. Fanny had a habit of changing her mind, so Justine answered.

"Hello?"

"Yes, hello," said a male voice, haughty but also base, a drill sergeant playing Henry Higgins. "Please connect me to Louis Borger."

"Lou? I'm pretty sure he's sleeping right now. Can I take a message?"

"This is a time-sensitive matter."

"Can I ask who's calling?"

"Go wake him up and place a telephone receiver in his hand. Now."

Justine put on a nightgown and hurried downstairs. Dot was on her divan, Dartmouth alongside her. Justine paused, as she always did when she went through the living room, to make sure Dot was all right. That she was alive. Justine stared until she saw her chest rise and fall. It seemed to take longer this time, and the rise was not as high. Justine went into the kitchen and tapped on the door by the pantry that led to the garage.

"Lou?"

"Come on in."

His voice was even and strong, not the voice of a person she'd just woken up. Justine opened the door. Lou was sitting on his cot, dressed in one of his two changes of clothes. His blankets were folded neatly and stacked on his pillow. Several full two-liter Coke bottles and a number of foot-high towers of Reader's Digest Condensed Books formed a modest rampart at the foot of his cot.

"Hi, Lou. Up, huh?"

"Yeah. Couldn't sleep."

"There's a guy on the phone for you. He says it's urgent."

"Thanks, darling."

"It's Sherpa, right? Is today the big treatment day?"

"I imagine it is the big appointment before the big treatment day. When he demonstrates the procedure and tells us what to expect."

Lou went into the kitchen and picked up the extension.

"Hello?" said Lou.

Justine opened the pantry and lurked there, reviewing the fare, while Lou said, "Yes, Sherpa," into the phone a few times, then hung up. He immediately picked up the phone again and dialed.

"Yeah, I need a cab going way south, to Slaughter Lane."

"Lou, I can take you," said Justine. "I have the day off. I have a friend's car. I just hafta stop at the store for a minute to put up a sign."

"That's sweet, but Charlotte's got the car today, so we're better off taking a cab. We'll be there awhile this time."

Justine shook a Pop-Tart at Lou.

"Hang up that telephone this instant because I am driving you to Sherpa's."

Lou hung up the phone.

"All right then," he said. "Let's go get ole Dotty bundled up."

Justine always waited in the car, but this morning she opened her door, looked down at the ground to make sure she wouldn't squash her tarantula, and stepped out.

"I'm coming in, too."

Lou carried Dot the whole way.

The house itself was a small, low, ordinary stuccoed ranch. A satellite dish beetled from an eave. An orange cat, balanced at the peak of the roof, watched them.

A man in his fifties came to the door. He was shirtless, lean, and weathered. He wore loose olive-green pants held up with dark red suspenders. The toe leather of his black lace-up boots was worn away, exposing battered and rusty steel toes. His forearms were tanned, broad, hairy; his chest tense, ribs asymmetrical, belly randomly scarred. He was not muscular, but clearly mule-strong. His hands were thick, and gray with calluses. His face, gullied with deep wrinkles, was flattened like a journeyman fighter's. His head was freshly shaved, but faintly visible stubble betrayed a hairline that crossed low on his forehead. His eyes glimmered with a mineral, transparent slate, like in photographs of Confederate soldiers. Under one arm he held an intelligent-looking, obviously frightened adolescent raccoon. The Sherpa held out his free hand, palm up. Lou's arms were full of Dot, who appeared to be asleep.

"Justine, baby," said Lou, "go in my coat pocket, this one here, and get out the money and the little photography things in there, would you? And give them to Sherpa? Sherpa, this is Justine, can she come in, too?"

Sherpa stared at Justine, saying nothing. In Lou's pocket, warm, humid, the lining torn, Justine found a folded stack of cash an inch thick, the outer note a twenty, and three black plastic 35 mm canisters with gray caps. She placed everything in the lifeless arroyo of Sherpa's hand. He turned and went inside. Lou and Dot followed. Justine did the same, shutting the door behind her. For a moment, all was black.

"Hurry," came the soft-hard voice of Sherpa from somewhere deep in the house. "Live or die?"

"Live, Sherpa," said Lou and Dot.

"What!" screamed Sherpa.

"Live, Sherp—"

"Shut the fuck up." A kettle began to whistle somewhere.

A yellow light resolved in the distance. Justine could make out the shape of Lou holding Dot, a pietà in silhouette.

Then, a paling squeak. The raccoon?

A sudden bright light blinded Justine. She blinked and wiped her eyes with the tail of her T-shirt, bending over so as not to expose her belly and bra.

The house was a single large room with a low drop ceiling of acoustic tiles and a plain white linoleum floor waxed to a hospital shine. The room was bare except for a large, empty kennel, and a small gas stove, kettle screaming on one burner. Sherpa lifted the lid, quieting the kettle for a moment, poured the contents of Lou's three canisters into the water, then replaced the lid. He turned around, and as if he had just realized a movie camera was filming him, exclaimed, "Well, hello."

"Hello, Sh—"

"Today I take you downstairs. You, pull on that."

With his elbow Sherpa pointed first to Justine and then to the baseboard by the stove, where a brass handle was visible. Justine pulled up the trapdoor, revealing wooden stairs that led to a cellar. Sherpa went first, then Lou and Dot, then Justine. The trapdoor fell shut behind her.

The cellar, also one room, was triangular, almost as large as the entire house above. The space seemed old, geologically so, like a cavern. The concrete walls and floor were painted a matte black. Against one wall stood an antique glass-fronted gun case with four identical rifles, a small black safe, a Styrofoam cooler, and a toilet with a floral, cushioned toilet seat, facing a large TV set. Against another wall was a stainless-steel counter, on which sat dozens of corked brown-glass bottles, a pack of balloons, and a stack of index cards. Against the third wall was a ratty blue couch.

"Sit on that," said Sherpa.

Lou put Dot down in the middle of the couch, and he and Justine sat on either side of her.

In the center of the room stood an enormous green-felted mahogany billiard table. At one end of the table, next to a coil of transparent plastic tubing, sat an odd device that looked to be contrived of the parts of a sewing machine and powered by a hand-cranked direct current generator of the sort used by Marxist rebels to set off dynamite or electrocute bourgeoisie. At the other end of the table lay an enameled-steel tray deep enough to hide its contents. Something about the way the felt deformed beneath the tray suggested it was not empty. The center of the table was barren, stained. Sherpa walked to the table and let the raccoon off there.

Sherpa went to the stainless-steel counter, uncorked a bottle, and tapped several small blue capsules into the palm of his hand. He walked directly over to Dot.

"*Aah*," said Sherpa. "*Ah*. Say *aaah*."

Dot opened her mouth, and Sherpa dropped the capsules in one at a time. He shut her mouth and held it closed with one hand, and rubbed her throat with the other.

Justine stood up.

"What did you just give her?"

Sherpa ignored her. He gave Lou two pills, which he also swallowed dry.

"What is that shit?"

"Justine," Lou said, cringing, sotto voce. "Please. It's all right."

"Girl," said Sherpa, "don't you take vitamins?"

"Don't call me girl," said Justine, grabbing Dot's hand and pulling. "Dot, get up. Time to go. C'mon, Lou, gimme a hand."

"No," said Dot, pulling her hand away. The strength and speed of her recoil startled Justine.

"Justine, please," said Lou, putting his arms around Dot. "We've been working on this an awful long time. Please."

"No way, this guy's a total fruit sandwich. C'mon."

"Justine, stop it," said Dot, her voice clogging up, maybe from the effects of the pills. "Just settle yourself. This is just a dress rehearsal. The show is soon, maybe tomorrow."

Justine looked at the raccoon, Sherpa, the staircase. Upstairs the kettle continued to scream. Justine sat down.

Sherpa came over to Justine, rattling blue capsules in one hand, like dice.

"Okiedoke. Aah."

"I'm not taking those."

"Oh?" said Sherpa. "Sure?"

"No way."

"Justine," Lou said. "Sherpa has cured more than a hundred patients. We trust him."

"That'll be just fine, then," he said. "Okay, everybody out."

From Lou and Dot simultaneously, "Huh?" Lou's eyelids were beginning to droop and his eyes to cross.

"Don't pretend you don't know the rules. Adios, kids."

"No, please, Sherpa, wait," said Lou, panic elbowing its way through his otherwise-drugged-neutral body. "Justine, darling, take them, they're purifiers, it's all right. Go ahead now."

"Too late, show's over," said Sherpa, walking over to the table and scooping up the raccoon. "Out, y'all."

The couch began to thump; once, twice, a third time. It was Lou, crying in single, compressed, quiet sobs.

"Kill the lights when you leave. Oh, turn off the fire under the pot upstairs on your way out, wouldja?"

"Please," said Dot, with what must have been energy borrowed from the gods. "Sherpa. Oh. Justine. Come on, now."

Justine had never seen Dot supplicate, never seen her beg, never seen her extorted. Justine imagined this was how it had been when under the sick thumb of her old pimp, Kelly Miller.

"Time for all y'all to fuck off now."

Justine kept quiet. She didn't stand up. Lou quit sobbing. Dot seemed to hold her breath. Presently, Sherpa put the raccoon back down on the billiards table. He walked over to his Styrofoam cooler and pulled out a can of Sprite. He approached Justine.

"Here, princess. Fucking take the fucking caps."

She put out her hand. He gave her two capsules. She didn't recognize them, and she'd been prescribed pretty much every mellower in the PDR, or so it seemed. They smelled faintly of finger paints. He opened the Sprite and gave it to her. She swallowed the pills.

The raccoon had shuffled to the end of the table to paw at something in the enameled tray.

"Gimme that," said Sherpa, walking back to the table and snatching something out of the animal's paws: a syringe. Sherpa scruffed its neck like a cat and dragged it back to the center of the table, and, with one hand, in one motion, popped the lid off the syringe and stuck the needle into the meat of the raccoon's hind leg.

The raccoon exploded in motive panic. Sherpa held on tightly. Ten seconds later, it was limp as a raw steak.

"Sux," said Sherpa, grinning widely, wrinkles forming at his stubbly hairline. "My concession to the mainstream. But you won't need it."

Sherpa took an object from the deep tray. It looked a little like a mother-of-pearl barrette. He performed a movement, and the object doubled in length. Oh, a razor, straight-edge, the old-fashioned kind. Justine screamed, but it came out comically diluted, a scream not screamed but said.

"Jesus, shut up. I'm not gonna hurt him, I'm just shaving a teeeeee*nine*sy bit of fur here off the hind legs so I can find a couple veins. The animal here will be himself again soon, cured of his little affliction. How's that sound to you?"

Sherpa shaved the raccoon's hind legs near the ankles. Lou watched, looking small, tired, hopeful, a gambler who just got dealt his first pair of aces in three days. Dot had fallen onto Lou's shoulder.

A strand of hair fell into Justine's eye, irritating her tear duct and vaguely nauseating her, but it seemed beyond human effort to reach up and brush it away. She could neither keep her eyelids shut nor prevent them from falling: they fluttered at half-mast by the involuntary power of their own tiny, drugged musculature. Justine's tonsils began to contract, signaling panic.

"I want to go home."

No one heard, or appeared to have heard. Had she even said it?

Sherpa went to the steel counter and opened the bag of balloons. They were long and slender, balloon-animal balloons. He wrapped one tightly around the raccoon's leg, then inserted a large-gauge needle with an orange plastic valve at one end into a vein just below the tourniquet. He did the same to the other leg, then removed the balloons with a snap. Into one valve he injected a clear liquid.

Justine's panic passed, giving way to a floating feeling of invisibility. Not a bad feeling, that. Maybe everything would be fine.

"Anesthesia, my own formula. You—Dot, right?—must be awake, so you will not need it, but the dumb animal—" Sherpa grabbed the raccoon's tail and shook it like a dinner bell "—would not likely understand that the transformation is for his own good. He would thrash."

"Makes sense, Sherpa," said Lou.

"Shut up."

With the shears he snipped a short length of fresh tubing from the coil on his table, then plugged one end into a valve protruding from the odd machine, and the other into the valve of the raccoon's right cannula.

Sherpa repeated the procedure with the raccoon's other leg, a new tube, a separate valve in the machine.

"Circuit completed," he said, giggling.

He opened a little door in the machine and placed an object of some kind inside. He began to slowly crank the machine.

"Now, this is purely for demonstration, remember," he said, continuing to crank. "The real business will be our next, and last, appointment. Louis, c'mere, crank."

Lou stood up, unsteady, like a film of a dying caribou played in reverse slow motion. He made his way over to the grinder and began to crank. Sherpa slapped him on the back of the head, the power behind the motion nearly knocking Lou to the ground.

"Counterclockwise, Jesus, man."

Lou reversed direction. Presently a fine meniscus of blood began to grow in the tube attached to the raccoon's left leg. It threaded through the tube, as thin and attenuated as mercury in a fever thermometer. It reached the machine. After a moment it reemerged from the machine and into the other tube, crawling the length of the tube and back into the raccoon's body, the blood somehow transformed, somehow purged of its muds and poisons.

Sherpa lit a cigarette.

"It will take forty minutes for a therapeutic percentage of the animal's blood to circulate and filter through the field. But, of course, *you*," said Sherpa, smiling, pointing his chin at Dot, "are sicker, larger, *bloodier*, and will take about five hours."

Upstairs, the kettle finally boiled dry. All was quiet but the crank.

Then they were in the car. Lou was driving. Justine was in the passenger seat, fully reclined, Dot limp across the backseat. A misty recollection of Lou carrying her. No one talked or moved. They didn't stop. They didn't do anything but listen to Don Gibson sing "Sea of Love" on KVET, and drive.

Justine struggled up the stairs to her room, locked the door, undressed with hands that felt not like her own but a lecherous stranger's, lay down on her bed, and called Troy, but there was no answer and he had no machine so she hung up. No matter, she might not have been able to put a sentence together, anyway. For more than an hour she masturbated with frantic, hard slaps and swipes of her stranger's fingers, a sensational guilt at her recent and present actions building along with the approach to the oasis of orgasm that would quench both. Finally, accomplishing neither, she stopped and lay as still as she could, counted the tickling drops of sweat as they ran down the shallow gullies between her ribs. The phone rang. She answered, her hands her own again.

"It's like two," said Troy.

"God, I need to talk to you," said Justine, sitting up, sore, lacquered in rapidly drying sweat.

"You forgot me. Stamp club ended like thirty minutes ago, and I'm sitting out here on the curb and Rogers LeRoi and Gary Fike are smoking and looking at me like they might be thinking about kicking my ass. Are you gonna come get me?"

"I forgot, sorry, but the weirdest stuff happened—I'm kind of freaked out."

"Really? Hey, what are you eating? It sounds soft. Donettes?"

"Nothing. I'm just slurring a little, from pills. I'll explain."

"Well, are you coming?"

"Leaving right now." She stood up, a bit dizzy, but without difficulty. It had been five or six hours since she'd eaten the blue capsules.

"Hurry up. Hey, do they know?"

Downstairs, a door slammed. It was Charlotte's peculiar slam. Home from the Wheelers', where she played pinochle on Sunday afternoons.

"Who? Know what?"

"That I'm coming over to meet everybody?"

"Oh god," said Justine. "I forgot. Look, that's not gonna happen, Troy. Everything's different now. Everything's weird, and I don't know what the hell to do."

Troy sighed. "What happened? No, don't tell me. Come get me, then tell me. Hurry. Rogers is gonna whale on me really soon, I know it."

Troy's green Dodge Aspen blew clouds of smoke as Justine drove to Austin High School.

Troy was sitting on the curb near the pay phones, intact. Rogers and Gary were indeed buzzarding nearby.

"He's scary," said Troy, climbing in and slamming the passenger door.

"What are they doing here on a Sunday?"

"I think they live at the school."

"Man, I'm glad to see you," said Justine. "You're the only normal person I know."

"Rogers is not like a good, heroic delinquent like Ponyboy or anything. He's more like Scarface. Drive away."

"Would you forget about Rogers?" said Justine, slipping the Aspen into gear and pulling out onto San Marcos Street. "He's nothing, Troy. But listen…"

"He has an Uzi hidden on school grounds, and he drives to Houston once a week to buy heroin to traffic to fourth-graders at Hyde Park Baptist. Ponyboy just had a broken bottle."

"You know Lou that I've told you about?"

"Damn hot today. What is it, like, March?"

"April 2. Will you listen to me? The scariest shit happened today—"

"Hot weather makes people like Rogers LeRoi want to subjugate or kill weak persons. And it makes weak persons weaker. Wimps, nerds, geeks. Stamp-clubbers."

"So roll down your window, Troy, Jesus."

"Wait. Look," he said, opening up his Liberty stamp album. "I traded my dumb Scott #524 to Sam for his mint #325 with a tiny, insignificant burn mark on McKinley's face, but you can still tell it's him. Sam's new at collecting."

"I'm driving, Troy," said Justine, beginning to roll her own window down. "I'll look at your stamps at the next light."

"Don't open your window, or my dupes'll blow away. Look what else, I got half a sixty-five-cent Graf, left half, the best half, from Orvance, who just gave it to me, he said it muddied his collection. But guess what, Hansika's stupid Uncle Vijay or somebody bought her a Scott #112, mint, no hinge or anything. I'll never have an Uncle Vijay. I'll never have a Scott #112. I'll never have a collection like Hansika. Me and Sam and Orvance and Willie are thinking about expelling her from the club. That'll make my collection the third best, next to—"

"Troy, shut up."

"What?"

"I have to tell you about what happened today."

"What?"

"It was so scary, I took Lou and his sick friend Dot I've been telling you about? to the so-called doctor they've been seeing and I hoped he was just a hippie all-natural guy or an acupuncturist or something, but he's a psychopath, just like I thought—"

"Now Rogers, there's your psycho."

"You haven't met them yet, but Dot means a lot to me, and I think this quack might kill her, literally end her life. And he's taking all their money."

"That sucks," said Troy, trying to fit a stamp with Skylab on it into a tiny plastic sleeve.

"Will you help me figure out something to do?"

"You want me to go kick his ass?"

Justine did want something like that. But Troy couldn't do such a thing, for reasons both moral and physiological. For a moment, she wished she were friends with Rogers LeRoi. She could barter with him. He gives Sherpa a nice throttling, Rogers gets a nice blow job. No paperwork.

"I don't know."

"*God*, I wish I had a Scott #112."

Justine opened her mouth to speak, but then said nothing. The light at East Eleventh and the frontage road turned red.

"Okay," said Troy, cracking open his album to near the beginning. "This is a really short light so I'll explain fast. See the picture of this square stamp? See? It's brown, really. Or buff. It's worth more than a hundred dollars."

The tears were coming. Old tears, cave-woman tears of aloneness and resignation. She had been expecting them, but they were coming too early. Troy, less than worthless when faced with lachrymose demonstrations, would either shut down completely, or, worse, would beg for a blow job.

The light at East Eleventh remained red. Justine shut down her throat, ground her incisors edge-to-edge, and pulled tight the threads of muscle across her cheekbones. If it didn't turn green soon she wouldn't be able to keep the tears back. Turn! The light's reputation as mercifully brief seemed now to have been a great municipal lie.

But it changed.

"Light, sweetie."

Justine stomped on the gas. The tears retreated back to their tear sacs or wherever it was they bivouacked when not dripping off her chin and the end of her nose.

"Home?" she said after a moment.

"Huh?"

"Want me to take you home?"

"No, Thundercloud. I need a shift, and I'm pretty sure Winnie'll give me one. I *must* own that #112."

"Thundercloud. Why didn't you tell me that? I wouldn't have come this—"

"Unless...," said Troy, pointing to the Tomby Motel, coming up on the left, where in 1973 the Rev. Richman Joe Mackelar got busted snorting gunpowder and cocaine out of the deep ensellure of a thirteen-year-old hooker, "you want to get a roo-oo-oom."

Justine ignored him. She turned on the radio, which was tuned to KVET, the station Dot and Lou listened to. KVET brought her down, so she twisted the dial in search of a better one.

"Does your silence indicate that you are you seriously considering my offer right now?" said Troy. "There's the Tomby. Look right there. There it is. Right there. Just hang a left. Quickly now. Left. Oh, you missed it. Now you'll have to pull a yooey."

Justine ignored him. She found a robust station playing country and western. She turned it up.

"I just don't get it!" Troy shouted, over Dolly Parton's "Jolene." "Am I grosser than Dick? You had sex with him on your first date."

"It wasn't a date."

Troy threw up his hands, banging a knuckle on the dome light.

"Ow. Not a date? You just plain had sex with him?"

"Why are you always thinking about sex when I'm extremely upset? I'm upset, you know. My granddaddy and my... Dot are doing something stupid and dangerous and I can't help them, because I need your help, but you're just a big waving boner."

Troy turned off the radio.

"I like that song!"

"I'm *always* thinking about sex, so it stands to reason that I'd be thinking about it when you get upset."

"You're so immature."

"I'm a virgin. What do you expect? Look, I'll be good. I've been reading up."

"On what?"

"Sexual themes."

"Where? Like in *Penthouse?*"

"No, a book. I got it at Crammed Shelf. *The Master Lover's Operator's Manual*, by Mellow. The only thing I ever borrowed without paying for, except that stale vanilla Charleston Chew I stole from a Toot'n Totum in Amarillo when I was three."

"Oh, Troy."

"I'm going to put it back. I read it twice, and I now know everything there is to know about pleasing a woman."

"I mean..."

"Justine, we're so close. Why not?"

"We're not that close, Troy."

"We can fart in front of each other. That's closeness. That's intimacy. I bet you couldn't fart in front of Dick."

Troy farted modestly.

"Roll down your window, now, asshole."

Troy shut his stamp album and rolled down the window.

"You should be sweeter to me, Justine."

On the Lamar bridge Justine tailgated a moped piloted by a large man in a business suit.

"Don't tailgate, please, it's illegal and dangerous. The legal distance you should keep away from the car ahead of you is d ≥ vc/10, where v equals velocity and c equals one car length."

Justine crept up closer to the moped.

"Hey," said Troy, "how about if we just drop the sex thing altogether and be friends?"

Justine knew Troy well enough now to recognize the primitive form of reverse psychology that he occasionally used in an attempt to manipulate her. He'd grown up without siblings or a mother and so had had virtually no remedial instruction in the art of control, let alone an opportunity to field-test the basics. Justine, on the other hand, was essentially postdoctoral. Usually she found his gambits innocent and endearing, soft, round bunnies of manipulation. But not today.

"*Good*," said Justine, swerving into the parking lot of the Thundercloud Subs kiosk on South Lamar and slamming on the brakes just in time to avoid hitting some clown staring at the sky with a pair of binoculars.

"Okay, good, me too," said Troy. "No more talk of that. So, can you get me at, like, nine?"

"Keep your stupid shitbox car."

Justine climbed out of the Aspen and slammed the door. A side-view mirror disengaged and fell to the tarmac with a rusty crunch. She turned her back on Troy, then began to walk north toward home.

* * *

Troy called late that night.

"What?" said Justine, who had been lying on her bed snipping visually compelling bits out of *Grunion Beat* and *Expectant Bride* and *Cigar Twee* and pasting them to a large sheet of watercolor paper for a work in five-point perspective whose theme was lustmord. Downstairs, Dot was asleep on the divan. Lou was out, somewhere.

"Hi. I'm calling to apologize?"

"What for?"

From a TV-dinner ad in *Mess*, Justine clipped a picture of a Salisbury steak whose mashed-potato area suggested the open mouth of a person screaming in ecstatic sexual pain.

"For nagging you about tailgating and sex."

Justine pasted the TV dinner next to a truffle pig.

"And for not paying attention to you about your bad day. But I had a bad day, too, you know, with the #112 and Rogers..."

"It's okay, I gotta go, homework, *Heart of Darkness*."

"Just rent *Apocalypse Now*."

"Don't they chop off a water buffalo's head?"

"Yeah, so?"

"I don't want to see that."

"You watched *Faces of Death*."

"And I still have nightmares. That *monkey*."

"That was awesome. So. I'm sorry about not being there for you today. What happened?"

"Oh, I don't know."

"Come on. I'm listening. No stamp talk. I put the collection away in the refrigerator for the night."

"What? Refrigerator?"

"That's where I store it. Low humidity; the stamps' gum won't activate."

"Oh."

"Some of my older specimens smell a little like luncheon meat, though, especially the imperforate National Parks series."

"Isn't this stamp talk?"

"Oh. So what happened?"

Justine took a breath.

"Well, this guy, Sherpa, is a paranoiac and con man, and he's lying to Lou and Dot about how he's gonna cure her."

"How do you know he can't?"

Justine sighed. "He can't, that's all."

"Maybe he's a prodigy of medicine, like Vesalius or Jonas Salk."

"He's not, okay?"

"Okay, okay."

"He should be dead. If I wasn't afraid of jail and getting interrogated by a corrupt detective and being put on the witness stand and rudely cross-examined, I'd shoot him."

Justine didn't really wish him dead, but her hatred felt pretty lethal. She wished she knew Rogers a little better.

"And," continued Justine, "he's scary, but weirdly attractive, like a really evil cult leader. He forced me to take two muscle relaxants or something, and did some kind of strange vivisection on a little raccoon that involved transfusing its blood back into its own body after running it through these weird 'fields.'"

"Jeez."

Justine snipped a picture of a high-tech quiver from an article on bow-hunting accessories in *Buckfeller* and inserted it into an X-ACTO-knife slit she'd made between the buttocks of a very suggestive peach she'd clipped from a schnapps ad.

"I knew a guy at ASH like him," she said. "He was, like, forty but looked seventy-five. He thought that the Smithsonian Institution was shooting fossil beams at him in order to age him faster. So he made parabolic mirrors out of Big Red gum-wrapper foil that he pointed in the general direction of Washington, DC, to gather the beams and refocus them into a single spot where they would slowly 'transgeal' into a mass that, when large enough, could be safely disposed of. And, once a week, using a forceps made of two Popsicle sticks, he would give the 'transjelly'—actually a small, hard ball of Play Doh—to Dawna, the head nurse."

"I can't think of anything to say."

"Johnny Ipolyte. He was harmless, and he really believed in what he was doing. But this guy, Sherpa, he's a mean asshole, just as nuts as Johnny, but cruel, too."

"So what do your granddad and Dot see in him?" said Troy.

"He manipulates. He's a psycho megalomaniac like Jim Jones. He makes them think he's their last chance. Dot says she's heard he's cured all kinds of people, that people've traveled from everywhere just to see him."

"So what do you want to do?"

"I don't know."

"Let's go out to his place and cream him."

"You sound suspiciously eager. Why?"

"I want to help."

Justine said nothing.

Downstairs, Dot moaned quietly. Dartmouth whined. It was nearly one in the morning.

"We can go right after school if you want. Justine?"

Cutting the little slit in the peach had made Justine horny, a condition that always inspired thoughts of Gracie Yin, with whom Justine happened to have an appointment tomorrow to talk about her college plans.

"I gotta go."

"Look, Justine, I'm really not doing this to make you give it up. I just want to help, and be friends again. I miss you."

"Gimme a break."

"*You* give *me* a break. I'm not such a perv as all that, jeez."

Justine sat up.

"All right. You'll come with me?"

"Sure. We'll get together after school and lay our best plans. I'll do anything you want. I hafta watch Garry Shandling at nine, though."

"Maybe you can meet Dot and Lou. Maybe you and I together can convince them that this guy's bananas."

"Okay."

Justine was excited. Tomorrow: Troy, the way she liked him. An adventure. Maybe a rescue.

And Gracie Yin.

IX

1978–1982

Murphy Lee Crockett was six and a half when he realized he had no purpose.

He and his best friend, Quince Waelder, had been riding the ill-greased Tarlton Park merry-go-round, trying without success to get it to spin faster by using old tennis rackets as oars, when Quince's brother, Travis, who was thirteen, emerged from the mesquite at the park's perimeter on his mini-bike, shirtless, shoeless, strong, squinty, mean, his face punctured with a mouth that could make a slur of any word. He skidded to a stop, sending a wave of gravelly dirt over Murphy and Quince.

"What're you two gays doing?" he said, revving his bike, which made an oval of sheet metal, emblazoned with the number 69 and fastened to the chassis, chatter like a high hat.

Murphy ignored him. Quince chirped, "Shut up" and took a swipe at his brother with his warped, slack-strung Wilson racket. It was a symbolic swipe; Travis was several yards away.

Travis shut off his bike.

All became quiet, except for the medieval Catherine-wheel creak of the decelerating merry-go-round.

Murphy and Quince scooted backward toward the center, where centripetal force was weaker and the median distance from Travis was greater.

"Chickens," said Travis. "Gay chickens. *Bok bok bok bgok. Bok bok. Bgawwk.*"

"Shut your trap," said Quince.

Murphy knew that if he jumped off first and ran for home, Travis would dog him on his bike, tackle him, and steal his shorts as a trophy. And that would give Quince a chance to run to his own house, where his mother would shelter him from his brother, at least until seven, when it was time for her to go play bezique at cousin Coretta's in Bastrop. Then Quince would be alone with Travis once again.

Similarly, if Quince took off first, Murphy could make it home unmolested.

"Quince, run," Murphy whispered into the back of Quince's neck.

"No way José," said Quince. "You run."

"No way José."

And so nobody moved.

"Hey, you guys," said Travis, "I know a way to make that go really fast."

There was a tone to Travis's voice, high and melodic, that Murphy did not recognize. It was *conspiratorial*.

Travis looked around, as though making sure they weren't being watched by thieves who might steal all the coming fun, then got off his bike and let it down gently to the ground. He grabbed a bar on the merry-go-round and let it drag him till they both stopped.

"Get off."

Murphy held his breath.

"C'mon, I'm not gonna get you, Jesus."

Murphy thought Travis sounded sincere. Murphy elbowed Quince, and they both carefully climbed off, being sure to stay opposite Travis.

Travis picked up his bike and walked it over to the merry-go-round. He positioned the rear tire tangential to the curve.

"Gimme a hand."

It did seem that Travis was contriving something that had nothing to do with capturing Murphy's shorts, so after a moment's consideration, Murphy elbowed Quince again. With bottom-of-the-food-chain caution, they made their way around the edge of the merry-go-round.

"Okay, Murph, grab the seat from underneath. Quince, grab the other side of the seat. Don't burn your knees on the exhaust pipe."

As far as Murphy could remember, Travis had never called him by his name. Maybe they were going to be friends. Have a club. Race bikes. Smoke marijuana joints and beat up Quince together. Steal shorts from big kids. From *girls*!

Travis grabbed the back wheel by the spokes.

"Lift."

They lifted. Travis guided the back tire and placed it carefully and precisely on the very edge of the merry-go-round, like a needle on a record.

"Okay, good. Now get on."

For an instant, Murphy thought he meant *on the bike*, but Travis got on it instead. He started it, and let it idle.

"Get on!"

Quince and Murphy climbed onto the merry-go-round.

"Okay, now get across from one another, near the edge. And get rid of the fucking rackets. You're gonna need both hands."

Travis slowly opened the throttle. The wheel spun on the diamond-plate steel of the merry-go-round, stripping off a little of what was left of the old blood-clot-colored paint.

"Murph, give the dirt a little push with your foot," said Travis. "A liiiittle push."

Murphy did.

"Now pull your foot back in before it goes under the wheel."

The merry-go-round started to slowly turn. Travis sweated and squinted, concentrating on keeping the rear tire straight and in even contact with the edge of the floor.

They picked up speed. Pitchfork-shaped systems of veins in Travis's hands bulged as he held the bike steady, staring over his shoulder at the rear tire.

"Hold on," said Travis, in yet another tone Murphy had never heard before, this one pitched at a note harmonic to the whine of the bike and conveying what Murphy decided was radical sincerity.

They were going almost as fast as Quince and Murphy could go under their own power. Soon they were going as fast as they had ever gone. Faster.

Murphy shut his eyes. He had been holding a bar by his hands, but now he had the crooks of his arms and knees around it. It felt like he was being sucked into a Boeing engine. Surely his knees and elbows would give out, his limbs torn away, his torso with its quartet of blood-squirting stumps flung a hundred yards into the scrub oak, where he would bleed to death, face up, and vultures would eat the eyeballs out of his head. Everyone knew that carrion birds ate the eyes first.

Faster. The bike's engine rose from a buzz to a hiss.

Then, a jolt and a scream. Murphy opened his eyes for an instant. Quince was gone.

Another jolt. Murphy's legs and arms opened out straight like switchblades, and then he was in space, an object in a chute of simple momentum.

He hit the ground, bounced back up with fresh topspin, and tumbled end over end like a baton. He finally came to rest by the warped slide that he'd poured Orange Crush down earlier in the day. He looked up into the sky. A cloud shaped a little like Oscar the Grouch floated by. Somebody was crying. Murphy recognized Quince's peculiar bawly gulps. No minibike engine hissing. A sudden stinging in one eye. Blood, from a split across the bridge of his nose.

Travis's head suddenly obscured Oscar.

"Got both you gays today."

He waved Quince's blue shorts in Murphy's face. Then he pulled Murphy's shorts off, lifting him momentarily off the ground. One of his Hush Puppies came off. He lay still.

"These smell like piss," said Travis, holding Murphy's many-pocketed tennis shorts by a single belt loop. "You *still* wet the bed, you weenie?"

Travis kicked him in the armpit, then disappeared.

Oscar had re-formed into a regular old cloud. Presently Travis's minibike could be heard. The buzz of the engine diminished as he drove off into the mesquite. Then silence again. Even Quince had stopped crying.

He waited for the cloud to change into something. Anything. A telephone, a Lucky Charm, a pineapple, a guillotine blade to chop off his head. But it didn't. It just stayed a regular old cloud, scudding peacefully off toward San Antonio.

* * *

When Murphy got home on his last day of second grade, he went directly to the kitchen and ate half a package of Pecan Sandies. Then he went downstairs to watch *Little House on the Prairie* with Granny.

"Do they get paid?" said Murphy.

"Who?" said Granny, who was sitting in a blue nightgown at the end of the divan with her feet tucked under her, drinking white sherry, smoking Vantages, and writing proofs in set theory.

"Those kids. On TV."

Thunder rumbled, far away and to the west, where thunder always first sounded in Austin.

"Acting is a job, so they probably get paid. Don't know what, though."

"Like a hundred dollars a day?"

"Maybe. Do you want to be an actor? You'd make a lot of friends."

"No way. Friends are gay."

"What about Quince?"

"Quince is gay. He's not my friend."

"He used to be," said Granny. "What happened?"

Hanging out with Quince had always been fraught with risk, reaching its piquancy with the merry-go-round incident. Murphy turned his back on him after that, and hadn't encountered Travis since. Each day without a debagging emboldened Murphy, and he looked forward to the day he would get Travis back. Murphy thought he would kill him if he could, and he watched for opportunities. He daydreamed about pushing Travis into a hole that went all the way to the Earth's molten core. He imagined hijacking a steamroller from a construction site and flattening Travis's whole house, with Travis inside. He imagined disabling the brakes on Travis's minibike and watching him helplessly run a stop sign and get mulched by a speeding cement mixer. He imagined setting him on fire.

Thunder again, closer, sharper. Lightning strobed the TV room.

"But you do want to become an actor?"

"No. I just wanted to know what they make."

"Do you want to direct?"

"What? Direct what?"

"Never mind. What *do* you want to be?"

"Nothing. I don't want anything. I don't like anything. I don't hate anything. Just nothing."

"Don't profess mathematics."

"Don't worry."

"Your I-am-Mr.-Spock-with-no-emotions tomfoolery is beginning to rankle me, young man."

The New Zoo Revue ended and a baloney commercial came on. Murphy hated ads. He liked *The Brady Bunch*, though, which came on next.

"Can you think of nothing?" said Murphy.

"No way to know," said Granny.

Granny always said stuff like that. It made Murphy want to pick up her stupid gold-leaf side table and hit her with it.

"Why?"

"I'll explain when you're older."

"I don't *feel* anything. So why can't I think about not thinking about anything?"

An ad for a set of Mahalia Jackson records ended and *The Brady Bunch* came on. Ooh, the one where Bobby turns out to be a pool shark.

"You're numb?"

And she always talked right when a show started. He fought fury.

"My show's on."

A snap of thunder and a bright bolt, only half a second apart. The wind picked up, and it became dark.

"I hope the damn lights—"

Another explosive crash and bolt, and the power went out.

"—don't go down."

"Oh no," said Murphy.

"Dammit," said Granny. "Murphy Lee, go get the flashlight out of my bureau. Top drawer."

Murphy'd been through all Granny's drawers a million times; he knew where the flashlight was. There were also empty pill bottles, full pill bottles, loose pills, a long, combination-locked wooden box that Murphy knew held Grampoppy's Korean War bayonet, a yellowing, vaguely sticky plastic bag of loose bullets and a dog tag, and a heavy rectangular magnifying glass with a slanted handle.

The flashlight was yellow plastic and held two D batteries. Murphy switched it on. A trembling yellow blip appeared on the ceiling.

Murphy pointed the feeble beam right into his left eyeball. It didn't hurt at all, and he could see fine afterward.

"Batteries are almost dead!" shouted Murphy.

"Dammit," came the opinion from downstairs.

Murphy shook the flashlight. He tapped it on the drawer. He unscrewed the end and rotated the batteries; all without improvement.

He picked up the magnifying glass and shone the light through it at the wall. As he approached the wall, an interesting effect: the light concentrated into a little bright dot. Granny would be able to see her equations at least. He could hold the magnifying glass and she could hold her pencil and the flashlight.

He put the magnifying glass in his pocket. He touched the wall where the dot was; it was warm.

The power snapped back on. Murphy went downstairs and showed Granny his discovery.

"And the sun'll start a fire," she said. "Why, Murphy, you look excited. Excitement is a feeling."

That summer Murphy carried his magnifying glass with him everywhere.

In the driveway he ignited the corners of books of matches and watched them jump as the flame reached the ranks of match-heads, lasered holes in Granny's stork bridge cards, vaporized ants and doodlebugs, exploded a fluorescent light bulb, heated up a ball bearing, and then burned his fingers trying to pick it up. He set an Excedrin on fire. He stuck a circle of Q-tips a foot across in the grass in the backyard, lit them like little torches, then put a toad in the fire jail. He burned an excellent likeness of Count Chocula on a plywood wall of a house that had been under construction and then abandoned more than a year before. In the mornings he would steam away the dew on the pomegranate-tree leaves, and in the afternoons he'd burn the leaves.

One scorching afternoon he found the neighbor's cat Styx asleep in the ivy behind Granny's house. With a stealth Styx himself would have admired, Murphy slowly snuck up and lit one of Styx's whiskers, which smoked and sparked and curled like a bomb fuse in a *Tom and Jerry* cartoon. Styx leaped and twisted and scratched at his face, then ran away, head low, tail flat down and straight. The perfume of the burn was delicious, but Murphy told himself not to enjoy it.

"This isn't fun, this isn't work. It's just time passing."

He looked at his watch, a Timex with a little rectangle that read the day and date, which Granny had given him as a Christmas present. It was August 9, 2:27:14 p.m. In an hour and a half it would be the hottest time of the day on the hottest day of the year so far.

Murphy sat in the yard and burned dollar signs into rotten pecans while he waited for four o'clock.

Travis raced by on his bike. It wasn't his dirt bike—he'd outgrown that—it was a real bike, a street bike. A Kawasaki 150. It was a nice bike. A week earlier, when Murphy had been in the yard melting army-men heads, Travis had raced past, a girl sitting behind him, holding him around the waist, head on his shoulder, eyes closed, barefoot, white threads from her cutoff jeans blowing straight back, chain grease on her shin, a rib-cage-shaped shadow of sweat on the back of her T-shirt. Travis had given Murphy the finger as he went by.

But today Travis appeared not to notice him.

At 3:54 Murphy walked the two blocks to the Waelders' house.

Through the picture window Murphy could see the top of Travis's stupid head about a yard away from their TV, which was airing an episode of *Mighty Mouse*, one of the old black-and-white kind that don't make any sense.

Parked in front of the garage door was the Kawasaki. With a few gulps and a deep breath sucked through the gap of his overbite, Murphy suppressed his excitement. He walked past the Waelders', then quickly cut through the Muñozs' yard into the alley, where he crouched down next to a dented trash can that smelled like a dead dog, and waited.

He couldn't see into the TV room any longer, but Mighty Mouse's sloppy alto came through just fine. The sweat from the crooks of his knees ran down his calves, washing away the dirt and leaving clean, branching channels that eventually soaked into the tops of his sports socks. A similar dynamic was in action on his arms and forehead. The skin under his watchband itched. The handle of his magnifying glass was almost too hot to hold. Thirsty. He would've sizzled a hole in his own fingernail if he thought it would somehow produce a can of icy RC Cola.

3:59:34

Murphy detected the faint musical signature of a Nestea commercial. Just before it ended, the volume spiked—Travis's show was about to come on. *The Brady Bunch.* It was the only thing they had in common.

Murphy snuck halfway back through the Muñozs' yard, then crawled under the hurricane fence corroded with morning glories that separated their yard from the Waelders'. He stood up. The sun slapped at the back of his neck as he looked down at the black shadow he cast over Travis's three-week-old Kawasaki.

...the youngest one in curls...

Murphy crouched down on the concrete driveway. He held out his magnifying glass, which immediately produced an immaculate seed of a sun on the sidewall of the Kawasaki's rear tire. Soon, the beautifully organic fougère of oxidizing rubber forced Murphy to have to restrain a sigh and a smile.

...man named Brady...

The tire disappeared. At virtually the same instant there was a loud *op*, and vulcanized shrapnel spread through the summer afternoon.

Murphy ran back through the alley in an aural vacuum. The world was bright, bright like a dentist's anglepoise, even under the dotting shade of the trees arched over the alley. Squinting bright. Headache bright. And silent.

He could barely breathe, but at the same time, he could breathe far more deeply than he ever had—as though his windpipe had dilated but his lungs had shrunk to dirty pink kitchen sponges, dried and slate-like from disuse.

He realized he still had his magnifying glass in his hand.

It was whole, uncracked. He kept running.

When he finally got home, he was alone—Granny wasn't back from tutoring yet. Murphy stood in the kitchen, closed his eyes, respired in his strange new way, and tapped on his skull with the magnifying glass, hoping his hearing would return.

The fake black-forest clock over the kitchen table chimed. He opened his eyes. He looked down.

His entire front, from V-neck to Hush Puppies, was soaked in blood.

He screamed. It came out hoarse, broken, frothy, like the howl of a rabid whippet. He searched for the source of the blood. He peeled off his shirt, kicked off his shoes and socks, tore down his shorts and underwear, and scanned himself. No cuts, tears, avulsions, holes; nothing missing. It was as if he were sweating blood. He looked at himself in the polished, convex flank of the four-slice toaster. There was something odd about his neck. He ran to the bathroom.

A nozzle, greasy and black, two inches long, stuck out of his windpipe. From the end of it, spit-thinned blood dripped; from the root of it, rich red channels pooled in his collarbone, spilled over, and fanned out down his chest.

He pulled out the tracheotomy tube.

And he fainted.

He spent four days in the hospital. Who cares; he had gotten away with blowing up Travis's precious tire. Supposedly Travis thought his tire had burst in the sun. It *had* been the hottest part of the hottest day. Obviously, he'd never noticed the splashed blood trailing through the gravel in his side yard and down the alleyway back to Murphy's house.

The official press was that Murphy had fallen on a slot-head screwdriver, which seemed to satisfy everyone except for a tall, skinny nurse named May who would come into his room, pinch his big toe really hard, and point at the ceiling.

"Ssss. Ss. Sss," she would say. "You didn't fall on no screwdriver."

Then she'd wiggle all his valves and slap his bag of saline solution.

"And let me add that you too old to wet the bed, young man."

Murphy hadn't wet his bed since Travis flung him off the merry-go-round. Murphy had regarded the side effect as freak luck, like when some people get struck by lightning and all of a sudden they can memorize a quarter million digits of pi or read minds.

But now he'd wet the bed every night since he'd been in the hospital.

Five weeks later, on another abnormally hot day, Murphy, with a new timbre to his voice that made him sound like Paul Lynde yodeling underwater, reported for the first day of third grade.

"Murphy Lee?" said Mrs. Santangelica. "Is that you?"

"Mmm."

"You sound different."

"Mmm."

"What happened?"

The attention of the other forty or so freshly advanced third-graders had turned to Murphy and Mrs. Santangelica.

"Mmnmnow."

The classroom sang with grade-school chuckling.

"Aren't you hot with that shirt buttoned all up?"

"Mnmo."

"Do you have the croup? Maybe you'd like to see the nurse? I'll excuse you."

Murphy said, "There's no excuse for me," but it came out sounding like an experimental dulcimer melody. His classmates abandoned chuckling for giggling.

"Blowhole," said Renée Tuttle, who was sitting directly behind Murphy.

Murphy had had Renée as a classmate last year. Over the summer, she had grown from a tiny, delicate, clover-like being, always overlooked, forgotten, ignored, in danger of being trod upon, to a *girl*—taller than anyone in the class, razor-chinned, strapped with long muscles.

"What'd you say, Renée?" said Mrs. Santangelica.

"I don't know, nothing."

"Be sweet."

Murphy'd heard that Renée's dad was a karate expert, and forged combat knives out of industrial hacksaw blades. He played high-stakes poker, smoked contraband cigars, and drove a yellow Porsche covered in STP and Pennzoil stickers that could go Mach 1. He played bass in a band and could drink a whole case of tallboys. He had night-vision goggles and a medieval crossbow. He once put a tapir in a headlock, and another time caught a baby that had fallen out of a helicopter.

Renée huffed and put her feet up on the back of Murphy's chair. She bounced her feet as fast as a drumroll until recess.

On the playground, Murphy went behind the jungle gym to explore a giant old pile of dirt that had sprung a copse of weeds over the summer. He climbed to the top and looked down. Dandelions, ragweed, hay, crabgrass. Nothing especially flammable; most of them, he knew from experience, would hardly smolder. And the hill's non-weeds were just as disappointing: broken glass, mashed cans, shreds of rotted rubber. Except for a confused or possibly insane locust pacing back and forth at the foot of the hill, there weren't even any bugs to vaporize.

Murphy euthanized the locust and sat down at the summit of his dirt hill.

He watched his classmates. They were the same kids as last year, doing the same things. They fired the same Nerf balls at each other, fought over the same Frisbees, sat morosely in the shade of the brick wall of the gym, stalked, screeched, snuck, hid, and spun like pulsars until their fuel of sugar was spent and they collapsed in flares of powdered dirt, where they would wait for a recess monitor to drag them away. All the same. Except now they were a little older and a little bigger, less frantic but more potent, less cruel but more cunning. Coarser. At home with premeditation.

Murphy got out his magnifying glass. He began to peel off a callus he'd recently developed on his thumb from sweeping Granny's walk every day.

The callus came off. He accidentally dropped it in the dirt.

"Shit," he said. *Chisth.*

"Watcha doing, blowhole?"

Murphy spun around. Renée.

"Mnupn."

"What's that? Magnifying glass? Give it."

Renée took his glass away, pushed him aside, and then immediately and expertly focused the sun on the cuff of her jeans. A tiny smolder only.

"Sucks," said Renée, giving Murphy back his magnifying glass. "My dad has an oxyacetylene torch. Fifty hundred thousand degrees. Hotter than the planet Mercury. Get rid of that dumb magnifier and get a torch. Bye, blowhole."

Renée shoe-skied down the dirt hill and ran off toward the slides.

Murphy searched for the callus with his glass. Desperate, he burned off a knot in his shoelace.

The bell rang.

Murphy began following Renée home after school.

He'd stay a block or so behind her, and when she turned the corner at the unfinished house, the one he'd burned Count Chocula into, he'd stop, watch her until she disappeared, then sit on the curb and flick lighted matches into the street until it was time to go home and watch *The Brady Bunch*.

Though it felt like he was abandoning tradition, he had retired his magnifying glass and switched to the sulfur match. Though likely not as much fun as an oxyacetylene torch, matches were efficient and immediately satisfying. They were also copiously available—Granny had accumulated hundreds of boxes and books of matches that she stored in a big aluminum suitcase of the sort secret agents use to carry dismantled sniper rifles. What's more, during the summer she had switched to a gold Zippo lighter one of her math tutees had given her. So, for most practical matters, Murphy now had his own metal valise of power.

"A nice smell, flint and lighter fluid," Granny had said, flipping open her new Zippo and snorting at the wick. "Smell, Murphy."

Granny leaned far over her legal pad of proofs to wave the lighter under his nose.

Nice, Murphy had thought, but nothing compared to the sweet, almost alcoholic top note of an oxidizing gelatin-phosporous-head match.

"Delicious, right?" said Granny.

Murphy nodded instead of speaking.

"Murphy, bed. Go."

Because he'd started wetting the bed again, Granny taught him how to use the washer and dryer.

"Don't forget to empty the lint trap. See? Just get a fingernail under the lint layer to get it going, then roll it off the screen. Feels pretty good to do. Lint rolling."

"Ymf."

"If you forget, the lint can catch fire. You heard me, Murphy?"

"Yp."

He wondered if laundering was his purpose.

Murphy squeezed the box of matches in his pocket that he'd selected that morning before school—a fat cuboid made of scabbard and paper that read in faded cursive THE SPODEE MOTOR LODGE WITH SWIM-POOL— and waited for the bell that would signal the last instant of school and the first of the Thanksgiving holiday.

Mrs. Santangelica seemed to be waiting impatiently, too—she unfolded and folded and emptied and filled and tested and retested her professional

Swingline stapler, until finally the bell rang.

Renée jumped up and was out the door first. Murphy waited ninety seconds and then followed her out into yet another ridiculously hot day.

As always, at the corner where the unfinished house was, Renée turned and was gone. This time, though, he wouldn't see her for five days, until school on Monday.

On the sidewalk across the street a bored-looking mourning dove pecked at an empty Skoal can.

Murphy had taught himself to shoot a flaming match twenty, sometimes thirty feet by first pushing the match head against the strike-paper with his fingertip, aiming, then flicking his finger. He got out his matchbox, calculated vectors, and let one go.

It landed well short of the dove, who paid it no attention.

Murphy turned to go home.

"Hi, blowhole," said Renée.

"Agh."

"Is your voice box ever gonna heal?"

Panic forced dots of sweat out of Murphy's wrists and forehead.

"Agh."

"I doubled around that skeleton house," she said, pointing at the half-finished construction project. "I wanted to ask you why you follow me every day. Do you like me?"

"Agh."

"Come over, and I'll ask my daddy to light his torch."

Renée lived in a big duplex, each half of which had later been halved, forming a fourplex; the Tuttles were domiciled in the second unit from the left.

"Where," said Murphy, carefully testing the word before he finished the question, "is your daddy's Porsche?"

"Your voice sounds a little better," said Renée, as she sorted through the half dozen keys she kept on a leather bootlace necklace. "Porsche is getting the double exhausts chromed. Come on in."

Mr. Tuttle, a large, down-comforter-soft man begrown with a mossy gray beard, was asleep in a fully articulated Barcalounger in front of a TV. He was shoe- and sockless, wearing a three-piece suit whose tie had been shed and had come to rest in a bowl of popcorn on the floor next to a four-tier pyramid of empty Busch cans.

"Daddy."

Mr. Tuttle opened one eye.

"Home?" came a voice from within his beard.

"Thanksgiving. Out early today. This is Murphy Lee, from school. Will you melt something with your torch for him?"

Mr. Tuttle looked from Renée to Murphy to Renée to the TV to Renée.

"Tired. Busy. Job hunting."

"Just a nickel?"

"Ballgame on."

"A fork?"

Mr. Tuttle shut his eye.

"C'mon, Blow. Let's go to your house."

On the way to Murphy's, they stopped at 7-Eleven to get cold drinks.

"Why do you like that stuff?" said Renée as Murphy picked a Pepsi out of the cooler. "Dr Peppers're better."

"They taste the same. Don't they?"

"God. No, they don't. Dr Pepper won the taste test on TV, so there's proof. Beat Coke *and* Pepsi."

Murphy considered this. Murphy considered his new friend. He considered fire, Granny, his new voice, his new friend's gender, her fresh superiority. He liked being Blowhole. Renée Tuttle didn't call anyone else by a cool nickname. He put his Pepsi back and chose a Dr Pepper.

"We should get something for your momma."

"Huh?"

"How about a Canada Dry? Old people like ginger ale."

Murphy froze. Only eighteen minutes into a new friendship and already conflict stood rampant, ready to disembowel him and scatter his tripe like grain. His real mother was considered peculiar, and lived in a booby hatch in San Angelo, where she tended a turnip patch and forbade visits. *Granny* was his real mother, but no one at school knew.

"Yeah," said Murphy. "Ginger ale. Momma likes that."

Renée opened her can and took a great gulp before they even got to the register. She bought all three drinks with a ten-dollar bill.

When they got to Murphy's, Granny was, mercifully, taking a nap. Murphy and Renée watched *The Flintstones* with the sound down low.

"Do you have Atari?" said Renée.

"No, but I'm getting it, really soon, next week or tomorrow," said Murphy, a lie.

"Good."

"Yeah."

"You know that little kid Quince, in first?"

"Uh-huh."

The gods could be so unkind.

"His big brother Travis has a Harley-Davidson hog *and* Atari."

From Granny's room Murphy heard the signature *plinkch* of a Zippo. The lighter's naphthalene perfume and Granny herself wafted into the den.

"Why, who is this young lady in my house?" she said.

"That's my momma, hi, Momma, this is Renée, Momma, from Ms. Santangelica's class. That's my momma."

"Well."

"Hi, Mrs. Crockett."

"Hmm."

"Murphy bought you a Canada Dry."

"Why, thank you. Son."

So magnificent, the sweet smiles of the gods!

Granny invited Renée over for turkey the next day. Through Renée, Granny extended the same invitation to Mr. Tuttle, but he was on Green Beret shark-wrestling duty in the Gulf, and was unable to attend. After dinner, Granny said she'd give Renée a ride home so she could stay later and not have to worry about walking home in the dark.

The next morning Murphy woke up and went downstairs to find the women in his life sitting Indian-style on the den floor before the TV set, on which a white blip whizzed and caromed against a supernaturally black background.

"Your mom went out and bought you Atari this morning!" Renée shouted.

Over the next few weeks Murphy and Renée played *Pong*, fired off match rockets, watched after-school TV, and waited every day for Granny to get home from Austin Community College, where she taught math, to make them Elvis sandwiches and virgin margaritas. When Christmas vacation started, Renée would come over early in the morning, and Granny would fry eggs and bacon for the three of them.

"You know, sugar," Granny said to Renée on the morning of Christmas Eve Eve as the three of them sat around the Christmas tree they'd all decorated with matchboxes and three-decades-old popcorn strings, "your daddy's welcome over here too."

"Uh," said Renée, "thank you, Mrs. Crockett."

"You can have other friends, too, both of you. Like your little friend Quince. Would you like to have him over, too?"

"No way," said Murphy.

"Okay," said Renée.

Two days after Christmas, Murphy and Renée were at 7-Eleven buying Mentos and Dr Peppers when a voice behind them said:

"Hi, Murphy."

Renée and Murphy turned around.

"Oh," said Murphy. "Hi, Quince."

"Hi," said Quince. "Your grandma invited me over to your house today."

"Grandma?" said Renée.

"Shut up," said Murphy. "Where's Travis?"

"Jail still," said Quince, biting hard into a Chunky he had yet to pay for.

"Good."

"You sound funny, like a donkey," said Quince.

"Well, you look funny, like a donkey."

"You still smell like tinkle, too," said Quince, who looked like he might cry.

"I don't either!"

"Why'd your grandma call him?"

"Because his mommy's crazy and lives at a bootie hatch."

"So who's that at your house?"

"That's his grandma."

A brief silence, largely occupied by a fierce staredown between Quince and Murphy, was broken by the 7-Eleven cash-register lady. "You kids pay for them treats first, then go outside and bicker."

Outside, Renée said, "What's Travis doing in a jail?"

"I don't know," said Quince, keeping close to Renée. "Mommy won't tell me."

"I hope I never go to jail," said Renée.

"I'd break you out," said Quince.

"Really?" said Renée, without a quaver of patronization.

"Yeah."

Murphy felt like shooting matches at Quince's hair. *Phoom!* Bald.

Renée pulled the tab off her can of Dr Pepper with one smooth move-ment, like an adult: no hesitation, no hitch, no labor. Then she dropped the curling petal of aluminum inside the can.

"What if you swallow that?" said Murphy.

"I won't. It sinks."

Both Quince and Murphy tried to pull the tabs off their cans in like fashion. Quince yanked hard, but the pull-tab did not uncouple; he flung his Coke backward into the open passenger window of a Wagoneer parked by the ice shed. Murphy ripped at his tab, but only the ring part came away: the soda inside was to be trapped forever.

Renée ran over to the big vehicle, opened the door, grabbed the Coke, slammed the door.

"Hey, you little turds," said an old man emerging from the store, presum-ably the Wagoneer's pilot. He wore a dirty felt cowboy hat and was missing a hand. Quince and Murphy and Renée ran.

They stopped in front of Murphy's house.

"I gotta go," he said. "Renée, you coming in?"

"I don't know."

"His house smells like tinkle 'cause he wets the bed," said Quince.

"I got Atari, nyah," said Murphy.

"I got Intellivision, nyaaaahh," Quince said.

"I thought you had Atari," said Renée.

"Atari's gay. Now I have Intellivision that I got for Christmas."

"No way. Golf?"

"*Sea Battle.*"

"I gotta go on inside," Murphy said again. He *did* sound a little like a donkey.

"Any other cartridges?" said Renée.

"No, but I'm gonna get them all."

"Let's go play."

"Renée, come on in," said Murphy.

"Should we get more Dr Peppers first?" Renée said to Quince, ignoring Murphy. "I have fifty cents."

"Yeah," said Quince. "I have forty-four cents. We could go to Lucky's instead of 7-Eleven so we don't run into that one-hand man again."

Renée and Quince started down the street, examining each other's pool of coin. Murphy watched them go.

Granny wasn't home yet. He got a handful of matchbooks out of the metal suitcase, a couple of coat hangers, Granny's yellow and blue plastic squeeze-bottle of Ronsonol, went out into the backyard, fashioned a kind of raised cradle out of the hanger, placed the Dr Pepper can with its inaccessible contents in the cradle, assembled a pyre underneath, squirted accelerant over the entire assemblage, then shot a match at it. Murphy ran and crouched behind Granny's big terra-cotta jardiniere and waited for the can to explode.

It did not. It merely turned black about its underside. Murphy kicked it into the ivy by the fence bordering the alley. Then, with adrenal rage, he leaned against the jardiniere, which had sat in the side yard for as long as he could remember, stagnating, nourishing mosquitoes by the cloud, and pushed.

A brackish fan of foamy water as dark as cuttlefish ink spread through the grass and immediately got drunk up by the dry soil, leaving above ground only a supersaturated balsa-wood toy airplane, hundreds of wooden matches, and two cue-ball-sized toads that at first appeared inert but soon began to hop away in opposite directions—one toward the alley fence, the other toward the porch.

Murphy got behind the toppled jardiniere and pushed and heaved until it finally began to roll. It crushed the porch-bound toad.

"Quince," said Murphy.

He then ran after the other toad, who had just about gotten to the fence. Murphy soaked the animal in Ronsonol and set it on fire. It hopped four more times, then stopped. Its skin bubbled. Its mouth opened. It shrank. It hopped once more.

"Renée."

He stomped on it. An orange finger of flame leapt from the frog's head;

Murphy stomped again. After all, he didn't want to burn down the whole neighborhood.

. . .

January. Renée had neither called nor dropped by since the Day of the Toads. She didn't play with Murphy at recess, she didn't pair up with him for science experiments, she didn't even flick paper footballs at the back of his head or put ice cubes down his shirt. She didn't wait for Murphy in the hallway after school, but instead went outside to find Quince, who was always waiting by the bike rack. They walked from school to Renée's house every day, something Murphy knew because he followed them every day, taking extra care to ensure he wasn't seen. Murphy would hide inside the abandoned house across from Renée's and watch for movement inside the Tuttles'. During his sentinels he would experiment with matches and a quantity of Ronsonol he carried with him in a twelve-dram prescription bottle that once held pills for Granny's flatulence, and wait for Quince to go home.

Every time he left Renée's, Quince seemed a bit larger, a bit taller. By Cinco de Mayo, Murphy noticed that the pair were the same height. Murphy was at least half a foot shorter.

One afternoon, as Murphy sat in his secret spot testing a contrivance of matches whose heads were tightly wrapped in tinfoil, heated until ignition, causing the contrivance to rocket in a satisfying but wholly unpredictable way, he heard a car start.

It was Mr. Tuttle, backing out of the driveway in his old Chevette. He drove off in the direction of Mueller Airport.

They were alone. Renée and Quince were *by themselves*.

A sudden wind blew the day's heat and gel-like humidity away. The gust was followed by a rolling tide of gray clouds lit from within by bright branches of lightning tinted red.

A yellowy light went on in one of the windows of the Tuttles', illuminating a ceiling fan. From beyond the frame of the window a hand appeared. It pulled a chain on the fan, which accelerated to a leisurely wobble. The light went off. Presently, a low, greenish-blue light filled the window.

The treetops waved. Twigs and leaves fell. It got cool and dry. The sky grew darker.

Knees bent, head down low, Murphy gritted his incisors, took a plumb, dizzying breath that made his scarred windpipe tickle, and crawled toward the Tuttles' like infantry.

He crouched under the window, his back to the nearly paintless wall. He listened, but the rustling trees, like thousands of sparklers, swallowed up every noise but the thunder.

He squeezed his matchboxes, felt the aliphatic chill of the prescription vial of Ronsonol in his pocket, then stood and peeked inside the house.

Renée and Quince were lying on the shag-carpeted floor with a black corduroy armchair pillow behind each of their heads while before them a small color TV played the *Brady Bunch* episode where Marcia gets kissed by Davy Jones. Murphy would never again watch *The Brady Bunch*. He would kill off each Brady in his mind until the archive in his brain was empty of that particular show.

The show ended in a commercial for Brawny. Quince pulled out from under the TV stand a flat brown and black box with many cords snaking from it: Intellivision. He plugged in the *Major League Baseball* cartridge. Breathtaking! Atari held no cards against the royal flush of colors, movement, and sharpness of Intellivision.

Murphy watched them play, one inning, two, three; he watched them grow more animated and shrieky, until the fifth inning, when Quince tripled off of a wobbly curveball, scoring three runs. Renée paused, then reached over and pulled Quince's shirt over his head. He responded by yanking off one of her blue Keds. By the time they were tied at six in the bottom of the ninth, both wore nothing but underwear, their shirts and shoes and socks and pants scattered here and there.

Renée appeared to be pitching, the winning run on second. She threw a couple of pert strikes. She squealed after each one; Quince groaned.

In real life Quince bore zero aptitude for any sport, especially baseball, but he had a built a reputation on his skills with the joystick. He knocked Renée's next split-fingered out of the park. Quince arched with victorious laughter. Renée covered her mouth with one hand, then rolled backward, kicking and shaking her head. She rolled onto her knees, grabbed an armchair pillow, and buried her head and shoulders underneath it. Quince stood up, grinning, jumping from one foot to the other, his fingers peace signs stabbing at the ceiling.

The wind stopped, as though by a wall, allowing an instant of placid quiet.
Quince chirping: "You gotta, Ren, you gotta, Ren."
Renée squealing: "No way, you suck."
The wind blew down its wall and the obscuring hiss of sparklers returned.
Renée threw her pillow at Quince, who ducked. He chased her around the
TV. She was scream-laughing under the din of the storm. He slipped and fell,
but caught her ankle as she raced by. She went down. He grabbed her panties,
which slipped and stretched unevenly down her legs, then caught at her knees,
where Quince ripped them off and waved them like a shredded battle flag.

Murphy ducked and ran. It began to hail.

The hailstones got larger. They hurt. Now instead of bouncing like teeth
when they hit the pavement, they shattered.

Murphy smelled smoke. It grew in pungency the closer he got to
home. Soon the smoke was visible; then it was bodied; then it was its own
weather—whorls of ash lit with tiny magma-orange live cinders. Then it
was no longer smoke but a nebula of heat. He stopped.

Translucent peach-marmalade flames squirted out of all the windows of
the north side of his house. Neighbors stood under the eaves of their porches,
forearms shielding their faces, watching. Presently sirens broke through the
noise of the wind and exploding hailstones, and soon there were yellow-and-
black-jacketed firemen swimming through the smoke and ribbons of fire
like storm-caught hornets, dragging ladders and hoses and axes.

Granny's Valiant wasn't in the driveway.

Murphy sat down on the sidewalk among the melting balls and shards
of ice and watched the flames reach out of the windows for the cedar fence
and the pecan trees and the resigned firemen with their arcing tubes of white
water.

A shaggy explosion made the firemen back up a step.

My matches suitcase.

The shredded victory flag would not leave his mind.

Hailstones broke on his knees.

The fire marshal came to Murphy and Granny's room at HoJo's to report that
it was most likely the dryer that had started the fire.

"Probably the lint trap," he said, accepting a Vantage and a light from

Granny. "Was the dryer drying?"

Murphy, who was pretending to watch *The New Zoo Revue*, felt Granny's glance like grasshoppers under his shirt collar.

"I leave it on all the time," she said.

"You gotta clean the lint trap."

"I know that."

"Y'orta save that lint. My nephew Ely, out in Gruene, can make paper out of it. He harvests lint from anybody's dryer in town who'll let him, and there's a lot of folks who will. He sells the paper to artists and whatnot for in the neighborhood of ten dollars a sheet no bigger than a welcome mat."

"I wish he'd come by earlier."

"How you holding up, boy?" said the fire marshal.

"Fine."

"Don't worry, you can get all new toys with your mama's insurance."

"You'll talk to Farmer's?" said Granny.

"Sure I will."

He left.

Granny turned off the TV.

"Hey."

"Did you hear what the man said?"

"No."

"Did you clean the trap like I told you to?"

"Yeah."

"Every day?"

"Yeah. Gah!"

He had cleaned it only once.

"Maybe," Murphy said, "you left a cigarette burning and it lit the other cigarette butts and then they lit your bridge cards right next to your lighter fluid and then the lighter fluid exploded and threw flames everywhere and then the house burned down. That's probably what happened. It was your fault. Can you please turn the TV back on?"

Granny clenched her neck and jaw. She turned the TV back on. Then she lay down on her twin bed and went to sleep.

State Farm paid out. Before Murphy and Granny moved into a small, newly constructed house off Chicon, they visited the remains of their old home. They waded through the charcoal and pools of melted and solidified plastic and metal. Granny recovered a skillet that had been her great-great-great-grandmother's and had survived another fire, a houseboat in Bayou La Batre in the 1840s. That fire spared nothing but the relative and the pan.

Murphy hoped to find his magnifying glass, but all he came away with was Grampoppy's bayonet. The fire had vaporized its box and its hilt, leaving only the fire-scaled blade and a three-inch tang that begged for a nice new handle.

"Don't you goddam dare let anything happen to that Jap-sticker, Murphy Lee Crockett," Granny had said, shaking her skillet at him. She was as angry as he'd ever seen her.

When Murphy was eleven, he grew out of his fire stage, shortly after he had made a lightbulb-filled-with-gasoline booby trap and screwed it into a socket in the disgusting bathroom at the Round and Round go-kart track. He hid in some nearby bushes and waited for a guinea pig to go in and flick the switch. He waited and waited. Didn't anybody ever need to take a shit in this place? Eventually he went in and flicked the switch himself. The bulb exploded perfectly, a succulent arson. On fire, he ran onto the go-kart tracks. The next thing he knew, he and his fire were being smothered under the weight of a giant, gristled good Samaritan. When Murphy had been sufficiently doused, the good Samaritan rolled off, inspected Murphy for serious burns (they were all superficial), and then showed Murphy a badge indicating that he was a police officer. Murphy went to kid jail, was bonded out by Granny—who sold her Valiant to do so—pleaded guilty, received three months in juvie and two years' probation. When he awoke on the final day of his period of probation, he was dry. His bed-wetting had finally ceased.

That day was also the first that he hadn't at least once thought of the shredded pink battle flag.

X

"Come in, Justine," said Gracie Yin, holding her office door open and inviting Justine inside with the wave of a manila folder. "Nice to see you again."

"Hi."

Justine sat down, smoothed out her blue skirt, and checked her reflection in the glass of Gracie's framed counselor's certificate over the file cabinet in her office.

Gracie sat down in a swivel chair and balanced the manila folder on the armrest.

"How goes it?"

Gracie wore a white fitted linen suit and a light blue silk blouse with the stitching of a breast pocket just visible under a lapel of her jacket. She wore a man's tie, saddle-tan with thin pink pinstripes, the knot tied loosely and hanging down to the second button of her blouse. Her brown suede kitten heels looked as light as cork and seemed so delicate that Justine wondered if she were to hook one finger between the leather upper and Gracie's instep and merely pull, would the shoe tear away like dime-store gift wrap?

"Fine."

"When was it we saw each other last? A little while after you returned to school after your hospitalization?"

"Yeah. I think so."

Gracie crossed one leg over the other. A run in her pantyhose disappeared into her shoe.

"How is the adjustment?"

"Fine."

Gracie opened the folder and studied something inside. Then she looked up at Justine.

"Your arm. And how is that?"

"Getting better."

"May I see?"

Justine's nipples hurt. The night before, after she'd hung up with Troy, the Christmas-morning-caliber anticipation, the woolly after-effects of the blue capsules, the imagery in her collage, and the horniness at the thought of seeing Gracie Yin had all combined to bring forth a creative lust that she answered by tying her nipples together with a length of grosgrain ribbon, holding the bight between her teeth, and pulling in the manner of reins; this proved to be an excellent addition to her workaday masturbation. And now, looking at and listening to the words tumble over Gracie Yin's lower lip, Justine's nipples started to harden and ache. She slumped forward so her hair would cover the front of her blouse, which would otherwise surely betray her. Justine unbuttoned her cuff and pulled up her sleeve.

"Hm. That's sure not just a cry for help," she said, rolling her chair back on the hard rectangle of clear plastic on the floor. "Thank you for showing me."

"Sure."

"Now, are you still thinking about UT?"

"I guess. I'm also kind of thinking about NYU."

"UT's harder to get into than it used to be, even if you're in-state, and out-of-state anything's going to be tough, and expensive," said Gracie, smiling, her mouth slightly open so Justine could see the wet pink of the inside of her lower lip. She had small, talc-white teeth edged with little serrations, except for her canines, which, even though vaguely yellowing, dully peaked, and barely a sixteenth of an inch longer than her incisors, were as subtly menacing as a cookie-cutter businessman with a faint smear of blood on his knuckles.

"I'm a pretty good artist."

Gracie again examined something in her folder.

"It's the grades I'm a little concerned with."

"I know. I'm trying to catch up. I missed a lot of school."

"What's your third-choice school? ACC?"

"I don't have one."

"What about extracurrics? Sports? Volunteer work? Girl Scouts?"

"Girl Scouts? Do they still have that?"

"Sure."

"No."

"If you can, Justine, try and do something outside of class. Start a reading group. An entomology club. Play chess. Join the cheerleading squad. That's the kind of stuff colleges look for these days."

Cheerleading! Did Gracie Yin think Justine was attractive enough to be a cheerleader?

"It's okay, it's okay," said Gracie with some urgency, as if she were thinking Justine might go south at that very moment. "Listen, do what you can. Meanwhile, did your parents go to UT? If you're related to an alumnus, that always helps."

"My mom did. She didn't graduate, though."

"Hmmm. Did she go to Austin High, too?" said Gracie, pointing to the floor with her thumb.

"Yeah."

"Dad?"

"I'm adopted. Livia—my mom—her husband died right after they were married."

Gracie leaned forward in her chair, put her elbows on her knees, and clasped her hands. Her pink and tan tie hung between her legs.

"We're going to do what we can for you, Justine. Look, see if you can join a club. Talk to Livia about writing a letter for you, for your UT app. And I'll help you with your NYU app. We'll get you into one or the other. Maybe both."

"Okay."

Gracie shuffled some papers and shut Justine's file.

"How are things at home?"

"Fine."

"You can confide in me. Guidance counselors aren't just for breakfast anymore."

"I don't know. I guess my grandmother's sick."

"I'm so sorry. What's wrong?"

"AIDS. She's a hooker. Retired."

"Oh. My."

Gracie crossed her legs the other way. Her shoe slipped off at the heel, but she saved it from falling by straightening out her leg. Her tiny, arched foot, a shoe hanging off the toes, was pointed at Justine's knees.

"Yeah."

"You sound like you admire her."

"She's pretty cool."

"How ill is she?"

Gracie allowed her shoe to hang off her toes. Slices of Coke-can-red toenail polish occasionally glimmered.

"Ms. Yin?"

"*Gracie.* I'm barely six years older than you, Justine."

"Uh, do you know a doctor who calls himself Sherpa?"

"Sherpa? Nope. Is he your psychiatrist?"

Justine smiled. Dr. Jumples, the shrink to whom she'd been assigned for post-discharge therapy, wouldn't have thought it funny to be compared to Sherpa. Justine had seen Dr. Jumples only a few times. He always looked like he was doing forced community service during their sessions, sighing and fidgeting and watching the clock.

"No, he's just a... guy. A specialist."

"How are things going with your doctor?"

"I quit seeing him. He's an idiot."

"I wish you'd go back."

"I'd rather see you."

"I'm not qualified, Justine, or I'd like to see you, too. We've got a rapport."

Gracie reached down and pulled her shoe back on with a pinkie, then looked at the clock on her desk.

"Let's make another appointment," said Gracie. "Two weeks?"

"Okay."

"What class do you hate the most?"

"French. Third period. And math analysis, fourth."

"Okay, Monday the seventeenth, at the start of third period. We'll have two periods, an hour and half. We can talk somewhere else, like a coffee shop."

"I... is that allowed?"

"Not really, but what're they gonna do? Meet me at my car, '73 yellow Subaru wagon shitbox, at the appointed time. We'll go to Jim's and order cinnamon rolls and coffee."

Gracie rolled her chair to her desk.

"Meanwhile, here's my card. I don't give it out often, but here you go. Give me a call if you want. Okay?"

Justine nodded.

"Listen, if Dick Seldom's out there, send him in, wouldya?"

After saying hi to Dick, who glanced at Gracie's door and then winked chastely at his old girlfriend, Justine hurried down the empty hall of the underclassmen's science building toward the bathroom, where she hoped to lock herself in a stall and pinch the itch out of her nipples, quickly masturbate, and then pee, before fifth period let out and the bathroom became a caucus of preening sophomores.

CLOSED MAINTAINANCE read the sign on the ladies' room door.

Muffled clattering: the bell. Students instantly filled the narrow hall like red cells in a capillary.

"Dammit," said Justine, hectic with manifold corporeal needs. "Dammit."

More red cells, sluggish now from overcrowding. Justine was trapped in the middle of the hall.

Justine felt the tail of her blouse being pulled out of the waistband of her skirt. She spun around.

"Hi, sweetie," said Troy, smiling.

"Don't ever do that again. Where did you learn that? Did you see Rogers LeRoi do that?"

Troy blushed and shifted and shrank.

"I don't know. Sorry."

"Jesus."

"I'm just excited. About messing up Sherpa after school. Hey, you look all red and hivey."

"I have to tinkle."

"You have lang. lab last period today, right? Want to meet there, then we'll blow this Popsicle stand?"

The crowd squeezed them together, face to face.

"Listen," said Justine, quietly, fiercely. "I'm ready."

"Ready for what?"

"I'm ready."

"Wha... really? You want to go to Sherpa's now? I don't know, you know, I can't cut class, I only did it that one time with that bad-influence kid Alan and I was a wreck the whole time, and besides I have a free period next and I wanna go work on the Circus Maximus model me and Rashad are working on I told you about, I'm making clay gladiators and I'm gonna paint them bloody and gory, and pull some arms off and scatter them around the arena, and I also decided to make a Cleopatra figurine and put her up in the stands with Caesar and Brutus—"

"Troy," said Justine, whispering in his ear. "Let's go to your house first. Then we'll go to Sherpa's."

A sea-salty, formaldehydic aroma began to rise off of Troy. A boner also rose in his chinos, which Justine could feel poking at her left acetabulum.

"You mean... you want to meet my dad?"

"I want to see your room. Your *bed*. Now."

"Oh."

"C'mon."

Justine reached down for his hand.

"We'll get in trouble, Justine. We'll get detention. With the burnouts."

"I need it, Troy," she said, realizing with a goose-pimpling rosewater blush that she had never said anything like that to anyone; had never even thought those words; had never acknowledged that there was something sweet but always on the lam that people called *it* when they needed *it* yet which could be hunted and caught and field-dressed only by a cooperating team whose prime directive was the pursuit of *it*. "And I know *you* do."

Justine put her hands on either side of Troy's neck, her thumbs just under his earlobes, and kissed him, hard, her mouth open, her braces tearing at the soft flesh inside her lips, tongue hard and arrogant, just like she'd seen

Rogers LeRoi once do, in the middle of driver's ed, to Lauren Pirckheimer, a red-haired girl who'd gone from zero to D-cup in the thirty days of the previous September.

Justine left several crisp impressions of her braces inside her lips.

"'Kay," said Troy.

Troy and Justine crawled on their hands and knees through the narrow, darkly shaded side yard that ran by the windows of Troy's dad's den. On their left was an ancient cedar fence ablossom with ivy and corticioids and molds.

"...the sun's not yellow it's chicken!" shouted a voice above them.

"That's Dad," he said over his shoulder. "Keep down."

"Duh."

As she crawled behind Troy, mildly repelled by the sole of one of Troy's Stan Smiths, which had a blackened wafer of antique gum embedded with a red toothpick sword and some grasshopper fragments, Justine paid careful attention to where she placed her bare knees so she wouldn't collapse a fire-ant mound—they were everywhere this year, and it was only April. Barely April.

They snuck through the utility room door in the back of the house, crawled up the stairs, and slid into Troy's room at the end of the hall.

"Whew," said Troy.

His room smelled of airplane glue and the peculiar sebaceous formalin-and–Dead Sea cologne his body produced when aroused.

"I'm glad we're doing this," said Troy, digging some *Spaceballs* sheets out of his closet.

"Quiet," Justine hissed.

"It's okay!" said Troy, shouting melodramatically. "He's deaf. When I told you Dad was deaf, I meant de-e-e-e-e-e-eaf!"

Justine winced and pressed the palms of her hands to her ears like she was trying to pop her head.

"Yodel lay ee yodel lay ee yodel lay ee ooo!"

Supposedly Mr. Bugler had lost his hearing from an accident at a stereo store many years before. He'd been listening to King Crimson on some bitchin headphones when there'd been a freak burst of sonic energy from a faulty something-or-other. His deafness was profound and permanent. He never sued the store or the manufacturer, because he didn't believe in litigation, having once been sued by a neighbor who'd had an anxiety attack after Mactard, Troy's sugar glider, bit him.

Mactard was still alive, and presently hanging out in his cage next to Troy's plastic globes of royal-blue and velvet-red bettas on his dresser. Mactard and the fish seemed interested in Troy stripping his bed of sheets and blankets.

"I wish we could go to my house," whispered Justine, still uncomfortable with the idea of not whispering.

"Your granddad's not deaf, though. We'd have to be mice there. We wouldn't be able to groan or make the bedsprings creak."

I bet Dot wouldn't mind.

"Dad's pretty cool, though, so don't worry."

Troy's dad could be heard downstairs, singing something rich and deep in German.

"He has a nice voice."

"Yeah. Dad's nice."

"What if he comes up here, just because?"

"Don't worry, my sweet. We can make sexual love all day and night. Dad doesn't come in here if the door's shut; he knows I need concentration when I'm gluing. And he hates the glue smell. Besides, he sings all the time; we'll know if he comes up the stairs. He sings *The Barber of Seville* when he's climbing the stairs."

Justine didn't know how *The Barber of Seville* went, but it did sound like Troy had the situation in hand. No siblings, one deaf parent. It was perfect.

Except Justine had lost the lustfulness which had so straitjacketed her during and after her appointment with Gracie Yin. She had been a pool of desire in the hallway at school but now she just felt gross and slick and clammy down there. Now she just wanted to have a bath and a peanut butter and banana sandwich and listen to Theatre of Hate and masturbate over Gracie and sleep until tomorrow. The idea of confronting Sherpa shut Justine down even more.

Troy kicked off his Stan Smiths. The shoe with the toothpick sword landed in a far corner, sole up. Troy struggled with a complicated-looking Boy Scout–type belt buckle in need of polishing.

"Where are the rubbers?" said Justine, testing out a normal speaking voice. "You said you have some."

"In the tank."

"What tank?"

"Toilet tank," said Troy, his trousers finally off, boner holding up a white cotton Hanes tent. "Perfect hiding spot."

"Serious?" said Justine, looking around and not looking at the boner.

Justine went into the bathroom and hoisted the ceramic lid off the toilet tank. There was a Ziploc, filled with light-blue Trojan-Enz, weighted down with a wrench. There were other things in there, each anchored with tools or flint rocks, but they were not identifiable, wrapped as they were in opaque balloons.

"This is disgusting."

Troy must have sensed some balking on Justine's part, so he jumped out of bed, still in his Hanes and socks, and tried to woo her.

"I've been waiting for this day since we started going out. Come to bed, my sweet."

He pulled out her shirttail again, but this time she said nothing and closed her eyes. She wouldn't really deny him now, in the state he was in; that wouldn't be a nice thing to do. She listened for Dot's voice in her head, telling her *Use, use, use.*

She left her blouse on. She turned her back to Troy so he could get at the tiny zipper of her skirt.

The sounds of zipping and of unzipping were different to Justine. The former was the harsh chord of a trial—putting on her too-tight jeans the day she returned to school, packing her suitcase for Camp Meredith in seventh grade, watching a paramedic draw the zipper of body a bag over the nose of a girl who killed herself on her unit at ASH. But *un*zipping: a music of release. Opening a vanity case in a hotel; *Sticky Fingers*; undressing for a bath; undressing for bed.

Who is that? It was Dot, in her head. *Whoever you want him to be.*

They were Gracie's hands unzipping her, pulling off her skirt, her panties, undoing her blouse, unclasping her bra. Justine turned around and kissed her.

They fell onto the bed, Justine biting at Troy's lips. The insides of her mouth were still tender and shallowly torn in places from kissing Troy in the hall at school. She bent one leg at the knee, hooked her toe under the waistband of Troy's Hanes, and then stripped them away. She looked down; it was the first time Justine'd seen his dick, and it did seem like a very nice dick, uniform and subtly arced, a Walt Disney dick, unlike the dick of that dick Dick, which was short and purple and torqued a half turn and veined like a weightlifter's neck. A banyan-tree dick.

"Wow," said Troy.

Justine plucked a very chilly rubber out of the Ziploc, wondering for an instant if temperature affected its reliability.

She realized she'd have to carry Troy through the next few parts, as he seemed to have seized up at the sight of Justine on her knees on the bed, naked, expertly stripping open a rubber.

"Did Dick teach you all that stuff?"

"Do you know how to put it on?" said Justine, closing her eyes again.

Shuck him, fuck him, do what you want.

Gracie was back, a perfectly symmetrical volcano with a slowly concaving surface, lava branching and channeling, a long pink and tan cleft, starting at the summit and trailing down to the tree line.

"Yeah, no, well..."

Justine became a lagoon.

"I'll do it," she said. "Lie back."

Justine straddled Troy just above his knees, put the rubber in her mouth, took Troy's boner in one hand, and bent down to put the rubber on him with her lips and tongue, like Dick the dick had taught her to do. But Troy, with a frantic, trilling huff, immediately ejaculated, getting some in her braces, some in her hair, but most she rerouted to the fresh, clean *Spaceballs* sheets. Downstairs, Mr. Bugler was singing "Psychotic Reaction."

"Oh my god. Oh my fucking god Justine oh my god. Oww. Ahh. Let go. Don't touch it ahh. Oh my god. Gahh!"

Lava. Justine let go, spit the condom out, turned around, backed up, and lowered her lagoon onto Troy's mouth.

"Nhrrt," said Troy, waving his arms around.

"Don't move!" shouted Justine, all at once not caring, excited that there was another person, an adult, in the house, singing psychedelic pop.

I can't get your love, I can't get a fraction.

Troy pushed up on Justine's bottom, perhaps to get a breath of air.

"Lick."

Justine ground herself onto his chin and leaned on Troy's stomach while he licked her in an ice-cream-cone sort of way. She grabbed his hands and brought them up to pinch her nipples.

"Squeeze!" she yelled, releasing, unzipping. "Crush."

She bore down on Gracie the volcano. A rocket appeared on the horizon. It screamed toward her.

Uh oh, little girl, psychotic reaction.

"Lick."

Troy licked. His boner began to regather against her chin. No, it was Gracie, touching Justine's neck with the tip of her nose. The volcano trembled, it roared in orange, it began to collapse.

Justine reached back, lifted up Troy's head by the hair, and tucked an ankle underneath. She moved her hips in tiny but explosive spasms along three dimensions. Troy's dick thrust between her cheek and shoulder. He ejaculated again, two, three, four, five, six long stripes across Justine's back, but this time he made no sound.

Uh oh, little girl, would you like to take a ride, now

Then, the familiar, almost-comforting black gauze of despair and self-deception that attended every orgasm like a widow's veil shook itself out and floated down to drape her. As it landed, a beautiful, wren-like warble rose in her ears.

"I'm gonna come!" cried Justine. *"Gra-a-a-a-a-cie!"*

Una voce poco fa...

Mr. Bugler came in. Justine screamed and jumped off Troy, landing knees first on the hard wood floor. Troy yanked a sheet over himself. The bettas darted, Mactard screeched and scuttled. Justine crawled into a corner, completely naked, smiling crazily, her butt touching the red toothpick on the underside of Troy's shoe. She grabbed the only cover within reach; the lid to the Game of Risk.

"Dad!"

Mr. Bugler stopped singing. His mouth hung open. He was holding a package covered in foreign stamps as big as banknotes. He put it down on Mactard's cage. He looked once at the ceiling, turned around, and left the room, leaving the door open.

Each alley appeared to feature its own cat.

The cat in the alley behind Troy's house, a short-legged, gray-striped female, paused in her dismemberment of a large salamander in order to watch Justine put her panties and skirt and shoes back on.

"Did you see us, too, cat?"

The alley on the next block was staked by a marmalade cat leisurely squinting on top of a discarded Easy Bake oven. He didn't even flinch when Justine cried, "Oh, gross" after realizing that her blouse, which she'd hastily pulled back on after Mr. Bugler left the room, was stuck to her back.

A wiry, flea-spiced, comically cross-eyed calico in the alley behind the video store made Justine laugh.

"You can laugh at me back if you want, cat."

A gamine, burnt-umber supermodel who reminded Justine of Prince whipped her tail in the shiny leaves of poison ivy and stared Justine directly in the eyes, seeming to shoot beams of shame at her. Justine repelled them.

"I don't care one damn bit that I got caught."

In the alley behind the old boarded-up murder-suicide house barely obscured by a jungle of honeysuckle on a wire hurricane fence, on top of a rimless yellow Camaro that had been there most of Justine's life, crouched a Maine coon cat with half a tail and a shred of gore stuck to his chin.

Justine tapped her own chin.

"Man overboard," she said.

The cat's pupils bloomed black.

And on the next block, out of a dilapidated shed at the side of the alley came a skinny black cat dusted with yellow-green pollen who walked up to Justine, stretched gymnastically, flopped onto his side, producing a little powdery cloud of ragweed spores and alley dust, and waited impatiently for Justine's full attention.

"You don't mind that I'm rubbing your belly?" Justine asked the black cat, who began to purr like a moped. "What kind of cat tolerates belly rubbing? It must be your secret."

The cat stretched out to the length of a loaf of French bread and yawned. It seemed as content as Justine was blissful. She could never have guessed that the finest antidepressant would turn out to be not Parnate or ECT or fifty-minute blocs of expensive, unwanted therapy, but the tawdry splendor of cunnilingus interruptus.

"And you're very dusty. I'm dirty, too. Hooray!"

He wore a red leather collar aspangle with dozens of stamped-metal tags.

"You have many medals. You must be very important."

The cat jumped up and walked away, tail in the air.

"It's nothing to be ashamed of!" Justine called after the cat.

In Justine's own alley, balanced with feral precision atop their cedar fence, and with its sites on a dove poking its head in and out of one of Charlotte's weathered bird feeders, was the Rooneys' whiny, compost-colored moggie, Rogelio.

When Justine carefully opened the gate, Rogelio and the dove scattered noisily. No matter—Charlotte was at the bank, tellering; so was Livia, skip tracing; Lou was at his job at the Registry. Dot was surely asleep. Justine could barely wait to tell her the whole story! Even Dartmouth was likely napping, probably at Dot's feet.

All Justine cared about at the moment was her tub. She would need two baths: the first to wash off all the sweat and fear and glazing fluids; the second to merely lie up to her nostrils in and review the day. And then, scrubbed and clean, she would call Troy and find out how much trouble he was in. Mr. Bugler sounded like a pretty cool dad, and hadn't done anything scary when he caught them. She couldn't really tell, though—the look on Mr. Bugler's face had been as unreadable as higher math. Maybe Troy wasn't in any trouble at all. Maybe his dad took him out for whiskey sours and a lap dance. Or maybe Troy was presently wrapped in canvas cerements, ready to be shipped off to a behavioral boot camp in some Canadian-border state free of corporal punishment laws. Whatever it was, they were unlikely to be going down to Sherpa's this afternoon. But they had to go soon; Dot's "treatment" was imminent.

A door in the rear of her house led to a tiny utility room, where the fuse box, water heater, washer-dryer stack, and metal shelves loaded down with cases of Tuborg, took up 80 percent of the space. There were two more doors inside the utility room: one that led to the garage—Lou's room—and another that went right into the kitchen.

Justine quietly snuck into the utility room, crouched down, and listened. The door to the garage was ajar. There was still an hour of school left; she was not supposed to be home. She especially wasn't supposed to be home panti-less, basted in semen, and practically jaundiced with embarrassed delight. If she had to, she'd squeeze behind the water heater and hide until she could gain her bathtub unnoticed.

She held her breath and shut her eyes. No sound at all.

Justine carefully tried the kitchen door: locked. She pushed open the door to the garage.

Lou and Livia stood in the middle of the garage, in a tight, full, motionless embrace, directly under the unshaded bulb, whose kite-string switch just barely touched Lou's shoulder.

Justine froze. Then she silently backed up, pulling the door so it was barely ajar. She watched.

"I'm glad you called me, Lou," said Livia.

The embrace remained inert, but potent; a pendulum stopped at its apogee. What were they doing here?

"We had bad luck, Lou. It's the only way to think of it."

"Bad luck," said Lou, deep into Livia's shoulder.

The soapy, vinegar incense of vodka reached Justine. A fifth of Smirnoff lay on its side against the rusting blade of an ax that as far as Justine could remember had never been used or even moved. The bottle appeared empty.

"Where's Dot?" said Livia.

"Car."

"Justine's boyfriend's car?"

"Sherpa's car. I took it. She's in the backseat. She's got her blanket."

Lou began to cry.

"He tied her down," he said. "With duct tape. Silver duct tape. He gave her those goddam pills. And I didn't stop him."

"You did what you thought was the best thing."

"And then he put the needles in her arms, big old needles, like ink pens, Christ mother. And I didn't stop him."

Livia patted Lou on the shoulder. She rubbed his arm.

"Then he turned on his machine, and Dot's bad blood ran up the tube. She wasn't knocked out, and she started to whimper, like her little dog."

Livia didn't say anything.

"And I didn't scoop her up and run out of there. I carried her two miles once, but I didn't pick her up when it really mattered. Oh, Livia. Oh, me."

"All right. All right now."

"He made her do something terrible then. He made her eat something. He called it communion, and I had to eat it, too, and so did he."

"What?" said Livia, more of a hiss than a whisper. "What'd he make you eat?"

Lou sobbed. The most terrible sound in the world.

"My skin," he said. "This cut, on my arm here, it wasn't an accident. He made me flay my skin and give it to him."

"How did all this happen to us, Lou?"

"Then Dot had a seizure. Her feet, just her feet, began to shake like a copperhead's rattle. The rest of her was still, frozen, all clenched up, her little hands clawed up like rakes."

"Why did all this have to happen?" said Livia, her voice rising, her own hands gripping her daddy's shirt.

"He got out a syringe and was about to shoot her with it, and I told him to stop."

"I think I did all this to you."

"He yelled at me to sit down, and I did. He gave her the shot."

"I'm sorry about what I did."

"Then she relaxed. There was blood dripping off her fingertips, but I couldn't tell where it was coming from. I got up, and he yelled at me to have a fucking seat, but I didn't listen this time. I went over there and pushed him out of the way. I pulled out the needles. The blood dripping off her hands was coming out from under her fingernails. *He did something to her so it squeezed the blood out of her own fingertips, Livia.*"

Justine couldn't feel her hands.

"I hit him with one of those brown bottles he had. He went down. I kicked him. I got one of his rifles out the case and hit him with it till he quit moving. I've never hit a man like that, and I'm sick from it. I picked up Dot. She was limp and cool and light as foam. I took her outside, but the cabbie who brought us down hadn't waited like he said he would. I put Dot down under a cedar tree and went back in for Sherpa's car keys. I found them but when I came back out, Dot was dead. There was already a hawk circling a hundred feet up. I drove us here. It wasn't even ten in the morning."

Livia took several steps back. She crouched down, her face in her hands, her fingers in her hair.

"I'm taking her back to New Orleans," said Lou.

Livia stood up. She ran toward Lou, embraced him, and kissed him hard on the mouth.

For one moment, an instant, a countable second, Lou did nothing, nothing at all.

Then he gently pushed his daughter away.

Justine soundlessly escaped the house and ran around to the front. In the street was parked a Monte Carlo. Across the backseat lay a figure covered with a blue-gray afghan. Justine banged on the window, but the figure did not stir. The car was locked. She fell to her knees in the road. She looked at her arms. She had left her backpack at Troy's; all her razor blades were inside. There was no glass or metal in the road, there were no sharp edges on the car, there was no way to leave all this. She hit herself, in the jaw, the eyes, but it didn't hurt, and could never hurt enough.

The front door of the house opened. Lou stepped out. Justine hid behind a tree. Lou came up to the car, fumbling with the car keys. She trembled as she watched him. Justine was enraged by his dense insistence on Sherpa's safe counsel; she hated them both for ruining their family just as it was coming back together; she was disgusted with herself for her pity for him and his daughter, she nearly choked on the acid surprise of seeing Livia passionately kiss her own father... behind the ancient sycamore she wept without control at the death of her best friend and the incest in her own house.

Lou got into the car, looked once into the backseat, and drove away.

Justine ran down the alley, back the way she'd come. She passed Rogelio, a rock dove in his mouth. The Maine coon cat on the old yellow Camaro had not moved, but the shred of gore was gone. The black cat hissed as Justine passed. The supermodel had disappeared. The wiry cat, now between the planks of a broken pallet, peered at Justine as she ran. The orange cat was staring down a mean-looking Siamese with gristly, corded muscles; neither paid Justine any attention. And the gray cat behind Troy's house stood in the dead center of the alley, grooming its apron.

No singing from the Buglers' house. Sticking out of the trash can in the alley was Justine's school backpack. On the ground below were her bra and panties. She retrieved only her backpack.

Justine went into Troy's backyard and crept up to his bedroom window. "Troy?"

She grabbed a handful of dirt and grass and tossed it at the glass.

"Troy?" she said again, louder. "Troy!"

She ran around to the front of the house, not bothering to hide. Mr. Bugler's Toyota was still in the driveway. But visible at the corner of the block was Troy's Aspen, just where they'd left it.

"Troy!" She banged on the front door. "I need you. Come on."

No answer. No movement at all from inside. A bluejay sallied down from a magnolia tree and plucked a hair out of Justine's head.

"Ah!" cried Justine, this time rattling the doorknob and trying to twist it with both hands. "Oh, Troy, Dot's dead. And my mom... oh, Troy. Oh god. Come out here. Please!"

The bluejay swept down again and plucked another few strands.

She ran to the backyard again, picked up more dirt—this time a larger and rockier handful—and threw it hard at his window. A single vertical, almost perfectly straight crack appeared.

"I'm all alone now, and I need you," Justine said, when nobody responded.

She tried the back door. "Just let me use your phone, then," she said to the door, which was scalloped with old gray paint.

She sat down in the grass for a moment. Fire ants found a bare, dirty ankle, and lit it up.

"Ah!" Justine jumped up and frantically brushed herself off. "Help me, Troy."

She ran around to the front of the house again. Mr. Bugler's Toyota was gone.

Down the street she saw Troy open the back door to his Aspen and put Mactard, in his cage, inside. He threw a rolled-up sleeping bag in the front. Justine ran toward him.

"Troy, Dot's dead, and I..."

Troy turned to look at Justine. His hair was wet and combed to the side. He wore a blue suit, wrinkled, dusty on the shoulders. His Stan Smiths were gone, replaced with stiff brown wingtips that looked four sizes too large. In one hand he had a box of Triscuits; in the other, his keys.

"Stop."

"Troy?"

"I have to go to my great uncle's in Deep Ellum."

"Let me come. I can't live without you."

"I can't."

"When are you coming back?"

Troy shrugged, then looked inside his car.

"What about your stamps?"

He shrugged again, then got into the car. Justine ran around to the passenger door, but Troy reached over and locked it. Then he twisted around and locked both back doors.

"Troy. Everything's falling apart. I need you."

He started the engine. Justine stood in front of his car.

"It was only *one hour* ago when everything was okay."

Troy rolled down his window a crack.

"I have to go. I'm sorry. It's all my fault."

"I don't have anywhere to go. Let me come with you. I'll stay in the way back. We won't tell anybody."

Troy smiled, a horizontal pink slash in his face. Then the smile vanished, and Troy put the car in gear.

Justine darted around to the back and opened the station wagon's rear door. She almost got inside, but there was nothing to hold on to. Troy stepped on the accelerator, and Justine fell back into the street.

Twenty-six blocks; twenty-six alleys.

Justine went into the drugstore through the service entrance.

"Good news, child," said Fanny, who was bent over her pill-counting tray, counting Tagamets. "Archibold Bamberger come by yesterday and buried some stuff in the yard, ChapSticks and dice and what-have-yous, and I'll be damned if I didn't dream sweet dreams all night. No Doc, no Johnny, no Sebastian Cabot, no Charlie Rich. Just clouds and King Ranch chicken and something about college football... sugar, you look awful."

"I have to call Charlotte."

"Sorry, no phone calls at work. What have you done to yourself?"

"It's no big deal."

"You tell me what happened. Wait. Vic, get your nose out the insulin refrigerator. No snacks in there, never have been, never will be. Get Justine some Neosporin and gauze."

Vic, Fanny's most senior employee, and the one in charge of payroll, instead brought Justine an envelope.

"Eighty-four fifty-five cash," he said, then returned to the insulin refrigerator.

Justine picked up the phone and dialed the bank, but the receptionist said Charlotte had gone home early. Justine hung up.

"Did you just disobey me?" said Fanny.

Justine ignored her. She went into her backpack, which had smears of garbage all over it from the alley behind Troy's, and found a business card. She dialed the number.

"Is Ms. Yin there?"

"Who's calling?" said a deep, male voice.

"You hang up that telephone receiver," said Fanny.

"Justine Moppett, one of Gracie's, ah, Ms. Yin's guidance, uh, subjects. At school."

"You can't call her at home."

"It's that Troy, I know," said Fanny. "Nasty influence. He wouldn't buy one candy bar, so you tell him..."

"I know, but she gave me her card..."

"Out of Neosporin," said Vic. "Out of gauze."

"Troy, right, sugar?" said Fanny. "I'm just trying to help here. Quit that fussing and hang up and tell me what's the story."

"She said I could call if I needed her, I'm a special case..."

"Bactine?" said Vic.

"You forgot that sign about Doc yesterday," said Fanny. "I had a lot of damage control to do this morning because of that, and I wasn't gonna say anything, but now you're being insubordinate, so you are removed from my grace, Justine Moppett."

"Please, can she call me? I'm at 453-1254."

"No."

"Antiseptic cotton disks?"

Fanny placed a finger on the telephone hook.

"I'm... in trouble, Mr. Yin, she said I could call her..."

"You are not welcome to call me Mr. Yin."

"I..."

"You're the cutter, right?"

"Hang up," said Fanny. "Now."

"Yes. I am."

"Sit down so I can squirt this at your knees," said Vic.

"Believe you me, Gracie does not want to talk to you."

"I need her," said Justine, exhausted.

Fanny leaned over and glared hard at Justine. Justine slapped Fanny's hand away from the telephone hook.

"Whoa," said Vic.

"Damnation," said Fanny.

"Right," said the deep male voice.

"I'll die," she whispered.

"I doubt it," said Vic, Fanny, and the deep male voice.

"I love Gracie."

"I love restraining orders."

"She loves me."

"She loves *me*."

Fanny pulled on the phone cord.

"I need my Humulin!" shouted Mr. Krupp.

"Isopropyl alc, three cases," said the deliveryman. "Nutrament, four."

"Fire-ant bites, too, down here," said Vic, glancing up Justine's skirt.

With a great tug on the cord, Fanny pulled the receiver out of Justine's hand.

"You are fired. Go away."

Two hours and five miles later Justine stopped at one of the two entrances to the multi-acre parking lot of the Santa Ana Apartments. She jogged up and down the rows of parked cars, pausing at one entrance or the other to watch the cars come and go. No 1970s yellow Subaru.

It was nearly 6:30. Maybe her car had broken down. Maybe she had already come and gone, and was on her way to Enchanted Rock or someplace with her mean boyfriend/husband. Maybe she had bought a new car or gotten a ride. Maybe she'd stopped at Jim's with another student she liked better. Maybe Dick the dick. Maybe she was having sex with him in her office at this very minute.

But probably she just wasn't home yet.

Justine couldn't watch both entrances at once.

Or could she? Next to a dirty perimeter fence stood an ash tree. She left her backpack at the foot of it and began to climb. At twenty feet, she found a large, semi-comfortable branch with a barely sufficient view of both entrances, and settled along it on her stomach, like a three-toed sloth.

Calm—the sort that makes sails droop sleepily and the ships below them drift in helpless circles—found its way through Justine. She allowed ants and caterpillars and spiders to cross her as if she were just another branch. Sunlight baked her in random patches. Mockingbirds ignored her; squirrels scolded; paper wasps evaluated her dirty elbows; ash borers went about their destructive business. She was safe here, safe from the terrible history of the day that eddied beneath her like a heavy, lethal, invisible gas. She was not known here.

"Justine?"

She contracted like a spring broken, nearly falling from her perch.

"My god, Justine. What are you doing?"

The bustling crowd of insects, alarmed, bit, stung, scattered. Justine shimmied down, nearly suffocating with relief, panic, and the loitering heat of the April evening.

Gracie helped her down the last few feet. Justine's blue skirt hiked up, exposing her body. The unforgiving bark met with her queasy shame.

"It's all right, kiddo, it's okay. Come, let's sit in my car."

Gracie had parked just under her tree.

"Sorry about the mess," Gracie added, clearing the passenger seat and floor of McDonald's bags and homemade Led Zeppelin tapes and stocking wads and sticky-looking travel mugs and *U.S. News and World Report*s and blackening banana skins, tossing them all like wedding bouquets into the backseat. Last, she flung her thin black attaché case into the back. A few manila folders peeked out of the mouth. "Sit."

She turned the car on. Frigid air conditioning and J. Geils exploded all over both of them.

"I saw the backpack," said Gracie, turning J. Geils down. "I didn't think anything of it at first, but something made me look up. I knew it was you right away. I remembered your skirt from today."

"Today," said Justine. "That was today?"

"What happened to you? You're an absolute mess."

Justine counted the blanching Chiquita banana stickers on the glove-compartment door.

"You were all right earlier," said Gracie. "Tell me what happened. Maybe I can help."

Gracie's inspection sticker had expired four years ago.

"Want me to run you home? I'd have to run inside and tell my husband a little white lie first, though."

They both smiled; Justine because of this free fall of absurdity she was in; Gracie, perhaps, to hide her desire to be rid of her troublesome counselee.

"I don't know."

"Troy's?"

Justine smiled again.

"No."

"Want me to call your psychiatrist?"

Justine shrank down in the seat, put the bony sockets of her eyes on her kneecaps, and shook her head.

"I'm just glad to be here right now."

"You really, really don't look well, Justine."

"It's all right."

They sat and listened to something rattle around inside an air-conditioner vent. The melody of "Centerfold" was still barely audible.

"I called you before I came, but your husband said you weren't home yet."

"A cleaning," said Gracie. She bared her teeth. The falling sun highlighted her incisors' tiny serrations, and made her canines appear yellower than they had that morning. Harder. More… *canine*. "I had a poppy seed between two molars. The tech said it'd probably been there for weeks."

Justine witnessed against a scrim of her imagination a sudden, unbidden film of herself kissing Gracie so deeply that their jaws, at right angles to each other, unlocked and stretched open like boas swallowing rabbits, each tongue now seated deeply enough to experience the warmth of the other's throat.

"I don't think he appreciated me calling."

Gracie leaned back and sighed.

"He doesn't like for me to bring my work home," she said, glancing back at her attaché case. "If I have work, I either have to stay late at school or go sit at Denny's. You want to go sit at Denny's and drink coffee?"

Justine shivered. She pulled her knees up to her chin and pulled the hem of her skirt tightly across her thighs. Gracie immediately turned off the air conditioning.

"It's about the only thing that works in this shitbox."

"I don't know what to do."

"Are you in trouble?"

"I don't know."

Already the heat was gathering again.

"How can I help you?" Gracie said, with what Justine thought was more than a trace of impatience. "How about that doctor you mentioned to me today. Sherpa? Can he help you?"

Justine shook her head.

"Want to go to the police?"

Gracie looked over her shoulder toward the apartment complex. Time and heat bore down on Justine.

"My grandmother died."

"Oh, Justine, I'm sorry."

"And—" *my adoptive mother kissed her own daddy, my granddaddy, hard, with lust* "—I got fired."

"Oh no."

"And Troy broke up with me."

"Oh, Justine," she said, touching Justine's shoulder while looking in the rearview mirror. "That's a rotten day. Come on, let me take you home."

"No. Please."

"Okay, Justine. But look. I'm going to run up to tell Curren I've got work, then I'll come back and drive us through someplace and get some food—"

"Don't leave."

"—and then we're going over to Old Navy and get you a new outfit. You're filthy. You don't even have any underwear."

Justine, wide-eyed, stared at Gracie.

"I saw up your skirt when you were climbing down the tree. Sorry."

When tears were impossible, or when they were simply overtaken by higher-dimension emotions that needed fuller expression, Justine's body would begin to involuntarily undulate along her spine, shallowly at first, then the peaks and valleys deepening, an emotional petit mal.

"Justine. Look at me. Were you raped?"

She shook her head.

"Okay. Good. Lemme go talk with Curren."

"Can I stay with you?"

"At my place? I wish you could, but it's just not possible."

My place.

"Can I just stay right here, in the car with you, Ms. Yin?"

"I asked you to call me Gracie," she said, checking the rearview again. "Shit."

Justine looked back. A tall man, tanned to the color of iron ore, long brown hair parted on the side, wearing a pink Oxford shirt unbuttoned to the solar plexus, khaki shorts, and dusty, unlaced docksiders, was heading toward the car with his head tilted a few degrees as if trying to get a fuller understanding of the betrayal in progress a few yards before him.

"Is that—"

"Shit, Justine."

"I—"

Gracie reached down to the side of her seat, feeling about for something. She gave up, cursed, kicked off her suede heels, then straightened her body out as much as she could in the cramped seat, lifted up her skirt to reveal, beneath her pantyhose, pale-blue satin underwear. She hooked her thumbs under the waistband and began to pull the hose and panties down, but had to stop when her thighs came up against the steering wheel. She sat back down, felt under the dashboard, pulled a lever, and lifted up the steering wheel until it locked into place at a higher angle. She straightened out her body again, pulled her panties and hose over her knees and feet, and then thrust them at Justine.

"Here," she said, rapidly smoothing out her skirt and pulling her shoes back on with her pinkie. "I don't know why, but I'd feel a lot better, Justine, if you had some fucking underwear. Hide it."

Justine wadded up the fabric into a spongy ball and stuffed it into her backpack just as Curren, smiling, appeared at her window.

"Roll it down," said Gracie, her head falling back on the hard, cracked vinyl headrest.

"Hi," said Curren, his breath smelling of tequila and Frito pie. "Who's this?"

"This is one of my guidance students. Justine? I was telling you about her?"

"Oh, yeah, we chatted earlier," said Curren, pleasantly. "How you doing?"

"Fine," said Justine, feeling as though she were trapped in a clear trash bag being shrunk by the heat of Curren's breath.

"She declared her love for you, you know," he said.

Justine couldn't tell whom he was talking to. Or about.

"I was just on my way up to tell you I've gotta run her home and then go catch up on some stuff," said Gracie. "But I'll be back lickity."

"You're going to have to find your way home, um, Justine," said Curren, sticking his head partway in the window, enabling Justine to see the tiny engraving on one stem of his sunglasses: Ray-Ban. "And Gracie? Come."

Curren withdrew his head, stepped back, and clapped twice, as though to call a ballplayer off the field and back onto the bench in a hopeless game.

"She's in some distress, Cur."

"It's Cuervo time." He clapped again.

"I can't leave her alone right now."

"Why can't you leave your work at work? Put the car in park, give her a dollar bus fare, then come inside and help me crush ice. Your fucking blender can't handle *ice*. It stalls. It makes the lights dim."

"Couple minutes?"

"You were supposed to be back two and a quarter hours ago."

"C'mon, Cur. I had the dentist today. I'm pretty sure I told you."

"Didn't."

The argument was civil, but its rises and syllable-punching were now picking up and volleying across Justine's forehead.

"Look, this is my *job*, Curren. I'll be back."

"Roll up the window, Justine," said Gracie quietly, putting on her seat belt.

Justine looked at her, the mixture of relief and panic and hesitation like grapefruit juice under her tongue.

"Go on, honey," said Gracie.

Justine began to crank as fast as she could. Gracie turned on the air. Curren ran up and smacked his palms on the edge of the rising plate of glass. Justine cranked harder; the glass rose a quarter inch, then another. Curren readjusted, shifting his entire weight to his hands on the edge of the glass. The right side of the car sank on its old struts. Something snapped, loud, like a breaking tightrope, and the plate of glass fell down inside the door. Justine screamed. Gracie gasped. Curren cried out and jumped back, losing his sunglasses, then looked closely at his hands. Then he rubbed them together and ran his fingers through his hair. He was shaking.

"Fuck *this*, Gracie."

"Come on, let's drive away," said Justine.

"Are you okay?" said Gracie; again Justine wasn't sure who was being addressed.

"We," said Curren, picking his sunglasses off the pavement, "are back to square one, Gracie. It's Halloween all over again."

"Oh, please don't say that," said Gracie, no longer reasonable, no longer in control.

"Go wherever you want now. Do whatever. Maybe we'll pick up again someday."

"No, Curren. C'mon."

"Go. Take her and do whatever you *want* with her."

"I can't go *through* that again."

"Too late."

Curren turned around as though to head back to the apartment building, but stayed in place.

"No."

Gracie turned to Justine and looked at her as though in famine. Justine returned her look; they both silently, brittlely beseeched the other: *Don't leave, let me leave, don't leave, let me leave.*

Justine shut her eyes for a moment, then opened them. She smiled at Gracie. Gracie peeled off her seat belt, opened her door, and yelled, "Curren, I'm coming, wait!" then she reached back and pulled six five-dollar bills out of her purse and put them in Justine's hand.

"Justine. You'll be okay, I know it. Take a cab home, or to that Sherpa's. I know there's someone out there who can help right now."

"What did he mean by Halloween?"

"Nothing. It's okay. Curren has to be my priority at the moment. Please understand. Come see me first thing in the morning, though, huh? Promise me you'll be all right."

"I don't know. Don't make me leave."

"You'll be fine."

Gracie kissed her on the cheek, right at the edge of her nose.

"Now go on," said Gracie. "You gotta slam the door, hard, when you leave."

"I can't leave, I need you!"

"Shit, Justine. Just get out. You'll be fine."

"Gracie, I can't go—"

"Suit yourself, then, Justine, Jesus Christ. Just don't fucking be here when I get back. Jesus."

Gracie got out and slammed the door. She took off her brown suede shoes and ran after Curren, calling his name.

At Luby's Cafeteria Justine ordered a fried-fish plate and a Dr Pepper and four different flavors of Jell-O, and, at a round, family-sized table against a wall of leaden gray-green drapes twenty-five feet high, she sat down, facing the restaurant, alone. As she waited for the round man with the old-fashioned monocle on a black string to come by with the coffee cart, she removed from her backpack a small, elegant stationery system that had been a birthday present from Charlotte, complete with felt calligraphy pens, handmade deckled paper, and a roll of twenty-two-cent stamps.

She wrote out two letters.

> I love you. I'm sorry I had to do this. Dot is dead because I didn't rescue her in time, and Troy broke up with me, and I'm so mad at Livia for so many things. And I'm mad at Lou too. Mostly I'm confused about everything. It's for the best that I'm gone. I promise that it didn't hurt. I'm in the yellow car in the alley. I love you. Love, Justine.

Justine wrote and rewrote the note several times, unsure of the proper verb tenses for this peculiar grammatical situation. Finally, satisfied at least that the message was clear without being cold, she placed the letter in an envelope and addressed it to Charlotte.

The second letter said:

> I saw you and him in the garage. I'm dead and it's your fault.

Justine did not have to revise this one. She folded it without care and placed it in an envelope, which she addressed to Livia, at Charlotte's house. She forewent capitalizing as a form of disrespect.

A full roster of eight-year-old baseball players in yellow-and-black uniforms streamed into the dining room like polluted floodwater. Each child screamed at a different pitch while racing around the tables, their plates of macaroni and cheese and chicken-fried steaks and pudding skidding around on their trays, sometimes jumping the trays' curbs and crashing to the floor.

Erkule, the coffee-cart man, came around again and refilled Justine's cup. His attitude earlier had been friendly, almost jolly, but now every time a baseball child came near he winced, as though he'd just gotten a surprise intra-marrow injection.

"Is it like this every day?" said Justine.

"Yes, yes," said Erkule. "But in wintertime? Football children, with helmets."

Justine left a big tip. She went into the bathroom. In a stall she took Gracie's panties and hose out of the pocket in her backpack and put them on. As she pulled up the hose, her leg stubble caught on the elastic web of fibers, causing a run and a not-unpleasant rasping sound. The run enlarged into a tenuous ladder stretching from her upper thigh to her instep. Then she left the stall, stood in front of the mirror over the row of sinks, and washed her face as well as she could with a wet paper towel. In her backpack she had a few paper-wrapped single-edged razor blades that she kept together with a blue rubber band. She removed the band and used it to tie her hair back. She counted her money, looked closely at her braces and the leftovers trapped within them, then picked up her backpack and left the ladies' room.

She paid, bought a couple of Andes mints, took a toothpick. Outside, she found a pay phone and called a cab, which was there in less than two minutes.

When they got to Justine's part of town she asked the cabbie, Stellamarie Sykes, if she would drive through the neighborhood post office.

"Mm," said Stellamarie, who pulled into the parking lot of the Speedway P. O. and stopped at the mailboxes. "Gimme your letter."

"There're two."

"Okay, gimme your letterzzzz*uh*."

Stellamarie Sykes reached over her shoulder and began a rapid pinching movement with her fingertips. Justine gave her the letters, which she examined closely.

"Same address—you waste a stamp," she said, flipping each envelope over and back again like fresh Polaroids.

216

"I know."

"Next time you got forty-four cents to throw away, you give me a call. I'll come by and get it."

After a brief but militarily icy stare at Justine through the rearview, Stellamarie dropped the letters into the mailbox.

"You want me to run you by a fountain you can pitch some money into?"

Justine sighed. She would not miss Stellamarie.

"Please just go three blocks thataway and drop me off."

"*Rmf.*"

Justine paid the $15.15 with a twenty and, without waiting for change, walked straight down the alley and past her house until she came upon the old yellow Camaro behind the spooky, long-abandoned, unsalable murder-suicide house. It was dusk and still hot. Insects wheeled around the streetlights. The Maine coon cat was nowhere in sight.

The old car had no hood, engine, side-view mirrors, bumpers, headlights, or wheels. It was equipped with heavily tinted windows and a two-part sunroof, one side of which Justine happened to know could be pried off with a slot-head screwdriver that was stuck hilt-deep into the ground by the fence, which was where she left it the last time she played in the old yellow Camaro, back when she was in the seventh grade and wanted privacy to experiment with grapevine-smoking.

And there it was. Yellowed, cracked acrylic handle with a shaft of corroded metal. The sunroof came off easily. Justine lowered herself inside and pulled the sunroof back into place.

Hot, black, quiet as a moon. Justine sat on the decayed, ceramic-hard vinyl backseat, waiting for her eyes to adjust, and to be stung or mauled by the present tenants.

Unoccupied, apparently; no biters forthcame. Interior details resolved: the yawn below the dashboard where the stereo used to be; the Ferragamo shoebox filled with fuses and Phillips 66 gas receipts on the passenger seat; a midrange speaker hanging from the driver's-side door by its weed-like wire roots; the floor of the backseat filled with old Miller High Life cans made of real tin and as uncrushable as mortar casings. On the back of the driver's seat was a poem that Justine had written with her first tube of lip gloss, Bonne Belle Lip Smackers (strawberry), which Charlotte's friend Nance had given Justine, saying it would go well with her green eyes and maybe the pink jumper she'd seen at the Mervyn's where she worked.

Justine sniffed at the poem: no longer fragrant.

> The clouds and the sun
> are fighting
> the earth,
> The stars and the moon
> are lighting
> the birth,
> Of the me and the you
> The we and the us,
> The scissors and paste and my
> ugly face,
> and the life
> not a pennysworth.

Oh dear. That's terrible.

Hot. She wished she had a Dr Pepper. In this stuffy silence she would be able to hear the minute explosions of carbonation tick musically against the inside of the can, while condensation on the outside collected into little rivers that ran down her forearm.

She lay down across the backseat. She opened her backpack, found a razor, and peeled off its paper wrapper. This particular manufacturer coated the faces of its razors with the merest skin of yellow machine oil, which stung when it got into a cut. Justine wiped the oil away with the tail of her blouse, then placed the edge at an angle on her wrist about an inch below the bottom of her palm and just to the left of the tendon.

During her hospital stay, Justine had roomed with a young woman, a UT doctoral candidate in astrogeology named Jessy Burke, who was wealthy and smart and cultured. She also had a great number of scars on her arms. But unlike Justine's, which were messy and random, Jessy's were neat, straight, parallel, and of uniform depth, breadth, spacing, and longitude. Yet they were not artificially so—she had used no ruler or compass. They were accomplished freehand. Artisanal slices.

"You never go across?" Justine had asked her one afternoon in the sofa room. "Or zigzag? Or just stab?"

"Oh no," said Jessy, admiring her own left arm, which was just as elegantly scarred as the right.

"How do you get them so straight and neat?" asked Justine politely. She secretly preferred her own scar maps.

Patients had begun wandering into the sofa room. Transition Group, for those fixing to be discharged into quarter-, half-, and three-quarter-way houses, was about to start.

"Are you in this group?" asked Jessy, glaring at some of the moderately smug Transition Group members.

"I wish," said Justine. "I'm gonna be here forever."

"Not I. I'm going to sign myself out today. I just come here to make my parents feel guilty for divorcing and remarrying Republican clods."

"Why'd they get divorced?"

"Daddy used to say it was my fault because I brought home my school friends who tempted him into straying and Mother used to say—or, rather, *scream*—it was because the house was a filthy mess. She always looked at me when she screamed that. And I guess the house *was* a junkyard."

"You rebelled by making super-orderly cuts?"

"I never thought of it like that," said Jessy. "Okay. Put your finger like that, like you're holding a... wait, what do you use?"

"Single-edges."

"Okay. Now, instead of moving the blade, move your arm. Like your pulling on a long white kidskin opera glove. Here, use this."

Jessy tore the flap off of her flip-top box of Marlboros and gave it to Justine to use as a prop.

"Like that?"

"Like that."

A fellow patient, Dean Schoomacker, approached them.

He said: "If you guys aren't here for Transition Group you better get the heck out because Transition Group is in the sofa room from three to four on Wednesday afternoons and I'm in the Transition Group so I can stay but everyone else adios amigos."

"So," Jessy said, addressing Justine and ignoring Dean, "imagine you're going to see *La Traviata*, you're in a Dior gown, opera glasses in your clutch, frangipani on your elbows, and a bunch of handsome gentlemen waiting down in the drawing room. You're almost ready."

"You guys are gonna catch heck," said Dean.

"All you have left to do?" Jessy whispered to Justine. "Draw on your long white kidskin gloves."

Justine pushed the corner of the blade into her wrist a millimeter, then two, three; the skin would not split. Four, five: a little blood, token, ran down her forearm, hot, poky—the pure opposite of the condensation from a cold can of Dr Pepper. Six: a thicker thread of blood. Then a giving, like the skin of a grape opening under the press of a jaw.

Would Dot allow her company? Would Justine apologize on behalf of all their survivors? She imagined Dot to be sitting on a stool at the end of a bar, it's the 1940s, she's fishnetted, tough, wily; a drained and upended bourbon tumbler touches her two diaries on the long, wet limewood bar... Dot is the divine issue of a union of Sophia Loren and Nefertiti and there are men and women prostrate before her on an earthen floor, clutching money and apologies and love letters, the great Sherpa and Kelly Miller each in a small, cramped cage swinging in the barroom rafters. Justine enters the bar, and Dot turns to look.

Don't pity me with your blood.

Justine stopped. Justine did not draw on the long white glove.

She sat up and threw the razor down into the compost of Miller beer cans.

"Help!" she screamed, as loud as she could.

She didn't actually want or need any help; she yelled in a pique of disgusted irony. A cry for help. She couldn't kill herself. She'd never really tried in her whole psychopathologically fertile life, never even really wanted to, except earlier today, outside of Dot's car, knees on the blacktop, the door hot against her face. She was a crybaby. She hated herself for her cowardice and hypocrisy, her virtuoso lies and simpleton's guile, her purposeless body and borrowed curiosity, her weedy bromeliads of hair and putatively electrifying green eyes, which to her just looked like botulinal oysters. Her "borderline personality." She'd never had a real reason to kill herself, just bothersome depressions and bratty outbursts of self-hatred that always ended, rapidly, following an intramuscular shot of major tranquilizers, firmly attached to a gurney in a five-point restraint.

Justine fell asleep.

She woke to the purr of a prowl car easing down the alley and pointing its spotlight into backyards. The spot swept through the Camaro, but did not fall on Justine. The prowler disappeared down the alley.

Justine climbed out of the car and replaced the sunroof, which popped into place with a Tupperware-like burp. She stabbed the screwdriver back into the ground. It felt good.

She stabbed the dirt again, and again, and again, then stopped in mid-stab.

She stood up, tucked the tool into the waist of her skirt, then walked back to the post office.

The mailbox containing her two letters sat directly beneath a streetlight that buzzed as though it was about to short out, and radiated a nauseating baby-aspirin-orange light. The hinged mouth of the mailbox bore a sticker that indicated the next pickup time as 8:15 a.m. Probably about three hours away.

Justine circled the mailbox. It was held together by rivets and bolted to a crumbly cement plinth.

She opened the mouth and stuck her arm in. Something occluded access to the letters inside. She pulled the mouth open wider; the occlusion grew more occlusive. She closed the mouth to a slit, reaching in as far as she could, but still, occlusion.

She braced a foot on the mailbox and pulled on the mouth-handle; she hammered the mouth with both fists; she slammed the mouth; she forced a small oak branch into the mouth. How loud it all was. But what of it? Who cares? Let 'em take me away to Del Valle. I'm not afraid of jail, you bastards.

The branch broke. Justine fell back with part of the branch in her hand. The mouth swallowed the rest of it.

The mailbox had no screws at all, just big blue rivet after big blue rivet. Justine wedged the head of her screwdriver under one of the rivets and hammered on the end of the handle with her branch. When it was wedged under as far as it would go, Justine pulled.

The corroded metal snapped; Justine fell and landed on her bottom in the concrete parking lot. The screwdriver had broken off unevenly, leaving the shaft with a shallow-beveled chisel tip, sharp as an obsidian arrowhead.

Justine sat down in the grass by the curb to cast loathing at the mailbox and to behold her new tool. She hated the mailbox. It seemed almost alive— it had legs, tiny flat feet, a torso, a digestive system, an empty, rudimentary head. It belched. It was as solid and obstinate as a bison, as arrogant and over-bearing as an ID-checker at a Sixth Street bar. Viewed straight on, the mailbox wore the same *golly* expression as may sometimes be seen of the faces of the very, very dim. It was warm. It had a small hole for the insertion of hard keys.

Justine stuck her screwdriver-shiv into the keyhole, and with the branch hammered as hard as she could.

Nothing happened. The lock did not give; the screwdriver did not break.

She looked beneath. The metal seemed softer, thinner. The underbelly. When she pushed on it, it gave a bit, like the lid on a tin of butter cookies, but there was not enough clearance to bang on it, stab it, or even squeeze underneath and bench-press the screwdriver up into the mailbox's guts.

Then, an idea.

She placed the point of the screwdriver into the center of the underbelly, and wedged the handle into the cement at an angle. The more she wedged the handle, the closer to perpendicular its angle became to the cement, the farther the point sank into the underbelly. She picked up her branch again and hit the side of the handle.

Pdnk. The point pierced the steel creature. Justine pulled the screwdriver out and repeated, over and over, until she had eight or ten tightly clustered quarter-inch holes. From inside it would look like a drain. Then, with some knuckle-flaying jabs and wrenching and torquing, she made a hole large enough to get three fingers into.

The first thing she pulled out was a squarish yellow envelope embossed with the Hallmark logo. It was from Lola Baumgartner to Master Kenny Keene. The extraction process partly shredded the envelope, revealing its contents of a fire-engine-shaped birthday card containing five mint-crisp one-dollar bills.

These were next, all mutilated to a degree by the jagged hole: a postcard in Czech, a phone bill remittance, a letter to the editor of the *Daily Texan*, a letter with a hockey card in it, some wit's sticky Icee cup, a move in a postal chess match (...f6!), more bill payments, a poem about Canada that one Connie Davis was mailing to herself as a form of copyright protection. A sonnet called "Pigeon Friends."

A package blocked the hole. It would not unblock no matter how she prodded or shifted or stabbed.

Justine sat back to vibrate in frustration, and to consider her federal crime.

She scooped up all the mail she'd ruined and wandered around the neighborhood, delivering each envelope to its return address. It took two hours. She returned to the mailbox and lay down in the dewy grass nearby with her backpack for a pillow. She tried not to fall asleep. Cars began to drive through the lot to stop and feed the mailbox. The sun rose. It grew warm.

Presently a mail lady cursed with a tiny Victorian waist and wearing a very wide-brimmed straw sun hat appeared, equipped with a canvas bag and a ring of keys. She stooped by the mailbox and began to hunt through her keys.

"Hello, miss?" said Justine.

"Eeeeee!" said the mail lady, tossing her keys in the air and falling backward into the parking lot. "You scared the hell outta me. Dammit."

"I'm sorry," said Justine, standing up. "Are you okay? I was just wondering..."

"Dammit." The mail lady found her keys. As she stood up, some Bonz fell out of her shirt pocket.

"Here," said Justine, picking them up and giving them back. "Dog biscuits are a good idea."

"Dammit."

"Ma'am, I need to get a couple of letters back I mailed by accident. They're probably right on top in there."

"You want me to *give* you some government property?"

"Well, no, I just need my two letters back, they're both the same, kind of creamy, soft envelopes, and I addressed them with this kind of pen..."

Justine disinterred her calligraphy felt pen from her backpack and scribbled on the palm of her hand.

"...and they just weren't ready to mail yet."

A long silver Chrysler was idling behind Justine and the mail lady. Clearly the driver was waiting for them to move so he could mail his letters.

"I'm not giving you anything in this box."

"I just live down the street. I'm mailing them to my own house and to a neighbor. Can't you give them to me?"

"If you live that close, they'll get delivered by noon. Just go wait."

Justine felt it would damage her case to explain she was never going there again, so she kept her mouth shut.

The mail lady was settling down. She renewed thumbing through her hoop of keys, keeping an eye on Justine.

"Please?"

"No. Begone!"

"I need them. It's a matter of life or death."

"Oh no it isn't."

"Oh yes it is too. If those people open those letters, they'll be so upset that there might be a death."

"So call them and say don't open the letters."

"If you knew them, you'd know that they'd both open their letters even faster."

Especially Charlotte. Livia would open hers immediately if she wasn't supposed to, the disobedience itself the reward, but Charlotte would open hers out of pure worry, mixed with a bit of Emily Post–era manners.

I was worried sick, she would say. *And, look, I was right—you were going to commit suicide and blame your mother, Livia.*

"You should've thought of that before you mailed them," said the mail lady, not softening at all, in fact growing more impervious, like ten-minute epoxy.

The Chrysler crept forward a few inches. A Roto-Rooter van got in line behind him.

"*I* didn't mail them," said Justine. "See, someone stole them. I got mugged, and the mugger stole my letters. And my billfold, and my car, and left me in some dirt to die. That's why I look like this. So I have to get those letters back because they weren't ready for mailing."

The mail lady's slacks were held up with a thick belt from which hung a flashlight, a little holster with some kind of black tube in it, and a pair of white, furry booties.

"I'm not lying," said Justine, stamping, and corrugating her face as if to warn of a tantrum.

"Did you really get held up?" she asked, leaning back and hooking her ring fingers in her belt. "What'd he look like?"

"Ah, he was big and tall, and he was wearing a shirt and some pants. Blue. And he had a gun. A Gatling gun, and a mask. Of pantyhose. I couldn't see his face."

There were four cars in line now. The last one was anonymized by black tinted windows and customized with hydraulics. It beeped and performed silly gymnastics.

"Why didn't he take your backpack?"

"Oh, he just went through it for valuables."

"Lemme go call the cops for you, then."

"No. No, they already know. I filed a report for the arraignment. All the cops are looking for him right now. Those letters are going to be evidence, you know."

The mail lady sighed and opened the belly of the mailbox. She began to stuff mail into her canvas sack. Justine nearly began applauding with relief.

"Hey," said Justine. "They were on top. You probably already put them in your bag."

The mail lady paused. She unholstered her black tube.

"If you do not leave, kid, I will mace you."

The Chrysler driver put the car in park and rolled down his window. The Roto-Rooter man got out of his van. The tinted-windows car jittered and rocked.

Justine backed up, tripping on her backpack.

"I hate you."

"What's going on here?" said the Roto-Rooter man, whose hair resembled Valerie Bertinelli's. "Why are you pointing mace at her?"

"Back off, fellah," she said. "Unless you want some, too."

"I just want my letters back."

The Chrysler beeped consumptively, then a crinkly old man emerged. He was wearing a strange, amply pocketed denim onesie, and holding a parcel tied with twine.

"Ain't nobody gonna squirt mace on nobody," he said, shaking his finger at both Justine and the mail lady.

"Is that more than thirteen ounces?" said the mail lady fiercely, pointing at his parcel. "You can't mail that in this mailbox if it's over thirteen ounces.

You'll have to wait for the lobby to open."

"I know the rules," said the old man, who had an embroidered oval patch over one of his breast pockets that said REALHAPPY.

"What happened to you, young lady?" said the Roto-Rooter man, pointing politely at the unfinished cut on Justine's wrist. "Would you like me to take you to a doctor?"

"No, I really just need my two letters back that I accidentally mailed. I—"

"You said they were stolen!" shouted the mail lady.

The bouncing car paused for a moment to let out a woman who also had superb hair, but more like Scott Baio's. She carried her own can of mace.

"Give her her letters back, look at her, she's loco, open your eyes."

"No. It's against the law, and I don't like her, anyway. She scared me and I fell over and sat on my flashlight."

"Serves you right for raising the postage again," said the Hispanic woman, her Mace trained on the mail lady.

"I didn't do that."

"Stamps went up again?" said REALHAPPY, who stomped with one foot, then the other, then looked up into the trees. "Goddammit."

"It went up?" said the Roto-Rooter man. "To what?"

"Quarter," said the Hispanic woman.

"Oh, goddammit everything," said the old man again, in a way that sounded like he'd been stunned by some federal surprise every single day of his life.

"Hey, that means I didn't put enough on there," said Justine. "You have to give them back to me so I can put more stamps on."

"I don't have to do anything," said the mail lady, locking the mailbox.

"Give her the letters, see," said the old man, like James Cagney.

"I think I'd like to talk to your supervisor," said the Roto-Rooter man, whose lovely hair shined and floated gently like a condor on a breeze.

"I don't have a supervisor. I'm the Postmaster General. And the Postmaster General says why don't all y'all take a deep breath and fuck y'allselves."

The mail lady held her spray in both hands like a cop pointing a pistol at a perp.

Justine, eyes shut, hands clawed, lunged for the bag.

"Hey!"

Justine, her face buried in the mail lady's tiny waist and her hands in her mailbag, heard the sound of hairspray spraying and felt a cool liquid soak into her hair on the back of her head.

Screams. Medieval-thumbscrew screams. The mail lady ripped her bag away. Justine turned. All three of her defenders were on the ground flopping and croaking like electrocuted game fish.

"Girl."

And with a jet of oleoresin capsicum the mail lady filled Justine's cool green eyes.

In less than fifteen minutes Justine was able to stand and open her eyes without retching. Her colleagues were nowhere to be seen, though their vehicles were still there; each was being loaded onto a flatbed wrecker by tanned men in sleeveless work shirts who ignored her completely.

The mail lady was gone.

Justine walked back home.

It was Tuesday. Charlotte's Fifth Avenue was in the driveway, as was Livia's Maverick. Justine had obviously been missed.

Justine crawled under the hedge marking a property boundary. She had spent some time in conference with trees and grass and bugs lately; the inside of a hedge was familiar if not altogether comfortable.

The effects of the pepper spray were largely gone except that Justine felt as if her lungs were enormous, capable of holding many cubic yards of oxygen and sustaining her if she chose at that moment to participate in an Iron Man competition.

She breathed deeply, slowly. She arranged herself so she could watch for Shook, the mailman, and intercept him. It shouldn't be more than a couple of hours. She would not fall asleep.

Justine fell asleep.

For the second time in just a few hours, Justine was awakened by a police car.

This one idled noisily in the driveway. The passenger door was open. The driver, a narrow-skulled cop who looked barely thirteen, was yawning so hard his eyes were tearing up and he needed both hands to cover his mouth.

Standing on the porch of her house was an older, larger cop, whose old, large face was decorated with a dense black toothbrush moustache. Next to him stood Charlotte, dressed only in her slippers and baby-blue bathrobe. Standing with them was Livia, who was wearing exactly the same thing as when she had kissed her daddy. Lou himself and Dot were nowhere in sight. Charlotte was holding a photograph. The cop was holding Justine's letters. Livia was tightly holding herself.

"Which are you?" the cop said to Charlotte.

"Charlotte," she said with an aged tremor. "Her grandmother."

"And you're…?" said the cop, appraising Livia.

"I'm her mother. Adoptive. Livia Moppett."

"Well," said the cop, holding up a letter in each hand, "this is for you, and this is for you. But you owe me three cents apiece first. Postage due. Lemme have the picture."

Charlotte found a coin in her robe pocket. She gave it and the picture to the cop. He gave them the letters, which they opened.

Charlotte covered her mouth and squeezed her eyes shut. Livia froze.

Charlotte dropped her letter and ran down the side yard toward the alley. One of her baby-blue slippers came off.

"Mother. Stop."

Livia picked up her mother's letter.

The expression she made was not one Justine had ever seen before, until recently. Where? Oh. On Troy. When he drove away.

Livia dropped her mother's letter, then ran after her. Before she could get far, Charlotte came running back.

"She's not in the car in the alley! What did your letter say?"

"The same as yours," said Livia, stuffing the letter into the pocket of her robe.

"Get my keys. We're going to go look for her."

The cop picked up and read Charlotte's letter.

"Klaus," he said, thrusting at the yawning cop the letter and a four-by-six-inch picture of Justine taken for her sophomore yearbook. "Let's go find her."

"What for?" said Klaus, still yawning like a sinkhole.

"She's wanted."

"For what?" said yawning Klaus.

"For one," said the toothbrush cop, "destruction of government property. For two, suicide-attempting. That's not allowed in Travis County or in the kingdom of God. For three, assault with intent to kill on a federal employee. For four, loitering. And there's littering and a bunch of other stuff. Plus, she's missing, also against the rules."

Livia came back out of the house with the keys. Charlotte was already in the passenger seat of her car.

"You go by yourself," said Livia, handing her mother the keys. "Someone needs to be here in case she comes home."

Livia went inside the house and shut the front door with a gentle *kalak*.

The yawning cop got into the backseat of the cruiser and lay down, and toothbrush got into the front. They backed out of the driveway and pulled away, lights and siren in full festival.

Both Charlotte and her car screamed into the street and disappeared into the deep arch of magnolias.

229

XI

April 1988

The bartender, a slight, makeup-less woman in her mid-fifties wearing a striped vest and a bow tie, issued Lou an ashtray, a bowl of Chex Mix, and a coaster emblazoned with a cute cartoon bat. The mammalian, flying kind.

The bartender leaned forward. Her nostrils dilated appreciably.

"Been barhopping tonight?"

"No," said Lou, which was the truth. He'd been drinking vodka he bought at Centennial Liquors off Fifty-First Street, which had been the first liquor store all day that hadn't turned him away for already being shitfaced.

The bartender leaned back and looked Lou directly in the eye. He hated looking right at people. It felt like they could read his mind and see the grotesque truths about him. It was much easier to stare at a neutral object, like a knuckle or a cue ball or a dirt clod, and maybe glance up now and then.

Lou tried to look back at the bartender in a sober, helpful way, but his eyes teared up and he had to look down at his bat.

"No vodka for you," she said finally.

"Well, that's fine. I'm pretty tired of vodka, anyway. Rolling Rock?"

She brought him one.

"Dollar."

Lou took a modest sip of fifty-ish degrees Fahrenheit beer. He looked back down at his bat again. He noticed that it had angry red eyes and little fangs; its cartoony cuteness was now just common malevolence. He placed his bottle on the bat, but still he felt it staring through the green glass at him.

"Whatcha got on tap there?"

"Seltzer," said the bartender.

Lou ate some Chex Mix.

"No TV, huh?"

"It's four in the afternoon," said the bartender. "Nothing on."

Lou thought that was a little presumptuous. Who was she to say what he liked to watch? It was April. There'd be baseball, surely. Why wouldn't he want to watch baseball? Poor Dot. She'd hated baseball. She'd hated it so much that she used to delight in ribbing Lou about how stupid it was. How disgusting, with the bilious tobacco sputum puddles everywhere and lip-readable cussing and choreographies of crotch-tugging. About how corpulent all the pitchers and coaches were, and what pussies everybody was, with big leather gloves and shin guards and hard hats and padded masks. About how long the games were. How *poky*.

"Unless you wanna watch *As the World Turns*," said the bartender, with a big, brown smile. "You wanna watch that? Hold on. Hey, Dizz. Dizzy. Wake up."

A man whom Lou hadn't noticed before and who was napping on the floor near the warbling video games sat up and rubbed his eyebrows with his palms.

"Dizz. Warm up that TV set. Our patron here would like to catch up on his stories."

Dizz reached up and flicked on the TV. He turned channels, passing a Rangers game, Charlie Hough on the mound.

"Say, I noticed a ball game," said Lou pleasantly. "Can we watch that?"

Both Dizz and the bartender turned to look at Lou. The bat was looking at him. Dot was out there in the parking lot, alone in the backseat of Sherpa's Monte Carlo, and here he was, Lou Borger, drinking warm beer and eating cold mockery.

The bartender snatched his beer away. Dizz, now fully awake and illumined by a soap opera, was the most menacing individual Lou had ever seen. He turned to As the World Turns.

"I think I saw this episode, so I guess I'll be on my way," said Lou, standing up and tipping the bartender a quarter. "I'm expected back home in Arabi, Louisiana, and furthermore I got someone waiting for me in the car."

"Sheik," said Dizz, who started to laugh like Horshack from Welcome Back, Kotter. "Ima Sheika Araby."

Lou backed quickly out of the bar.

He climbed into the blue Monte Carlo. Dot was lying along the backseat, covered in her old favorite sun-bleached afghan. Lou had put her green marabou slippers on her feet before they'd set out that afternoon, just after Livia'd kissed him in the garage and he hadn't stopped her.

Lou parked at the same Centennial again and bought another quart of Smirnoff from the same clerk who was still trying to load the same spool of register tape into the same cash register that he'd been trying to load it into when Lou'd come in four hours before.

Lou pulled onto I-290 east. He sighed at the micro-orgasm of the bottle's metal cap and tax label cracking open, and the coital slipperiness of the first swallow.

He signaled when he changed lanes. He drank through the side of his mouth so the bottle wouldn't obscure his view of the road. He drove three miles over the speed limit—the precise speed, he'd read somewhere, that was least likely to toll a cop's bells. He did not tailgate. With both hands he squeezed the hard blue sparkly steering wheel. He did not fall asleep. He tuned into and turned up loud a three-hour commercial-free heavy-metal marathon. And, with every muscle and neuron, Lou fought the Weave.

On the other side of Houston, Lou entered I-10 east toward New Orleans. It was getting dark. The temperature dropped. The vodka was nearly half gone. Lou was sleepy. He did not want to stop, even though he could feel that he was losing the fight against the Weave.

"A test," said Lou. "A couple-hundred-mile-long goddam test."

Lou squeezed the steering wheel harder. He held his breath and clenched the muscles in his neck and shoulders and face, making his eyes bug out. I could sure use a cup of coffee. And maybe a cheeseburger. And a commode.

He let his breath out. He was even sleepier than before.

Ahead, dots of bright color. They resolved into emblems on towering poles: McDonald's, Exxon, Waffle House, and another... it looked familiar. Lou squinted.

"Wendy's!" Lou shouted. He glanced over his shoulder to tell Dot but remembered she was gone. When he turned back, the steel letters *GMC* filled most of the window. Lou crushed the brake with the heel of his boot to avoid rear-ending the pickup and swerved into the breakdown lane. A little orange Ford Fiesta was there, its hood up, its backseat alive with children and dogs.

Lou pleaded guilty to all charges, including five counts of vehicular homicide, and one count of abuse of a corpse. (It was not illegal to kill a dog in Texas.) Though the jury's recommendation had been "forever," Lou was sentenced to twenty-two years of sober, hard labor, to be served at the Louisiana State Penitentiary at Angola.

XII

May 2004

Driving home from Planned Parenthood, where she went at least once a week for a proper pregnancy test—fuck that e.p.t. noise—April Carole rolled down the window of the black Mini Cooper once owned by her now-dead sister, Bryce, and shouted at the scudding-by world, "I wonder who it was!"

There were a dozen or so possibilities, given the window of time during which conception might've occurred. It could've been the short guy who resembled Tom Hulce. He had been able to achieve the male's goal thrice, without withdrawing, in less than ten minutes, every second of which April admitted to both herself and to him (as a rule she did not compliment her lover's performances or moan overmuch during them) that she enjoyed quite a bit, particularly the unexpected basal flares and unusually brisk thunder that his weird barley-twist penis had been capable of provoking.

Twinges and twangs, and occasionally thoomps, constituted April's principal sexual jolts, and were really the only things she was able to enjoy during her swiving marathon, except for Scrabble-ating every single one of her conquests, which caused many of them to want to show her a thing or two about dominance. April, and probably all the men, bandied dominance and virility.

Or it might have been the too-tall guy with the graying, moustacheless beard whose semen production, though dispensed only in a single dose, was delivered with substantial volume and muzzle velocity, and somehow felt *on target*.

Or it had been the predictable, almost-forgettable guy she'd met on Atlanta Craigslist who arrived at her apartment to find that April had inked superb drawings of raspberries and stinging nettle and red clover all over her pelvic region in red and green ballpoint because she had been wondering whether *renditions* of the so-called fertility herbs would have more of an influence than the plants themselves, which had, so far, proved powerless.

Or maybe it was the Russian exchange student, a basso profundo with exactly the same hair as April's, whom she'd cornered at one of the UT practice rooms and who claimed to have once paid a disbarred surgeon to open him up while a local tattooer inked his liver with a likeness of Maria Callas. He showed April the scar. She thought she would like to have a child with Veniamin. She liked him. She'd swallowed her very last tiny egg just as he came.

Or it could have been one of the five nearly identical sailors who drank every beer in the refrigerator and wouldn't leave until April'd cherry-popped their one reluctant comrade, Morris, who, as it turned out, happened to be in control of a very sweet kissing style that April might've come to like had she not been on a mission.

Or it was Ryan, over whom April shook the powders of mercy during the salient period.

Whoever. April was now, officially, a mom-to-be. She looked down at her belly. She took her hands off the steering wheel and briefly used her belly to steer her Mini Cooper up Airport Boulevard.

"Whaddaya think of that, Montserrat! Or Ricky! Like driving?"

Presently April arrived at the Parallel Apartments, parked her car, and walked up to her efficiency, in which she found Ryan asleep on the futon.

"Wakey!" she said. "Guess what?"

"Nlph."

"Just fourteen hours ago, I fucked my last stranger, the nine-hundred-sixteenth, some Kerneth Hanger, plus, just forty-five *minutes* ago, I got back a pregnancy test. And..."

"Mf. And... what?"

"Two guesses."

"...positive?" said Ryan, now wide awake and sitting up.

"That is correct, motherfucker!"

Ryan jumped up and ran to the kitchenette. He returned with two bottles of beer. April knew that part of his enthusiasm was genuine happiness for her conceiving, but an equal if not larger part was the revived hope that April would now be available to him. But April had plans to be only with people she had real feelings for. And the only one of the 916 that she had crushed on was Veniamin.

Ryan handed her the beer.

"*Slainte mhath!*" said he, tapping the body of her bottle with the heel of his and taking a long pull. April herself took a modest sip, her last for a long while, then smiled and reached up to kiss him on the cheek.

"You're my best friend, Ryan."

"I know," he said, two-thirds of his beer drunk up.

"You really know how to take care of a person," said April

"I am really very good at that," said Ryan.

"You stuck with me through all the year, all the slutting."

"Yeah."

"I'm done. I'm fine now, I think."

"What do you mean?"

Ryan's beer was now gone.

"I can take care of myself."

And April sent Ryan away.

The freedom accompanying escape from an existence whoring yourself out for more than a year, for *nothing*, is not just the snug, violet-scented solitude of your own apartment evacuated of all past evidence, but also a tower from whose highest point you can view both your history of compulsive promiscuity and your escape from it, without judgment, without falling back into the mire, without a crushing penalty waiting for you. That freedom, though, requires maintenance, protection, and a handler practiced in issuing firm *no*'s, and it must exist in a hostile world that makes its isle of freedom worth wanting.

April lived snug in her apartment for months, living off of a surprisingly lucrative and easy three-week temp job at the Texas Department of Public Safety (offices of Concealed Handgun Licensing) that she'd completed just a few days before she'd been declared pregnant. After the assignment, April began filling her now-wide-open schedule by not drinking alcohol, reading baby books, surfing baby sites, singing to her baby, doing scales, playing White Stripes records for the baby, regularly eating the vitamins she was supposed to, and carefully restoring her antique bassinet with new twigs of wicker, painting them with acrylics mixed in sympathy to the original palette of woody yellows, light browns, and straw. The bassinet and its baby developed apace.

April also watched in her mind vivid films of her year-and-more's worth of horizontal labor, which she finally escaped by achieving what she had worked for. April thought that she might've worked harder than anyone in history to get pregnant, and she deserved her freedom and solitude now. Especially immunity from the phone, which rang all day, still, the calls always from past conquests who had fallen for her and/or felt they deserved a little more, like, *Where was the fucking blow job?*, or from hopeful new "referrals" who sometimes left their entire credit-card number on voicemail, or from Ryan, just checking in to see if she needed anything. She never called anyone back. She never called anyone, period, except, once, the Time Warner guy. April needed him to come get her Dell Latitude back online. She had research and maternity-dress shopping to do.

April loved anything that verified her status as carrying, be it the praiseful smiles of gynecologists; be it her favorite articles of clothing encountering the new snugness at her waistline; be it the pregnancy mask so dark that a four-year-old child at the Highland Mall asked her if the rest of her body was black; be it April's neighbor Porifiro knocking on her door with a cream puff from Central Market in one hand and a card in the other, a homemade congratulatory card that opened onto a Crayola meadow of pop-up sheep and pigs and goats and chickens, each wearing a hat made of an origamied five-dollar bill.

"Jesus, Porifiro, you *made* this?" April had said.

"Yep. I just found out about you, uh, your, uh…"

"Shit, who told you? Nobody knows but doctors. It hasn't even been five months."

"I saw you at a coffee shop one day, reading that baby book *What to Expect* or something. Then I saw you toting that big old Graco baby stroller up the stairs. Looked like a chuckwagon. 'Member, we waved. Then I saw you sitting in your car one day and you're busy listening to your stomach with a stethoscope. So I was pretty sure, and I figure if come to find out I'm wrong, twenty bucks oughta fix the damage done."

"You were watching—"

"Hey, I'm no stalker. Just a busybody who spends a lot of time looking through his blinds. To, you know, keep the Parallel Apartments safe from crime and all that."

April smiled and looked at her card again. Oh dear. The baby goat. The baby goat was so cute it pushed April onto the entrance ramp of a highway that might lead to tears. She couldn't remember the last time she'd felt the imminence of the horrible grief hiccup in her chest that was the wall between tears and no tears, but, she thought, here it comes. And it arrived. She hugged her neighbor. His T-shirt smelled of dryer sheets and Pop-Tarts, and she soaked it in the wet of a monster cry.

"Okay, okay," Porifiro finally said, pushing her gently away and back into her apartment. "That's fine. Thaaat's fine."

April invited Porifiro in. He declined, but asked her to always wave when she saw him. April promised to do so. April said she'd wash his shirt for him if he liked, and he said he might bring it by. She shut the door, sat down in the middle of the floor between a stack of never-unpacked boxes and the telephone, opened her card again, which read "*A New Baby, HooRah April!!!*" She removed the pig's money hat, carefully unfolded it, and then tried to fold it back, without luck. She tried with the chicken hat, but couldn't refold that either. She struck out with the sheep, too, even accidentally pulling her off the card altogether. She wasn't going to monkey with her baby goat's money hat no matter what. What if she tried and failed? Then no one would have a hat. April stood her card up against the base of the cordless, laid the detached sheep in front of the card, picked up the receiver, and dialed the obvious number.

"Hello, Caroles."

"Dad?"

"*Bry*—?"

"No, April."

The unintentional slight didn't bother her in the least. She felt at peace with her sister for the first time ever, and she was going to make it so with her parents.

"Oh god, sorry... April, how good to hear your sweet voice."

"You, too."

Silence.

"Everything all right?" Archie Carole finally said, his words slick with worry, as if he'd just remembered that his estranged daughter would only ever call him if she was in some seriously hot water. "Are you in jail?"

"No. Is my mother there?"

"Yes, but I don't think this is the best—"

"Harry?"

"Uh, school."

"Oh. Well, can I come over?"

"Now?"

"Yeah, now."

"Well... of course, April. Come on over."

"Thanks, Daddy."

April cradled the receiver and jumped up to dress. She was definitely showing now—how could a belly like that *not* crack her mother's endless mourning, if only for a few minutes?

A red ribbed tank top she'd bought at Old Navy two years ago seemed to provide adequate coverage, ventilation, and elasticity, and would also favorably feature her boobs, which, though a little tender and itchy, had enlarged at least a cup size. She didn't know why she wanted to show her parents the embonpoint of her late-fourth-month bust, but she did.

April pulled on a long pleated unbleached-linen skirt embroidered with blue sharks, slipped into a pair of flip-flops, and went out to the car. In the rearview she did her face and plucked her brows. She started the car. As she began to back out, a terror came over her. It felt like a thousand spikes of razor-sharp glass from a hundred busted bottles pouring down and slicing into her from a bucket tipped thirty feet above... she jammed on the brakes. *Where's my baby!*

Then she remembered. Ah. Ha. Hahaha. A chuckle escaped, but the trauma of the razor-glass shower stayed with her, cutting, stabbing, until she reached her parents' house in Bee Cave.

The house, a low brick ranch situated so close to the road that the driveway lay parallel to the facade, leaving no room for any sort of lawn save two strips of ill-tended monkey grass, had been April's home since birth (she and Bryce had been born in the tub—April was nineteen minutes older), until she enrolled in UT's School of Music in '98. The front door was never used, so April, after parking bumper to bumper behind her dad's Cadillac, walked through the side yard to the back door. Still shaken by the vision of the rain of razor glass, she knocked, an action she'd never before committed upon this door, and waited. She could see movement inside, but it was a full thirty seconds before anyone came to let her in. It was her father who did.

"You didn't have to knock," said Archie Carole, not smiling, not frowning.

"Yeah. Hi, Daddy."

"Hi. Long time no see."

The tired salutation used to enrage April. He always used it, no matter the visitor, no matter the time passed between visits. But this time April was not enraged. She wondered if, by becoming pregnant and escaping her disgusting, open-legged servitude, she had also left behind a canyonful of resentments and hatred.

She wished Bryce were here, too, mutually contrite, in all her beauty, sitting at the dining-room table with their mother, who always received guests while seated at the head of the table, as if she were the duchess of the room, unwilling to rise for subalterns. Bryce would be sitting next to her, leaning toward her mother, her agent, informer, confidante, the two a team, or even a single being, invulnerable.

But Blaise was not at the table. She was standing near the gas stove, expressionless except for a tightly ruffed brow, arms crossed, dressed in a light denim skirt, her weight borne by one shoeless foot—in other words, just as she'd appeared ever since Bryce died.

"Hi, Mom."

She smiled politely but did not speak or move. April walked up and gave her a hug, being sure to press their bellies together.

"You're pregnant," she said, after returning the hug with one arm only.

"Yeah."

"You're not married, though."

"How do you know?"

"Is it Ryan's?"

"No," said April. She had been planning to lie and say her nonexistent boyfriend, "Laurence," was the father, but a lie now would force an endless stream of them, whereas one simple truth now would say an awful lot about her life yet not invite many questions, given its indecorous nature: "I don't know whose it is."

"I... would you like a beer?"

"No beer for me, thanks."

"Of course, how stupid of me," Blaise said, smacking her forehead with the heel of her palm, an action whose harshness probably exceeded in vigor its intent. "I'm sure you've stopped your pills, too."

"Yeah, but not till I found out."

"So you were on... what? And for how long?"

"The same old stuff. About five weeks."

"You didn't stop when you missed a period?"

"I never missed one. Happens."

"I'm sure it'll be fine."

"How do you feel without them?" said her father, assuming his typical stance as monitor of healthful practices among his family and friends.

"I'm fine, seriously, don't notice anything at all. I just wanted to come over today to give you the good news, about the baby, and to apologize for how I treated you both and how I treated Bryce, and to just basically apologize for me."

April stood, head slightly bowed, expecting a tentative but warm welcome home.

"Welcome home," her parents said, coolly, and awkwardly out of sync.

"Thanks." April fought a fidget. "Just know that I'm doing everything right to be a good mother."

"I'm sure you'll be a wonderful mother."

"Thanks. How's Harry?"

"Becoming a boy," said Blaise.

April tried to suppress a giggle, but failed.

"What?" said Archie, beginning to smile. He looked at his wife, who was not smiling.

"The way you said that," said April, between stitches, "it sounded like Harry used to be a girl."

Silence. Then Archie roared, a genuine belly laugh. Blaise blushed and almost smiled. April found herself at the starting line of a long stretch of guffaws. Eventually her mother joined in, impotent to suppress a laugh. The three of them went on long enough to give April a stomachache.

The tempest passed. They all sat down on the kitchen floor at the same time, heads down, grinning, each busy investigating something—her mother, the hem of her skirt; her father, a thumb wart; April, a giggle-pulled muscle in her side. She had not laughed that hard since her cat Clavamox fell in the toilet.

"I'm at more than four months," said April, noticing that the aroma of roasting meat was filling the room. "What're..."

April was going to say "we," but realized at the last moment that it would've sounded presumptuous.

"...you having?"

"Pork loin," said Blaise, still rosy from her fit. "Soon you can get an ultrasound and find out its gender."

"I know. But I don't wanna know till he or she is born."

"Why don't we all sit at the table?"

April and Archie sat on either side of her mother's seat at the head of the already-set dining-room table. Presently her mother arrived with the tenderloin and set it between them. She left and returned with green beans and a salad. One more trip brought salt and pepper, butter, and two bottles of Shiner Bock.

"What would you like to drink?" said Blaise.

"Me? Root beer?"

"Archie, we still have a case of Bryce's A&W, don't we?"

"Yeah, I'll get a can."

"We have a little news, too," said Blaise, when Archie had left the room. "We learned that Bryce had been secretly married. The father came forward. After producing a marriage certificate and demanding a paternity test—it came back positive—he—Clare—yes, Clare was his name—was awarded by a court—Judge Polemp's—Bryce's estate, including Harry."

"God."

"Got it," said Archie, returning with a can of A&W from whatever domestic vault the memories of Bryce were stored in. "Let me get some ice."

"I'll take it warm."

April opened the two-year-old can, poured the fizzless liquid into a glass, and took a sip. It tasted like sugar water amplified with tar and lemons—the flavors that carbonization apparently curtained.

The house itself was brick, but the interior walls were of particleboard, the doors light and hollow, the central air vents virtual ear trumpets, amplifying and distributing among the rooms every conversation, groan, curse, murmur, aria, fart, lie, moan, and collision; there was little question whether Archie had heard Blaise tell their daughter about Harry. Proving this, he said:

"And it looks like he's going to come get your car."

This news didn't upset April as much she would've expected. She still had her old Mazda. And she wouldn't have to worry about somebody stealing the desirable little Mini.

"Oh, okay."

"Really? Okay?"

"Yeah, I understand. Can I cut the pork tenders?"

"We have to wait fifteen minutes. It's carrying over. Still cooking."

April's stomach growled. The pulled muscle ached. The atmosphere was cooling more rapidly than the meat. Four wordless minutes passed.

"We've really missed Harry," said Archie.

"I bet," said April. The uncarved meat screamed in conspicuity.

"Clare said we can see him when we want," said Blaise.

"He's a nice person."

"He's been in prison and rehab," added Archie, managing to simultaneously direct the comment toward Blaise with acrimony and toward April with compassion.

"He's sober and free."

"He's on parole and drinks beer."

"He works for IBM now."

"In the mailroom," said Archie. "He works literally *in the mailroom*."

"Do you guys think it's been fifteen minutes?"

"Soon," said Blaise.

April's stomach was beginning to cramp. More than just her stomach. It felt like her whole middle, lungs to perineum, was starting to fold itself into eighths.

"Can I go ahead and have beans?"

"Can't you wait?"

"Yeah." April drank down her A&W, but it didn't help the intensifying cramp. She felt a shift in her uterus. That was new. April stood up. "I think my baby moved, for the first time!"

"Let me feel," said Blaise, with what seemed like suppressed excitement. Blaise held her daughter's hips and pressed an ear to her belly. April noticed that her mother had gray roots: she had evidently begun dyeing her hair after their estrangement. So much had been lost by vice of April's selfishness, hatred, resentment. It might not be fixable.

But maybe it was. She would bring her baby over to her parents' every day. She would arrange playdates for Harry and his new cousin. She would have her people over, cook for them, sing them songs. She would think about, maybe even write about, Bryce. She'd get back in touch with Ryan, bring him over. He'd make a good father. Maybe she could fall in love with him. There were philters and berries and spells for that kind of thing. Maybe they could all live in her parents' house together. *Maybe she'd have another child.*

"I don't notice anything yet," Blaise said. "But it's still a tiny bit early for kicking."

"I felt something."

"Maybe you need the potty," said Archie, eliciting crisp stares from both mother and daughter.

But maybe she did need to go. She excused herself.

Even though it had been recently papered in a vinyly crocus print that April did not hate, the bathroom, historically *her* bathroom, seemed utterly the same—all at once welcoming and repellant, asylum and gaol, vacant and spirited. It had always been the most acoustically secure room in the house, and April had spent a lot of time here.

She sat. She doubled over, winced. Nothing happened. She took off all her clothes, turned on the shower, lay down in the tub, and let the water cool her down. She began to bleed from her vagina. She reached up and grabbed a towel, and screamed into it. The cramping localized, then she experienced what she imagined a contraction to be.

"Okay in there, honey?" said her mother through the door. *Honey.*

"Fine, out in a minute, start without me."

April was certain that her mother was at the door during the entire four minutes that it took to miscarry her baby. A girl.

Montserrat.

XIII

March 2004

Together Marcia Brodsky and Casey prepared to lift Rance off of the low, vast bed in the boudoir where he performed his services, Marcia holding his feet, Casey at the business end. Usually Rance could walk on his knees to the bathtub by himself, but Rance had damaged some critical piece of circuitry while screwing a state senator, deactivating himself. That had been an hour ago.

"Ready?" said Marcia.

"Yeah," said Casey.

"Okay, one, two, three, lift!"

The naked 110-pound doll, in its unconscious mode, was quite limp. As Marcia and Casey slid him off the bed, he dipped in the middle, hitting his butt on the floor rather hard.

"God, he's not that heavy," said Marcia. "We're such pussies."

"What's the big hurry, anyway?" said Casey. "Why can't we just take a night off?"

"Because the tech guy'll be here in less than an hour, and they said

Rance had to be spotless. Plus, tonight there's gonna be nine clients in just twelve hours, our biggest night yet. And I have intelligence that suggests one of them is going to be a *Chronicle* reviewer. We're up for Best Austin Whorehouse."

"Do you think he's broken?"

"If I busted him I'll—"

"I wouldn't worry," said Casey. "I assure you he's been pounded much harder than that."

She let Rance's legs down. "How are we gonna do this?"

"Can't drag him, he might get a rash. Or a tear."

"We could if you put a tarp or something under him."

"You have a tarp?"

"Well, how about a shower curtain?"

With this method they got him all the way to the tub, but could not hoist him up and in.

"What now?"

"I hate Senator John Hill. He's never invited back."

"Why don't you call tech support again?"

Marcia refused to do that. She had immediately called tech support when they realized Rance was not responding to stimuli after his rendezvous with the senator, and she had not liked speaking with Miss Chassen, the damage, malfunction, and tune-up liaison at HoBots, LLC.

"I've only had him a month," Marcia told Miss Chassen. "He's been great up to now."

"Have you been mistreating him?"

"No, I have *not*."

"Our chief tech," she said, "Mr. C. P. Horn, has chartered a jet at Houston Hobby. He will arrive at your residence within an hour."

"Wow."

"Please clean your HoBot before Mr. Horn arrives."

"Okay."

"Thoroughly. Mr. Horn won't work on it if there is any gradoo in evidence."

"Okay."

"I mean it."

"Okay!"

"Miss Brodsky. Settle down. Do you have time for a quick survey?"

"How 1—"

"Two minutes."

"Yeah, sure," said Marcia. It wouldn't take long to scrub ole Rance down. If they could get him into the tub.

"Very good. First question: how many events in an average week?"

"Events? You mean like… coituses?"

"And any other form of intimate contact."

Marcia thought about it. Eleven clients the first week, two the second week, twenty-four the third, twenty-six the last. Word had been getting around. Rance had been programmed to ask each date, after the main event, how they'd heard of the Dollhaus, and more and more were saying "a friend's recommendation" or "*Chronicle* ad" or "My shrink told me to come," or something other than just a happenstance of internet-hooker-searching, or a direct invitation from Marcia or Casey.

"Fifteen or so, I guess." *Not including my own personal Rance time.*

"My. Sounds like you and Nicaise have a very special bond."

"*Rance.* Yes."

Marcia did not elaborate. She did not want to tell Miss Chassen the numbers were so high because she also *sold* events, often to strangers. Though, in all truth, Marcia did love Rance. They engaged four times a week, usually around 5 a.m., after the last client had left for the evening. Rance would groom himself while Marcia put fresh sheets on the bed. They would sleep till eleven, romance again, then get to work for the day.

The other three nights were Casey's.

"Thank you," said Miss Chassen. "Next question: have you ever used an automatic companion from another manufacturer?"

No, she had not. The internet informed her that there was nothing else like Rance in the world, and there were only a few dozen of him. And, as far she could see, no one else had set up a brothel around their HoBot. She was an industry leader, and would, hopefully, open Dollhaus Too in San Antonio before long.

"On a scale of one to ten, what would you rate his average performance?"

Marcia chuckled. All she could think of was Nigel Tufnel. *These go to eleven.*

"Ten, I guess."

"You must be easy to please."

"Okay, screw you."

She hung up and screeched, alarming Casey, as well as Schmidt, her dog, who was tied up outside. Schmidt had shown some aggression toward Rance, which Rance one day returned twofold, scaring and embarrassing Schmidt, who later tried to leap into the house through an open window to enact vengeance upon Rance, but was defeated by a screen.

"What was that for?" Casey said.

"I hate that woman."

"Why?"

"She was rude."

"Marcia, do not alienate tech support, for god's sake!"

"Just help me get him into the tub."

Rance, lying crumpled and gel-like on the floor of the bathroom, gravidly refused to cooperate in his transfer to the tub.

"You know what," said Marcia, sitting on the floor, examining Rance's head to make sure he'd received no bruises there during his move, "this isn't the first time we've needed help. Muscle. A human forklift. I think I'm gonna hire somebody. Right now."

"No," said Casey. "I forbid you. They'd steal your business model, and maybe your business. Then where would you be?"

"Just a minute."

She stood up and went to her computer, typed a name into Dogpile, and was rewarded with a phone number, which she called.

"Yeah?"

"Porifiro?"

"Who's this?"

"Marcia Brodsky, remember I took pictures of you on your trike last month."

"Yeah. How you doing? I like those pictures a lot. I'm having one blown up and I'm gonna have a painter paint the Astros in the background."

"Say, do you need a job?"

"Working for who?"

"Me."

"Why? I don't look like a man that's got a job?"

"I just figure you spend a lot of time on your trike so you might—"

"Okay, I could use one. Ole Tom Mix caught diabetes and I have to give the little man two shots a day and feed him the most expensive goddam store-bought dog food you buy at the vet."

"There's a catch: it starts right now."

"I'll be over there in six minutes."

Porifiro showed signs of neither disgust nor daunt; he simply picked up Rance, stepped into the tub, put him down gently, and stepped out. When the robot was clean, Porifiro carried him to the boudoir and laid him on the edge of the bed.

The tech guy arrived. He looked like T. S. Eliot, and dragged behind him a wagon of repair crap. He uttered not a single word. He simply waited until Marcia led him into the boudoir, where he went to work on Rance, hanging IVs, setting out palettes of surgical tools, meters of all kinds, vials and syringes, and a laptop. Marcia left him alone and returned to the kitchen, where she sat down with Porifiro and Casey. They looked like they'd been ignoring each other.

"Okay, that was easy," said Porifiro, declining the hundred-dollar bill Marcia offered him. "That's all I gotta do? Shuttle that floppy doll here and there? What's it pay?"

"Forty dollars per hour."

"Right on!"

Casey groaned, dramatically, as though he'd just been presented with his mother's head in a Frisbee.

"But only ten hours a week to start," said Marcia, crunching Casey's toes under the table with the wooden heel of a platform. "And honestly, I don't know what I'm gonna have you do. We've only been in business a month, and we're still figuring stuff out. So maybe I oughta ask, what can you do?"

Porifiro stroked his chin for a moment, and said:

"Well, I can build a good trike. I can bench 310. I have a good collection of baseball cards. I have good people skills. I can really fuck a man up if I get mad enough. I'm a good salesman. I can do eBay, and PowerPoint, and Excel and Word, and all that computer shit. I bodyguard, used to work with Anthony (Tony) Robbins, no shit. I speak Spanish and Portuguese. And I'm a good dog-man. You have a dog, right? I see him pissing in the side yard sometimes."

"Yeah," Marcia said. "Schmidt could use some company. I have to keep him in the yard so he doesn't get at the merchandise."

"What the hell is it you guys do?"

Marcia told him. Casey remained sullen the entire time. When Porifiro finally left for the night, Casey exploded. "How the fuck do you know that guy?"

"Whoa, Casey—"

"Why are you inviting a total str—"

"He's not, he did some work for me once. I've known him for years. He drives his trike around the neighborhood every day."

"That's *that* guy? That guy's insane!"

The tech guy came out of the boudoir with his wagon.

"How's Rance?"

"Fixed."

Marcia tried to give him a hundred-dollar tip, but he waved it away.

"So, what was up with him?" said Marcia, stuffing the bill into her shirt pocket.

"Lateral PMDV-board overload causing intraspinal seepage that arced the MamaHelpMe circuit in the sixth pelvic conduit, ultimately blowing the alternator."

"Oh. What caused it?"

"Blunt force trauma, replipenis. Probably a bite. It's been replaced."

T. S. Eliot left. Presently in came Rance, walking on his knees. He couldn't actually walk; that was still beyond the technological acumen of HoBots.

"Better?"

"Yes, I am," said Rance. "I want to make love to something!" He began to hump the divan.

Marcia used her remote to send him back to his boudoir.

"Our first client of the night will be here in ten minutes," said Marcia, finally alone with Casey.

"I'm going home," he said, putting on a silly porkpie hat he'd lately grown attached to.

"Get back here. I don't understand what you're so pissed about."

"Bye."

"You know what? I think you feel threatened by Porifiro."

"Ha!"

"Or else you've got a crush on him."

Both, as it turned out.

Over the next few months, Marcia, on the advice of Porifiro, raised the price of a date from $300 to $750 to $1,200 to $1,500. Traffic increased. Marcia was now serving thirty-five to fifty clients a week, bringing in several hundred thousand bucks a month. She paid off her credit-card debts, one at a time, starting with the lenders that had been the nicest to her during their debt-collecting years. Bank of America and Wells Fargo were last. She paid her last penny of debt on August 7, 2004, and by October she had two hundred thousand in a brand-new bank account at the Texas Federal Credit Union. She would be able to pay her 2004 income taxes in full, and still have enough to give both Casey and Porifiro big raises.

Porifiro was making as much as Casey now. Casey did not like this. He pouted, picked fights. Porifiro was doing more work, too. Casey did not like this either. He slacked off more, picked more fights. Casey was becoming redundant. Not that Marcia would ever fire him. Or would she?

The last thrust-and-parry between the two men occurred on October 16, 2004.

Marcia had left for a day of shopping, planning first to drop by Home Depot to buy a handheld spray attachment that she could plug into the showerhead in order to give Rance localized attention to the parts of himself he could not easily clean on his own. But when she got to the register, she realized she'd forgotten the damn hundred-dollar gift card she'd accepted as payment from one client, Miss Tramp, who had paid for her date entirely with gift cards, some fifteen hundred dollars worth of virtual cash from Neiman's, Best Buy, Crammed Shelf, Chuy's, Twin Liquors, and, of course, Home Depot. Marcia carried other bearer instruments on her person, but she wanted to spend the damn *card*.

Marcia growled, then smiled at the clerk and told him she'd be back.

She arrived to an empty house; Casey and Porifiro wouldn't be here till five. She heard noises coming from the boudoir. It sounded like Rance and a companion were on an exceptionally fine and rowdy date, considering the volume of porcine grunting emerging from the room, loud enough to penetrate the acoustic buffers between the boudoir and the house. Rarely could she hear anything going on inside the boudoir without her headphones. What the hell was going on? There were no dates scheduled during the day, and, besides, Marcia was always home, in control, madaming, whenever Rance was on a date. It was *her* company: she screened the clients, she made the daily cash deposit, she organized the schedule, she eavesdropped on every date. Part of Marcia's job was to listen for signs of discord, cardiac arrest, malfunction, and Rance's peculiar, and thankfully rarely uttered, safe words, *Mi madre*.

The headphones were as intrusive as she allowed herself or her staff to be, with one exception: the occasional use of a hidden, closed-circuit night-or-day-vision eye-in-the-sky that she only ever turned on when she heard irregularities.

Marcia put down her purse, got the house gun out from under the divan cushions, and, at the continued *eeyi*s, *oh god*s, and *fuck me*s coming through the walls of the boudoir, Marcia flipped the camera on.

Porifiro.

Porifiro, who had declined the job perk of free Rance time; Porifiro, who didn't like to deal with Rance directly at all; Porifiro, who had more than once poked a bit of not-so-lighthearted fun at Casey's gayness, which Marcia usually overlooked and Casey never seemed to hear; Porifiro, who was straight.

Marcia left the house, finished her shopping, and came back home around four. No one in the house or boudoir. It was still an hour before her bickery and tedious employees were due, and two hours before the arrival of tonight's date, Hymie Jeffs, a repeat customer who had paid the discount rate of fifteen thousand dollars, in advance, for a twelve-hour all-nighter, most of which he usually spent dozing and snuggling.

Marcia checked in on Rance. He sat up in bed and said, "Hello, darling. I can't wait for tomorrow morning, when we'll be together again. Would you like a quickie right now?"

"No, thank you, darling. How did you enjoy your afternoon delight with Porifiro?"

"Oh dear, that was supposed to be a secret."

"I didn't know that Porifiro was gay," said Marcia, taking a seat at the edge of the bed.

"We've been together many times," said Rance. "Perhaps he's a straight man who loves bottom-love. On the other hand..."

"What?"

Rance leaned over and whispered something into Marcia's ear.

Casey arrived at Marcia's a few minutes early. She sat him down at the kitchen table.

"I caught Porifiro with Rance."

"*What?*"

"In a very compromising and submissive position."

"No way. He's totally a breeder."

"Yes way. I saw him."

"Fire him."

"I'm just gonna ignore it," said Marcia. "Let him have his privacy."

"I hate closet cases."

"You were one till you were twenty-eight!"

"And I hated myself."

"Here he comes. Don't say anything."

Porifiro knocked and let himself inside.

"Yo," he said.

"Porifiro, I heard you got reamed and rimmed by Rance."

"Casey, goddammit!" said Marcia.

"Wha...? I wouldn't get with that thing, that's for you two to do."

"Porifiro," said Marcia, "I saw you. You don't have to lie. You're among friends here, we won't say anything. You can even have regular nights with him. Casey and I will each give you one of our nights. Three for me, two for each of you."

Casey stood up, wan with indignance. "I am not giving up one of my nights to this fucking case!"

"Whoa, and I don't want no nights, I told you I'm normal. I don't go for that ole mud-tunnel shit, man, it's pussy for me all the way."

"Little fucking liar," said Casey.

"Stop it, Casey. Porifiro, what if we just never bring it up again, and you use Rance whenever he's free."

"Like I said, I don't go that way."

"Okay. Whatever you say. I don't like being lied to right to my face, though."

"*Casey*'s been lying to you," said Porifiro. "Ain't that right, man?"

"I don't know what you're talking about."

Porifiro said, "He tells you he runs that robot's diagnostic machine every day, but I know for a fact he don't do it more than maybe once a week."

"You shit."

"That true?" said Marcia.

"I don't know, mayb—"

"So you both lied to me."

"I ain't lying, just him," said Porifiro.

"Forget about it, now why don't we just move along, we need to talk about Mr. Jeffs tonight—"

"I oughta get up and kick your faggot ass, man."

"Go for it, queer," said Casey.

"Porifiro," said Marcia, "I can't believe you said such a thing. Apologize to Casey. And you apologize, too, Casey."

"You ain't my fucking mother."

"You're fired, Mr. Mirrin," said Marcia.

"Good, gimme my pay."

"Out!"

Porifiro stomped off, slamming the door on his way out.

"I hate that guy," said Casey.

"Well, he doesn't hate you."

"What? What's that supposed to mean?"

"Rance told me that when he was with Porifiro, he kept calling Rance *Casey*."

"You... you're making that up."

"Go ask Rance."

"That bitch."

"Don't call him that!"

"I'll call him what I want."

"Say, why don't you take some time off."

"You're firing me, too?"

"I'm putting you on indefinite administrative leave."

"*Why?*"

"Because you're angry all the time, because you might be a little deceptive, because you're mean to Rance and call him names."

"Fuck you, Marcia Lathers Brodsky. I quit."

XIV

July 2003

Murphy was thirty-one when he learned about the Big Three. Knowledge of the Big Three gave Murphy, for the first time ever, a Purpose.

For the past four years Murphy had been laboring below poverty level as an unprized, overburdened book buyer at Crammed Shelf, a three-floor used-and-new-book shop wedged between a decrepit, poisonous health-food franchise and a parking garage on North Lamar not far from the Colorado River. His job consisted of evaluating stacks of books brought in by estate-sale agents, clerks from other bookstores, shoplifters, or cash-poor desperadoes certain that the James Pattersons and Dan Browns they'd pinched from their parents' bookshelves were worth at least a few dollars apiece. To perform the evaluations, Murphy simply multiplied the retail price of a book by .03 on a pocket calculator powered by a moody solar element that he had to go to a window to activate. One thing Murphy liked about his job was watching the exquisite variety of appall the human face was capable of expressing when offered sixty cents for a brand-new hardcover.

Another part of the job Murphy liked was Sousou, one of the weekday register operators. Cynical, gloomy, lazy, promiscuous, larcenous, well read, forgetful, brilliant, nippy, sexy, unhealthily crushed out on Bob Newhart, betrothed to a local Satanist, tattooed from earlobe to instep with wandering, particolored scrolls and long vines of mysterious rhetoric that crept beneath the cuffs of her cutoff overalls, then emerged from under the collar of her T-shirt and circled her neck a few times before disappearing into the hairline behind her left ear... Sousou was the bookshop's premiere draw, its nuclear glue, its anima, perfume, index, aurora, cortex; she was its mirth and gravity. She was also its fourth in command, reporting to a fierce but lovable Central American, who was in turn supervised by Embree, the general manager, who himself was puppeted about by the owners, Mmes Blake and Wintry, a pair of elderly lady "companions" whom no one had ever seen.

Embree was a tyrannical, endomorphic blowhard glazed with Joycean spectacles and piled with a spongy meadow of black chest hairs so springy that they made his partly unbuttoned Hawaiian shirts float an inch above his skin. Whenever he moved, his chest hairs audibly tickled the polyester in crinkly tones, which, to Murphy, sounded just like what frying bacon would sound like if frying bacon could stage-whisper. Murphy sometimes thought he would like to kill Embree. Murphy sometimes thought he would like to kill some customers. Murphy often thought he would like to fuck Sousou.

Embree decided each day when his employees would break for lunch. Today he decided Murphy's lunch would begin now, at 8:00 a.m., about fifteen minutes into his shift.

"Sous," said Embree, "eat when you want."

It was no secret that Embree also wanted to fuck Sousou. But Sousou apparently wanted to fuck only her betrothed, Mandune, a fellow no sensible person would ever cuckold: he had once pulled out his own pinkie fingernails so that he could get "Vlad the Impaler" and "Nostradamus" tattooed on the beds of exposed flesh. None of this mattered, though: Mandune or no Mandune, neither Murphy nor Embree was going to get any Lebanese pussy, ever.

"Clean the shitter first, Crockett," said Embree, pointing at the bathroom but staring at Sousou's thighs.

Murphy growled quietly; he didn't want Sousou to see him pissed.

On the way to the bathroom Murphy grabbed his *Once and Future King* lunchbox and a book he'd purchased yesterday from some penniless dipshit: *Wet, Set 'n' Slay*, by one Dr. Winnie Slarchj. It was about murderers. Serial killers, specifically.

Murphy read on the commode. Maybe the book would have a steamy passage he could masturbate to.

But no. Dr. Slarchj's book concentrated on what the thinkers at Quantico had known for years: that the childhoods of virtually all serial killers have three things in common: bed-wetting, animal-torturing, and fire-setting. Dr. Slarchj examined the twisted formative years of such giants in the field as Dahmer and Gacy and Bourke. She spoke with psychiatrists trained to watch for these despicable symptoms in children, in slim hopes of being able to prevent the formation of a serial killer. Did Dr. Slarchj offer any hope for future generations? Can one learn to not be a serial killer? Or was it a destiny, unalterable?

Yes, says Dr. Slarchj, it is one's lot.

Yes.

Murphy reviewed his life. Fires, check; bed-wetting, check; those Quince and Renée toads he'd killed. And countless insects. Check.

It was clear. Murphy had a purpose. A career. A meaning. An excuse. For the first time since Travis Waelder stole his pants at the playground in 1978, Murphy could *be*.

Murphy emerged from the bathroom, walked behind the cash wrap, and slapped Sousou on the ass twice, once per buttock. If Mandune sought to avenge the assault, Mandune would suffer bloody dispatch at Murphy's hands, maybe with his grandfather's war bayonet. Murphy, his hand buzzing from the force of the spanking, walked into the little office by the literary-journals wall, where he encountered Embree sitting, like a minor Caesar, cross-legged on the floor and squinting contentedly at a first edition of *In a Narrow Grave* that Murphy himself had bought from some ignorant relic for a dime. Embree looked up and was promptly advised by Murphy to go fuck himself. Murphy left Crammed Shelf for what was to be the last time.

* * *

A year later, Murphy Lee Crockett was watching out of a crack in his blinds for a delivery truck to pull into the parking lot of his apartment building, the Parallel Apartments.

Delivery trucks brought Murphy things all the time, mostly books he planned to resell. Today, though, he was expecting something special: Murphy had told the eBay cutlery vendor SlicenDicenJulian that he'd needed his reproduction Nazi dagger immediately, that's why he'd fucking used the fucking Buy It Now option of $29.95 and had also PayPaled an extra thirty bucks to pay for overnight shipping. But that had been four days ago; SlicenDicenJulian hadn't answered his emails, and no razor-sharp reproduction Nazi dagger with a spring-action Nazi flag feature had been placed in his hands by any of the great, heaving courier services.

Maybe when I get my dagger I'll just hunt the fucker down and lance him into little meat cubes.

Because Murphy didn't want to miss his package, he hadn't walked down to H-E-B for Rolos and pork skins, and he hadn't gone down to the mossy washing machine in the apartment complex next door to wash his underwear, and he hadn't gone over to the East Side to visit Granny in the Home. Granny had gone downhill over the last year, ever since he did the Take This Job and Shove It at Crammed Shelf. Granny had survived two recent mastectomies, and a bad, rib-snapping fall, and had confided in Murphy that she'd begun to cough up blood. She didn't have to tell him what that meant. She did make him promise not to tell the Home's doctor, and he had kept that promise: the sooner Granny died, the sooner he got his inheritance, whatever that might be.

A UPS van shot down the street in front of Murphy's apartment, disappearing around a corner.

He jumped up, opened the front door, leaned over the flaking iron balcony railing, and shook his fist.

"Where's my parcel, you United Parcel Service driver bastard! You have my dagger. I hate you."

The door to the apartment next to Murphy's opened and a young, wiry man of twenty-five or so, also in his boxers, emerged holding a bottle of Miller in one hand, and in the other a fierce little dog of mixed provenance. It barked.

"Stop shouting, man, you're freaking out Tom Mix."

"You shut up, Porifiro, or you'll be next."

Tom Mix barked and barked.

"*You* shut up."

"No, *you*."

"*You*, man."

"I hate Tom Mix and your beer and you, too, Porifiro."

"Man, you need to get laid. All that gnarly rage'd dry right up."

"I need my dagger, to stick in your ass."

"I know someone, Murphy Lee, she's fi-i-i-ne, and she likes independent-bookseller bachelors."

This was the third time Porifiro had tried to set him up with a girl. Maybe Murphy'd take him up on it one day. It had been a long, long time. Never, that's how long.

"I get plenty of pussy," said Murphy.

"Brother, you've never had a piece like this."

It was not clear to Murphy why Porifiro wanted to set him up. He didn't like Porifiro, and made that clear whenever he got the chance. Maybe he was just a nice person. No; more likely it was a way to get back at Murphy for the years of belittling and slander. Maybe the girl was a man, or had AIDS, or worse.

"Wanna see a picture, Murphy Lee?"

"Go stick Tom Mix up your ass!"

Murphy was just about to go back inside and slam the door when a big orange, white, and blue van pulled into the parking lot.

"Look, said Porifiro. "*Somebody*'s getting something."

"Me. Me."

Murphy ran down to the FedEx truck and danced lightly from toe to toe waiting next to the driver's door for the driver to climb down with his box. The driver was preoccupied with some kind of paperwork, and did not even look up. Murphy tapped on the window.

"Sir? Sir? Sir? You should have been here three days ago."

The driver opened his door. He had dark brown, unblinking eyes and hands like catchers' mitts. He held a single, thin, overnight express envelope in one mitt.

"Just a minute."

He scribbled on his clipboard. His pen looked like a thermometer in his huge hand.

"That's not mine," said Murphy. "Mine's thicker and at least a foot long, and..."

The driver glared down at him, eyes turning yellow-black. He bared his teeth.

"Say again."

It didn't sound like a question.

"My box?" said Murphy, beginning to jump up and down. "Please, god, don't tell me you don't have it."

"You Porifiro Mirrin?"

"No."

"S'me," said Porifiro, who had followed Murphy into the parking lot. Murphy's misfortune seemed to change in direct proportion to Porifiro's merriment. The driver gave Porifiro his envelope.

"Orestes Minoso," Porifiro said, transferring his beer to his Tom Mix hand so he could sign for the delivery. "Rookie card, *mint*. From eBay. Man, I motherfucking love eBay."

The driver slid his door shut with a crunch, put his truck in reverse, and began to back up. Murphy gathered up a handful of pecans off the pavement and threw them at the FedEx truck. The driver grinned at Murphy, put his truck in gear, and drove slowly away.

Murphy headed up to his own apartment, planning to make a couple calls and send a few emails to that larcenous eBay fascist. Porifiro followed him up, balancing his FedEx envelope on his fingertips, like a pie.

In front of Murphy's next-door neighbor's door paced a gray and black bobtail cat, yawning and meowing passively. Murphy'd seen it before. The door opened and the cat squeezed inside at the same time a young woman's head peeked out.

"Hi, Porifiro," said their neighbor, waving.

"Yo, April, how you doing?"

"Oh, you know."

"You come bang on this door if you need anything," he said.

"I will."

"Don't go bang on *his* door, though," he added, gesturing to Murphy. "He's liable to ruin your day."

Porifiro laughed and went inside.

Murphy knew this woman was a student of music at UT. German arias sung with significant pulmonary force often found their way into his apartment. And, somewhat incongruous to his idea of practitioners of classical music, the woman also seemed to collect boyfriends. She had so many that sometimes three- or four-way fistfights between them erupted in the parking lot. More than once Murphy had been awakened in the middle of the night by the sound of whimpering, which upon investigation turned out to be a rejected boyfriend prostrate before her door, an empty fifth of tequila at his feet, weeping about love and death and need, and trying to force his body under the door.

Such a scene hadn't played out in a while. Maybe she'd gotten religion or something. Or a steady boyfriend.

Murphy ignored her. He hated her for no good reason. Well, maybe because she never invited him over to fuck her like all those other guys. Murphy had often considered making her one of his victims, but attacking a neighbor was asking for trouble: what do cops do first after a crime? Canvass the neighborhood. And they'd knock on Murphy's door first. What if he couldn't keep a straight face? Or had overlooked a dot of blood or gore stuck to his forehead? Besides, she had the wrong name. It did not fit with the theme he'd chosen for his first serial-killing program.

"You're Murphous Lee Crockett, right?" said the neighbor.

Murphy looked at her, appalled to hear his given name spoken aloud. He'd seen her only at night, really, when he watched all his neighbors come and go, doing fun, social things. She was sorority blond, Dallas blond, beauty-pageant blond. She wore a long, faintly stained white T-shirt she'd probably slept in, and wore one of those intolerable yellow Lance Armstrong rubber bands around her wrist.

"Yeah..."

"I'm April," she said, slurring her words a bit, possibly from drink, probably from drugs. "A package came for you a few days ago, but they left it in front of my door. I should have given this to you earlier, but I kind of forgot about it. I was busy with a personal matter."

Murphy did not ask what that might be. She told him anyway:

"I just lost my child. After trying to get pregnant for more than a year. I'm not feeling well."

Murphy had encountered this type before, the one that immediately upon introduction unpacks level-three personal information, and often asks the same of her respondent.

"I'm... sorry," said Murphy, though a fuck not did he give.

"Thank you. She just came out, ten days ago, a little lump with eyes. It's my mother's fault. And my dad's."

"Oh."

"And Bryce's."

April disappeared back into her apartment, leaving the door open. Murphy walked up slowly. The cat poked its head outside for an instant, then ducked back inside.

"It's here, come on in," came her muffled voice. Murphy did.

A gapless tesseract of paintings and posters of classical musicians covered the walls, and the ceiling was decorated with a huge poster of an Eastern European peasant woman with her mouth open, obviously belting something out, perhaps *Matka, Maruša, Alois Hába*, which were the words printed along the top of the poster. In one corner stood a wicker bassinet on wooden wheels. In another, dozens—hundreds?—of cardboard Mutter's Crystal Lager six-pack totes were stacked, ready for recycling.

On a low futon lay a gigantic naked man, face up. A bust of Liszt tattooed on his chest stared up at a dormant, grime-caked ceiling fan.

"That's Ryan," she said. "Ignore him." She picked up a cracked jewel case of Phyllis Treigle's *Medea* and threw it at him. It bounced off his head with a pleasant tropical tympany, like a coconut. "He deserves to be ignored."

The cat was rubbing itself on Murphy's bare leg. Animals are supposed to be able to sense evil, thought Murphy. What the hell's wrong with this thing?

Murphy hissed at the cat. "I. Am. Evil!"

"And that's little Clavamox," said April. "She goes to the vet a lot."

"Mmm," said Murphy.

"I think I'm going to kill myself soon, maybe tomorrow."

"Uh, don't do that," said Murphy, worrying that this crazy chick might keep his package—his dagger, he hoped—if he offended her. "Just keep trying, you know."

April bent down and pulled a long box out from under a knot of disemboweled audio components and stringed-instrument strings. "And here it is."

She presented Murphy with a narrow, triangular cardboard box, more than four feet long.

It was a fairly heavy box, and solid—no movement inside. There was no reason to ship such a small thing in such a long box. Except to suck a higher handling/packing/shipping fee out of him. Greedy eBay hammerhead.

Ryan stirred. He rolled onto his side, drew his knees up to his chin, and threw up.

"God!" screamed April. "Pig!"

"I love you," said Ryan, barely.

"*You* poisoned my baby!"

"You're getting weirder, April, I just want…"

Murphy backed out, shutting her door behind him. The apartment building began to vibrate from a royal bitching.

Finally at home, Murphy shut the blinds, shed his tennis shorts and tighty-whities and T-shirt stained the color of Mountain Dew at the armpits, set up his card table, and placed upon it his diamond whetstones, his home-made calfskin strop, and the titillating box that loopy April had kept hidden from him, the whore.

He fetched a large, shrink-wrapped ham from the refrigerator, unwrapped it, and placed it on his futon. It sweated and dripped in Murphy's humid efficiency.

If the dagger was made of really good steel like SlicenDicenJulian said, then it should hold a nice edge. Murphy's plan was to sharpen the point and edges to Oriental keenness, then stab and slice at the pork ball—the very best simulacrum of the human corpus—over and over and over.

He began to carefully open the box; no point in tearing it open—he had all day to savor his new toy. Besides, he'd hang on to the box—he might be able to recycle it, if ever he needed to mail a severed limb to the FBI.

Murphy extracted a long object wrapped tightly in Bubble Wrap.

It was not a Nazi dagger. It was a Japanese sword.

He put it down. He stood up. He paced. Back and forth, from futon to potty. Then he stopped, lay down on the floor, and, *sotto screeche*, began to curse. "Liar. Cheat. Thief. Die."

He jumped up, sat down at his computer, and wrote a hate letter to SlicenDicenJulian. He left libelous feedback.

He linked to SlicenDicenJulian's other items for sale. He still had half a dozen Nazi daggers for sale, and he'd lowered the Buy It Now price to

$24.95. Murphy shouted at his iMac. Spittle dotted the screen, leaving it decorated with tiny, colorful buttons.

But SlicenDicenJulian also had another Japanese sword for sale, just like the one he'd sent Murphy. It was $1,299.95.

Murphy paused in his fury. Perhaps there had been a Bank Error in His Favor.

Murphy considered his sword. It was heavy. The hilt was sturdy, and wrapped in what looked like silk cords. It slid out of its sheath soundlessly. A beautifully wavy bevel line ran to the tip.

He tested the edge with his thumb, which opened up immediately; blood ran down the steel and dripped onto the stale, gray carpet. It had happened so quickly and painlessly Murphy thought it might be a joke, a self-detonating squib. But a closer look verified the red smile of a deep, oblique cut.

Murphy wasn't sure if he was going to be squeamish about the blood of others—he hadn't succeeded in actually killing or even harming anyone yet—but historically he was definitely squeamish about his own. And so he fainted.

When he awoke, he was lying next to his new sword. He did not look at his thumb, which complained with a deep laceration's particular, nauseating thump. He crawled into the kitchen, found a dish towel on the floor, and, with his eyes closed, wrapped up his thumb.

He stood carefully. He drank a pint of half-and-half. He ate six Advils. He ignored the blackening stain of blood his torted thumb had left on the dish towel. Okay. It would be okay.

He picked up his sword. Very carefully, he touched the edge with his other thumb. It opened up like the first one. He fainted again, woke up, found another dish towel, and bound up the almost hemophilially dripping gash, downed a pint of kombucha mushroom juice, and ate ten Advils.

He picked up his sword again. He could barely hold it without the use of his opposables. This time he just looked at the edge.

"The chosen people."

He moved one of his thumbs the tiniest bit, causing a sub-dermal tectonic shift. He nearly fainted again. It wouldn't do to fall on his sword.

He went to Porifiro's and kicked the door. Porifiro answered, looking peeved. Tom Mix barked and barked and barked.

"What're you nekkid for?"

"Look, help me put on my shorts and drive me to St. David's. I need stitches."

"What happened?"

"I cut myself on the sword I'm going to unman you with if you don't take me to the ER right this minute."

"That was a sword in that box?"

"You were watching me?"

"Yeah, man, that's my job here."

"It's sharp as a laser. Now c'mon!"

"I can't take you on my trike. You'll bleed on it."

"Get the keys to my Chevette, duh. They're next to the computer."

"You gonna owe me," said Porifiro, beginning to giggle.

Murphy was going to shout after him, *Don't touch my sword!*, but Murphy thought better—maybe Porifiro'd cut himself, too.

"Weren't you here a few weeks ago?" said the doctor or nurse or whatever the man examining Murphy's left thumb was. "You look familiar."

Murphy *had* been to the emergency room a couple of times in the last few months. This was his third visit, all for career-related injuries. So to speak.

"Concussion," said Murphy. "Twisted ankle."

"Right, right, you fell and hit the back of your head. Trying to kick something, right?"

Murphy had been trying to kick an old lady in the temple, but there had been an issue with precision, which sent Murphy to the linoleum in the old lady's kitchen.

"Yeah," said Murphy, staring flatly at the doctor's hypodermic needle. "Is that gonna hurt?"

"Pinprick."

He injected some kind of -caine into the meat of Murphy's thumb.

"Haah. Aah."

"Needle stick," said the other medical person, on his right. She stuck a hypodermic needle into his other thumb.

"Meeyi," said Murphy.

"I remember him now," the left medical person said to the right. "Maxine, remember, he was here the same day as the lady with the weird snelled dart in her ass?"

269

"Oh. Yeah." said Maxine. "That was the gnarl. I don't remember this dude here, though."

Murphy looked at his right thumb just as Maxine was lifting up the parabola-shaped flap, revealing flesh with the subtle marbling of toro sashimi.

"I'm going to throw up."

"What'd you cut yourself with? Fuck, there's no ragged edges at all. Buddy, what's *that* sharp?"

"Do not call me Buddy," said Murphy, swallowing his nausea.

"Not talking to you, dude," said Maxine, forcing a threaded semicircular needle into the parabolic flap.

"Only thing this sharp," said the other medical person, Buddy, "is an obsidian knife, like the Aztecs used to use to remove beating hearts from teen virgins. And maybe, maybe, some very special Japanese swords. Sit still. Both your cuts are almost identical. You some kind of performance artist?"

"Gon' barf."

"Come on, pal, you're completely anesthetized."

"Feel tug... tug... tugging. Tugging feeling."

"Wait a minute," said Maxine. "I think I remember this guy now. Is he the one who was in for a bumped funny bone? Yo, I checked the records afterward—he's the only person ever to be admitted for that."

"It was severely painful," said Murphy.

It had been. A few weeks earlier, late on a warm night, Murphy'd been perched up in a magnolia tree just outside the second-floor open apartment window of a woman named Jan Bardee whom he'd found on MySpace and had been following for two months, his homemade bamboo blowgun with its batrachotoxin-tipped dart perfectly trained on her sleeping body, enjoying his moment of truth, when his target unexpectedly woke, got out of bed, and began to walk out of the room. Afraid he wouldn't get another chance, Murphy quickly blew a dart; it stuck neatly into her left buttock.

Murphy had not been prepared for the magnitude of Jan's scream. It, in confederation with the tiny recoil of the propulsive blowing action, proved sufficient to tip Murphy backward off the magnolia branch and into space. His trip to the ground was fairly short but still ended in a great agony almost exclusively focused in his right funny bone, which he'd hit on a defunct, half-buried sprinkler head.

It turned out that the poison dart frogs Murphy'd bought at Herpeton, and from which he'd harvested his "poison," had been raised in captivity and had thus manufactured no toxins at all. They were merely dart frogs. Murphy had introduced no poisons into Jan's buttock, only harmless frog sap.

It had been his fifth murder attempt, and fifth failure. He was not a serial killer, but a serial failure. But there would be no more. Failures, that is. His new sword would assure the world of *that*. His sixth attempt would succeed. He would spend at least six months finding, researching, and stalking her.

Maxine finished her stitching and started to wrap up his thumb. Then she put on a splint and wrapped that up, too.

Buddy was still tugging at his needle and thread.

"Aieee," said Murphy.

"C'mon, now."

"I have a low pain threshold,"

"Tell me about it," said Maxine and Buddy at the same time.

Buddy finished up, wrapping his right thumb up as Maxine had.

"How *is* that old funny bone?" asked Maxine.

"Fine," said Murphy. Truthfully, it still hurt sometimes, and the last two fingers on his right hand always felt buzzy.

"That's wonderful," said Maxine. "Keep your thumbs elevated. I'm gonna write you two scripts: for pain and infection. Be careful now. Don't want to see you in here for a brain freeze."

Maxine and Buddy laughed. They both patted Murphy on the back.

"Take care, little guy," they said.

Assholes. They'd obviously never had a really serious brain freeze.

In the waiting room Porifiro was asleep in a chair. Murphy kicked him in the kneecap.

"You look like a man on a runway directing planes with orange flashlights," he said.

"Shut up. Take me to Walgreens."

Back at his apartment, Murphy contemplated the ham on his futon. Flies had already found it.

His hands throbbed. He took a couple of codeinated Tylenols, and waited patiently while they took effect. He began to feel light and confident. He pulled the sword out of its sheath. With both hands he raised it over his head. He would've preferred to be able to bring it down with the force of a

Tudor executioner, but he couldn't, with his thumbs in the state they were in. So he just let the weapon fall.

It slipped through the marionberry-julep-smoked H-E-B bone-in ham like it was an aspic, quailing the accumulation of meat flies, which promptly settled again on the two halves. The sword had sunk into his futon, down to the beechwood frame, where it lodged. Murphy worked it out, carefully wiped it clean on his boxers, and sheathed it.

"I shall call you Zordmurk," said Murphy, kissing his sword.

He lay down on his futon with Zordmurk and the ham.

He should've thought of the sword method sooner. It was so much more elegant than a stupid blowgun. Or any of his other serial-killing attempts.

The first "victim," a lawyer named Peter Bradley who specialized in Chapter 11 (farmers) bankruptcy and who, a month's worth of tailing would reveal, liked to hire plump, red-haired hookers to visit him at work after hours. He had opened his office door one evening, probably expecting to see his escort, but had instead beheld Murphy, dressed in black, fully balaclavaed, and armed with a halberd acquired at a Renaissance Faire in Buda. Murphy, similarly, had not expected Peter Bradley to answer the door fully chain-mailed, with the exception of a hypnotically tumescent, cobra-like penis sticking out of the chain-mail's fly. For a moment or two, both men regarded each other in curious silence. Then Murphy jousted, but Peter's heavy, tight-linked mail repulsed the replica halberd. Murphy ran away; behind him, Peter, furious, screamed something about "recent surgery." Later Murphy read, in *News of the Weird*, that an Austin lawyer who'd donated a kidney and then suffered a near halberd stabbing, damaging his remaining kidney, had successfully sued to get his old kidney back, rendering the former donee dead. Though through Murphy's actions a man had died, Murphy could not smell the coppery glory of the slaught; he smelled only the familiar halitosis of utter failure that so befouled every single goddam thing he tried.

Murphy's second intended victim, a collector of math texts, had approached Murphy at his booth at a book-and-ephemera fair asking if he happened to have a copy of Volume 141, No. 3 of the *Annals of Mathematics*.

"With Wiles's proof?" said the collector, a little old lady of the gentian-violet-haired tribe. She clasped her hands in antiquarian anticipation.

"Does it *look* like I carry math magazines?" Murphy said, gesturing at his stock of modern fiction. "I have only perfect copies of the very best literary firsts, MacLean, Crichton, Crouch, Bach, Ros, Waller, etc. Math is neither literary nor collectible, no offense. Go ask one of the many minnow-mongers stinking this book fair up."

"Oh," she said. "I see. Well, we must be content to disagree. May I leave you my name? Just in case you come across one?"

Murphy huffed mightily.

"Fine."

She dug around in her little-old-lady purse, located a Tiger Mart receipt, scribbled thereon, and handed it to Murphy.

Cynthia Braden
3903 North Loop
City, 78751
455.6702

"This is your real name?"

"Why, yes. Oh, I forgot to mention I will pay up to a thousand dollars for a good copy."

This got Murphy's attention. He would ask Granny if she knew about this stupid magazine. Maybe she even had one.

And she did. She *had* owned the *Annals* going back to about 1940.

"But those burned up after somebody forgot to clean the lint filter," she said, looking peeved and uncomfortable at her forty-five-degree angle of repose in the big, adjustable sick-person bed. "I had to start again. That issue's probably in the attic. Don't make a mess."

"I won't! Jeez!"

"What do you want it for, anyway?"

Murphy explained that he wanted to loan it to someone.

"A woman? Murphy, have you got a special lady friend?"

"No way!" An image of himself doing it with Cynthia Braden, her pink bun rhythmically whacking a headboard, came unsolicited. He shuddered. "Never!"

"What about that darling Arabic girl at..."

"Granny!" Murphy had never told her he'd quit Crammed Shelf to become a serial killer.

"Well, you make durn sure you get that journal back."

Granny began to cough, jiggling her "boobs." She'd had her second mastectomy a few weeks before, and had taken to wearing, beneath her rather snug nightgowns, prostheses that Murphy estimated, based on his deep acumen of internet porn, to be at least double-Ds, and, given the slight lag between a boob's action and its reaction, he suspected they were composed of a heavy material such as silicone. If Granny wanted to spend the rest of her meager life with a nice rack, more power. Murphy wondered what they cost. He wondered what they looked like. He wondered what they felt like. Were they just water balloons in a bra? Or were they stuck to her somehow, installed beneath some skin grafted from her ass? Or maybe they just hollowed out the originals and filled them with something else, turducken-style. Could a fellah put his dick between them? Cameth then an image, also unsolicited, and just as unwelcome, of himself in a jiggly three-some with Cynthia and Granny. Murphy clawed at his face and groaned.

"Oh, stop that, Murphy Lee," said Granny, reaching for a bottle of water on her bedside table. "Open this for me."

Murphy did. She took a long drink, right from the bottle. When she put it down, Murphy noticed that the water was tinted red.

"Jesus, Granny, you're bleeding."

"I—"

"Is that from coughing?"

"No, it's—"

"It is."

And so began a short ado that ended when Murphy agreed not to tell Dr. Moutmelth about her lung-cancer symptom, and in exchange Granny agreed to transfer Volume 141, No. 3 of the *Annals of Mathematics* into Murphy's permanent custody. Win-win, psych!

Just around dusk on a hot night some days later, Murphy paid Cynthia Braden a visit. She greeted him with delight, made him a cup of tea, wrote him a check for a thousand bucks, accepted the valuable journal, turned away, and began to rifle through her kitchen cabinets, where she was sure she had stored some peach preserves; at this instant Murphy stood up, clicked his heels together, which caused a four-inch stiletto to spring from the toe of his right shoe, took sight of Cynthia's right temple, stepped back, wound up, kicked, and missed, succeeding only in ruffling her gentian-violet bun with the gentle breeze of failure. The momentum of the unexpected follow-through (1) disengaged Murphy's knife shoe, which went sailing out an open window into the night, and (2) spun Murphy 270 degrees while his left foot remained stationary, twisting his knee and ankle and sending him to the floor, which greeted him with a concussion.

Cynthia brought him to the hospital, evidently without ever having any idea what might have been.

Her check bounced.

The third "victim," Bobby Brudi, whom he'd found listed in an old-fashioned paper phone book in probably the last phone booth in Texas, was a "technical stylist" at Trim and Pluck, a depilatory spa in North Austin near the I-183 overpass at Burnet Road that specialized in Hollywood waxes for men. Inspired by a trademark method of an infamous hit man, Murphy decided he would dispatch Bobby with a squirt of cyanide salts right in the face. After getting ripped off a dozen times by internet cyanide dealers trawling for desperate dupes on provocative suicide websites, Murphy finally got lucky, receiving genuine cyanide salts in the mail for less than fifty bucks. He prepared a small spray bottle of the salts dissolved in acid, put on his standard black beard, sunglasses, and ball cap disguise, allowed himself to be waxed by Bobby—easily the most excruciating pain of his life—then tried to squirt him, but the nozzle was aimed sideways so nobody got offed. Murphy bolted to his car hidden behind the strip mall and drove off, his crotch still screeching helplessly at its recent brimstone rapine.

Murphy's fourth attempt was an actual firearms assault on a certain Grady Gregg, a bouncer, ID-checker, and noted asshole, whose shift at Antone's ended around 3 a.m., at which time, Murphy had discovered after several weeks' surveillance, the man would walk to a dark, deserted street corner nearby, the same one every time, lean against the street lamp there, light and smoke a cigarette in a rapid, assholey, cool-gesture-polluted way. Murphy planned to extinguish this Grady Gregg in an AK-47 strafing from his Chevette parked forty yards away. But when the time came, Murphy missed with every single shot in his thirty-round magazine. Later, in his apartment, Murphy disintegrated the disappointing instrument with a hacksaw and sledgehammer, and, as a final rain of disrespect, threw its fragments into the tub and urinated on them.

* * *

No more. The next victim, whom Murphy Lee Crockett would start looking for tomorrow, would die, maybe sooner, maybe later, but definitely, and definitely in pieces. It would be his first try at up-close, blood-spurting despatch.

PART TWO

XV

June 2004

Justine had now been at the Frito Motel for more than a month. She watched her bank account drop and credit-card balance rise, weekly, by the price of two Mr. Gatti's three-topping pizzas or a Sonic #2 Combo or a twelve-pack of Dr Pepper cans plus forty dollars cash back. She visited Amy the desk clerk once a week to tell her she was staying, and she called Middling Car Rentals in New York every two weeks to renew her car lease. She collaged, she slept, she masturbated, she contemplated suicide, she rented movies from I Heart Video, she bought books at Crammed Shelf about pregnancy and childbirth and abortion and adoption. She solved Black Belt Sudoku with a rapidity and accuracy that made her wonder whether she had found something she was good enough at that she might take it up professionally, become wealthy from international tournament wipeouts, and famous and lovable for her humble beginnings, so famous that she appeared on an episode of *Letterman* that Livia and Charlotte happened to see and which made them feel awful and guilty and penitent.

One morning Justine parked on Threepenny Street in front of the house she'd been conceived in, thirty-five years ago. Where Livia had screwed her three-day husband, Burt, and gotten Justine started.

A flat ranch, small and brittle-looking. Torn screens, cracked windows, clots of mud-dauber nests stuck to the gutters.

Justine knocked. When nobody came to the door, she took the hot, corroded doorknob in both hands and twisted, but it wouldn't move. After a careful look around the seemingly dead and unpeopled neighborhood, Justine climbed over the iron railing at the end of the porch and dropped into the weeds. She felt her way around the perimeter. In the back was a large window, partly open.

She climbed inside, finding herself in the kitchen. A ray of sun illuminated the stirred-up dust motes. She headed toward the east end of the tiny house, pausing every few steps to see if anything felt familiar. Nothing did.

A closed door. Justine pushed. It opened soundlessly into a small room, the walls pierced with hundreds of thumbtacks, some pinning down torn corners of paper. From the ceiling hung a fan, one of the ornate, shoddy fake antiques you can buy nowadays at Home Depot for thirty bucks. The room was emotionless, without personality, memory, import.

A bed—a made twin bed—sat in the middle of the room. Red, white, and green comforter, lacy bed skirt, healthily fluffy pillows leaning against the headboard. Surely not the original bed, the one in which the regrettable conception must have occurred thirty-five years ago. Burt, no longer Livia's obscure and revered three-day hubby, but Justine's fucking *dad*. A few moments of newlywed flailing, and Justine was started.

Justine mourned for her stupid, naive self. For disfigured Quentinforce. For her soulless, hateful *real* mother. For her weakling *real* grandmother. For dead Burt. For insane Betsey, who was not her mother, but who loved her.

No one would hear her threnody here. She wrecked her throat with dry screams at the airless, dirty box broken up with a perfectly ordinary bed and sophisticated with a shitty fan.

Justine left, feeling like she'd committed a rape.

In the afternoon she drove to her old neighborhood. She turned down an alley. Unlike much of the city, this alley was unchanged. As was the next, and the next, and the next. Soon she was in her old alley.

It was not much changed either, but the yellow Camaro was gone. It had apparently been taken away long ago; there was no evidence that a car of any kind had been there.

Justine idled by the Camaro's old spot.

She got out and crawled to the fence, where she found a three-inch gap. Justine chamfered her fists into her eye sockets. She bit her cheek and issued a low, private growl of resolve.

Something growled back. Justine noticed racing toward her across the lawn the soggy black muzzle and pork-pink tongue of a graying, incontinently excited pug dog. Justine willed herself to look only at her dog; she wasn't quite ready to scan the back of the house for the wandering, smoking figure of her grandmother. She put her hand through the fence; Dartmouth instantly demerged it with stringy slop.

She thought about kicking out a slat and stealing him so they could live at the Frito together, but Dartmouth remembered something and evacuated the yard in a sandy blur.

She glanced. Just a sliver of an instant, and then fists back in the sockets, but a glance nonetheless. The Château Frontenac, visible in the moonlight. Overgrown yard. Charlotte's picture window. In the window, the edge of Charlotte's table. And the old refrigerator. The same one, with rounded corners and a big handle shaped like a 7. Something about the quality of the light inside suggested it was just Charlotte and Dartmouth who lived there, that she had never married. But today no Charlotte was in evidence.

Justine got into her car and drove back to the motel. Inside, she undressed, reached for the remote, and turned on the weather. She pointed and fake-clicked the remote at various imperfections in the Room—the blinds, which, infuriatingly, never quite closed, the lampshade vaguely smeared with a fawn paste, the derailed sliding closet door, her belly, and, in the corner over the closet, the small flag of soiled, artificially linen-grained wallpaper that had recently peeled away from the wall and was now flopped over itself like a Rottweiler's ear.

Maybe there was spatter on the walls behind the wallpaper. Justine wished she'd been one of the victims. Being a murder victim was one of Justine's principal nonerotic fantasies (along with auto-da-fé, post-Armageddon survival, and being the world's first trillionaire so she could help defeat AIDS and malaria and order all the billionaires around). Murdered: so many problems that would solve!

Justine watched the wallpaper ear for a blinkless minute. She fell asleep. In the morning she went downstairs.

"There's a book on it," said Amy, whose ring and middle fingers were splinted together with an apparatus of sheet metal and blue foam. "I can't remember what it's called. The pictures are really nauseating. I can't look at it."

"I need the book about the murders at the Frito Motel, please," said Justine, addressing the man behind the welcome counter at Crammed Shelf Books.

"Bag," he said. On his wrist a bruise-like tattoo of a crucified grotesque was uttering something in Latin.

"Bag... of Fritos?" said Justine. "No, murder. Motel Frito. Book, about. It."

The welcome man lowered his eyelids until one eye was just barely open, like someone under general anesthesia. Then he snapped awake and pointed at Justine's big, brand-new straw purse, which she'd bought as a consolation after her screamy meltdown at the house on Threepenny Street. A costly, fettering consolation from Urban Outfitters.

"*Bag.* Check your *bag.*"

"Oh."

Justine handed him her purse, and he gave her a laminated tarot card (two of cups) with a clothespin stuck to it.

"Title."

"Uh, well..."

"Author?"

"I..."

"Genre? Publisher? ISBN? Editor? Color? Format? Thickness? Odor?"

"All I know is that it's about the Frito murders..."

"No such occurrence. No such book."

"It's over there," a voice behind her said.

Justine turned. Behold, an extraordinary creature, dressed in white shorts and a red-and-blue-striped FC Belize shirt, pointing into the distance like a sylph in a bas-relief by Saint-Gaudens.

"In the true crime section," said the extraordinary creature. "Behind the papoose straps. Author's Witt MacKaraher."

"You think you know everything, Rose," said the welcome man, a subtle, die-sunk anger in his eyes. "You haven't even been here six months."

"You don't even know where fiction is, Matt," said Rose, who then turned toward Justine. "I've been here seven months, just so you know. Follow me."

Justine did. At the back wall of the first floor, near the elevator, the extraordinary creature Rose crouched down and pulled a paperback off a bottom shelf.

"This is what you want. Check out this guy's crazy haircut."

Rose flipped to a fuzzy halftone photo in the middle of the book and showed it to Justine.

"Gilley Dade," said Rose. "I went to Austin High with him, in the mid-nineties. Heard of him?"

"Me, I'mn hisoom. Him. Rhoo. Oom."

"His room? At the Frito?"

"Yp."

"That's creepy. Does it smell like blood?"

"Np."

"The murders were awfully gruesome. Here, the book tells it all. Start at the beginning. What's your name, anyway?"

"Justine."

Rose smiled, said Justine's name, and disappeared.

Justine was just about to sit on the floor to look at the pictures but realized that Rose might disappear forever before she got another look at her. She might clock out and then decide on her way home to quit Crammed Shelf without notice and move to Oatmeal, Texas, or maybe she'd get seduced in the parking lot by a magnificent stranger and embark on a shut-door, phones-off, windows-blacked erotic safari and then marry him, or maybe she'd get the flesh-eating disease later today and be too ashamed of the ravages of the bug's predation to engage the public or jump into a long-term affair with anyone ever again.

With her book in one hand Justine paced the aisles, looking for the Pernambuco hue of Rose's skin or the red/white/blue of the weird, shiny soccer ensemble, all the while trying to avoid squashing underfoot any of the unpredictable members of a modest plague of crickets that had colonized the store.

"Rose works in receiving," said a voice behind her. Justine turned around. Matt. "She only comes downstairs to annoy me, or to try to set me up with somebody. Rose thinks she's a matchmaker."

"Oh, I'm not looking for her. I'm—"

"Of course you are. Everyone is. I can tell."

"No, I'm—"

"You can't go up to receiving. You'll have to wait until Rose's shift is over."

"Wh—"

"Nine."

"Is she—?"

"Not a she."

"*You* said 'she.'"

"I am not an unprivileged out-country gawk—"

"I'm *from* Austin. Why are you being mean? I don't even kn—"

"—like yourself."

"Do you—"

"Rose does not—"

"—ever let anyone finish a sentence?"

"—ID. And you should've known the title and author of your book before you came in."

"IthinkyouhaveacrushonRose," said Justine. "That's what I think."

"I like girls, not dykes or men or ungendered persons. Or butter-haired women."

"I am not butter-haired. My hair is 'wheat.'"

"Butter."

"Oh. Okay. I'm going to sit down now."

"Rose is in a relationship. Go home to your crime scene."

Justine could never be a lawyer. She never won arguments or contests of wits or verbal recontres. She couldn't yell very well or hurl clever invectives or even tell jokes. She hated Matt because he was mean and because she couldn't tell him go to hell like she wanted to. She could only turn red and steamy and say: "No."

She plugged her ears against whatever riposte Matt was composing and ran off to find a comfortable spot in which to pass the next four hours.

She found a chair, sat down, and opened the book at random. The imagery made her quickly forget about Welcome Matt. It even made her forget about Rose.

It was a mug shot of a grinning, blood-soaked Gilley Dade. He was wearing his apparently infamous bird-of-paradise hairdo—seven inches tall, according to the height chart on the wall behind him. And opposite the mug shot was a photo of the inside of a room, #233, according to the caption. Her room, at the Frito. The walls were covered in professional-wrestling posters that were in turn covered in blood. The floor was disordered with uncategorizable lumps of some kind, also glazed in blood. At the bottom of the page was a gallery of four separate pictures, a woman and three men, all unnamed. The woman was shelved with muscle and snarling with thespian menace. The three men were distinguishable only by Vandyke density.

Justine had always thought there was a property of photographs of people that, even out of context, communicated the subjects' current vital status. Justine was sure that the four people at the bottom of the page were no longer vital, and she thought it fairly likely that they were the ones who sourced all the blood and lumps.

Justine hunted through the rest of the pictures looking for more shocking stuff, or at least something explanatory, but apart from a kind of blurry image of a cop dangling a shiny brown sawed-off shotgun from his pinkie by the trigger guard, most of the pictures were of florid deputies, sleepy judges, unhinged relatives, and silvered-haired, fiftyish attorneys with neat parts and open mouths half obscured by bubbly fences of reporters' microphones.

Justine would have to read the damn book to find out what had happened.

Before she started she checked the clock on the wall over the elevator that Rose would emerge from after the shift. Justine sighed to calm the whipping butterflies between her lungs, then began.

According to the book, Gilley Dade, along with his girlfriend, Kate the Chin (née Heather Keeton), the semiprofessional wrestler well known and deeply unloved for her ability to reduce to a crawling shiver even the gristliest of opponents by lustily driving her mallet-hard chin like a wedge into their bodies, had enterprised to make a few extra bucks by renting a room at the Renaissance Hotel downtown and inviting people to drop by and, for a fee, either wrestle Kate, bet on the outcome, or both. Gilley, her manager, advertised only by word of mouth.

Apart from having to find a new hotel room somewhere in Austin every few hours (due to evictions or environmental breakdowns), their enterprise was working out great.

But Kate, unbeknownst to Gilley, had begun another venture. It was similar to her and Gilley's racket, except Kate's venture added nakedness and sex: if you beat her, you were allowed to do it with her. She occasionally faked a loss if she was wrestling a cute guy, partly because Gilley was rotten in bed and smelled like pickle juice, and partly because an occasional defeat would bring in the business.

Kate hosted matches just once or twice a week, on her days off, in out-of-the-way motels, with clients she was sure had no knowledge of her "day" job with Gilley. But as her venture became popular, it seemed inevitable that Gilley would find out.

So she decided to quit—after one more match.

Of course, Gilley did find out. And he drove out to a little back-lot hut on Burleson Road where his granddaddy had collected a stash of guns and fertilizer-bomb materials for the Texas secession bloodbath he was planning. Gilley picked out a greasy break-action, then sawed the barrels off so close to the chambers that the shotgun was really more of a directional mine. He pulled one arm out of his T-shirt and lifted the bottom hem over his shoulder. In this improvised baby sling he wrapped a hundred buckshot shells. Then he drove out to the Frito.

Kate had also added required nudity to her big match, so when Gilley crashed through the window of the motel room (instead of blasting open the door—he wanted to use as many shells as possible on soft targets), he was met with a room full of men with boners pointed at the sweat-primed interlocking of Kate and a certain fellow later identified by a shoe as one Kurt Kane.

The book analyzed in detail the facts of the two or three minutes that followed Gilley's ingress. Justine was disgusted with her lust for these details, but she didn't stop reading. Later, all she really recalled was that there were four fatalities—Kate and the three similar men—but that the dozen or so survivors had lost limbs and parts and chunks while escaping. Kate and the three unlucky men had been shot over and over, dozens of times, so that very few recognizable human elements remained.

Eventually Gilley ran out of recognizable targets and so took off east down Concordia Avenue until he found refuge in a forsythia bush. But it was false harbor; he was easily caught because of the trail of blood. Gilley was now on death row. In Texas, a state that liked to execute. Gilley would not be around much longer.

Justine looked up. It was 9:22. She was sure she hadn't missed Rose coming out of the elevator. Or had she?

"You missed her," said Matt, catching Justine jog-walking through the aisles.

"I don't like you."

"Here's your tacky bag. Gimme back the tarot card."

Justine headed home to the Frito Motel to lament and examine her room more closely, and perhaps peel some wallpaper.

But when she arrived, she simply lay on the bed and went immediately to sleep. She dreamed of hummingbird eggs, of David Beckham, of pools of melted iron a hundred thousand miles deep, of horses made of grass, of stalled and crowded freight elevators, of crushed ice in empty Dr Pepper mugs. Of Mariarosa Balaguer, bookseller.

There was no way Justine was going to go back into that store to be molested by Matt or to get caught sneaking glances at Rose, by Rose. And since there was no practicable spot from which to spy on the front door to wait for Rose to emerge, Justine decided she would first find Rose's car—if she had one—with the idea of secretly following her home after she got off work. Justine's courtship methods had always centered around the discipline of gentle, distant stalking, so the plan seemed comfortably consonant.

Of course, she had to find Rose's car. Justine was pretty sure that retail employees were required by the retailer that employed them to park as far away from the entrance of the store as possible so as not to fill a parking spot that might be taken by a viable shopper who otherwise might flee to another store and spend their money there. And since Justine was sure Rose was a responsible employee, possibly even devoted, Justine began her search for Rose's car at the remotest reasonable location: the top tier of the Crammed Shelf/HealthMuffin: Organic Grocery Adventureland parking garage.

The structure's aphelion car was a college-guy Jeep arched with roll-bars and macho-ed with a fluorescent Titty Bingo bumper sticker. Justine continued on, watching for an automobile whose form was taking shape so quickly in her mind that by the third tier she was certain that it couldn't be anything but a dented light-blue Celica on a pronated chassis, its paint all sun-crisped and its tires so treadless from wear they looked like

Scooter Pies; *futbol* bumper stickers and, should Justine dare to get out and look, blankets and shoes and soccer balls in the backseat. In the front, on the floor, tapes. Not CDs, tapes. Caseless, tantalizingly unidentifiable TDK-60s.

No such car appeared, nothing even similar, and soon the garage disgorged Justine and her Meagre. She went home and tore off the exorbitantly cute Urban Outfitters smock she'd bought just in case she ran into Rose by surprise, and placed it on top of the TV.

The next day, the same outfit, the same grade-school-caliber stalking, the same unbreathable disappointment. She came home to the same frond of peeling wallpaper, the same talcy knoll of poison in the ashtray, the same long night of TV's engineered realities.

The following week, all the same. Rose obviously had no car, or else something *had* happened to her. Maybe Justine had even caused Rose's misfortune simply by imagining it. Hopefully it wasn't the flesh-eating disease—that really seemed unbeatably awful.

On Bastille Day, instead of constructing a fetching outfit, Justine stayed in bed. She reached down and grabbed a big Jerry's Artarama bag off the floor and dumped the contents into her bedspread-covered lap. Foam board, glue sticks, squeeze bottles of rice starch paste, Rapidographs, a spectrum of gray Pantones, rulers, razor blades, a lazy Susan, silhouette scissors. Another big bag contained a bunch of magazines she'd quarried from the Dumpster of a big Half Price Books on South Lamar. She poured these out next to her and began to thumb through them, snipping out bits of red and white imagery she planned to accrete into an abstracted bloodbath with overtones of youthful, Milton Bradley–style innocence. It was to be a hinged mourning diptych to go on top of the TV. It would take, Justine figured, about two weeks to complete, during which time, she promised herself, she would exorcise Rose, she would forget her stupid family, and she would decide about the baby's life. And her own.

Just thinking about the import of the collage made Justine sad and tearful, and this impaired the surgical temperament needed for magazine snipping; she accidentally pared off a tiny spear of thumb cuticle.

"Ow," said Justine, even though it hadn't hurt at all. "Ow."

A rapid knock came at the door, and then keys in the lock. The door opened four inches and then stopped at the length of the chain.

"Oh, sorry, no sign on the door," said a dark eclipse that blocked out half the light from the sliver of open door. "Okay?"

Justine didn't move. Usually when the maids came by, an instinctive spasm of modesty caused her to pat at her messy hair, draw up the covers, turn the channel to something neutral, smile in divine serenity, or anything else that made it seem she was at the pith a demure but efficient regent of her little motel realm rather than her real persona, which Justine had lately been imagining as a guilt-clamped, sod-dwelling creature with lots and lots and lots to hide.

"Washrags? Soap bars? Tissue?"

"No, thank you," said Justine, grinning like a sweating serial masturbator.

"Sugar Babies? I found a whole box left by someone in 227."

"No, thank you."

"I'm new. I'm Lacey. They told me you been here awhile."

"Hi."

"Don't forget to put your placard out next time."

With a little wave Lacey pulled the door shut. Justine relaxed. With care not to disturb her piles of glossy red and white fragments excised from *Marie Claire*, *Bizarre*, *Gol Nogomet*, *World Domination Sudoku Swimsuit Issue*, and *Knit Praxis*, Justine climbed out of bed, put out the placard, and did up the other two locks. She tinkled, got a Dr Pepper out of the her ice-filled Styrofoam chest, wiped off some greasy mare on the TV that had been smearing about an eighth of the screen since she'd moved in and that had been driving her crazy but never seemed worth getting up to clean and besides was kind of disgusting, then got back into bed.

Then somebody knocked again. Justine got up and looked out the window, expecting to see Lacey's hamper-wagon, but it was not in evidence. The placement of the window revealed only the edge of a blue-rayon-cloaked shoulder blade and a white, shorts-covered buttock. An excellent white buttock, thought Justine. Incomparable. Well, that's just great. Now Justine would have to avoid Lacey in order not to fall in lust with her, muddying further her already well-muddied emotional psychology. And what if she fell in love? That would be devastating.

Justine noticed a car down in the parking lot. A Jeep. A college-guy Jeep. Pink and green neon letters on the back bumper confirmed the vehicle to be the same one that lived on top of the Crammed Shelf parking garage.

A knock again, hard.

Justine grabbed the phone and ran and hid behind the bed. She was going to be killed by a UT football monster who had obviously seen her eyeing his Jeep. She grabbed her scissors, holding them dagger-like over her head.

The college guy's fist hammered at the door.

Justine was about to dial 911 but it was not at all clear how to do so on the complicated hotel-room telephone. So she called the lobby.

"Amy," Justine hissed. "Someone's trying to get in. Call the police."

"Who is it?"

"Justine. Moppett."

"No, I know that, who's at the door?"

"I don't know."

"Maybe a copycat killer," said Amy, gorgeously excited. "A lot more common than you'd think."

"Call the cops."

"We really will have to raise your rate if anything happens to you."

"Help," said Justine, dropping the phone, climbing on the bed, and banging on her neighbor's wall.

"Justine?" shouted a voice at the door. "Matt asked me to come by and tell you he's sorry. He's feeling bad about being mean. Don't be shy."

Justine stopped banging.

"Okay in there?"

Craft supplies and raw materials lay in wrinkled chaos all over the bed and the floor. The Dr Pepper had leaped off the side table onto the bed and was pooling around her feet and between her toes.

"I have to tell you something else, too. Open sesame."

"I'm glad you're still here," said Rose. "I figured you might've checked out already."

Justine and Rose sat on either side of a booth at the diner next door to the Frito. A quick, pleasant waiter named Wart (or at least that's how he was addressed by the outraged-for-obscure-reasons cook) sat down on Rose's side and took their orders for ice waters and cups of coffee and Texas toast and chorizo-potato-egg breakfast tacos. Justine ordered a cold Dr Pepper in a can for herself. She had been so looking forward to the one that, during the short peril a few moments earlier, had been irreversibly leached by her motel bed.

"Matt's not so bad usually," said Rose, biting off half of a taco, chewing twice, and swallowing. "But he confessed to me he was kinda mean to you. And that you had never come back."

Justine stared at the extraordinary creature before her. This was a prank of some kind, or a mistake, or a parallel fantasy universe that would fold over on itself and snap into infinite disappointment at the same instant it convinced Justine of its reality.

"He's just mad because of the last girl I set him up with," said Rose, vanishing the other half of the taco. "I eat fast, I know, I'm in trouble with everybody for it, especially my aunt Olympe. I'm just hungry. I wait too long to eat, and then overcompensate."

"I don't mind," Justine managed to say. She added, in a sort of hemi-sequitur, "I like junk food and candy."

Justine noticed that Rose had skin a shade or two darker and warmer than that of Sugar Babies. She would have to ask Lacey if she had any left.

"Anyway, in spite of himself I think Matt may have done us a favor," said Rose, slicing open another taco and flooding it from stem to stern with habanero Tabasco.

The words *us* and *favor* elevated Justine from a state of agitated confusion to one of hopeful agitated confusion. Rose took another big shark bite of taco, and smiled in a Mona Lisa way. Justine recalled that at one time a theory that the real Mona Lisa might have been a man had gained some merit among scholars. She smiled back, rigidly self-conscious about what felt like it must be a whole patty of chorizo stuck to her front teeth.

"I guess we should start at the beginning," said Rose, using her forearm to squeegee away the table's spreading tide of ice-water-glass condensation. "Because no matter where you start, that *is* the beginning. Right?"

The mystery and improbability of the situation at hand, along with the shape of Rose's nose, were creating in Justine a sexual demand. It—Rose's nose—was regally wide across the bottom, saddling out to a parabolic low that seemed to invite one to roll little orbs of mercury off of it. Justine wished mercury wasn't deadly poison, because it really was sexy stuff.

"Right."

"Except for a few times when I was little, I never did any matchmaking," said Rose. "Those really early times all I did was marry bugs to spiders, toys to toys, weeds to flowers. It wasn't until I was seven that I first felt this weird urge. It was sudden and strong. I guess it's similar to how some seven-year-olds suddenly, desperately need to take ballet or own a lamb, but my urge didn't feel material. It was—and is still—an urge to make whole."

An obscure thing began racing around inside of Justine that might've been just smittenness but was probably a relay team of lust and need and hope and love and disbelief passing her heart off to one another like a baton. What a raw-bait tiger pit this Rose Balaguer visit was turning out to be. Visitation, more like. She did not seem like the kind of being who paid mere visits. If Rose appears before you, you are either in her grace or in deep trouble.

"Back then there was this grumpy old guy who ran a 7-Eleven in Laredo," Rose continued. "We called him Ivan, Uncle Ivan, though he wasn't my or Olympe's uncle. One day when I was in the store buying Lik-m-aid with a quarter I'd found, something in my seven-year-old head told me that Uncle Ivan was unwhole, and needed something to make him whole. Something else told me that that thing was Mrs. Ayers, my Sunday-school teacher."

Rose browbeat Ivan, a then-forty-six-year-old paradigm of the commitment-avoiding male, into going on a pizza-and-rollerskating date with Rose's freshly widowed catechism teacher. En route to the Skatodrome, the couple broke down and had to call Puny's Wreckers to tow their borrowed Volvo to a Swedish-car specialist in Beaumont. The tow-truck driver, one of the violinists in a three-string klezmer act, invited the couple to ride with him on the drive, as long as they didn't interrupt his song composing, a process that he felt creativity most favored when driving his tow truck. During an air-violin arpeggio, Hilyard, the driver, lost control of the wrecker, totaling it and the Volvo, and blamed the collision on Mrs. Ayers, who in turn blamed it on Ivan. This exquisitely rotten date graduated to pure enmity, with both Mrs. Ayers and Uncle Ivan blaming each other, for years, for the date's failure. However, Rose's aunt Olympe blamed the situation not on the fledgling marriage-bawd Rose, but on Rose's grandmother, a self-serving harridan who had tried to awaken the matchmaking talent she felt sure lay dormant in the child.

Not incidentally, it had been Olympe's Volvo the daters had borrowed.

"Come to find out," continued Rose, "the urge I'd felt was, specifically, the urge to match-make. Many people have it. My grandmother,

her mom, and her grandmother, etc., all were partly controlled by that particular gene."

Why at this moment Justine began to feel the black suck that only romantic doom can apply, she could not say. The "us" Rose had referred to earlier was not, Justine felt certain, the two persons in this diner booth.

"It wasn't your fault, then," said Justine, with a conversational steadiness that surprised her. "It's in your genes."

"That is right," said Rose, with a spank of indignance. "Matchmakers make matches. We guarantee nothing, and we aren't relationship counselors."

Rose stood up. She drank the rest of her water, and Justine's water, too. "You done?" she said. Justine nodded.

While Rose was at the register paying the bill, Justine picked up Rose's water glass and licked, inside and out, the place on the rim that had rested on Rose's lips. The immediate shame this lecherous act brought served to clarify the imprecise black sucking Justine had felt earlier. Though still wet and blurry, it was steadily precipitating into something well infused with a loneliness even deeper than the one in New York she'd recently fled. Once, while sitting at a free lecture on medieval tempera-painting techniques at the Morgan Library, Justine had been able to secretly masturbate by sitting in her chair, Indian-style, like now, and slowly rolling the heel of her Cydwoq shoe against her crotch. It had been a pretty damn good orgasm. She very seriously considered doing the same right now. It would take only a moment, given the effect of the mildly habaneroic flavor of the ice-water glass.

"C'mon, Justine," said Rose after she paid. "Let's go outside. It smells like sheep in here."

They sat out in the diner parking lot on one of those concrete logs sometimes found at the end of a parking spot. Justine finished her Dr Pepper and casually placed the can down as close as she dared to Rose's complicated, heavily laced soccer shoe. Justine wanted to hook a finger under the hem of Rose's green-silk soccer shorts and lift to see if the skin of her way-upper thigh was the same brown as the rest of her, or if there was a tan line, or what.

"You might be wondering what makes a match between two certain people!" shouted Rose, barely audible above the groaning, split-level roar of the interstate less than twenty yards away. "A good question. Okay: I have a large mental file of people I've met—I never forget a face or a disposition or a perfume or cologne or favorite book or coffee drink or pet. Or income or job or arrest record or anything else I find out about them."

Ah. That's why she's here. Duh. Rose was not here for Justine. Not really. She was here in blind agency of her own instinct; she had a match in mind for Justine, who now considered leaping into traffic to die.

"So when I meet somebody new, I run their profile against my database, looking for potentials. I always find at least one. But most never get off the ground, for practical reasons. Can't find someone, they're in jail, or Sweden, or dead. However, if they're in a relationship already, that won't stop me. If I get the bingo feeling, I have to act on it."

"Bingo?" Justine shouted.

With her traffic death pending, a sudden freedom to think what she wanted, no matter how ugly or depraved, was granted to Justine. The first thing she wondered was whether Rose wore a jockstrap. After all, Justine was still not certain what Rose was, what those shiny soccer shorts concealed. Agh. Why was lust so often attached to pain and death?

"Bingo. Like just when you're playing and waiting for the next number and they call I-20 or whatever and you get a step closer and then G-51 makes your Bingo. It's a thrill covered in suspense and uncertainty—maybe they made a mistake, maybe they really said G-61, maybe you really just fell asleep during *Wheel* and dreamed it all.

"So," continued Rose, "if I meet someone new and then race through my files and a name and a face comes up that shouts *Bingo*, then I figure out how to get them hooked up. That's the fun part."

In high school Rose made many matches, including a complicated one between Candace, a slow twenty-year-old senior with two lethal boyfriends and tens of thousands of suitors, and Punch, a precocious freshman who had skipped, based on merit and the opinions of his tutors, the first half of high school.

"It was one of the most intense bingos I ever got. It was a complete surprise—I saw Punch in line to register for the SATs and ran him through the database, strictly routine, and I got a blow-me-down match with Candace. I'd never come up with such disparate matchees. I called my grandmother in Honduras to find out what to do. My grandmother is really a horrible person—I'll tell you about her someday."

Someday? You mean I'll see you again?

"But she shared a few secrets—including potions. I know it's a shitty stereotype that Latin Americans always have mystical relatives, but in my case it's true. Before long, Punch and Candace—who I'm sure never would've met—met."

"So how'd it turn out?"

"Oh, not so great," said Rose. "Pretty terrible, to be frank."

Rose had been talkative and liberal with information up till now, but she suddenly quieted down. Her Sugar Babies hands dropped dusty chunks of gravel into Justine's can.

"I talk a lot, I know," said Rose. "Anyway, it wasn't as lousy as my Matt match. I'm blaming him for fucking it up, though. He doesn't know what he had."

Of course. It hit Justine like a bare fist. Rose was going to set her up with the person in Austin for whom her distaste was freshest.

"A while back me and Matt and some other Crammed Shelf people dropped by a Cinco de Mayo party at somebody's house after work. It was late, really Seis de Mayo by that time, and much alcohol had already filtered through the partiers. New relationships were being formed everywhere you looked.

"A van-load of Aggies crashed the party. They came inside the house wearing conical party hats and pinching bottles of beer out of a big ice-filled plastic trash can in the kitchen and counting down from five to one and then hollering 'Happy New Year!' Then they ran around the house, wetly and dramatically kissing everyone on the lips.

"A silly man with a scratchy moustache kissed me, almost completely missing my lips," said Rose. "But I wasn't really paying attention to him. I was watching the room, watching for bingos.

"And there one was: in the corner of the TV room, a tall woman wearing a T-shirt and black pegged jeans and no shoes had gently placed Matt against a stereo speaker and was sucking at his neck like a vampire.

"I thought those two would catch fire," said Rose, shaking the Dr Pepper can like a martini mixer. "Such a wicked, sparkling bingo."

But the woman vanished, leaving Matt slumped in a corner, drooling, head lolling against a lowing woofer. Rose was still in the silly embrace of her own New Year's Day celebrant.

"I had to hit him in the ribs, but he let go," said Rose. "And then I ran off down the street after the van, which was already up to Riverside. It turned into traffic, but I kept running and running and running. Finally, you won't believe it, but I caught up with it at the light just before the I-35 on-ramp. The tall woman was driving."

Rose upended the Dr Pepper can and shook the rocks out into a little knoll. It reminded Justine of the piles of dirt that fresh-dug graves produce.

"Let's just say my evening ended with the tall woman—Evenie—driving off in my Jeep with Matt, still intoxicated with passion and malt liquor, buckled into the passenger seat. I was so excited I couldn't sleep at all that night. I was dying to call him but I held out. The next day he wasn't at work. I didn't know whether to be worried or ecstatic."

"They can feel the same sometimes," said Justine.

Rose paused to put her head on Justine's knee and smile at her just long enough to make Justine wonder what the hell was going on. Justine swallowed wrong and began hacking away in the dusty parking lot.

"So," said Rose, whacking Justine on the back, "early the next morning, about an hour before he was supposed to be at Crammed Shelf, he called the store. He was at his great-granddaddy's ranch outside of Norman, Oklahoma, sitting on a metal stool in a barn, milking a cow. He told me he hated me."

Rose had later found out from Evenie that she and Matt had gone to her place, had lain down on her genuine Tabriz, and watched *Shaun of the Dead* together, cheek to cheek, on her tiny iPod, then had pretty good sex right there on the floor.

"But then," Rose continued, "Evenie, pointing out that since it was the first time they'd ever met, neither of them had anything to lose and everything to gain by admitting to and experimenting with the private, taboo fantasies and kinks that were the *true truths* of their real sexualities, to see if they really had what it took to embark on a genuine, truth-based eros-governed relationship. Evenie told me that Matt, with a devilish, de-Sadian look in his eye, said he liked sucking on women's toes. Evenie told him to knock himself out. When he was finished, Evenie said that she had always wanted to bind her lovers with zinc bobwire, face-up, to a big beechwood workbench she had in a shed out back and then irrumate them with a saguaro-like strap-on she'd picked up from a Japanese sex-toy test-marketing firm."

Justine wanted to hear no more. She wanted to kiss Rose goodbye, and die before Matt could suck on her toes.

"Evenie tied him up, explained about safe words, and he whimpered and cried while a varicose erection tossed and turned on his stomach. She went to work. But, in spite of the new experience and notable orgasms had all around, Matt, after being disbound, accused her of rape, accused me of facilitating rape, and hated me for setting him up. I promised I'd make it up to him, even though I think he was the one who fucked it up. After all, he could've stopped whenever he wanted, and I think he was having a great time even though ashamed to admit it."

Justine despaired. Mixed in with her loathing of Matt was some empathy for the guy. Still, she did not ever want to see his thrumming erection.

"So that's why he was such a dick to you. I think he sensed that I might be formulating you as a new match for him. Justine. Justine. Justine. Justine... what's your last name, anyway?"

"Uh, I'm not sure. Maybe Moppett. Or Johnsonson. Or Durant."

"You'll explain that to me sometime."

"Okay."

"So, Justine Unsure, here's the thing."

I know. I can't do it. But I will, for you, Rose.

"Justine, you have air conditioning in your Room?"

"Yeah..."

"Take us there, so I can finish my story in the cool and quiet."

Justine did.

"Are you really, really full," said Rose, sitting next to Justine on the floor at the end of the bed and squeezing off channel after channel with the remote control, "or might you be pregnant?"

"I'm..."

How quickly circumstances can change. Rose had prevented Justine's half-serious traffic-suicide plot, and was now touching her hip with her own.

"Can I stop here?"

"I love *Law & Order.*"

"Me too. So, which is it?"

Rose pointed the remote at Justine's belly and clicked the FFWD button over and over.

"A little of both," said Justine.

Justine realized that this was the first time anyone had asked, and the first time she'd ever told anyone. Except Franklin. Justine hadn't been to see an obstetrician or even a GP, not once. Even Amy downstairs had never seemed to notice, and it was hard to hide a fifth of a volleyball stuck to your belly in the middle of summer when thin, snug cotton was the chemise de rigueur. But maybe Amy was just being polite.

"I can't get pregnant," said Rose.

"Why?"

"I'm kinda guevedoche, but different."

"What's that?"

"A little of both."

"Oh."

"But me?" said Rose, leaning in to Justine a little. "A *lot* of both. Most guevedoche are kinda a little of both, and none of it works all that great. But *all* of mine works. Except for the getting-pregnant part."

"Oh?"

"Yes. I'm really my own thing, not gueve at all. I'm terribly rare and valuable, and in great demand."

"Oh?"

"And everything works. Uterus, clitoris, lots of semen, lots of sperm. And I'll never go bald. Just no eggs."

Rose fell sideways, letting her head come to rest delicately on Justine's volleyball, ear down. Matt, and his thrumming erection, seemed far, far away.

"Any kicking or hitting? What month does that nonsense start? Boy or girl? Or is it too soon for that? Who's your boyfriend? Where's your boyfriend? Hubby? Any other kids? How far along?"

Rose's voice made Justine's body vibrate in such a pleasant, extrasensory way that she wondered if there weren't an actual sixth sense, an additional bodily sense, whose organ, perhaps effaced inside the body just at the base of the spine, registered only sub-tangible vibrations. If so, Justine was now experiencing the jasmine, the northern lights, the pure cane sugar of all vibes.

"About eight weeks."

"So you're due...?"

"January 14. But I'm not sure I'm going to keep it."

Instead of sitting up Rose spun a quarter turn and was now facing up, the back of her head pillowed between Justine's belly and the tops of her thighs.

"My big fat head won't hurt the baby, will it?"

"Oh, no."

"What's your sperm-dispenser say?"

"He doesn't have any."

"Sperm?"

"Say."

"Well, *I* hope you keep it. Babies are fun. I'll be a godparent if you don't already have one."

Where was Matt? He seemed to be turning into less of a factor in the algebra of Rose's visitation.

Rose turned to give her attention to Richard Belzer, who was discussing his father's suicide with another cop, but Justine's thighs were in the way. Rose pushed them apart like reeds.

"Thank you," said Rose. "Don't you think the Belz is kinda hot? In a way?"

Justine couldn't move or speak. She was aware of the mortifying possibility that her vestibular perfumes, less than four inches from Rose's sexy nose, might betray her stellar arousal.

But if Rose did sense anything, she said nothing. She rested, breathed, occasionally chuckled or gasped at the minor levity and major horror that most *Law & Order: SVU* episodes comprised. Justine tried to follow her cues. What if Justine gasped at something Rose found funny, or, worse, chuckled at something horrible? Her parted thighs began to cramp along the adductors.

Something needed to be done. If Justine waited (and she always waited—waiting was her nature and foe; to allow; to pass by the scene, rubbernecking), Rose might sit up and kiss her and take off all her clothes and show Justine how their parts would work so well together and then give Justine a fucking that was precisely the kind Justine was sure could never happen—a clear kind, lieless, with huffing and *yeses* and fresh sorts of trembles.

But, on the other hand, it was possible that if Justine waited, Rose might turn around, begin to discuss the logistics of Justine's upcoming date with Matt, and leave, taking her flirty, black-tar-heroin vibrations and better-than–Sugar Babies skin with her, leaving Justine as alone as she'd ever felt.

But what if Justine *didn't* wait; what if she acted—say, reached down and took Rose's hand, or gave her earlobe a little pinch, or said, *Ow, my bottom is falling asleep* during a Viagra commercial—Justine might destroy what was only ever supposed to have been a sweet little innocent acquaintanceship.

But no. This was no sweet little innocent anything: Rose was lying with her head almost in Justine's lap, Justine's legs spread at an angle large enough that it subtended a thirty-six-inch separation of her knees. An *invitational* angle. And, if a mouth and a vagina—no matter how thick the material hiding the latter and deflecting the former—were as close as theirs were now, there should be no question about *whether* it was just a friendship, but *when* it would prove itself more than.

Justine waited anyway. *SVU* ended. A *Criminal Intent* began, ended. Rose scarcely moved. Justine didn't move at all. She couldn't tell if Rose had dozed off. God. Justine. *Act*, you sheep.

Justine continued to not act. She let her head fall back against the bed. Something hard and angular was there, poking at the back of her skull. Oh, the corner of a magazine. Big, thick. Maybe *Brides*. She let her head rest on the sharp corner. She watched the curl of delaminating wallpaper. She prayed for help, for a sign. She prayed for an angel with a pair of scissors to squirt out of the ceiling and snip off all their clothes and then order them to lick lick lick. She prayed for Dot to speak into her ear, to tell her it was okay to—

Rose sat up.

"You know why I'm here, of course."

"Ah…"

"When I first saw you standing at Matt's welcome desk, I ran you down my list, looking for Bingos. And guess who I found."

"Matt."

Rose took off her jersey. Her torso was like a male butterfly swimmer's, flat and smooth, except her nipples were womanly, berrylike. Still sitting, she pulled off her shorts and panties. Her penis was erect, curved, and nearly touching her solar plexus. She stood up.

"Me!"

Justine began to suspect "Rose" was an apparition. A ghost with a message.

"I watched you lick my glass. In the mirror over the lunch counter."

Rose put one leg up on the edge of the bed, lifted her scrotum out of the way with one hand, and with two fingers of the other spread open the vulva of her small, delicate vagina.

"*Vive la difference*," said Rose.

XVI

October 2004

On the one-month anniversary of Montserrat's death, April filled a plastic
bowl with Three Musketeers and Dots and Tootsie Rolls and grocery-store
suckers. She opened the door to her apartment and placed an old air conditioner box out on the balcony. She sifted through the bowl of candy until it
was all mixed together, then put it on top of the box. She shut herself inside
her apartment. It was unlikely that anybody would trick-or-treat at this
shitty apartment complex, but putting the last of her food (if you wanted
to call rods and bars and balls of sugar food) out where anyone could take
it gave her comfort, which in turn gave her the confidence to proceed with
the evening.

Instead of putting on the Dora the Explorer wig and costume and going
downtown to meet Ryan at the Vinyl Bar on Fourth, as planned, April
changed into sweatpants and a T-shirt, placed her laptop on the toilet lid,
drew a hot bath, eased into the water fully dressed, unwrapped a sterile
seventeen-gauge needle she'd stolen from Planned Parenthood, seated it
expertly into a vein in her right arm, and watched her blood drain into

the hot water in convect volutes. She would be empty in less than ten minutes, long enough to start a Scrabble game. She set it to "expert," and was immediately able to play *CENTRAL* for 74. The computer countered with *COQUETTE* for 94. April welcomed a thrashing, which is what she usually got when playing at this difficulty level. When the score was 202 to 189, computer winning, April played *PET* just over *CENTRAL*, also making the words *PA* and *EL*. It didn't put her ahead much. April was growing lightheaded and a bit nauseated. The water had become a uniform, transparent vermilion. April lifted her arm out of the water. The blood flowed steadily, like a urination, out of the thick needle. The computer passed its turn. April stared at her letters. *AAEOOKU*. She was about to play *UKE*, but stopped. She stared at the board for a long time, re-reading the words. Portent spilled from them. She would never have expected a message *now*. Was she being tricked?

After a moment's hard staring at the board, she decided that no trick was being played on her. And if she was being tricked, she could always come back to this suicide business later.

She stopped the game. She got on the internet. She found the website for Central Market. The event was on Thursday. Tomorrow. She shut her eyes and remained quiet for a couple of minutes.

This would work.

On the verge of unconsciousness, April plucked the needle out of her arm. She lay in the cooling water and waited for her body to utter new blood into her veins. She slept. Many hours later she awoke, carefully stood up, drained the tub, shucked her soaked pink T-shirt and sweatpants, and showered. It was three in the morning. She dressed and drove to Walmart.

Back at home April opened the box with her costly new baby doll, an uncanny replica of a six-week-old baby. She swaddled it so its little face barely peeked out at the world. She donned a Baby Björn, a large, roomy one, and placed the doll in it. She walked around the room, lightly rocking the doll, looking in at it, cooing at it. She took the Björn off, dressed in jeans and a brown sweater, did her face, put on the Dora wig, slipped into a pair of worn brown moccasins, picked up the Baby Björn with the well-wrapped doll inside, found a screwdriver, and walked out the door. The candy was still there, apparently untouched. April descended the stairs. Still no one had come to collect Bryce's husband's Mini Cooper, which sat in the parking lot, unused, eddies of dirt and twigs surrounding each tire. Another auspicious sign. She removed the license plates, then drove the car to Central Market, where outside in the small park that flanked the upscale grocery store, a monthly get-together of moms and babies and dogs was taking place: Babystock & Petpalooza. April had been to this event before, two or three years ago, to look at babies (but not to shop!), but she had forgotten about it until the Scrabble board reminded her. April put on her sunglasses. She parked in a spot close to the store, rear-first, leaving the doors unlocked.

April did not stand out among the many dozens of mothers. In the park she walked slowly among the mothers and strollers and dogs and children and Central Market employees and shoppers. No one looked at her, no one asked to peek inside her Björn, no one stared at her wig.

She sat at a picnic table with two other mothers, each in control of a double stroller, which they were rocking with their feet. The women were sharing a Caesar salad and a rotisserie chicken sandwich. One mother, who was sitting on April's side of the bench, bounced a well-wrapped baby on her lap. In the double stroller, which was parked between April and the mother, facing April, remained a loosely bundled baby, so thoroughly covered against the chill early November air that April couldn't see its face. At one edge of the park was a small stage upon which a violinist and an oboist were preparing to perform. They began to play a composition that April had never heard, but that was surely old; late-eighteenth-century German, possibly. She listened, her eyes closed, for several minutes. When she opened them, the mothers at her table had finished their salad and sandwich and were both working intently on their smartphones. April furtively adjusted the baby doll in her Björn, making room. She swung her legs over the bench seat, crouched down, deftly picked up the baby in the stroller, tucked it into her Björn with the doll, quietly stood, and briskly walked to her car. The baby was silent and still on the ride home.

She had done it. She had been calm the whole time, but the thrill of it, delayed until this instant, made her shudder.

At the Parallel Apartments, April carefully maneuvered the car so it was precisely where it had been before, its tires crowded with flotsam from rainstorms and time. It looked as though it had never moved. She put the license plates back on, climbed up to her apartment with the baby, and locked the door shut behind her. She lay on her futon and began to unwrap the baby.

What is this? A furry blanket, deep in the layers? The furry blanket was warm. It moved. A small dog poked its head out. A Lhasa Apso. It looked up at April and whimpered. April stared at the animal. She dug deeper into the blankets, but there was no baby.

XVII

1985–2004

By the time Mariarosa Balaguer was six, her aunt Olympe had accumulated three good reasons to move them both from Tegucigalpa to Laredo, Texas: (1) so Olympe, a cordwainer by trade and descent, could "work" for the border town's premier boot maker, Sir MacCrear, with whom she had recently begun a correspondence that had quickly risen from strictly professional to flirty professional to racily nonprofessional to lovey-dovey desperate; (2) to give Rose better access to doctors who were more likely to know how to treat a guevedoche, especially when the unique miseries and elevated medical risks of puberty arrived; and (3) to get Rose away from the rest of her greedy, brutal, and wildly superstitious family.

There had been guevedoche in the family as far back as anyone could remember, a scatter of unbranched, barren twigs at the reaches of the complicated family tree—an actual document, 340 years old, drawn originally in oak-gall ink on amate and colored with red earths and fading purple woad, and, in recent years, appended with names penned in ballpoint and colored with scented Crayola markers or dime-store poster paint. It now hung in the kitchen of Rose's grandmother's house, a brick box on the edge of a semi-fashionable but declining area of Honduras's capital. Until Rose, Grandmother Balaguer was the most enthusiastic matchmaker of all her forebears and descendants, having successfully united no fewer than four hundred persons into no fewer than two hundred betrothals, reunitings, reverse estrangements, kiss-and-make-ups, and vivid one-nighters.

The document in Grandmother's kitchen had been, as many old manuscripts covered in paleographic mysteries are, bestowed with a magical quality (as far as matchmaking was concerned), and was often consulted by Grandmother when she was confronted with a matchmaking conundrum. The document was, in a way, an oracle speaking of, and to, its own future.

But Rose's birth flagged Grandmother's confidence and enthusiasm for matchmaking, as guevedoche could not reproduce (nor had they ever shown any matchmaking tendencies, at least not in *her* dynasty): the long line of matchmakers looked to be at a monstrous end, a failure Grandmother blamed herself for, as she had been responsible for the union of her son Aaron and a local cookie-and-cracker vendor named Beatrice, who had then produced Rose. The pain of Grandmother's loss of confidence she transduced into cruelty toward Beatrice; this cruelty Beatrice reflected onto Rose—first just neglect, then slaps, then throttlings, then beatings. By the time she was five, Rose was a limping scape of bruises and scars. Eventually the abuse transcended into exploitation: Beatrice and Aaron had begun to exhibit their child in a dope-shellacked tent on the ugliest edge of Tegucigalpa's worst slum, pricing the peeps according to the flesh the peeper wished to see. Very few wanted to see less than every inch of five-year-old naked Rose Balaguer, and so the box office quickly took in a fair amount of money.

Somehow, though, the child remained good-natured, gregarious, even bubbly. Moreover, Rose, in buck of family history, began to exhibit some matchmaking urges. She performed an elaborate wedding between Diarrea—a neighbor's incontinent bunny—and Carlos, an old, clear-plastic toy camel that had somehow acquired an interior puddle of greenish water that foamed dramatically when shaken. After the wedding, which had featured boiled eggs as bridesmaids, a cardboard chapel, a tiny gold band (a jewelry finding unearthed in the muddy road) for Diarrea's ring-phalange, and a lingering kiss, Rose drove the newlyweds in a wagon to Diarrea's hutch.

Even though the marriage ended a year or so later with Diarrea's matriculation into a purse and some stew, Grandmother considered it a success—a portentous success. The end of her lineage might be in sight, but by god it had not yet arrived. She decided to apprentice Rose, and turn the little freak into greatness. In a kind of reconciliation with Beatrice and Aaron, Grandmother approached them with the idea of adding another dimension to their sideshow: matches for money. Rose Balaguer, the latest in a four-century line of matchmakers, and the first guevedoche to bear the sacred mantle, would, for a small fee, find you a mate, patch up a separation, pacify a business partner, reconcile internal family feuds. The little sideshow began to take in more money than ever.

But not enough, at least as far as Beatrice and Aaron were concerned. Grandmother had not objected to exhibiting Rose, but they had not told her about their newest sub-venture, which had been suggested to them by some of the peep show's more impassioned and hard-to-please clientele. They complained that their yen for more than just a show was ruining their health and vitality. They suggested some contact, to be remunerated, depending on the intimacy of the act, at five to ten times the price of a close look.

And so, for ten months in 1984, Rose's parents whored her out to the worst of the worst. Rose remembered very little. The older she got, the less real what had happened to her seemed, until it became a fiction, a suite of scratched, ill-lit black-and-white cartoons of men playing with a doll, rocking her in their laps, feeding her, tickling her, filling her with things, holding her so tight she couldn't breathe.

Eventually, even the cartoons rarefied into single snapshots, these in turn slowly abstracting to meaningless grays. But it had all happened: Rose's anus was scarred and distended; her rectum colonized with irrepressible venereal warts, her vagina lacerated, her perineum split and sewn up and split and sewn up, three generations of keloids holding it together, her uterus punctured, her throat ulcerated, and her pelvis distorted, it having once been broken (by a violent man later murdered by his wife for the crime) and then healed at an anatomically incorrect angle, giving her a pronounced pigeon-toed walk.

How she had grown up so emotionally stable was as much a mystery to her psychiatrists as her body was to her physicians. There were doctors who considered her normalcy an impermeable shell, a maturing embryo of hatred and fury within trying to peck its way out. They thought of Rose as a kind of time bomb and themselves as the bomb squad, and told her as much.

Aunt Olympe, Aaron's sister, lived on the other side of the city, having long ago left the poisonous Balaguers. The birth of Rose was the first reason in years that she'd had to visit her family. She fell in love with the child, and visited as often as she could after that.

It was on a visit in 1985 that Olympe discovered (the fruit of a snoop through the family account books) Aaron and Beatrice's public and private exploitations of her little niece. Within thirty minutes of this discovery, Olympe had seized Rose, a suitcase of her things, and the account books, and was soon speeding toward Nuevo Laredo in Olympe's grumpy little Fiat. Some days later, a border crossing brought them to Sir MacCrear's Belt 'n' Bootery in Laredo.

Discounting the persistent curiosity and intrusion of the medical community, a relatively ordinary upbringing followed, its adolescent component not appreciably worse than the average teenager's. Soccer, library science, *Harry Potter* fan fiction, and matchmaking consumed her college years (Texas State); her sexual life, which in another age would have been at best lonesome and humiliating, was, thanks to the internet's agency to like communities, neither. She was surprised to find on her very first internet search dozens of websites devoted to atypical love connections. She joined a couple, and was soon crowded with people who wanted to date her. Some even declared love. And there was the occasional other who became infatuated, sometimes to a creepy, frightening, illegal degree.

Even the internet could find no one else quite like her, physically, anywhere. Every other kind of sexual rarity she read about or became acquainted with was, simply, less. She was the lone, fully ambisexual human being of the world.

The Room's overachieving air conditioner kept Justine and Rose safe from heatstroke as they spent every day fucking and confiding, confessing and fucking, declaring love and fucking some more.

They put all else on hold. For Justine, there wasn't much to put off— maybe collaging and sleep. And confronting her treacherous family. And thinking about the birth or death of her child.

But Rose, she had to pause all of her many hobbies and avocations, not to mention her job.

As conscientious an employee as Rose was, she had not seemed at all compunct about calling in fake-sick (mucopurulent double pink eye, a potent, convincing fiction), day after day, in order to stay in the Room with Justine and engage in their sexual *Cirque de Soleil*, from which they broke only to eat breakfast tacos or to power-nap or to track down Lacey for more sheets and towels or to hike over to Squealers to shop for restraints and chrisms and erotic simulacra or to share with each other their sins and secrets. Some of them, anyway. Justine confessed her affairs with Fleur de Lis and others while Franklin was in prison. Rose, cheating once—but only to win a soccer game; Justine, a sick hamster she'd tried to euthanize in a freezer but which had merely hibernated for the three cold months, emerging alive but sicker than ever and had had to be put down by a vet who did house calls, carrying out his ghastly work in an unmarked van, and whom Justine had paid with two convincing "twenties" she'd made herself with the color photocopier at Kinko's; Rose, skipping a funeral to go on a date in which good sex was assured, and another time skipping sex to go to a funeral; Justine, vividly wishing her mother dead; Rose, that she was presently two years into a three-year probation for assault (she socked a bartender who wouldn't give her the happy-hour price on a pint of Shiner exactly ten seconds after happy hour ended, but whose real crime was his known hatred of non-heterosexuals and who'd had a cold-cock coming for a decade); Justine, stealing from Midgie and then quitting without notice; Rose, that she'd been prostituted by her family for part of her early childhood; Justine, her family.

Of this last Justine held nothing back. Lou and Dot, Lou and Livia's devastating kiss, 9/11 and Valeria, the recently uncovered truth of Livia's being Justine's mother, and the mystery of why Charlotte and Livia had contrived such an extravagant, hideous lie to hide this truth from Justine.

"That's why you came back to Austin?" Rose asked one afternoon as she dabbed at the little dots of prolonged-standing-up-sex sweat that kept appearing on her forehead. "To confront all your people?"

"It's why. Mostly. To leave Franklin, too."

"And find Gracie?"

It was the one subject, the one word, that caused a hiccup in Rose's general good-naturedness.

"No, of course not. She's married anyway. I bet. No, here to confront the Durants."

"What are you waiting for?"

Fear was the answer, but Justine told Rose she didn't know. Moreover, she didn't know why she'd just lied to Rose.

"You ought to just call them up. *Hey what's up with lying about me being adopted,* Mom? *Why'd you aid and abet,* Gramma? You could tell them to go fuck themselves in the same phone call, then hang up. Confrontation over. On with your day. On with us."

"Maybe," said Justine, yanking out a hospital corner of the bedsheet to dab at her own sweat-points. "But maybe I don't really want to know."

"Or I could intercede. I could get all y'all back together. Intercession is a close relative of matchmaking, and I'm quite good at that, also. We could all have a big sit-down. You could tell them about the baby. Babies on the way can be a nice glue for broken relationships, you know. Even tricky, multipronged relationships, like yours."

"I just don't know," said Justine. "I just don't know, don't know, don't know."

"Well, I recommend it. Hey, I think I bruised my butt bone on that doorknob."

Justine said nothing.

"Oh, darling," said Rose, getting into bed. "Come lie down. I'm going to have to lie on my stomach, though, to let my butt heal in the open air."

During the next several weeks the duties of ordinary living grew more and more pressing. Rose had to return to all the matchmaking projects she'd deserted. She had soccer games to ref or compete in. Rose was also finally obliged to return to her noon-to-nine shifts at Crammed Shelf.

Justine spent the lonesome, Roseless hours in one of two distinct states: sleeping and pining. There had been no talk of moving in together, as powerful as their relationship felt—Justine endured as August and September burned themselves out. Sleeping was the obvious way to pass the hours, but that was not so easily done, because pining kept her awake.

Pining itself consisted of imagining Rose in the embrace of other lovers who were more attractive and stabler and happier, and who were, unlike Justine, terribly excited to be expecting.

The principal (and touchiest) subject of their growing relationship, and the most likely to cool their otherwise-substantial ardor, was the fate of the baby. Rose wanted it. Justine, who would have done anything to please Rose but had—as always—profound ambivalence about whether to keep her baby, expertly dissembled whenever the subject came up. That Justine was beginning to resent and hate the child inside of her was becoming the only real secret she kept from Rose. A practical corollary of this secret (a lie, in fact) was that Justine had kept her stash of mifepristone, even though she'd told Rose she'd gotten rid of it. "It's way, way too late for that stuff, anyway," Rose had said. "It would just make you sick and hurt the baby. Maybe kill you both. So I order you to flush 'em."

One afternoon in early September, while Rose was on her knees on the floor of the Room, naked, ironing a shiny soccer shirt, and Justine, in bed, was watching the shadows wiggle between the little muscles in Rose's shoulder, Justine was most distressingly visited by the idea of Rose's leaving her for another lover if she gave up the baby.

"If it's a boy, I like the name Walter," Rose said. "And if it's a girl, I like Babette."

"Are we together?" Justine said.

Rose stopped ironing and stood up straight on her knees.

"What?"

"Are we a thing?"

"You mean in a real relationship with meaning and a future and monogamous underpinnings?"

"Yeah."

"You betcha. I was planning to go home and tell my old landbitch I'm outta her moldy roach hovel, fuck the security deposit."

"Oh, Rose."

"So we can go apartment hunting on Saturday. It's about time to say adios to the old Room. What about that?"

"I love you."

"Baby, you should've told me you were feeling so insecure."

Rose climbed onto the bed and got under the covers with Justine. "Look. You can stay home in our new place and play Spider Solitaire on the computer and read all the uncorrected proofs and advance-reader copies I get from work and think up new sexual adventures and just generally mellow out in maternal repose while I work and bring home the bacon."

"But what if you meet somebody and when you're going through your files you find out *you're their* match?"

"Don't worry. You're her. You are she."

"So we are a thing."

"As far as I'm concerned we've been a thing since I got my Bingo over you and then came over and seduced you during *Law & Order*."

Justine felt Rose's erection filling out against her leg. Rose quickly arranged a couple of pillows in a formation that best supported the version of 69 they'd discovered together, with Rose on top, her penis between Justine's breasts and her tiny, nearly invisible but highly passible and charged clitoris just flush with Justine's lips. This was how it should be. This close, always.

"Sure I'm not hurting Walter?" said Rose, pausing to gather up a knot of bedspread to tuck under Justine's rear end.

"Positive."

bite lick play flick rub fuck

"Mng."

Rose pushed herself back into Justine's lips and spasm-shuddered in the peculiar, arrhythmic way that allowed Rose to stimulate both her sexual organs at once, and, occasionally, come with both. Like now.

Rose flooded Justine's solar plexus, semen spilling down her sides like opium-poppy milk. Rose lifted herself up, slowly, and lowered her erection into Justine's mouth.

"Wow," said Rose, not even slightly out of breath. "That was quick. See, I can only come like that if I'm in a real relationship, with love and commitment."

"Mlt."

"Baby, don't talk with your mouth full."

Baby.

Along with Rose's cock, Justine swallowed her own rising and filling-out idea that Rose really was an apparition; her perfect human, available only in the form of a skittery ghost, easily scared away, easy to lose forever.

In early November, Justine and Rose moved into an efficiency located on the second floor of a Motel 6–style apartment building of the sort replicated at least once on virtually every street within three miles of the UT campus and which collectively domiciled quite a few of the university's fifty thousand students.

Rose and Justine's building, the Parallel Apartments, was demographically typical in that it housed mostly students, but it was atypical in its percentage of asocialites: there were far more chess phenoms and shell-shocked cuckolds and shifty, deadbeat dads and warrant-dodging speed eaters and overworked Mexican graveyard-shift grocery-store stockers and lonesome mezzo-sopranos and corrupt eBay rare book dealers and whoever-else-have-you than most other apartment complexes around. The singer was especially noxious; she seemed never to quit practicing, and she lived just two doors down.

Rose and Justine's unit was tiny, but neither owned much. Justine had only what she'd brought from New York, a couple new outfits and purses, and a Styrofoam cooler she'd picked up at Academy months ago to keep her Dr Peppers cold. All Rose owned was a wall's worth of books, a drawer's worth of clothes, an old PC equipped with a 0.9 kbps dial-up modem, a few boxes of papers and correspondence from the physicians and specialists and photographers and sideshow scouts that had taken an interest in her over the years, a one-drawer metal file cabinet filled with the plans and details of her past matchmaking triumphs, and an aromatic double bed as concave as a radio telescope.

Rose also owned about eighty soccer trophies, which took up a good third of the apartment. One was a gold and ebony colossus nine feet high that had to be wedged into a corner at an angle. When Justine was alone in their new home, pining while Rose was out doing her many things, it was the sight of the colossus canted over its busy kingdom that brought her own lonesomeness into sharpest relief.

"Just before Walter's due," Rose said while rearranging her trophies to make room for a new one that she had just won, a fake-brass three-footer fangled as a coffin standing on end, Death perched on top, a soccer ball impaled on his scythe, the monument just acquired as champion of the East Side Halloween Torture Dungeon Round Robin, "we'll put all these in storage and park his little bassinet here."

Justine fell heavily onto the unmade bed. The pining bed, the sex bed, the collage bed. The bed with a history. Justine often wondered who else had slept here, bawled here, dreamed here, gotten fucked by Rose here. *Who'll be after me?*

"Or Babette," Rose added. "And I'd like to remind you of your promise to go see Dr. Nomb and at least get a checkup and find out the sex of the baby. Dr. Nomb'll love you; she loves me. My aunt and I have been seeing her since the eighties."

"I have to go job hunting. My credit card is full."

"No, you don't. You're expecting."

"They make women work until the last possible moment," said Justine. "Until you can practically *see* the baby."

A knock at the door. Thank god. Anything to interrupt this unnerving talk of pregnancy and birth and doctors. Justine got up and answered it.

A young woman, early twenties. Ah, their two-doors-down neighbor. The mezzo-soprano. She was holding a plastic bowl of Tootsie Pops and suckers and other Halloween leftovers.

"Hi," said Justine.

"Hi yourself," said the woman, offering up her bowl of candy. "I'd like to officially welcome you to the Parallel even though I know you've been here a little while already, haha, sorry, I was busy looking for tricksters."

There was something proprietary about the way the woman held the bowl, as if she were waiting for Justine to contribute rather than take a sucker. Justine picked one anyway.

"Thank you."

"Hi," said Rose, from her prostration on the apartment's gross carpeting.

"Hi. We're a family here at the Parallel, a big, wonderful family, and I'm so happy to have a new family member. Or," she said as she bent down to look closely at Justine's round, Frank Frazetta T-shirt-covered belly, "is it two?"

"It's *three*," said Rose. "Jan 14."

"How wonderful," said the woman. "I lost mine, almost five months along. They were just playing tricks on me. I didn't get back in the tub, though."

She put her sucker bowl down, put one hand on her own flat belly, and the other on Justine's. Justine jumped back.

"Oh, sorry," she said, blushing and covering her mouth with both hands. "Just excited."

"Okay," said Justine, embarrassed that she'd jumped. "I'm really sorry to hear about your—"

"I just can't believe this," said the woman, looking over her shoulder. "The board never said anything about this."

"Board?"

The woman's disposition turned in an instant from a cool autumn afternoon to a predawn summer storm. She said:

"This is a trick."

Her eyes began to wander; she seemed to be watching the movements of something inside the apartment that was visible only to her. Then she focused on Justine's belly.

"What?"

"Isn't it. Careful, I'll know if you're lying."

Justine opened her mouth to speak, but said nothing. She looked at Rose, who shrugged with her eyes. Justine covered her belly with both arms.

"Uh, I'm not lying about anything," she said.

The woman looked Justine up and down. She seemed satisfied by Justine's response.

"Okay, maybe it's for real," she said finally. "I'll check on our little'un again soon. Now I have scales."

She smiled. It was a weird smile, shaped like a punctuation brace turned sideways, the point up. It was distinctly forced, imperfectly hiding something; the smile of one pausing in the middle of a much grander emotion to deal with a trifling of some sort.

"Okay," said Rose. "Thank you for stopping by."

"Not too far away, is it?" the woman said, looking at Justine's belly again. "I'm so excited. I just love these messages!"

She left, taking her unsettling mouth, her bowl of junk, and her babel with her.

"What the fuck was that?" said Rose.

"What're scales?"

"I don't know. I hope you didn't just catch them."

"A little loony."

"What was that shit about tricks?" said Rose.

"And calling me a liar?"

"Weird."

"Yeah," said Rose, getting up on all fours and starting to stalk Justine like a lion after an ibex. "You'll never trick me. Haha. Raor."

"I don't…," said Justine, jumping up on the naked bed.

"Rumbling purring sound like jungle cats make."

"…think…"

"Nothing hides from Jungle Cat."

"…want it."

Rose stopped mid-slink. "What?"

"I don't want this. Baby."

"What? Why?"

"Because I couldn't be a good mother. I come from bad mothers. I wasn't good. My Valeria died."

Justine expected to begin crying immediately, but nothing happened.

"You're a wonderful mother. You'll be a beautiful, sweet, hip mother."

"No, my baby will be a tiny little blue wreck and die young and in agony, I know it."

"Oh, Justine," said Rose, crawling up onto the bed next to her. "If you really believed that, why didn't you get an abortion?"

"I don't know. I couldn't decide. And now…"

The ducts were filling, finally.

"What?"

"…it's even harder to decide because I'm worried you'll leave me if I don't have it."

Justine expected—hoped—that Rose would pshaw the notion. But she did not.

The neighbor began to sing. Her powerful voice, modulated with long pauses as if in a phone conversation, seemed to come from the walls, as if she were trapped behind the drywall with a microphone. Opera. A genre that Justine simply did not get at all. It made her feel dim and left out. All that yodeling and showing off. The timbre of the granite German lyrics was nearly as depressing as the conversation they had interrupted.

"But," shouted Justine, "if I do have it and it survives it'll grow to hate me and then you'll start to hate me because I'll hate *it*."

Still Rose didn't counter.

"So that's why I can't decide. It feels like I have to choose whether I lose you now, or later."

Justine felt as if she were choking.

"Rose, say something. Tell me I'm wrong."

Still Rose was silent.

"Rose. Help me. I love you."

The singer sang a single note, an endless G major. The tone, which reminded Justine of emergency rooms for some reason, seemed to force its way into the apartment through the drains and air-conditioner vents.

"Rose, god, please say something."

Rose got off the bed and put her hands on her hips.

"Before we do anything else," she shouted, "let's go see the doctor!"

The neighbor snapped off sharply, as if hit in the mouth by a closed fist, mid-warble.

Three days later, Dr. Nomb, Rose's friend, champion, and GP since the age of six, confirmed the health of the baby, although it (Justine bitterly refused to learn its sex), appeared a bit small and possibly undernourished, and so advised Justine to lay off Dr Pepper and Doritos, and to add fish-oil gelcaps, prenatal folic acid, and DHA to her diet.

"And of course no drinking, smoking, or drugging," said Dr. Nomb, with a tone that suggested Justine might regularly commit all three prenatal crimes. "This is to include caffeine. Hear me?"

Justine nodded. Rose radiated nearly pure happiness, its small impurity being disbelief. How had she been so lucky to get a girlfriend *and* a baby? She wished Aunt Olympe were around, but she'd moved to Liberia to help the many limbless with their new prosthetics. She would be so proud. True, the pride would've broken up into pessimism pretty quickly, citing Rose's low matchmaking success rate. The magnitude of Rose's enthusiasm for her inherited compulsion was equaled only by the number of failed matches she'd arranged. On second thought, maybe it was better that her naturally doomsaying aunt was unavailable. Who needed a discouraging bummer of an aunt, always there to remind Rose of her most colorfully catastrophic matches? Rose would make her little Justine-and-Babette/Walter family succeed if it fucking killed her.

Right now, in the comforting, adult audience of Dr. Nomb, was the most confident Rose had felt since she first saw Justine, at Crammed Shelf, in dire need of rescue from Welcome Matt, in need of a book, one that Rose happened to know well, and which she could find on the shelf in the dark. Rose had been a wreck all the rest of that day, and the day after that, and every following instant, each of which seemed to increase the probability that Justine would disappear forever. That Justine had still been checked into the Room two weeks later was lucky; that she'd answered the door, that she'd blushed maroon at the sight of Rose, that she'd not screeched in fear or wrinkled in disgust or broken into giggles at the presentation of Rose's unique physiology, was luckier still; that she was going to bear them a baby, that she seemed to love Rose back without the intrusion of the creepy "love" she got from most lovers, all of whom were interested only in *la difference*, that she had those pretty mermaid eyes... incomprehensibly lucky.

"Dr. Nomb?" said Rose. "What about... relations? Is that okay?"

"Sex is fine. Limit acrobatics."

"What if I wanted to abort it?"

Rose gasped. Dr. Nomb seemed unmortifiable, but Justine's question obviously came as a surprise.

"It's too late for that."

The doctor, communicating with only a single, subtle crimping of her left cheek-apple, added: *And that's final, young lady.*

"The internet says it's never too late."

"The internet is wrong. The internet is the worst thing to happen to the profession of medicine since sympathetic powder."

"What?"

"Just do as I say."

XVIII

September 1969

When Lou Borger had gotten arrested for driving under the influence of beer, he'd had nearly four dollars in his billfold.

That was three weeks ago, and he was sure that the four dollars would disappear sometime while his billfold and all his personal belongings were growing moldy in some locker at the Texas City jail, an institution to which he had been sentenced to serve twenty-one days, the penalty Judge Melville Lipscomb had handed down.

"Also," said Judge Melville Lipscomb, who was sweating through his robes in the un-air-conditioned courtroom, "your pickemup truck is sentenced to one year in impound. Yonnastannat?"

"Yes, Judge," said Lou.

"And I am revoking your license. Yonnastannat?"

"I understand, Judge, thank you, sir."

The three weeks had passed quickly. Too quickly; Lou really had no desire to be out in the world again, as it meant job hunting. The night before he was arrested, he'd been fired from his offshore work for drinking on the job; this state of affairs led to more drinking—twenty-four hours' worth—and, ultimately, another DUI, another city-jail stretch, and another pending release into a world that demanded he have a job. In order to obtain a job, it was best not to be drunk. So, intent on making the best of his release, Lou made an oath to quit drinking. More specifically, he had sworn in the presence of Leghorn, his cellmate, in jail for chicken fighting, that he'd do his level best to honor it.

"Leg," Lou'd said, removing an issue of *Texas Monthly* that Leghorn had fashioned into a little tent and placed over his eyes in order to simulate night, "wake up. I need you to be a witness to a new leaf I'm fixing to turn. I finally crossed that line—they got my truck and my license to drive it."

"Go away," said Leghorn, turning over on his lower bunk to face the wall, which was covered in newspaper girdle ads. "I am having a pleasant dream of a magical machine that is vending large Clark Bars, and po'boys with large shrimps, what is in the velvet lobby of a magical whorehouse, where I am welcomed for free every day by women of the Amazon."

"Look here," said Lou, flapping an envelope over Leghorn's face. "I wrote it down. Listen: 'I, Lou Borger, of Left Prong Molasses Bayou, Texas, USA, hereby will try as best I can to never empty another bottle of beer or glass of vodka or wine or highball, because I am always finding myself in jail after, and now I have no truck because of it. It is not good for my future.' So, look. Wake up and notarize."

Lou poked Leghorn behind the ear with the envelope.

"Ow. Later, man."

"No, now, Leg," said Lou. "My sentence is almost up, and I need a witness. It'll just take a minute. Just read it, then sign it down here at the corner. Then bite the paper someplace to make little divots in it, like a real notary stamp."

Leghorn growled and sat up.

"You will let me return to my dreams?"

"Why, certainly," said Lou.

"Give me your paper."

Lou gave it to Leghorn, who signed it, and then bit it, leaving a moist semicircle of irregular, carious dents in the lower right corner.

"Here. Now go away."

"You got the paper wet."

"Please tell Dot that I miss her."

The jailer appeared at the cell door.

"Borger," he said, "you're done here."

On the way to freedom, the jailer handed Lou his jeans. Lou dug around in the pockets.

"Here's my pencil," said Lou.

"What luck," said the jailer.

"And, by god, here's my goddam billfold. Lord, here is my four dollars. That means beer and freedom, amigo."

Of course his driver's license wasn't there any longer.

"Looks like I'll be walking to Kelly's, though."

"Tell Dot I say hello," said the jailer.

"Or maybe I'll just go on home," said Lou, sighing dramatically, remembering the oath he'd made barely ten minutes before.

On the walk home from the jail Lou passed the impound lot where they'd brought his truck after he'd driven away from Kelly's soon after closing time and purely by accident driven into a divan that some clod had carelessly left up on the sidewalk for the trash man.

Behind a tall chain-link fence coiffed with barbed wire, way in the corner of the lot, hemmed in by a scorched tractor and a police car with an arrow sticking out of it, was Lou's truck, a 1953 Ford. One door ajar, one tire flat, one light smashed, one fender staved in, one side-view mirror hanging by a shred of rust, one puddle of oil in the dirt, six crimped cans of Pearl wedged between the dash and the windshield.

Lou'd gotten ten or twelve DUIs in the past, but this was the first time they'd ever taken his truck away. Or his *license*, for chrissake.

He took out his comb and scraped it across his scalp, pulled out his money and counted it again. He did not take out his oath and re-read it; he instead calculated how many cans of beer four dollars could buy. At least twenty if he bought them at the grocery store, many fewer if he bought them at Kelly's. If he couldn't drive, then what harm were a few beers?

"What harm?" Lou shouted in the direction of the metal shed that sheltered whatever individual was in charge of the impound lot. But no one emerged, with or without a retort. Lou picked up a mashed spark plug off the sidewalk and threw it over the fence. It bounced off the roof of the shed and landed in some yard dog's water dish. He picked up a paper cup and threw it, but the wind caught it and placed it back where it had been. Lou crushed it with the heel of his boot.

Lou stopped at a railroad crossing to wait for a pokey train to pass.

As the cab finally went by, the cab man, who looked like he had met with neither soap nor comb nor luck since youth, stared at Lou as if he knew Lou was fixing to break his oath.

"I may be foul and matted and cursed, but I am a man of my word," the cab man seemed to say.

Lou stood for a moment, watching the end of the train shrink in the distance. He took out his oath and read it again, wishing he'd been more precise in the wording.

Okay, then, I'll go right home and tend to my affairs. I'll march right past Kelly's. Maybe I'll march right on past and stop for a haircut at Pendrick's, then pick up some Cheez-Its at Murra's, then go right on home and fry that pork chop waiting for me in the freezer.

Lou marched into town. When he reached Kelly's, at the corner of Spindrel and Farquhar, he marched right on past without even looking at the barroom door. He stopped for a trim at Pendrick's, tipped Pendrick a quarter, then stood outside the barbershop, stretching and breathing in the moist, coastal perfume of freedom in Texas City, Texas, USA.

Lou glanced back down the street just in time to see his old pal Dot go into Kelly's.

"Dot!"

He walked quickly back the way he came. He paused for an instant in front of the bar.

What if I just enjoyed a Coca-Cola and maybe said a quick hello to old Dot? That wouldn't break my promise, would it?

Lou took out his oath one more time. He was so sweaty and the air so humid that Leghorn's notary stamp had not dried; in fact, the whole envelope was now limp.

A little boy walked by. Lou looked at him, pointed to his paper, and said, "Nothing here about how I can't go into a saloon." The boy ran away.

Lou went in.

He stood inside the door and waited for his eyes to adjust to the dark. Presently he could make out the people sitting at the tables, and the ball game flickering on the coffin-sized TV console that Kelly's father, Bogue Miller, had gone to some trouble to hang from the ceiling before he died. Ah, there's Kelly's Gidget sculpture, emerging from the dark like a sunrise. And the figure of Kelly himself, tapping draft beer behind the bar.

Kelly was in his early thirties but looked ten years younger. Bamboo-skinny, big-eyed, plush-lipped, his melon-like head shingled with stiff plates of red hair, his skin so pale he appeared to fluoresce in the dim bar. This hangdog mingle of features begged insults, flimflams, and beatings. But only newcomers and fools were ever led on by his meek appearance; the regulars knew Kelly's aspect belied a belligerent, uncharitable nature that best went untested. There were plenty of tough folks in Kelly's, with a lot of time spent in jails and other locked places, but they did not antagonize Kelly, partly out of respect for his deceased father, and partly out of respect for their own health. Kelly carried around a big rusty socket wrench, with which he had over the years splintered many a wagging jaw. When he was in junior high he'd maimed a classmate with a winch chain over an auto-graphed Stan the Man baseball and got shipped off to reform school. It happened to be the same place that Lou had been sent for impregnating his girlfriend, Charlotte; he and Kelly arrived on the same day. Though they'd never been friends, it was Lou whom Kelly had chosen to accompany him on his escape a year later, mainly because Lou was good-sized and strong, and would be able to carry a big bag of Kelly's clothes. Kelly was something of a clotheshorse, or at least thought himself so.

Kelly certainly hadn't changed much in three weeks. Today he wore 1930s-style suspenders over some kind of shiny shirt. He looked like a dolphin that also happened to be an attorney.

Kelly had taken over the joint a couple of years before, after his father died following a sea-nettle sting. Bogue had been a truly fair and generous man, who had over the years extended to Lou, and quite a few other patrons, carelessly generous tabs. Lou's tab had amounted to $4,940, or at least that was the number Lou recalled Bogue last mentioning to him, which had been about a month before the sea nettle lanced Bogue's beer belly.

Kelly had never brought up the subject of the delinquent tab to Lou or to any of the other betabulated patrons after he took over, so Lou figured the numbers had been mercifully lost in probate. Or maybe Bogue had never written the numbers down in the first place; maybe he'd just been a specialized idiot savant and kept the sums in his head and they had been buried along with the rest of the man. Either way, it looked like the days of bar tabs were over: Kelly, on his first day as the new owner, announced in his high-pitched Piney Woods bray that no one gets a tab.

"Nobody," he'd whinnied.

"Even Dot?" somebody said.

"Nobody."

Bogue hadn't kept a tab on Dot; he just gave her whatever she wanted, and had done so ever since she first set up business at the jukebox end of the bar, ten years before. Bogue claimed that it was just sound business to underwrite a whore's drinks, but his real reasons were probably much more soft-hearted—everyone knew he adored her.

"I worry, I *worry*," Bogue would fretfully say to anyone who was too drunk to escape a conversation with him whenever Dot was out on a service call or just taking the day off. "She's like my only daughter I never had instead of the son I did. Oh *me*."

Dot's eyes were just like Sophia Loren's, and she moved with the grace of Audrey Hepburn. Dot was legendarily rumored to have entered the service industry because she liked it. She said it made her wealthy enough to be able to pursue her hobby, which was collecting first editions of fiction by women.

One day she brought in a nice *Mockingbird* to show Bogue, but he wasn't there. Kelly was there instead. He pushed a Tom Collins across the bar.

"Daddy's dead. Funeral's at Emken-Linton. This is your last one on the house."

Paying for her own drinks—expensive, complicated mixed beverages, the recipes for which Bogue had often had to look up in a tattered copy of *Cocktail Boothby's American Bartender*—forced Dot to raise her rates, which in turn made her less accessible and more desirable. These circumstances excited discontent among the patrons, a state to which Kelly responded not by refelting the pool table or sharpening the darts or updating the jukebox, but by raising the beer prices, rationing the swamp cooler, taking away the baskets of free pork skins and substituting nickel baskets of humid popcorn, and, most memorably, removing the free-coffee station and in its stead installing a knee-high cinder-block postament upon which he had placed a life-size fake-marble sculpture of a nude, ill-proportioned Gidget lying

Madame Récamier on a fake-marble surfboard, the whole installation footlit with soft incandescents.

Lou stepped down into the barroom. He felt the spongy give of spilled stale popcorn underfoot. He detected the vague vetiver base note of Dot's Chanel No. 22. Dot herself was nowhere to be seen, but her purse was on the bar next to one of her leather diaries and a fancy-looking mixed drink.

Many of Lou's friends and acquaintances were sitting around, drinking beer, watching a Braves-Giants game, and rapidly eating what looked like beer nuts. Scattered among the patrons were half gallons of milk and rolls of paper towels. This was all new in the last three weeks.

Lou sat down at a table with his old drinking buddies Doak Boyle and Tom Vlodzny. On one arm Doak wore a cast with hundreds of little dollar signs drawn on it in Magic Marker.

"What's the good word, Lou?" said Tom.

"What's this? Eggnog?" said Lou, picking up a milk carton and sniffing at it. "And, what, no popcorn? What're these things? What's got into Kelly? What happened to you, Doak? Where's Dot?"

"I wasn't ready for a pop quiz," said Doak.

"It's not eggnog," said Tom. "Milk."

Doak took the carton out of Lou's hand, took a big pull, ate a handful of the beer-nut things, drank half a bottle of beer, then pointed to a roll of paper towels. "Hand me that Bounty."

Lou handed the roll over. Doak pulled off a few sheets. He swabbed his forehead, dabbed at the tears on his cheeks, and blew his nose. Finally, he took a deep breath. Then he ate another handful of nuts.

"Beer nuts're a pretty extravagant change for Kelly," said Lou.

"These're little peppers," said Tom. "Pequins. Tasty. Warm. Habit-forming. The milk's to cool yourself down and neutralize the digestive fireworks. Works better'n beer. Bounty's for stanching the sinuses, and for swabbing the brow."

"That right," said Lou, tossing a modest handful of peppers into his mouth. "That was charitable of Kelly."

"Not really," said Doak, panting and wiping the sweat off his neck. "The pequins and the Bounty are free. But the milk's five dollars a carton."

"That's criminal," said Lou. "I'll bring my own damn milk if I need it, a dollar a gallon. Or I just won't consume little dry peppers. They're pretty fair, though. And warm."

Anita, the waitress, appeared at the table with another bowl of peppers and a beer, which she set before Tom.

"I seen you had come in, Lou, want me to find a Pearl for you?"

"Thank you, doll," said Lou. Gums scorched, throat anesthetized, he reached for Tom's beer. Tom snatched it away and hid it under the table.

"Mine," said Tom.

"Warm, huh," said Doak.

"Kaw," said Lou, reaching for Doak's milk. Doak took it away and hid it under his arm. Tom did the same with his milk.

"Eik," said Lou, standing up, looking around desperately. Everyone in the bar grabbed their milk to protect it from theft. One man took a small revolver out of his pocket and set in on a table.

Lou staggered up to the bar, behind which Kelly was standing on a small stool, tacking a Deutschmark to the ceiling.

"Ik."

"Lou," said Kelly. "Howdy. Did your time? How was it? See old Leghorn? Good, good. That's fine. We're sure happy to see you here at the saloon."

"Nlk," said Lou, finding his last two dollars and slapping it onto the bar.

"What? Tequila? Coming right up."

Lou shook his head. Tears and snot ran freely. His eyes were nearly swollen shut. Terrible, sharp metal doors slammed in his intestines.

"Ik." Lou stabbed his money with his finger.

"Oh, milk?"

"Gnnnn," said Lou, nodding like a pumpjack.

"Surely. Quart? That'll be $5,091.55."

Kelly unfurled a long roll of cash-register paper with tiny pencil markings on it. At one end it said LOU BORGER in big block letters.

"I'll start with these two dollars," said Kelly, snatching up Lou's money. "And believe me I will collect every motherloving cent from you, Lou Borger. And every other gin-soaked pecker in here."

Lou fell to the floor. His eyeballs felt like pickled eggs. He rolled over onto his back and looked up at the barroom. He surveyed the undersides of the stools and the distant, blurred green rectangle of the game.

"Goddammit, Kelly," Lou heard someone, a woman, say. "He just got out of the goddam joint."

"He always just got out, Dot," said the other voice.

"Gimme some milk," said Dot.

"No."

Somebody stepped on his Lou's triceps. Then, a voice in his ear.

"Lou, stand up."

"Aht?"

"Yeah, it's me," said Dot. "Let's go."

Dot guided Lou along the sidewalk as his vision and his ability to respire slowly returned. He spit out sheets of flesh that the peppers had burned off the inside of his mouth.

"Dah," said Lou, regretting it instantly, as a new blaze broke out in the back of his throat.

"Be quiet," said Dot. "I'm going to run in here for some things, then I'm taking you home. Just sit yourself down here on the curb."

Lou watched her go into Murra's. She came out with a carton of L&Ms and a half gallon of milk.

"Here," she said handing him both. "They're out of Cheez-It."

He looked up at her as he drank the milk. The sun was directly behind her head. He felt like he was staring into an eclipse of a thousand-foot statue of Cleopatra.

"Thank you."

"You in a lot of trouble with Kelly," Cleopatra's statue said. "He means to collect. Doak only owed him nine-hundred dollars for his bar tab, but Kelly got somebody to break his arm. Doak paid him half of it right away. Kelly won't let you off."

"My truck's gone. What am I supposed to do? I lost my offshore job."

"He already started to collect," said Dot, glancing behind her, in the direction of Lou's apartment.

"What's that mean?"

"Let's get you home first."

Dot helped him stand up, and walked him down to his apartment on Flangit Street.

Scattered around the tiny cement courtyard that served as Lou's front yard were three weeks' worth of *Galveston County Daily Newes*. Below the picture window next to a partly vaporized geranium plant that kept coming

331

back to life year after year was the baby pool that Lou used for relaxation. It had been hot lately; only two or three inches of water remained. Lou noticed that there was a hot plate in the pool, and scads of bottle caps, some of which were facedown, floating like tiny rafts.

"Hey," said Lou. "That's my hot plate."

"Lou…"

"And those… that's my goddam bottle-cap collection."

Lou looked up at Dot, and then at his apartment. The door was just ajar. Inside was a darkened ruin.

"Try to keep an open mind here, Lou," said Dot, following him inside.

His phone was gone. His TV was gone. His hi-fi and collection of country and western records were gone. His painting of bluebonnets. Both his electric fans and his percolator. On the kitchenette floor were the contents of his icebox—a pooling Velveeta, a jar of olives, a measled pork chop convulsing with larval beings. The icebox itself was gone.

All his work clothes were still on the floor where he'd left them, but the three-piece suit he kept on a hook on the bathroom door was gone. The pistol he kept in the drawer in the table that he put his alarm clock on was gone. The alarm clock was gone, too. They'd taken all the light bulbs, and his electric shaver, which had cost him nearly fifteen dollars. The jar of pennies he kept on the mantel over the fake fireplace was gone. The first edition of *Jude the Obscure* that Dot had given him was gone.

"Oh, fuck all this, Dot. Look. They took the book you gave me."

Lou grabbed the sides of his head and moaned.

"It's okay, settle down," said Dot. "It's just a book."

Lou didn't mention that that was where he kept his only picture of Charlotte.

"Aagh." Lou tugged at his ears.

"I told you. He means it."

Lou sat down heavily on the divan.

"He got my pennies and my .38."

And Charlotte, he got my Charlotte.

"Maybe you should commit a small crime and go back to jail," said Dot.

"Merle Haggard's gonna write a song about me."

Lou got up, went outside, and gathered up all of his newspapers. He came back in and dropped them all on the bare tile floor. He noticed that the circular rug made of yarn that he'd found in the bed of his pickup one day was gone.

"My little rug's gone."

Dot kicked off her shoes, tiny green mules, and made herself comfortable on the divan. She peeled open the carton of L&Ms, opened a pack, tamped a cigarette against a front tooth, and looked around on Lou's coffee table.

"I'm sorry, baby. Got some fire?"

Lou went into the kitchen and returned with a box of strike-anywhere matches, which he tossed in Dot's lap. She lit a cigarette and offered it to Lou. He wasn't much of a smoker, but he took a long drag anyway. "I hate Kelly."

"Sit down, baby."

Lou picked up Dot's feet, sat down on the end of the divan, and replaced her feet in his lap.

"Lou, you might want to think about New Orleans."

"I don't like to think about New Orleans," said Lou, which was very true; he'd been there four times, and only once had he returned with any memory of what he'd said or done there, and that time he'd fallen off a balcony onto a mobster, who'd pummeled him with Lou's own shoe until they were interrupted by a policeman on a horse who arrested both of them and put them in the same cell, where the mobster completed his task by pummeling Lou with his other shoe and poking him in the eyes, Three Stooges–style. Lou, temporarily blinded, had had to be chaperoned back to Texas City by a couple Eagle Scouts who found him bumping into poles in front of the jailhouse after he'd been let go.

"A judge would have to sentence me to New Orleans to get me back there."

"You can't stay in Texas City," said Dot, trying to light a match with her thumbnail. "You know Hoyt Delahoussaye? He only owed Bogue a hundred and some-odd. And nobody's seen him in a week."

"You think Kelly *killed* him?"

"Did I say that?"

Dot's feet in his lap initiated an erection in Lou's pants. Not that anything would come of it. They didn't exactly mesh as lovers. Lou didn't enjoy blow jobs in general, even though it was well documented that Dot could accomplish them in a variety of epic ways. And regular sex never really worked out between them. She liked to be on top, and Lou had no trouble being on bottom—the role fit his nature—but Dot liked to bounce hard and vigorously, with great amplitude, and Lou sometimes slipped out when she was at the peak, at which time she would slam back down quickly, once catching the tip of his penis and folding it in half. This had necessitated a trip to the emergency room, ruining the mood. It had complicated every one of Lou's penis-related activities for more than a year.

He leaned over and picked up a newspaper off the floor.

"Look here, the Padres are in last place again," he said, mentally commanding his erection to revert to flaccidity. "Wait. That was a couple weeks back. Let's look at today's standings."

Dot got the match lit, but the flaming head broke off and shot into the kitchen, where it landed in the pool of Velveeta and sizzled out. The room smelled briefly like a grilled cheese.

"Here it is," said Lou, slapping the newspaper on the table. "Today's goddam paper."

"Lou."

"Oho," said Lou. "Still in last place. I hope they get so far behind they wind up first place in the minors. I hate the Padres."

"Lou! Are you listening? I think the man may really put the hurt on you."

"Don't worry about me. I won't ever go back in there again. Look, I made an oath to quit drinking, anyway."

Lou reached into his pocket for his envelope and gave it to Dot, who declined to read it.

"You ought to mind me," she said instead.

"What about you? Why don't you go to New Orleans?"

"I can't go. This is where my business is, this is where I'm from, goddam Texas City. I can handle Kelly. You're between careers, and you're really from anywhere."

A few moments passed. Lou studied the newspaper, trying to ignore his erection. Dot looked around for Lou's ashtray, a two-foot-high sand-filled brass compotier on a clawfoot stand, but it was nowhere to be seen. She stubbed out her cigarette on the coffee table.

"Well, why isn't he making *you* pay?" Lou finally said. "Those were some costly philters you had old Bogue mix you over the years."

"Kelly's collecting on me three times a week. Hour at a time."

"Oh, goddammit, Dot, don't tell me that."

"He makes me call him brother. He calls me sister. Because of Bogue always telling him that I was like a daughter to him."

"Son of a bitch," said Lou. The idea of Kelly touching her repulsed him. His erection began to renege. But before it did, Dot noticed it with her foot.

"Hey, are you up?" she said, feeling around his crotch with her bare feet. "You are!"

"No, no, I'm not, I mean to say I was, but it's ending now, and it was an accident in the first place, but it's——"

"You son of a bitch," she said, yanking her feet out of his lap. "You like that? You like thinking about me and Kelly? I oughta——"

"No, Dot, you've got the wrong i——"

She kicked him in the jaw with her heel, hard, producing a bony *chrk* sound.

"Urln!"

"You... you... Did you know I've been working extra with Kelly to pay off *your* tab? You fucker. You're on your own now, man."

"Wait, now, just hold——"

Dot stood up, slipped on her green mules, and left, leaving the door wide open. Lou didn't run after her. They often had communication misalignments, and they often ended in minor violence, Lou always on the receiving end. Most times he deserved it. This time, though, he hadn't been guilty of what she thought he had. Kelly made him sick. Lou didn't have the guts to stand up to him. Which was too bad, because giving Kelly a good throttling would be a fine way to make up with Dot. As it stood, though, it seemed unlikely that Dot would forgive this anytime soon.

Lou poked at his chin, rubbed his jaw, stuck out his tongue. The bottom half of his skull sang like a tuning fork. Something fell out of his mouth. A tooth, of course. A fine specimen, a shiny alabaster molar. Lou took care of his teeth. He tried to replace it, but it wouldn't stay. On the coffee table he noticed one of those little strips of red plastic that one pulls off a pack of cigarettes to open it. He picked it up, wrapped it around his tooth, then wedged it back in its socket.

A little girl, nine or so, appeared at the front door. His neighbor, Belinda.

"Hi, Mr. Borger."

"Whaddaya say, Bee," said Lou.

"Why'd Dot stomp off like that?"

"We were engaged in a brief misunderstanding."

His tooth felt funny. Maybe it wouldn't take root again.

"Oh. You're bleeding."

"I know that. What's on your mind, young lady?"

"Momma needs your *TV Guide* to look for *Room 222*."

"I don't take the *TV Guide*," said Lou, poking at his tooth with his tongue. "You can have the TV section outta here, though. I'm keeping the local news part, though."

"Okay."

Lou subtracted the entertainment section from the paper and handed it to Belinda, who bore a poultice of some kind on one elbow.

"What happened to you?"

"I fell off LuLu's ten-speed."

"Who's LuLu?"

"My visiting cousin from Bossier."

"That's just fine."

"I hate LuLu."

"That right? What for?"

"She stole my Sno-Caps and fed them to Marvin."

"Who's Mar... oh, never mind, okay, then, run along, I need to cry and sort out my life."

"Okay. We're having corny dogs anyway. Bye."

Belinda left the door wide open. Why women often left doors wide open was a mystery he could find no patience to contemplate at the moment. And he was too tired to get up and close it.

He turned to the funnies. Then he remembered that the goddam funnies were on the other side of the goddam TV page, which he'd just given to a nine-year-old, goddammit.

"Goddammit."

Lou wadded up the paper and threw it at the pork chop. He picked another paper off the floor and opened it at random. Obituaries. Opposite was a list of Texans recently killed in Vietnam. One fellow, an unlucky GI who'd never even made it out of boot camp, had been bitten by a wandering spider.

But this was what got his attention:

DURANT Mrs. Louisabelle "Mère" née Desqueyroux, 55, of Austin. She is survived by a daughter, Charlotte Durant, and a granddaughter, Livia Durant Moppett, both of Austin. Services for Durant will be held at Weed-Corley-Fish Funeral Home at 4:30 p.m., Thursday, September 12.

Lou stared at the paper. Livia. A daughter. He closed his eyes and examined the afterimage of the black-and-white print inside his eyelids. He opened his eyes. He read the obit again. He put the paper down, went outside, looked at the sun for a minute, tapped his baby pool with the tip of his boot, making little ripples that caused the floating bottle caps to bob, went back inside, went through his divan and chair, where he found ninety cents and a gold earring he didn't recognize, crawled around the apartment looking for change on the floor, paused at the pork chop to marvel at the biology at work in his home, stood up, read the article one more time, jammed his tooth more firmly down into its socket, and went outside again, where he sat on the curb and watched Belinda fire bolts from a bright green water gun at a fifteen-year-old-or-so girl riding a pink ten-speed down the street.

"Kids!" hollered somebody. "Dinner!"

LuLu and Belinda dropped the bike and the gun and ran toward the voice.

Lou stood up. He walked over to the where the girls had dropped the bike and gun. The front wheel on the bike spun freely. There was evidence that the decorative, streamlining plastic tassels had been cut off of the ends of the handlebars. He picked up the bike. He got on. He wobbled a few feet, experimenting with speeds and brakes and keeping his jeans' cuffs out of the gears. He picked up a little speed down the slight incline of Adelaide Street. At the corner, he turned west, and disappeared.

XIX

September 1969

Lou Borger sat on the shoulder of Morris Avenue just west of Alvin, legs spread, thumb in the air. LuLu's bike lay in the gravel nearby. He figured he'd ridden more than twenty miles, the last four being a comprehensive review of all possible pains a pair of legs could suffer, until they seemed to jelly, and Lou went down.

A locomotive-like semi, pulling an unoccupied flatbed, roared past him, kicking up a zero-visibility storm of gravel and colachi. When it blew away, Lou notice that the truck had stopped on the shoulder a hundred or so yards away. It began to back up. Presently it stopped next to Lou. Stripes of ash-colored bird shit covered the windshield, except for the double arc of the wipers' purview. The girth and lumpiness of the streaks suggested vultures were the source.

A window rolled down.

"What happened to you?" said a voice in the cab.

"I grew tired of pedaling," said Lou, not moving.

"Where you ride from?"

"Texas City."

The trucker was silent for a moment. Lou could not make out his face; only a big grizzly jaw, chewing something.

"Where you headed?"

"Austin."

"Looks like your handlebars need retasseling," said the trucker.

Lou had been sitting on the shoulder for an hour, and this was the third traveler who had pulled over and mocked his bicycle. The other two had driven off after Lou strafed their cars with fistfuls of gravel. Lou was hot, sunburned, thirsty, and had decided that he would not rebut the next person who stopped to smart off.

"Yessir," said Lou.

The trucker chewed.

"Austin," he said, matter-of-factly, "is uphill from Texas City."

"Yes, sir."

Chew, chaw, chew.

"Well, okay, then," said the trucker, opening the passenger door. "Climb on up."

"I can't make my legs move."

Chew.

"Can't you pull yourself along, then hoist yourself up and swing on in?"

"No, sir, I can't get a purchase, what with the gravel and everything."

Chew, chew.

Lou heard the driver's-side door open and shut. Under the cab, the largest feet in the largest cowboy boots Lou'd ever seen landed in the gravel. They then carried the largest man in Texas around the truck and placed him in front of Lou.

"You're gonna have to ride on the bed," said the trucker, who then crouched down and picked Lou up like a sleepy four-year-old and lifted him up onto the flatbed trailer. "Just grab onto that rope yonder."

"Can't I ride in the cab?" said Lou.

"No."

"Why not?"

"Your legs're paralyzed, maybe your bowel controls're paralyzed, too. Can't risk that."

"I'll need my bicycle," said Lou.

The trucker picked the ten-speed up with one hand like it was a squash racket and put it on the trailer next to Lou.

"Hold on tight," he said. "We'll be to Austin in about four hours."

When they got to town, around dusk, they pulled into the big dirt parking lot of a roadhouse.

Lou sat up, undid his ad-hoc rope harness, and poked at his thighs.

"Well, we're here," said the trucker, who was just climbing out of the cab. "You got people here you want me to telephone?"

"No, not really," said Lou, carefully bending one knee, then the other.

"Want me to telephone the handlebar-tassel limousine?"

"I'll find my way," said Lou, who scooted over to the edge of the flatbed and slowly let himself over the side. With his feet a few inches or so off the ground, he let himself drop. His feet hit the dirt, then skidded away from each other, causing the splits. He screamed.

"Ow," said the trucker.

Lou started to cry.

"Quit that, now," said the trucker. "No-o-o crying now, you're just fine, yessiree."

"Baaah," said Lou.

"Settle down now, fellah. Look, you thirsty? How about a nice beer?"

Lou calmed down a little, and looked up at the trucker.

"That sound good?" said the trucker. "Nice cold beer?"

Lou whimpered. "Okay."

The trucker picked Lou up again, grabbed the bicycle, and carried them inside the bar. He set the bicycle down and engaged its kickstand. He balanced Lou carefully on a barstool. He put a dollar on the bar.

"This man needs to sit here in this beer joint until his legs deparalyze," said the trucker, wagging a souvenir-baseball-bat-sized finger at the bar at large. "Those are *doctor's orders*. Now, I gave him some starter money, but his subsequent beers shall be sponsored by the publican and the patronage. Y'all heard me?"

A murmured *yessir*.

"Okay, fellah, you on your own."

The trucker left.

The bartender, who had been leaning over talking to a young woman at the end of the bar, stood up and brought Lou a bottle of Pearl.

Lou reached for the beer, then realized that he had so far honored his oath, however inadvertently.

"Bartender, I think I'll have an RC instead."

"No refunds," said the bartender.

"That's fine," said Lou. "Just donate this beer to someone and sell me a goddam Royal Crown Cola."

The bartender slid the beer down the length of the bar, like in the oaters. The young woman at the end caught it without looking up.

Lou drank down his cola, then whacked himself on the thigh with the empty bottle. Slowly, sensation was returning. He rotated his ankles. He swung his legs. He kneaded his calves. He curled up his toes, massaged his kneecaps, pinched his hamstrings. Holding on to the bar, he carefully slid off the stool onto his feet.

It was all right. It would be all right. He let go of the bar, waved his arms for balance, and took a small step. Then another. Soon he was heading for the men's room all by himself.

He administered to himself a faucet bath and combed his hair with his fingers. He examined his tooth in the mirror. The cigarette-pack strand was holding the molar in place. It had stopped bleeding.

When he returned, there was a fresh RC Cola at his barstool, and the young woman from the end of the bar was sitting on his bicycle, squeezing the hand brakes.

"I had one like this," said the woman, who Lou realized couldn't have been more than twenty-five or twenty-six. She rang the little thumb-operated bell. "I'm going to ride it."

She climbed down, kicked up the kickstand, then wheeled it out the door.

"Okay," said Lou, to no one in particular.

He grabbed his RC off the bar and prepared to follow the woman outside.

"Don't you pitch no woo her way, pardner," said the bartender, pointing at Lou, and then at the door. "That is a *married woman*."

"I just want my bike back."

Outside, Lou found the woman riding around the dirt parking lot under the floodlights. Her shoes, black high heels of some kind with little buckled straps, lay in a tiny patch of low weeds up against the wall of the bar. She was working hard, standing on the pedals in her bare feet, and had picked up enough speed so the wind lifted up her long black hair.

Lou watched her circle. She wore loose black slacks that must have been made of polyester—they glittered faintly under the bright lights. Her blouse was black, fitted, with three large buttons. One shirttail was out. She went faster and faster, never looking at Lou as she passed. Pinheads of sweat were visible on the bridge of her nose as she went by; then, on the next pass, a vein in her forehead; then, a button missing; then, threads of makeup-tinted sweat on her cheeks, eyes staring at nothing, toes bloody, fists bloodless. One more circle and she looked as fierce as a crusader.

The cuff of her slacks caught in the chain and she went down, sliding headfirst, wrists grooving the dirt, the bike twisting once, twice, then coming to rest on top of her.

"Hey," said Lou. "Jesus Christ. You okay?"

The fall stopped her silent raging. She pushed the bike off, sat up, and began yanking at the cuff of her pants, which had twisted into a tourniquet around her calf.

Lou broke his RC Cola bottle on the wall of the bar, picked a sticky shard of glass out of the dirt, then as fast as he was able staggered over to her, got down on his knees, and sliced open the rock-hard knot of material. She examined her wrists, which were both skinned and peppered with dirt.

"I fell down in the dirt today and hurt myself, too," said Lou.

He helped her stand up. One of her shirttails was still out. Lou wanted to either tuck it in or pull the other one out. Instead, he studied the arc of her nose while she appraised her wounded wrists. She reminded him of Charlotte. And of Dot, who also reminded him of Charlotte. Lou's chest started to hurt. *Now* he needed a goddam beer.

"I need my shoes."

Lou creakily walked back to the weedy spot. He picked up the shoes, which were spattered with syrupy RC Cola. In the toe of one was a scalpel-like shard. Lou extracted it without cutting himself, threw it at the bar, then turned around.

She wasn't there.

"Hey."

He looked around. No one at all; just parked cars ringing the parking lot like spectators, watching him and the distaff bike.

"Hey."

Lou hobbled to the ring of cars, and began to search between and around each of them.

"Miss."

Lou stopped and listened. A sound, nearby: murmured song.

He cupped his hands against the passenger window of a ruined Catalina and peered inside. No one there, just what looked like a whole family's worth of laundry.

Hushed singing.

He peered into the teardrop-shaped window of a Chevy van.

"Miss? You in there?"

He put his ear against the dusty vehicle. Her singing came through, warm and rich, as though he had entered a symphony hall. He walked around and knocked on the driver's door. The singing stopped.

"I really ought to run you to a doctor," Lou said through the closed door. He thought how nice it would be to drive instead of walk or pedal.

He opened the door. The keys were in the ignition. He leaned inside and looked into the black cave of the van.

"I'll drive you," he said, climbing into the driver's seat. "Ready?"

"'Kay." Her voice was shaky, small.

Lou started the engine.

"Which way to a hospital?"

"Take me home."

"Want the radio?"

"'Kay."

"What's your name? Kay?"

"Cherry."

Lou looked into the cave. A vacuous light came through the teardrop. Cherry was lying on a mattress.

"Like 'cherry Coke'?"

"Except capitalized."

"I'm Lou."

"I've never met a Lou," said Cherry.

Cherry had apparently fallen asleep, as she no longer gave directions or responded to requests for them. So Lou drove around town. He relaxed and listened to a country and western station on low volume.

He'd lived in Texas for almost all of his thirty-two years but had never once been to Austin City. He was a reader of newspapers so he knew what went on here, more or less. He followed state politics, Longhorns baseball, high-school football. More than once he'd been tempted to come and find Charlotte, but he knew how that would turn out.

Every few years he'd call. But Mère always answered, like she was waiting for him. He'd always imagined Mère sitting in a wicker chair in a kitchen under a dirty white telephone, waiting for him to call and then have the number traced so she could send some thugs to give him a thumping, or worse. So Lou always hung up. At least the number had been the same since 1951.

Now Mère was gone. Even though he was broke, jobless, homeless, and sober, and there were most likely men plotting his assassination, Lou felt as free and happy as ever he could recall.

Lou had been driving for more than two hours with no feeling for where he was when he found himself driving past the roadhouse again. All at once a sense of direction came over him.

LuLu's bike was no longer in the middle of the parking lot, but was instead leaning against the wall where he'd broken the RC Cola bottle.

He didn't want to stop and get the damn bike. He never wanted to see that bike again. He'd make it up to LuLu somehow. Maybe someday he'd buy her a real bike, a Husqvarna or something. A Moto Guzzi. All Dubble Bubble pink and royally betasseled, a rocket with a glittery vinyl seat.

Now and then Lou caught sight of the University of Texas tower. The top was lit up orange; somebody'd won something big. But for Lou it couldn't be a symbol of victory any longer; he could see it in his mind only as a watchtower behind a scrim of TV static, a tiny figure near the top holding a black stick.

A bright street, Lamar Boulevard. Look, a funeral home. Weed-Corley-Fish. Maybe Mère Durant was in there already, her organs gone and her lips peeling back from her teeth and embalming fluid curing in her veins. Adios, Mère.

Lou found himself in a part of town where the streets were numbered and alphabetized, and dark as a Transylvanian forest. He pulled the van over. He quietly got out and stretched. He walked carefully down the street, then around the block. There was no traffic. The only sounds were the whinnies of eastern screech owls, dogs growling lazily behind honeysuckled fences, silly chirping tree frogs, and, once, a distant train. A large one, judging by the rumble. The Missouri Pacific, probably.

He got back to the van, climbed in, rested his head on the steering wheel, and just about fell asleep when he heard:

"Lou."

"Wha?"

"You can lie down back here if you want to."

"This suits me fine."

Cherry said nothing.

He put his head back on the steering wheel.

Somebody honked.

"Jesus Christ," said Lou, the hairs on his neck standing up, sharp as cactus spines.

"Your sleepy head slipped and honked the horn and scared both of us," said Cherry, from in the cave. "So come lie down."

Lou stumbled into the back. He found the vacant side of the mattress and lay down on his back.

"Here's a pillow."

From the dark something soft and smelling of pot and baby shampoo landed on his face.

"Want some blanket?"

Lou was still sunburned and itchy from his travels, and imagining being covered by a blanket in this humid metal casket made him think of secret police and illegal interrogation techniques and live burial.

"No, you have it," said Lou.

"I don't want it, I'm burning up. Where are we?"

"Uh, don't know. I think Avenue B."

"Oh, we're near not too far from my house. How'd you know?"

He thought about Cherry's shirt button. He imagined it, lying in the dirt of the parking lot, a pickup about to crush it; he imagined diving for it, saving it, giving it back to Cherry. He imagined helping her sew it back on.

"Didn't," said Lou, aware of her shifting on the mattress, which caused the van to creak faintly on its struts. "Never been to Austin."

"What are you doing here?"

Lou did not want to mention Charlotte, or that he had a daughter. He did not even want to think about Mère.

"Had the idea of looking up an old-time used-to-be."

"Oh."

"Yep. Long time ago."

"Find her?"

"I just got to town."

"Where are you staying?"

"Haven't worked that out yet."

Cherry sat up, then climbed into the driver's seat. She started the engine, drove a few blocks, and parked. She switched on the dome light, then turned back to look at Lou. She was awfully pretty, all that black hair.

"You can stay in here if you want." She got out. "Or you can come inside with me."

"Ah, Cherry?" said Lou, sitting up. "What about your husband?"

Cherry leaned back inside.

"What?"

"The bartender told me to let you be, that you were a married woman."

"The bartender," said Cherry, "was wrong."

"Oh." Lou was tired and hot and did not want to think, especially about bartenders and their ways.

"Coming? Or not?"

"I'm an old man, Cherry."

"You couldn't be more than thirty."

"Two years more."

"I'm plenty old enough, already robbed from my cradle long ago."

"Now hold on, I'm just here—"

"Why don't you tell yourself you're just coming in to use the shower? Just keep it down."

"Roommates?"

"Mother."

"Aw, hell, I better—"

"We keep to our own sides of the house. Now, are you coming in on your own, or do I have drag you by your hair?"

* * *

In the green-tiled bathroom next to Cherry's bedroom, Lou quietly took off his boots and jeans and socks and underwear and T-shirt. He stared at the pile of his dirty clothes and considered their recent history. They had been semi-clean when he'd been arrested and put in jail three weeks ago, but they'd acquired a jailhouse musk while waiting stuffed in a locker for their owner to be turned loose. Then he'd put them back on, spent the next few hours sweating his way around Texas City, making enemies, rolling around on barroom floors, and losing teeth, and had then bicycled and hitchhiked to another city. His clothes were no longer semi-clean. His clothes were dirty. It was good to be shut of them, even if only for a few minutes.

Lou stepped into the cold shower like it was another dimension. A nice, hygienic dimension.

When he started to shiver, he turned on the hot water, squeezed Johnson's baby shampoo onto his head, and scrubbed all over with a brick of strange black soap. He opened a safety razor he found on the rim of the tub and rinsed out the tiny thin black tusks he conjectured to be a woman's leg hairs. He wondered if they were Cherry's or her mother's. He took out the blade and rubbed it on the smooth tile to restore an edge, and shaved, mirrorless.

He stepped out. Except for his boots, which were standing neatly next to the commode, his clothes were gone. Hanging on the bathroom door was a red robe that had certainly not been there before. A fat pink towel balanced on the edge of the sink.

After drying off, he wrapped himself in the robe, tying the sash across the erection that had been keeping him company in the shower. He opened the door, glanced around the hall, and ducked into Cherry's dark bedroom.

"Cherry?"

"Get in bed with me."

Lou followed the voice. He found the edge of the bedspread and climbed under, remaining as close to the edge of the mattress as he could without falling off.

They were both still and quiet. Presently Lou became aware of a wet rumble: a washing machine. It stopped.

Cherry got out of bed. She opened the bedroom door, flicked on a hall light, which momentarily silhouetted her body, then shut the door behind her.

He heard a muffled *tktk ttk tk* that could be nothing else but the metal zipper of jeans in a dryer. Almighty God, what was he doing here?

Cherry returned, presenting her silhouette for another quarter second. She could be Charlotte. Maybe he would pretend she was. Cherry got back into bed.

"Hold my hand," she whispered.

He did. It was small, soft, and strong. She turned toward him and put her head on his soft terry-cloth-covered shoulder.

She fell asleep.

At dawn Lou woke to the sound of high-voltage electricity spitting out of a downed power line.

He opened his eyes. A ceiling fan with blades like cricket bats spun lazily overhead. A red cloth was twisted tightly around his body. His legs were alarmingly immobile, yet alive with a deep, intramuscular throbbing, as though run through with kebab skewers.

Facts slowly returned. Jail, Dot, Charlotte, bike, bar. Cherry.

He turned. Cherry was leaning on one elbow, watching him.

"What's that electricity noise?" he said.

"Shh," whispered Cherry. "Those're grackles."

Cherry kissed him hard and pulled at the collar of his robe. She swept the blankets off of both of them with one wide, hard swing of her arm. With both hands she loosened his sash, without ever taking her eyes from his.

"My legs are achy," said Lou.

"Sh."

She straddled him. As she leaned over to kiss him again, her long hair draped around his head, concealing both their faces from the brightening morning. She kissed him harder. Lou felt a foreign shifting in his jaw. Cherry drew away from him, opened her mouth, reached inside with two fingers, and removed a tooth. Lou's. She studied it for a moment. She smiled. Then she began to silently laugh. She buried her face in a pillow and laughed hard for a good two minutes. She resurfaced, placed the tooth on a nightstand, and resumed kissing. She tasted of whiskey and tangerines.

"I like the taste of blood," she said.

She put her hand under his head, her fingers in his hair, and pulled him harder against her mouth. Her kiss was almost painful, and absolutely silent, as though she were holding her breath. There was silence everywhere, Lou realized—the grackles were gone, the bed did not creak beneath them, no scrape of traffic. He opened his eyes. A tiny slit in the thick private curtain of her hair opened, letting in a thread of morning light. Cherry's other hand moved lightly between their bellies until she found him and put him inside her. Lou shuddered, and Cherry answered with a shudder of her own. She put her fingers, wet with her lubrication, between both their lips. As she began to move, the tiny slit in her hair began to close. Lou felt as though he were falling into a deep crevasse, watching the wound of light overhead diminish and collapse to black. She moved, unpredictably, perfectly silent, without a word or a sound, and he came. He grew limp and fell out of her. She shifted, found his jutting hip bone, and pressed herself into it. She held herself above him, becoming a low bridge touching him only at the mouth and hip, her nipples sometimes brushing over the hairs on his chest. She began to move faster, in spasms and starts. How could she remain so silent? He felt a warm, smooth wetness; his semen falling out of her and down between his legs. She stopped, her tongue deep under his, her lips swollen and trembling. She slowly let her breasts down onto his chest, spread her legs farther apart, and began to move her hips in tiny half circles, one way then the other, like the mainspring in a watch, her clitoris a feather on his raw hip. She lifted her head, raising up her thick drape of hair. Her eyes were closed, tears snared in her lashes. She took a deep breath, opened her mouth, and screamed with no sound at all. Lou thought for a moment that he'd become deaf.

But then Cherry whispered: *"Lou, I like you, Lou."*

"Me, too," said Lou. "I mean—"

"Sh."

Lou fell into a light sleep. When he awoke, Cherry was gone. According to an old-fashioned alarm clock on a windowsill, it was nearly 10 a.m. The room, apart from the bed and curtains and Cherry's torn and dirty black clothes and underthings, was bare.

Cherry came back into the bedroom, naked, carrying a huge armful of linens and towels, which she dropped on top of him.

"Warm," whispered Lou.

"We're alone," said Cherry in a normal voice. "Help me fold. Your articles are in here."

They folded towels in silence. Lou hated all other aspects of textile maintenance, but towel-folding made him happy, and he considered himself uncommonly talented.

"What about your old flame?" said Cherry, sitting on the edge of the bed, back straight, pulling a pillowcase onto a denuded and faintly stained pillow she had tucked under her chin.

Lou did not mention that she reminded him so much of Charlotte, and that Cherry had, in a few hours' time, almost replaced Charlotte in his head. The few women who'd ever allowed him into their beds had, afterward, *always* reminded him of Charlotte.

"Don't know."

Cherry tossed the freshly cased pillow to the end of the bed. Lou tried to concentrate on a large Pepsi beach towel that seemed to be wider at one end and was proving a challenge to fold.

"Want me to drop you off at her place? Here, this is yours."

Cherry tossed Lou a pair of holey and permanently stained briefs that time had rendered completely inelastic. Lou blushed.

"Ah, thanks."

"How do you keep those from falling? A little cotton belt?"

She leaned back on her elbows. She looked at Lou with an expression he could describe only as mournful. Her eyes began to darken. Her tears fell in the same way Charlotte's used to: from the outer corners, the right tears following a shallow arc over her cheekbone and then reversing back until they disappeared over her lip and into her mouth; the left was a perfect mirror. But unlike Charlotte, who wailed like a twister siren, Cherry cried like she came: in perfect silence.

Lou looked away. He picked his jeans out of the pile of clothes.

"Your pocket stuff is on the bedside table. You don't have any money?"

Lou observed his pocket things. He still had the ninety cents he'd found in the cushions at home.

He stood up and put on his underwear. Holding them up with one hand, he worked his jeans on.

"Wah."

"Legs ache?"

"Dammit. Ow. Yeah."

"Mine do, too. But from sex, not pedaling."

She smiled. The tear tracks were still there, drying in hourglass symmetry.

"I did accidental splits, too," said Lou, not knowing what else to say. "Hey, does that hurt?"

He pointed to a bruise circling her calf.

"No, but my wrists do a little."

She sat up and put her hands out, palms up. Lou sat on the bed. He held her wrists.

"I like you, did I mention that?" she said.

"I like you, too."

"Don't go see her."

She kissed him, softer this time.

Lou didn't know what to do, so he began to admire his stack of expertly folded towels. Cherry swept them off the bed.

An hour later Cherry pulled the van into the parking lot of Kincannon's Pawn and Pistol.

"What do you think you can get for it?" said Cherry, turning an earring this way and that to catch the noonday sun. "It doesn't look all that valuable."

Lou had the feeling she wanted to know whose it was, but she didn't ask. Which was good, because he didn't know. It wasn't Dot's style; she favored thin silver hoops with dangling things. This was gold, heavy, solid, unremarkable.

"Don't know. It's pretty hefty. Ten dollars I'll be happy."

"Why don't you let me give you a couple of dollars?"

"Don't know."

"Why don't you let me give you my number?"

Lou blushed. He'd just spent a night and a morning having awfully good sex with this woman, without blushing, and now the blood in his face felt like it would make his whiskers pop out and rain down into his lap.

"Look in there for a pencil," said Cherry, indicating the glove compartment. "Unless you can remember it."

"I better write it down."

Lou looked around. Pink traffic tickets, yellow traffic tickets. Unfoldable road maps stamped with sneaker prints. The mattress. The pillow. A squashed cardboard box marked "hall closet" in a child's hand. At Lou's feet, a tidy stack of brown, smoothed-out Hershey-bar wrappers and a paperback on figure skating. But nothing to write with.

He looked on the floor while Cherry looked in the back of the van, but there was nothing.

"What about a lipstick?" said Lou, excited by the idea of having a beautiful woman's telephone number written in fiery, fragrant wax on a thirty-dollar speeding ticket.

"Not here. Look, give me those candy-bar wrappers."

Drawn in pencil on the white side of the lowermost wrapper were the numerals and iconography of a five of diamonds. Lou looked at the next wrapper: the jack of spades. Jack resembled Brenda Starr, Reporter. So did the queen of spades.

"My mother taught me how to draw funnies when I was little."

Cherry went through the deck and selected seven non–face cards, rearranged them, squared them up, and handed them to Lou.

"Keep them in order," she said, "until you memorize them."

Lou began to flip through the Hershey-bar-wrapper cards, but Cherry put her hands over his, stopping him.

"Not now," she said. "Don't forget to call me when you get settled."

"I won't."

I really won't, thought Lou.

"I mean it," she said, withholding a kiss.

Me too.

The man in the pawnshop gave Lou six dollars and seven cents for his earring.

"This is a ten-dollar piece of gold," said Lou.

"That is a six-dollar-and-seven-cent piece of semi-gold," said the man behind the counter, who looked like a cadaver of Jack Ruby.

"How about a trade? I need a suit."

"Ain't got suits. Why, we got rings and electric edgers and tennis rackets and pistols and One-Steps and... wait. We do got a diving suit. Comes with a spear gun and flippers. 'll that do?"

"I have to go to a funeral."

"You can have it all for fifty-five."

"I need a six-dollar-and-seven-cent-suit that is not composed of rubber and zippers, and that comes with a tie, and what will not stand out in a crowd at a boneyard."

Both Lou and the pawnshop man leaned over the counter, studying the earring between them.

The pawnshop man picked up a phone.

"Helga, put that son of a bitch you married on the phone."

Lou ran a fingertip along the sharp crease of the seven folded candy-bar wrappers in his pocket.

"Look here, Lyle," said the pawnshop man into the phone. "Go in the den closet and get your Haggar Sunday suit and run it down here to the store. I got a man here who, unlike your shiftless Presbyterian self, will wear it."

A few minutes later a man entered the store with a brown suit on a hanger.

"What took so goddam long, Lyle, goddammit?"

"Helga made me iron it."

"Go away," said the pawnshop man, taking the suit. Lyle went away.

The slacks were too small, but the jacket and white shirt and green tie fit fine. Lou tucked the shirt into his jeans.

"Too bad about them cow kickers," said the pawnshop man, indicating Lou's flayed boots. "You can polish up that belt buckle, though."

"Which way's Oakwood Cemetery?"

With a fountain pen the pawnshop man carefully drew a detailed map.

"Pawnbrokering might not have been your first calling," said Lou, admiring the man's cartographic draftsmanship.

"I know that," he said.

The pawnshop man pushed Lou the finished map and seven cents, then sent him away.

The funeral was still hours away.

Lou sat down under a tree at the edge of a parking lot to rest. He took off his jacket and loosened his tie so he wouldn't sweat right through them before the funeral. The jacket seemed to be made of fine material, and Lou felt sharp. He wished he had a comb, but the combs at the Standard station he'd stopped at after his visit to the pawnshop were nine cents apiece.

"Your hair looks fine as it is," the girl at the register had said while Lou stared at the spinning comb display. "Really."

She smiled. She had many dimples. Lou left the station in an excellent mood. Austin, Texas, was going to be his new home.

The parking lot was crowded, and getting more so. The drivers seemed ornery, and there was occasional yelling. Lou couldn't tell what they were all doing there; the building that the parking lot appeared to service was free of identification. The people coming in and out looked either furious or depressed. A few looked addled, like those war veterans you see on street corners or sometimes in grocery stores, staring timelessly at the cabbages.

Two men burst out of the doors, fighting like hockey players. Their shirts were torn. They let go heavy but badly aimed swings at each other's heads. It looked like it was going to end in a draw, with both foes prostrate on the parking lot, spent and bloodied, but then one man slipped on what looked like a Vienna sausage, falling hard and smacking his head, audibly, seismically, on the curb. The other man stole something out of the vanquished's hand, then went back into the building.

Lou got up, put his coat over one arm like a French waiter, and went into the building. He found himself in a large room with a few rows of folding chairs in the center. All the chairs were filled, and many other people were sitting on the floor, some in sleeping bags. The graying head of a middle-aged fellow was visible through the slit in a pup tent. One wall of the room was fenestrated with a half dozen clerk's stations, their glass barriers scratched and yellowed. A despairing citizen slouched before each of them.

Oh. The Department of Public Safety.

Leaning against a wall near the door was the man who'd recently prevailed in the parking-lot mixitup. He was concentrating on adjusting his nose, which had apparently been knocked out of alignment. In his lap was a slip of bloody paper numbered 88.

"Eighty-two!" shouted a resentful government voice.

A woman lying on a blanket in the corner of the big lobby leaped to her feet.

"That's me," she announced to the room as she sauntered victoriously to the newly available clerk's window. "Out my motherfucking way."

After a moment's thought, Lou took a number. In Austin, Texas, not only was his luck with women proving quite excellent, but he felt much smarter, too. Lou took four more tickets. He sat down next to the man who'd won the parking-lot fight.

Lou looked at his tickets: 21, 22, 23, 24, 25. He put his head on his chest and tried to sleep.

Hours later the government voice said, "Seventeen."

The funeral was still an hour away. Lou had no intention of arriving before it started. His plan when he arrived was to skulk humbly next to an appropriately distant cemetery tree, then, just after Mère and her hopefully worm-porous coffin disappeared beneath the ground, he would emerge, and wait for Charlotte to see him.

"Eighteen."

Lou went outside. He put his tie and jacket back on, and stood next to the door.

A woman carrying a damp-bottomed sack of groceries approached. She appeared to be in charge of twin girls, five or six years old, deep into a teary bicker. Lou opened the door for them.

"They're up to number 18 in there," Lou said to the woman. "I've got number 21, right here. Just five dollars."

The woman gave him a look one might give a pervert or a tax auditor. The two girls stuck out their tongues at him. They went inside.

After a moment, one of the little girls came out with a five-dollar bill. Lou gave her the 21 ticket.

Lou sold 22, 23, and 24 the same way.

He raised his price to ten dollars for ticket 25.

An elderly man afflicted by an oystery cataract in one eye, and a young woman in a meager burnt-orange minidress both came up to Lou with tens in hand.

A fight all but started.

"Wait," said Lou. "An auction is the only answer here."

"Fifteen," the woman instantly said.

"Twenty-five," said the man, with the kind of eerie calm that attends financial confidence.

"Fifty." The woman hissed at the old man. He hissed back.

"One hunnert dollars."

He took a wad of cash out of his pocket and skinned off a hundred-dollar bill. The wad looked like it contained many, many of them.

The woman began to tremble, then cry. She kicked feebly at the old man, who just smiled at Lou.

"See ya later, alligator."

The woman trudged into the DPS building.

"Here, son. Hand 'er over."

The deal was done.

"Sir?" said Lou, trading the golden ticket for the hundred. "What time do you have?"

Lou stood under a prairie oak about fifty yards from the ceremony. There were at least two hundred people there, virtually all dressed in black, and many of the women veiled. Melodramatically veiled, thought Lou.

The crowd was standing around a mahogany casket that hovered over a big rectangular dirt doorway to hell. How could there be that many mourners for the woman? Maybe some are here to rejoice, like me, thought Lou.

There: Charlotte? Her back to him. Dressed in a loose black dress and a wide-brimmed hat; veilless. Men and women on either side of her. Who? Any one could be a husband, a lover, a friend. A *daughter.*

The woman turned to her right.

Lord. She was the same. Her profile was exactly as he remembered it, except her cheekbones were now sharper and limned with maternal peach, her lips less full, as though from years of overindulgent kissing, and the slope of her nose, outgrown of its little convex arc, was now straight, its angle of decline like the bannister of a very steep staircase.

Charlotte turned her attention back to the casket, which had begun a vagrant descent. Does Charlotte hate her like I do? She kept us apart. That was—is—love, you old crone. Like Romeo and Juliet. Bye, Mère. Welcome to your skeleton.

Lou felt like a fool. Brown jacket, jeans, boots like ruined Pop Warner footballs. Stalking a lusty memory just hours after screwing a distressed woman at least six years younger than he. Why reunite here? At a *funeral?* What if everybody hates me? What if nobody does?

Lou ducked back behind his tree.

He had a hundred and something dollars. He could get a nice room with a swamp cooler and an old easy chair for that. Maybe even a duplex. There, Cherry could find refuge from whatever it was that so troubled her. They could play cards and make love and go to Longhorns games. He would confess his catalog of misdemeanors. He would tell her about Charlotte, and Dot.

What the hell was he doing here? Lou reviewed his life and realized he had never been so jammed full of mixed feelings. He might have fallen in love with Cherry. He might have fallen out of love with Charlotte. He might be in love with both at the same time. He might have lost his best friend. The only comfort he could find was imagining some boneyard functionary dumping him in Mère's grave. That would serve him just right—another eternity with Mère.

Lou sat down. He took out his hundred-dollar bill and put it up to the patchy sunlight coming through the leaves to see if it had an anti-counterfeiting strip embedded in the paper like it was supposed to. It did! Relieved, Lou put the banknote back in his blue-jeans pocket, right up against the Hershey-bar wrappers.

An aptly cheerless hymn started. Lou couldn't make out the words, but it sounded as if the mourners knew them—there was a lot of discordant *la-la*-ing.

One singer, a woman, was a little louder and a tone sweeter than the others: Charlotte. He stood and peeked around the tree, watching her from behind. Again, she turned to the right. Lou saw and heard her sing the only recognizable word in the hymn: *love*.

When they were in school in 1951, they talked about love a lot. When Charlotte said it, her deep, warm *l* cozily flowered into the sexual sigh of the *o*, which, with a gentle bite into her lower lip, fell into the dark well of the *v*. Underneath a table perched on the school's vacant theater stage and covered with a long tablecloth that hid Charlotte and Lou from the rest of the school, Charlotte had told him she loved him, but he hadn't had time to say it back, because the theater had begun to fill with what sounded like teachers and, as it turned out, an even larger authority: Officer Kerr Furr, who threw back the tablecloth, dragged Lou out by his shirt collar, and hissed like a house cat at Charlotte. Lou had not seen her again. Until now.

The funeral was over. The crowd subdivided into cliques, each heading toward their cars in the freshly blacktopped parking lot. Charlotte, accompanied by a group of older women who kept whispering and smiling, and by a man built like Gorgeous George who was holding a squat, ice-filled glass that looked like it might've recently been full of bourbon. They were all headed toward a gray Lincoln. Gorgeous George hugged her, then got into the Lincoln and drove away. The older women dispersed. It was just Charlotte, alone, standing in an emptying parking spot, looking left to right, behind her, obviously waiting for someone.

Lou came out from behind the tree and stood at the edge of the shadow it cast, looking at Charlotte. He began to walk toward her. He straightened his tie. He wished desperately he'd written to her over the years, the letters disguised as gas bills so Mère wouldn't suspect.

Then, two decades of wishes and shame—from the day he was sent to reform school until three hours ago, when he last saw Cherry—fell down on Lou like hail. The candy wrappers in his pocket felt profane, punishing; a cilice.

He was less than ten feet away when Charlotte saw him, and less than five when she recognized him. He stopped.

"Hello."

"Lou Borger."

"Yes, I know."

"Are you here to rejoice in the death of my mother?"

"'Course not, she was a fine—"

"Come on now."

"Well, I guess I'm glad she's inert."

"Watch it. They haven't even buried her yet."

An engine started somewhere. A muddy backhoe operated by a skinny man with very black skin appeared from around a corner and began to crawl heavily toward Mère's ditch. It scooped up a jawful of earth and dropped it into the grave.

Lou didn't say anything, but he imagined the falling earth, gravelly and moist, wrecking the finish on Mère's coffin.

"You better be here to be a daddy to your daughter. Did you know she buried her husband yesterday?"

"Aw, hell," said Lou, despairing, feeling strange, atypically strange, more so than the sum of all the recent strange things. "No, I didn't know that."

"And she could bury me tomorrow, and be without any people at all."

"Don't say that."

"Why didn't you come for me?"

"I was afraid of Mère."

"I knew you'd say that. Mère was all sound and fury signifying nothing. You could've gotten ahold of me if you'd wanted to."

"I could say the same. But we were both cowards under Mère."

"Well, she's gone now. I imagine you're here to propose."

"I—"

"You're not married, are you? Remember, you may have only one wife at a time."

"No, not."

"All right, then. Go ahead."

He thought of Cherry. He thought of Dot. He wished he were dead. He thought of his daughter, Livia. He was glad he was alive.

"Will you marry me?" The Hershey wrappers seemed to tear themselves in half in his pocket.

"Yes, I will, Lou. Now, I want to introduce you to your daughter, Livia Durant Moppett."

Lou smiled.

"Okay."

"I want you to tell her that you love her and that you're sorry and you'll be around from now on."

"I will."

"Livie," said Charlotte, looking beyond Lou, "there you are. Where have you been? I thought you'd fallen into a grave. Now come here and say hello to your daddy. Say hello to the man who's going to marry your poor spinster mother."

XX

In Dr. Gonzales's waiting room, where Charlotte was seated next to Livia—who seemed to be holding her breath—and waiting impatiently for Alva to slide her window aside and call Charlotte's name, she looked down at her hands, wondering why they were stained red and blue. Oh yes: gnomes. Fimo clay. She had spent hours molding and baking those gnomes today. And when Livia had come over to give Charlotte a ride to the doctor, she gave her mother nothing but grief about the little figures.

"Durant, Charlotte Gue!" shouted Alva. Charlotte leaped.

Without a word of greeting, Dr. Gonzales took Charlotte's purse away from her, dug around till he found her pack of cigarettes, and wadded them up in front of her, flakes of tobacco snowing onto the clean white floor of the examination room. She submitted to a blood test and a few gruff questions about her symptoms, then Dr. Gonzales sent her away.

That was twenty-five minutes ago; fifteen minutes in the car with Livia, and ten minutes walking toward home after she abandoned her daughter at a construction site. Her feet were beginning to hurt.

On the other side of Forty-Fifth Street, Charlotte stopped at a tiny neighborhood store that she'd driven past thousands of times but had never entered.

"I would like a pack of Belair cigarettes, please," Charlotte said to the clerk, a child of ten or so.

The child stepped up on a crate of empty Dr Pepper bottles and reached up to get the cigarettes. Charlotte could not decide upon the gender of the child.

"That's four dollars and seventeen cents," said the child, whose voice gave away nothing.

"You know, I really shouldn't be smoking, darling, but…"

Charlotte reached to unzip her black patent-leather purse, but it wasn't there. A feeling of sudden, hot nakedness came over her, as if an antimatter pantsuit had by chance collided with her matter pantsuit, annihilating both.

The child had eighty-three cents out on the counter, ready for a five.

"I believe I've left my purse in my daughter's car. Did you know, I've never forgotten my purse. Ever."

"Oh."

"I'd sooner forget my own head. Ha ha!"

They both eyed the cigarettes.

"Or my daughter's name."

"What is it?"

"Livia."

They smiled artificially at each other for a moment.

Then: "Daddy daddy help crazy lady stranger danger hurry!"

Charlotte darted out the door. She began to run.

After never running in her life, this was the second time she'd been forced to run in as many months. The last time was to catch a taxicab that had arrived at her house after midnight to take her to the downtown Marriott, where she was to meet her old pinochle partner, Bull Wheeler. Charlotte had not been quite ready—she had been experimenting with bras—when the cab arrived, and it took her a good five minutes to choose a slightly padded and seamless pale-green article, and finish dressing. When she finally opened the door to leave, she saw the cab begin to drive away. She took off her heels, chased it, and finally caught it.

Charlotte had been having an affair with Bull for decades. They used to meet once a month in a nice hotel, sometimes in Houston or San Antonio, but lately they'd been meeting every few days. Charlotte wondered how much Livia knew—her remark about Charlotte's having the number memorized had rattled her. On the other hand, who cared?

On the night she'd had to run to catch the cab, Bull had been in an especially good mood.

"Church bells need a-ringing," Bull had said, standing naked on the edge of the trampoline-like queen-size bed, holding a Tom Collins in a paper cup in one hand and the ceiling fire-sprinkler in the other. His testicles, like racquetballs in a tube sock, pendulated beneath his eager, unfellable, non-Viagral erection.

"Bull, you'll activate that sprinkler if you don't let it go," Charlotte had responded, while adjusting her pillows behind her head in order to read the room-service menu in comfort. One pillow had a curious hard spot, as if there were a lemon inside it.

"If I let go I might fall off the bed and snap off the old oyster spoon."

"Get down, and pull those drapes. The people on First Street can see your penis."

"What? Please speak into the microphone."

"I'm tired, and my feet hurt. And you've made me itchy again."

Bull let go of the sprinkler and immediately slipped off the bed, landing hard, pecker side up, on one of Charlotte's high-heel shoes. He squawked once and passed out.

She called room service and ordered chicken Kiev and a slice of blueberry cheesecake. Then she called downstairs.

"Front desk, Nathan."

"This is room 1214. I would like to register complaints. The grout... can you hear me?"

"Yes, ma'am," said the clerk. "...the grout in the tub is mildewed. There is also a suspicious lump within one of the pillows. And the handle on the commode is ice cold and covered in dew."

The desk clerk said he'd immediately send up another pillow, but added his regrets that the black grout and the condensation on the toilet handle were not things he had any idea how to fix.

"Would you like another room?" offered the clerk, who had a Longview drawl that reminded Charlotte of Burt Moppett.

Charlotte had been cranky when she called, but the clerk's voice made her soften. She liked to think about Burt.

"No, no, darling, never mind," said Charlotte. "I think I would like you to send up a tube of Preparation H from the gift shop. Is it still open?"

"Yes it is, ma'am."

"You shall be discreet."

"Yes, ma'am. Is there anything else?"

Charlotte paused to analyze the clerk's voice for smart-aleckiness or false sincerity or giggle-suppression. None.

"That is all. Thank you."

Charlotte got up. She put a pillow under her lover's head and covered him with the bedspread, which, as it settled, assumed contours similar to Mount Fuji's—Bull's erection had not wilted, even with the dormancy of its steward.

Soon a pair of service personnel arrived. The first was a grumpy, cylinder-shaped woman carrying a black steel toolbox. The other, a short man with a red, shiny, closely shaved face, carried a plastic-wrapped pillow in one hand, and with the other guided an unstable cart burthen with Charlotte's dinner.

The cylinder and her toolbox disappeared into the bathroom. Soon the no-nonsense percussion of tools filled the hotel room.

The waiter, ignoring the gin-drowned person before him, parked the cart with one caster touching Bull's ear.

"May I replace your pillow?" said the waiter.

Charlotte nodded, indicating the lemon pillow.

The waiter unwrapped the new pillow, vigorously fluffed it, then took the bad pillow and placed it under the cart's tablecloth.

With an emcee-like gesture, he then said: "I present your dinner."

On the cart were four metal domes, each ventilated with a finger hole. He stuck his finger into the largest dome and snatched it away.

"Voilà," he said. "Chicken Kiev."

He similarly discovered the cheesecake and the toast. The last dome had not a finger hole but a little knob.

The noise in the bathroom stopped. The waiter stepped back, apparently finished with his presentation. The maintenance lady emerged from the bathroom and joined her colleague by the dining cart. Bull snored, a rubbery flapping.

Charlotte gave them each a dollar, and they left.

She lifted the last dome. Her Preparation H.

She ate her dinner, then went into the bathroom to draw a bath. The maintenance woman had somehow managed to remove every speck of mildewy grout. The knob on the commode had been covered with a tiny baby sock.

After her bath, Charlotte applied her H. Charlotte especially liked the feeling of Bull's testicles slapping at her bottom during sex, but afterward her anus was always raw and itchy.

Bull was still on the floor, Mount Fuji undisturbed. She shivered, and so took Bull's bedspread for herself. Charlotte, about to get under the covers, stopped for a moment to appraise Bull.

It was against her bon ton to have sex after a bath, but Bull's erection, with its urethral opening that ran perpendicular to the normal, vertical opening and reminded her of a mopish, eyeless Charlie Brown head, invited her to fuck without, as it were, Bull and his sophomoric dirty talk, and so Charlotte climbed on. She was not a woman who'd ever had a problem with vaginal aridity, and Charlie Brown slid right on in. She could take another bath. There had been periods of wrath and dolor in her life that only long hot baths could soothe, and there were days she took several. After finding a position where neither her knees nor her aching corns would suffer too much, Charlotte leaned on Bull's chest and began to fuck him.

He didn't wake, but some deep id caused his hips to thrust and his hands to grope for Charlotte's breasts. He ejaculated, and soon after, Charlotte had her first orgasm of the evening. An attractive feature of this hotel was its old, thick, soundproof walls, the sort that would keep the vocalities of orgasm from reaching prude, judgmental ears.

Charlotte bathed again, then got into bed next to Bull, who had somehow pulled himself onto the mattress while she was in the tub.

She called downstairs again.

"Front desk, Nathan."

"This is room 1214," Charlotte said. "Thank you for attending to my complaints."

"You're welcome," he said. *Oh, how much like Burt Moppett he is.*

"I'd like to order a 5:30 a.m. wake-up call."

"Certainly."

"Good night, young man."

Charlotte switched off the light, and turned away from Bull Wheeler.

* * *

When Charlotte got home, she was out of breath from running away from the cigarette store. She found a Tuborg in the refrigerator, and located her emergency carton of Belairs. Charlotte ignored Dr. Gonzales's rolling voice in her head and instead listened for the serrated whine of Livia's Nissan, a racket as unique as a thumbprint. But only the whispery din of distant traffic on I-35 made it through the filter of several blocks' worth of trees and houses. In her youth, when the neighborhood trees were slimmer and the houses fewer, sometimes the screams of the deranged could be heard coming from the asylum two blocks away.

Charlotte hauled Lou's old suitcase in from the den and dropped it onto her grackle-watching table. No grackles in her yard, no squirrels.

Inside the suitcase were the two brownish-black leather diaries, their covers flaking and reddish at the extremities, the spines corrugated with vertical creases. Charlotte sucked hard on a Belair and blew a cone of smoke at the kitchen ceiling.

The first diary was filled not with words but with bristly and faintly wavy black lines, more than a hundred on each page, that reminded her of long, very narrow pipe cleaners. She looked close, squinting: ah. They were words. The lines were sentences, penned in the smallest hand she'd ever seen, though not quite as small as those in the microprinted *Oxford English Dictionary* she'd gotten for joining the BOTMC a quarter century ago. *How in the world can I possibly read this handwri—*

Charlotte jumped up and ran to the shelf in the den. She might never have had much need for the big dictionary itself, but at last its attendant magnifying glass would be put to use.

The first entry explained the diary's genesis:

> December 25, 1957. Dear Diary, Today is Christmas day. This is my first diary page. I got these books from Fatty Marlon Chessman as a present because hes a book binder and knows how to make books a girl could like. They have 2 thousand pages each and the paper is thin like a Bibles so the books arent too fat. Fatty is the best baby in my book. Hay I dont mean this book but that other book haha. Fatty is a doll baby. Hes a face man and so I might let him go at it for love. This sharp fountain pen is nice too. I cant wait for tommorow

to write in you Dear Diary. Ill tell you about Rabbit Comiski. The are so many things to tell you so many babys to tell you about I cant hardly wait.

Charlotte sucked on her cigarette. Charlotte squeezed her eyes shut. She felt a little like she had when she read *The Prince of Tides*—she was dying to get to the end but if she skipped ahead she *knew* the end wouldn't be as satisfying as if she'd just stuck with it. So she'd read *Prince* all night, called in sick to the bank, and read the last words around lunch. Her eyes had burned, one elbow was chafed and scaly from leaning on it, her left thumb developed a strange cramp from holding the stiff paperback open—an ache that lasted for weeks afterward and that renewed itself whenever she sat down to read. Like now.

She skipped to the entry a couple weeks before Mère was buried.

August 29, 1969. DD, Lou is gone. I hope Kelly didn't get him. Maybe he is safe back in the joint. Maybe he just got tired of Texas City and left town again and went to New Orleans even though he doesn't like it there, he knows the place and could hide easy, not like Texas City where everybody knows where everybody is all the time. But he sure always had bad timing if he went there with that hurricane a couple of weeks back. I wished I did'nt kick him in the face like I did, I kicked him harder than I was meaning to, I know he was just being Lou. Maybe I'll leave too. I just hope he didn't go up to Austin City, with all that old trouble there waiting on him.

He did, though, didn't he, goddam him.

Ah, the Nissan squeal. It stopped, followed quickly by a hammering at the door.

"Mother! Are you in there? Open up this instant!"

"I'm busy right now," said Charlotte, just loud enough for Livia to hear through the door.

"Busy! What's got into you? Why are you behaving like a lunatic?"

Charlotte ignored her.

"Are you reading those diaries? Let's read them together! Mother! Open up!"

But Charlotte wasn't listening.

XXI

September 1969

"Livie," said Charlotte, looking beyond Lou, "there you are. Where have you been? I thought you'd fallen into a grave. Now come here and say hello to your daddy. Say hello to the man who's going to marry your poor spinster mother."

Charlotte took Lou by the shoulders and spun him a half turn. His body was normally tense and solid, but it relaxed and yielded at her touch, just as it always had. She left her hands on his shoulder blades. Then, just as she was about to give him a gentle push in Livia's direction, he froze up solid again.

"Go," she said, pushing a little harder. "This is all a big surprise so let's just get it over with and go home and catch up."

Livia had also stopped, mid-step. She and Lou faced each other, three strides apart.

Charlotte gave Lou one more gentle shove, allowing her fingers to arc just enough where it felt like she was getting a precious handful of him, but he wouldn't move.

"This is him, darling," said Charlotte, letting his deltoids go and standing off to his side.

Pretending to be bored and annoyed, Charlotte gestured at Lou. "I told you you two didn't look a whole lot alike, but believe you me, this is the man."

Charlotte couldn't pretend nonchalance any longer. She clasped her hands together like Mary Poppins. Her smile broke out, bright and white, under her black, wide-brimmed hat.

"Lou. Livie, darling. Oh my."

Charlotte grabbed each of them by a hand and pulled them into a three-way hug. She held Lou across his wide back, her red nails gaffed into a belt of muscle; Livia she held around the waist. Charlotte's head was between them, tears mixing with the sweat of her daughter's bare collarbone and spreading into the starched cotton of Lou's shirt.

She raised her head.

"Livie, Lou proposed to me. I made him."

Father and daughter looked at each other. Then Livia looked at her mother with an expression that reminded her of a woman being dragged into hell by the devil in a sixteenth-century painting.

Livia began to cough. It was a smoker's cough, abdominally deep, with sustained, staccato exhales, but Livia had never smoked. Not as far as Charlotte knew. Charlotte let go of Lou and began to clap Livia on the back with her palm.

"Wrong pipe," Charlotte said to Lou, who still had not moved. Even his face seemed cured solid, like ceramic.

Livia kept coughing. She fell to her knees, then to her hands. And then she stopped, in mid-hack, as if her fit were just a vinyl recording, its needle lifted away.

Sudden panic made Charlotte's hands cold.

"Are you choking? Liv!"

Livia's hair fell all around her face. She made no sound; the needle was still raised.

"Lou, come here and help me."

Lou still did not move, except to touch his forehead and then look at his fingers, as if he expected running blood.

The needle came down: Livia resumed the long, lone cough as though it had never been interrupted. It diminished into a tiny cry that reminded

Charlotte of an orange kitten she'd found in a ditch when she was five, so little its eyes had yet to open. She had named it Polka Dot.

"Liv, darling, it's all right. It's a shock to me, too. But it's all right. It's all right. Lou?"

Charlotte looked up. Lou was staring at his hands.

Livia sprang. She ran off toward the parking lot. After a moment, she ran around the corner of the gravedigger's stone house, and was gone.

Charlotte said, "It's all right, Lou. Let's just leave her alone. She's a wreck right now. Burt's gone—old Burt. You'd've liked him. He was a good boy, a good man."

She took Lou by the hands and put them on her cheeks.

"You didn't ever forget me, did you?"

"No," said Lou. "I never did."

Charlotte took his cheeks in her hands and gave them a little squeeze.

"Your hair looks pretty good," she said.

"Well, I got it trimmed yesterday."

"I'm going to cry pretty hard in a minute."

Since Livia had apparently disappeared with the car, Charlotte asked Merlin Waller, the gravedigger, if he'd give her and Lou a ride home.

Merlin shimmed them into the backseat of his Charger. By the time they were nearly home, Charlotte's tears had dried, and all she could think about was the glittering glass needles in her thigh—the one that was touching Lou's.

"We ought to just run over to a church and see if there's someone around that'll marry us right now," said Charlotte. "Merlin, would you drive us to University Baptist, first?"

"Y'all have y'all blood test?" said Merlin.

"Mind your own beeswax," said Charlotte.

"Y'all can't just get married," said Merlin. "They forms. They tests. They *laws*."

At that moment, Charlotte realized she cared less about marriage than she did about sex. Marriage, she figured, could wait a couple of days. Plus, it wasn't as if she had to choose. Why, she could have both.

"Better just take us home," she said.

Merlin pulled into the driveway. Charlotte giggled. She hadn't giggled in twenty years, and it felt like she might've torn a muscle.

"Merlin, sweetie, I'll make it up to you," she said. "Out, Lou."

She pushed on his shoulder as an excuse to touch him. She planned to start a pillow fight later, as an engine of seduction. The method had been used with great success by a female character in a novel she was reading, *Bosom Riseth, Bosom Falleth*, a romance. Charlotte opened up an exquisite giggle again. An outside observer would not guess she'd buried two loved ones in three days.

Lou would not get out. Charlotte pushed harder, then gently, gently pummeled his rigid shoulders.

"Out, Lou. I want to show you around."

"I'd better just—"

"Out, or I'll get Merlin to yank on your arm."

Lou climbed out. Charlotte followed. They stood in the driveway. Lou considered the gravel. Charlotte considered the cable-like tendons in her fiancé's wrist. She barely noticed Merlin backing out of the driveway.

"I need to—" said Lou.

"What? Tinkle? Let's go inside."

"I need to—"

"There's a lot to discuss, but I don't want to discuss anything right now. It'll all come out. We just need to all settle down first. Livie'll be back fairly soon, with all her composure. She's a composed girl. Now come *on*."

She took Lou by the wrist. The tendons gave, but just barely, like bass strings. Charlotte pulled him inside as though he were a balloon in a breeze.

"Please excuse the horrible messes everywhere; I just can't keep up with the second law of thermodynamics."

"Everything looks just neat as a pin."

"Oh, no, it's all a horror. Anyway. Mère moved us into this very house after I had Livie. That divan behind you there that I'm going to ask you to sit on was the first piece of furniture we got, except for Livie's bassinet. There was a time when there was nothing in this house but we three women, two pieces of ugly furniture, two decks of cards, and beer."

Charlotte went into the kitchen and opened two bottles of Coors.

"Our neighbors, the Rooneys," said Charlotte, peeking back into the living room to make sure Lou hadn't gone anywhere, "kept our beer in their icebox. Wasn't that kind? We'd sit and visit every day. When was your first beer, Lou?"

Charlotte couldn't stop chattering. It had been like this when they were in school. Lou, quiet; she, mouth amok. But, back then, Lou had never been somber like this.

She went back into the living room and handed Lou a beer. She stood before him, examining him for cracks of happiness in the hard ceramic of his features.

Do you have someone special?

"Don't listen to me, I'm just chattering," said Charlotte.

Who have you been with?

"Isn't Livie just a beauty?"

Have you touched them the same way you touched me?

"Nobody can get between us, now, Lou."

Mère's dead. Don't be afraid.

"Is your Coors cold enough? The icebox is not that devoted to its job. I could put it in the freezer. Or you don't like Coors? I have Miller, but it's tin-canned."

"I stopped drinking yesterday," said Lou, staring down the neck of the bottle, as if looking for a genie. "It had gotten me into some hot water lately."

"Well, good for you," she said, taking the bottle, brushing his hand, just barely, in the process. The glittering needles. "Livie'll drink it."

Lou looked toward the staircase.

"Let me show you around," she said.

"No, no."

"Mère didn't own much, but you might remember that TV," said Charlotte, pointing at an ancient boxed-in screen so convex it looked like half a crystal ball. "Same one she had twenty years ago. It receives Lawrence Welk and the Emergency Broadcast System and snow."

Lou nodded.

"There are all her *Reader's Digests* and Agatha Christie books. Only Hercule Poirot. For somebody so against the race of men, she loved Hercule Poirot. Read them over and over."

It occurred to Charlotte for the first time that Mère had loved *three* men— Big Red, Hercule Poirot, and Burt Moppett. Maybe Mère had been all hot air. The idea made Charlotte even happier than she'd been five minutes ago. Amid two still-warm deaths, Providence hinted at rebirth.

"I'm tired, Charlotte," said Lou, not moving.

Was that the first time he'd said her name since he got here? The first time in twenty years? *Say it again.*

"Let me put you down, then," she said, feeling the same sunless disappointment that used to chill her when she couldn't find him in the hallways at school. "But just a short one. We need to catch up."

I need us.

"All right."

Lou leaned back and rested his head on a blue afghan draped over the back of the divan.

"You couldn't be comfortable. Come with me."

"I better go get some rest at a motel. I'm all lathered and I'll be in the way here."

"You'll do no such thing. Come with me."

Charlotte took Lou's hand and pulled him off the divan. She led him up the stairs and down the hall to three closed doors.

"Bathroom's here," she said, pointing to the middle door.

She opened the right-hand door. "Livie's room, for now. It was the guest room, but since Burt died she hasn't wanted to stay in their house over on Threepenny Street, so she's been in here for a couple nights."

She shut the door, then opened the left-hand door. "Here's me. Go lie down."

She shut the door, went back downstairs and sat on the warm spot where he'd been sitting on the divan, and watched for Livia to come home.

Charlotte woke sharply. It was nearly dark. The cicadas screamed among the leaves. She realized she'd fallen asleep waiting for Livia.

She sat up. Her tendency in such situations was to worry herself into catalepsy, but this time she closed her eyes and forced herself to be cool and circumspect.

As she got up to get another beer, Lou came out of Charlotte's room. *His* room. *Our* room. But he went straight into the bathroom without even glancing down the hall. He was fully dressed: tie, jacket, and soft, worn boots.

Charlotte switched on the living-room lamps and sat back down on the divan. She held her breath, listening for any sound from the bathroom.

She quickly jumped up again and turned the lights back out—darkness, somehow, always seemed to sharpen subtle acoustics. Her beer fizzed. She stuck her thumb in the neck to damp the sound. A car went by outside; she cursed its meddling din, which seemed to last a full minute. Then another one. Charlotte growled, *"Damnation,"* pulled her thumb out of the beer bottle, and took a long drink.

Yet another car. But this one did not drive past. It slowed, then turned into the gravel driveway.

"Hello, Mother," said Livia, coming into the house, her black heels in one hand and her veiled hat in the other. "What are you doing sitting in the living room in the dark?"

"I am a nervous wreck and I am about to explode with both joy and worry."

"Is L... is my da... is your fiancé here?"

"Oh," said Charlotte. She had not thought of herself as a fiancée. There were a *lot* of angles she hadn't yet considered.

"I'm just getting my clothes and makeup—I'm going home. To Burt's and my house on Threepenny. I can't stay here. Will you go up and get me a change and my makeup? And my Playtex. It's on the floor."

"Your daddy's in the bathroom, I'll get him." Charlotte jumped up. "There's an open beer in the icebox, Livie—Lou wasn't thirsty, so he wanted you to have it."

"I want you to go up there and get my things, now."

"Why are you speaking to me in that tone?"

"Please."

"You sit down."

Charlotte put her hands on her daughter's shoulders and led her to the divan. Livia shook her mother off.

"Leave me alone."

"You have an odor... what is that on your dress? Is that throwup? Darling, you *were* sickened at the cemetery. This is all too much for you. I'm so sorry."

"Get my things."

"Lou will be out in a moment."

"Get my things."

"Now, you sit."

"No."

"Sit, dammit."

Livia sat down on the divan. She dropped her shoes and hat.

Charlotte, trying to remember when she'd last hollered at anyone, let alone her daughter, ran upstairs and tapped on the bathroom door.

"Lou, darling, Livie's here, your daughter, let's visit. Hurry, everyone's getting cranky. It's been a long day."

The shower went on.

"Lou?"

Charlotte came back downstairs and sat in the brown wicker chair across from Livia.

"He's bathing. He's exhausted. So how are you feeling, darling? We were so worried about you, but I told Lou you'd be fine, that you were simply reacting to another strange twist of fate. Lou cannot wait to sit down with you. He is appalled with himself for missing your childhood."

Livia said nothing.

"I believe we're going to run over to the First Baptist as soon as we can. How long did you and Burt... oh dear, I don't mean to be so insensitive. I just can't believe a little good luck rode right on in behind the bad. Can you?"

The shower ran.

"Let's try to forgive him. He was a child, and Mère—frankly—was an ogre to him. He was a frightened child. Now he is an adult, ready to return to his family, to be a husband to me, a daddy to you, and maybe even a daddy again. A younger sibling. Darling, I can't stand the sight of you with throw-up on your bosom. Let me get a rag."

Livia looked at the floor. Charlotte went into the kitchen. She wetted a dish towel, got the opened beer out of the icebox, and returned to the living room. Livia hadn't moved.

"We haven't discussed another child yet, but he appears capable."

A sudden, profound blush swept over Charlotte. She had never used such provocative language around her daughter. Or anyone. She hoped Livia didn't notice. She didn't look as though she'd heard.

"I want to go home."

The shower ran.

"Why don't you want to stay and chat with your daddy?"

"I don't know."

"He's a gentle man, Livie. Now take this dish towel. Dab, don't rub. And drink your beer. Your daddy opened it for you."

"You never told me anything about him. You never even showed me a picture of him. I thought you'd come to hate him, and now you think he's great."

"I've told you that Mère wouldn't let me keep anything like that around. I wasn't even allowed to mention his name."

"All because you *slept* with him?"

"Livie."

"You had me because of him. Does—did—Mère hate *me*?"

"Of course not. She loved you. And me."

"Why didn't she make you abort me?"

"That was unthinkable. It wasn't done. It isn't done."

"I hate her."

"Don't be ugly."

"You should hate her, too."

The water heater, nearly empty, thumped at its pipes.

"Watch your mouth, young lady. She took care of me when I was a thirteen-year-old mother. Most girls my age would have been *sent away*. Do you have any idea what that meant in 1951?"

Livia looked at her shoes and hat.

"This is happening, isn't it," she said.

"I don't know what in the world you mean," said Charlotte.

The water went off.

"Mother," she said, backing toward the front door, "go upstairs and get my things. I can't stay."

"My child," said Charlotte, "if you go now, it will crush me."

Livia ran upstairs to her room.

Charlotte heard her tearing open drawers, clicking the little chrome locks on her suitcase. In the bathroom, the sink water went on; its pipes had always sounded different than those of the shower or toilet. Then it went off.

Both doors opened at once.

Livia carried her suitcase in one hand and a wadded-up bra in the other. Lou was fully dressed. His hair was not wet, he was not shaved, his tie was precisely the same slack Y it had been when Charlotte first saw him.

He and Livia looked at each for an instant.

"I am sorry, Livia," said Lou.

He went back into his room.

Livia turned and walked down the stairs, then out the door.

Charlotte, confused, angry at her daughter, impatient with Lou, went upstairs.

"Now, you didn't even get under the covers," said Charlotte, pointing at the side of the bed Lou had obviously been sleeping on. "How can one get any rest on top of a bedspread?"

Charlotte did not ask why he had drained the hot-water tank without ever showering. She did not chastise him. She did not tell him to not break her heart again. Instead, she smiled and began to unknot his tie.

"We'll sort everything out tomorrow," she said sunnily. "Everyone is just bananas right now."

"I'll get it."

He pulled off his tie. His large hands were sunburned. The opening of his shirt collar revealed thin, light hairs on his chest below his collarbone. It was not the chest of the fourteen-year-old Lou that she remembered. It was the chest of stranger.

"I wish I had some pajamas for you."

"I don't need any," said Lou.

Charlotte shivered. She lubricated so fast it was as if a tiny robin's egg had broken inside her.

"I'd like to just sleep down on the divan," he said, stepping carefully past Charlotte. She gently grasped his jacket cuff. And he gently took her hand away.

"Stay up here, Lou. It's so much more comfortable. Now please help me with the clasp."

Charlotte turned her back to him and lifted her heavy black hair off her neck.

"I can't believe I've been in this horrible black weenie casing all day," she said, looking in her vanity mirror to see if Lou was looking at her. He wasn't. "I'm exhausted. I expect I'll fall to sleep the instant my head hits the pillow."

Lou undid the hook and eye at the neck of her dress. He pulled the zipper down to her bra strap. She turned around and allowed her dress to fall to the floor. Lou had already turned away.

"I've come to enjoy sleeping on divans, Charlotte," said Lou, heading towards the door. "We'll visit in the morning."

Charlotte grabbed a pillow by a corner and boomeranged it at Lou at an angle that caused it to land on his neck with a delectable *ntph*.

"Ha."

"Hey."

Charlotte giggled and ducked behind the bed as if to parry a pillow, but Lou didn't return fire. He simply held the pillow by a corner, then dropped it onto the bed.

"I'm tired," he said.

Charlotte stood up. She was wearing only a bra and panties and gartered stockings, all black. She had worn them for Burt's funeral; afterward she had come home and stripped bare, leaving all her clothes on the floor. Then, two days later, she'd picked the same clothes off the floor and put everything back on again for Mère's funeral.

"Lou," said Charlotte, reaching behind quickly to undo her bra clasp before he could leave. "I look good, Lou. I know I do. Turn around, goddammit. Men want me. Burt wanted me, though god help me if Livia knew that. But I've been waiting for you. Lou. Dammit. Come on."

Charlotte had been waiting for Lou, that was true, but she'd slept with several men in the parenthesis. Ernie, the cookie decorator with jailhouse man's-ruin tattoos all over his body; Carver, the ne'er-do-well oilman's son from San Angelo who made up extraordinary, bewitching fables that he would whisper to her after they made love; Gilberto, the confused, excitable Richie Valens lookalike whose knees were just splinters from jumping out of C-119 Flying Boxcars during the Korean War; a man whom she only ever knew as Numie, who had once so assiduously licked her anus while she was bent over an iron-battened treasure chest (that he claimed he'd pulled out of a sunken xebec on the floor of the Libyan Mediterranean) that she ejaculated a small quantity of urine as she experienced orgasm, prompting a visit to her female-issues doctor who explained that minor cataracts of that sort were not terribly uncommon and certainly nothing to worry about. Charlotte could not think about Numie without blushing like a plum and needing to tinkle.

And, every now and then, she fooled around with Bull Wheeler. She'd been doing so for years, the most recent encounter being late last week, before everyone was dead.

"I can't have you," said Lou.

"What does that mean? Turn around."

Charlotte had removed her bra and was bent over trying to undo the plastic garter stays, sharply conscious of the sagging-breast gene that had come from Mère's mother, Wuthering, leaped right over Mère, who was enviably perky the whole of her adult life, landed hard on Charlotte, and bounced, so to speak, right over Livia, whose breasts' alertness was as noteworthy as their fullness, and would land again on Livia's child—that is, if Burt had been able get the work done in the few days between his nuptials and his death.

The stays would not unstay. Charlotte stood up straight and drew her shoulders back, like she'd seen Livia do when boys were around.

"Lou!" she cried, collapsing into a supplicating hunch. She began to crawl across the bed towards him.

But Lou left, closing the door behind him.

Charlotte turned on her back and lay in the warm spot where Lou had been resting. She lit a cigarette. She had read in *LIFE* that cigarettes burned at around 800 degrees Fahrenheit. Without warning, she felt a sweeping and entirely novel urge to burn her breasts. With the cigarette between her lips, she guided the hot, trembling tip of it, which trembled all the more as she tried to steady it, down to within a quarter inch of her nipple. She held it there until the ambient heat scorched her. She quietly yelped, then sat up, feeling polluted and irredeemable, as if she'd been dreaming of horrific crimes she planned to commit.

She smoked three cigarettes while staring at the window, imagining that a Peeping Tom had been watching from the moment she'd let her dress fall. She imagined the Tom was disappointed with everything he'd seen so far.

I'm bored, said Tom, *and it's all your fault. You can't see, can you?*

Charlotte, unnerved, got up and pulled the blind. She turned out the lights, sat down at her vanity, and smoked in the dark, listening for the sound of Lou's breathing.

She realized she had no idea what his breathing sounded like: they'd never slept together. There had been plenty of incautious, emergency sex, often interrupted by a school bell or a car pulling into a concrete driveway or the house lights at a picture show, but they had never had the luxury of falling asleep together, naked, spent.

She got up, put on her yellow nightgown, and opened the door. The hallway was black dark; Lou had turned off all the lights. Charlotte recalled it was a new moon: there would be no seeing tonight, at least not without flooding the living room with the margarine glow of the hall ceiling light.

She went into the bathroom, not turning on the light until she'd shut the door. She ran the faucet, but the tank hadn't yet refilled; the water was no hotter than a puddle in the sun. Her nipple was beginning to itch, so she got in and lay down in the cool water, allowing it to rise until it touched her chin. She turned off the faucet with her toes, and listened to the *pyik poyk* as the water leaked through the imperfect seal of the rubber stopper and dripped into the abyss of the old copper plumbing.

She relaxed. She let her arm dangle over the edge of the tub, waited until her hand drip-dried, then reached down to the bath mat and found her cigarettes.

It will be all right.

In the morning Charlotte would let Lou sleep as late as he needed while she Easy-Offed the oven and opened condolence cards. She'd call Livie at her house on Threepenny; Livia would answer on their brand-new wall-mounted telephone and in the warm lullaby voice she used when she felt sheepish would tell her mother she didn't know what had gotten into her last night, that so many things had happened all at once, but that she'd be over after she put on her face and ironed her blouse, and Charlotte in turn would counsel her to give freedom to the yoke of noisy lovebirds that her new, well-meaning neighbors had negligently given her as a token of their condolence, and to not invite Burt's bandmates—Jerry, Gary, and Larry—over because they'd just smoke marijuana joints and argue over which of them Burt's Vox and Silvertone guitars should descend to; and then Charlotte would advise her to come over and allow Lou to take Burt's place as the man in her life. Charlotte would remind her: he is a good man.

She scratched at her nipple. She wished she'd turned the light out; a bath in the dark was something she liked to have during troubled times.

She wished Lou would come in and sit on the edge of the tub and tell her about himself. Tell her about the women he'd loved; about his job, his pets; does he still collect bottle caps; does he still like the smell of tornadoes, of kerosene; has he kept in touch with his uncle Georges, or with Win Chambers from the football team, or with Cyndy May from Boston; has he heard about fat old BamBam Dworchek and the big St. Louis Hotel fire; has he been back to Wichita Falls; does he have a car; did he ever go to a doctor about the whistling in his head; is his little toe still numb; did he go to war; is he still afraid of bugs and spiders and the sight of blood; what beer does he drink; has he heard of Ye Moppe Hedds—they got a record contract, you know, Lou, they're on the radio sometimes—do you still draw pelicans and explosions and pocketknives and P-38s in the margins of newspapers; why do you smell briny, do you live near the ocean; is there a baseball team where you live; do you have friends or do men still frighten you; do you have any children; are they boys or girls; do they look like Livie; do they look like me; where are they; do you see them; do they call you Daddy?

Charlotte got out of the water. She looked at the mirror and was surprised—shocked, really—to see her reflection; the glass was always hopelessly steamed over when she got out of the tub.

She looked at herself closely. Her eyes were marbled with wandering, red-black veins, her nose was red and swollen, more on one side than the other; she had a moustache that seemed to grow swarthier every week; a weird mole had sprung up in her hairline; the skin across her breastbone had attenuated as though her falling bosoms were pulling on it like taffy; and her teeth were not so white anymore.

She wrapped herself in two towels, then went back into her room, this time not bothering to edit herself for the sake of Lou's sleep.

She sat at her vanity, looking at herself in the far more flattering light of her two fake art deco lamps. She smoked. She ignored her nipple. She thought of Livie, by herself in her and Burt's queen-size bed under the beautiful quilt their neighbors the Rooneys had gotten them from Mervyn's as a wedding present. Charlotte wondered if Livie slept naked now that she didn't live at home. She wondered if Livie *needed* Burt.

Of course she did. At least she could have her daddy back.

Charlotte stood up, dropped her towels, and went downstairs.

But Lou was gone.

XXII

May 2004

Charlotte picked up Dot's diary again.

September 19, 1969. DD, I wish I could call Kellys to leave a message for Lou about me being here in New Orleans but if Kelly found out he might come and hurt Lou, then there wouldnt of been any reason to leave Texas City in the first place. So far everybodys viscious here and carries a knife theyre not afraid to show you. I have more than a g but I hid it all in a old crabmeat can under a board by the Mississippi River which looks like just a big muddy field, because I am afraid somebody will slit my throat for it. I think they slit throats for a nickle here. I hope Lous not too dumb to figure out this is where I am even though he might think I went someplace else because of Camille. I dont think he is too dumb, we talked about New Orleans all the time and Camille missed anyway and hit Mississippi instead, those poor people there.

ps. DD, can you believe I know how to spell Mississippi because of some old song.

ps. DD, Im staying in a room in a part of town called Treme, you say ay at the end but I can see the beer joints on the edge of the Quarters. I watch for Lou out my balcony.

Charlotte had no idea how to prepare for what she knew was coming. She didn't know exactly what it would be, or where it would strike, but she was fairly sure it would sicken her. Only something sickening could be reason enough to have messed everything up like it did.

September 26, 1969. DD, Thought I saw Lou driving a yellowcab on St Claude so I chased it down but it wasnt him. This morning this fellow Loup-Garou, he told me how to spell it with a dash and everything because I asked him once well, he came by really early knocking and I told him I was off the clock so go fuck your mama and that made him awful mad and he banged on my door til it broke and he whupped me pretty good too. I have a yellow eye all bloodshot and he pulled on my hair in back so it feels like the skin peeled off my skull like a orange peel. So I got 20 dollars out of my crabmeat can and got a little pistol. The pawnshop man told me to shoot at the door to his backroom that there wasnt anybody in there, so I'd get the hang of it because I told him I only ever fired a shotgun and that was Lous. So I shot 8-10 bullets at his storeroom door and it echod pretty loud in his pawnshop but he said I was a pro and gave me fifty bullets too. He didnt ask for some throat. Maybe he didnt know what I am. He is handsome. His name is Heron Scaro.

Charlotte wished she'd kept a diary. Dot's life was more real than her own. If Charlotte had kept one, she could pick it up anywhere and read and pretend that maybe she'd lived a real life, too.

Her eyes burned from the smoke and from squinting through the magnifying glass under the lone sixty-watt kitchen bulb. Dot's grammar and syntax were really beginning to bug her, though she had to admit her spelling was awfully good for a hooker.

"Heavens."

She stood up, stretched. She opened a kitchen window. She was fairly sure Livie wouldn't sneak in through an open window, but if she did, Charlotte would simply go to a motel. She would finish the diaries and contemplate her new condition there.

In the bathroom she tucked the diaries under the sink, drew a bath, soaked for an hour, followed up with an hour-long sleepless nap, then got up and dripped some Visine into both eyes. She recalled buying the Visine from a Randalls that had closed a decade ago. Perhaps Livie would come home to find her mother crawling around in the yard, blind, howling, and eating ivy and dirt clods.

She moved the diaries and impedimenta to the floor in the hallway, where visibility, if she had the lights on in all three rooms at the end of the hall, was much improved. She found five pillows and a blanket, a couple of fresh ashtrays, the rest of the carton of cigarettes, and a cold beer, then made herself comfortable on the hallway floor.

October 20, 1969. DD Im sorry I forgot to write yesterday but I was in such a hurry to see Heron I forgot. He still thinks Im a lady and he gets all anxious around me. Yesterday I know he wanted a kiss but I got confused and went home. Gee why is it harder to kiss a man than give him a knob job, beats me. Hes going to find out and that will be that. No Lou yet, maybe he went to Boston, I heard him say something about that one time.
ps. Short date with a bus driver he gave me a brandnew tenner. Come to find out there were two stuck together they were so brandnew, lucky me.

October 22, 1969. DD, Heron came over today, I didnt think he knew where I stayed but I don't think he made me even though I had all my spikeheels and garters all over Creation. He had flowers pink, and yellow, but no red. At Herons place where we went after dinner at Tujagues we didnt kiss and it got time where I had to skdaddle. Because I had a long date with some john my nieghbor Ivette gave me, his name was John too, for real and no kidding he showed me a card with his name right there, that happens sometimes. He went for a old fashioned and afterwards hit the hay for good, lucky me again.

October 24, 1969. DD, Heron brought me a little holster for my pistol that goes on my thigh. I told him he could put it on me if he wanted but he just went to pieces again and went home. I made up my mind the next time I see him Im gonna kiss him and show him my leg with my new holster.
ps. Loup-Garou and some friend with a ugly rug turned up early again. It was raining so hard I didnt want to go all the ways across the Quarters to make

a withdrawl from the crabmeat bank so we had a shorttime circus for 50$. I dont like Loup-Garou and his friend. I had my little pistol just by the bed under the rug but they didnt hit or holler this time.

October 26, 1969. DD, Maybe Lou won't make it after all Maybe he fell back in love again with that oldtimeusedtobe he told me about that time a long time ago at Peggy's when we got so soaked in gin we wound up sleeping on her bar room floor underneath the jug band stage. Hes afraid of her mama though so maybe he just went to Houston and thats that. If he comes back I just hope him and Heron get along.

October 27, 1969. When Heron came over I took away his flowers and kissed his mouth and got him over on the bed. I cleaned up the room before and Ivette let me use her electric sweeper and I put clean sheets on the bed before, too. Heron got awful excited awful quick and turned rabbit before I even could work his belt off. Then he got real sad, I don't know why some men are like that. He said he loved me and after that he was real gentle and quiet. He smelled nice. I told him I loved him too. I say that all the time to johns and I don't mean it and now I don't know if I mean it or not. I sure hope I do Dear Diary.

October 30, 1969. DD, Heron hasnt been around and his shops closed for two days nearly. Where is he?

November 3, 1969. DD, I sure missed you because the pigs tossed me in the wildlife preserve for three days. They caught me three dollar upright with a poor old fellow in Saint Louis 2 I don't know what they did with him but me, I got out at last and went home and there was Loup-Garou who had brung himself and four boys couldnt of been more than 12-13 years old. Those children turned out there pockets and nickles dimes pennies and wad up dollar bills spilled all over. Loup-Garou showed those children my pussy and said thats what yall are gonna fuck but Im going first so pay attention. Thank heaven all those children were little rabbits. Then they set down Indian style like they were at a camp fire while surprise, Loup garou poked me down south. I didnt want to holler at him in front of those children, if I was gonna holler Id of rather shot him. Then Loup-Garou pitched more scratch on the floor and told me to teach those boys French and they would be on their way. I start on the second littlest boy and he took my back of my head and slammed it right up my throat like ladies had been knobbing him his whole life. I gave him a good slap and he started crying. Surprise, the biggest boy gets hold of me and stuff it up from behind and Loup-Garou slaps me back and tells me orbit the littlest boy deep and surprise a knock comes at the door and Loup-Garou answers it! Its Heron Scaro hes got his hair combed and in a suit and red roses in a jar and he sees me. Loup-Garou gets right up in his face and hollers Busy! and pushes Heron down the hall. DD, I don't think I'll ever see Heron again. I cried a lot later on.

November 4, 1969. DD, Herons pawnshop was closed up today. I put some scratch in my crabmeat bank.

November 4, 1969. DD, its really the fifth because its so late. Its raining and Im watching the beer joints across North Rampart but, Heron don't patronize beer joints.

November 5, 1969. DD, I can't sleep and I sent off two johns that came knocking for morning knobjobs before work, I coulda used the money too. The east morning sun is so bright it makes my eyes water.

same day 10 minutes later, Oh brother That sun made me cry for real. I otta kill that Loup-Garou and Im not even gonna write his name out again I hate him so much.

November 5, 1969. DD, A john who says he works for Mister Marcello came by and told me he could help me. Brother I know what that means, that means he was gonna be my pimp, so I told Ivette so long and now here I am in a room over a lunch counter down by Lee Circle and I already have two new gentlemen that promise to be regulars. I get a free chickenfry downstairs once a day if I keep up the rent.

November 5, 1969. DD, I was busy all day so Heron didnt come up in my mind much but later on I laid down on the bed and cried out my eyes so hard I nearly threw up.

Nov 8 Lous here! Lou! Lou! Lou! Lou! Oh I saw him on the street car right out my window and I chased it down and jumped on even though it was still moving. He's here with me now, asleep on my bed.

November 10, 1969. DD, Come to find out Lou was up in Austin City and he looked up old Charlotte. He said it didnt work out and something bad happened but he didnt say what instead he just started crying like a sick child, it sure surprised me, and he didnt want to stop so I let him cry even though I had planned to be the one crying and cry all over him when I saw him again. He beat me to it I guess.

November 11, 1969. DD, The fun wore off and Lous on my last nerves again like always. Except he wont get out of bed even to eat. I told him about Heron too and that just made him cry more and more even though Im the one who was wanting to cry like I said.

November 12, 1969. DD, Hes always right there on my bed until its time for bed then he gets in the chair. He wont talk. I send him downstairs to the lunch counter when I have company.

November 26, 1969. DD, Been real busy making some good dough. I had to send off old Lou. He just mopes and sleeps and hes in the way here.

December 1, 1969. DD, Damn Heron damn Lou breaking my hearts like that.

Charlotte bit her thumb as hard as she could stand.

She took another long bath, got out, and drip-dried in front of the mirror, watching, as the fog receded from the center out, the revelations of her sixty-six-year-old body.

She lay back down in the hallway, naked this time, and read on.

December 26, 1969. DD, Lou paid a visit today, hes looking a teeninesy bit more spry than hes been looking and he found himself a position with a glass company, putting big ole windows up in office buildings. And brought me a present, thats a bottle of purple ink Im writing with right now. Pretty, don't you think, Dear Diary?

December 29, 1969. Just like I knew it all along! I thought if I didnt even write it down in you that maybe it wouldnt be true but goddammit I am pregnant. Today I paid Ivette a visit and she said right away when she let me in Shit I know that face, you got a Irish toothache. So Ivette give me the name of a man out in Bogalusa, thats a town way across the big lake Pont Chartrain. Lou will go with me.

January 22, 1970. DD, Brother I put it off and put it off but here me and Lou are sharing a big chair in a office at a yellowcab dispatch up Bogalusa and Im nervous. Oh there he is, bye DD

January 22, 1970. A whole hell of a lot sure can happen in 3 hours. For one thing the man wouldnt let Lou come in the backroom with the old pool table covered in newspapers Brother that made me more nervous than anything else, I felt like a old fish laying up there. It hurt but it was all over pretty quick and the man gave me Bayer Aspirin pills and a wad up old shirt to catch the blood and sent me back out to Lou then gives both us a ride in his yellowcab over to a motor lodge by the bus station. Lou tucks me in but Surprise he says he can't handle his secret on his own any more. I say What secret and he tells me a whole story about how a while back when he was up in Austin City he slept together with a pretty woman, only come to find out the next day at a funeral that she is his daughter he never met before, Livia. Brother that knocked me down. Lou just melted in tears and now hes asleep. I'm going to eat a few of these Bayer Aspirins and do some crying myself now. Good night, Dear Diary.

XXIII

January 2005

It was past one in the morning. Rance was cleaning himself after an erotic throwdown with Lalique, a Fort Worth socialite who wrote love letters to Rance, and thought he was writing back, but it had actually been Casey at the other end of the correspondence. Casey could write a moving love letter.

The next client was due at two.

For months Marcia Brodsky had been running the Dollhaus alone, without the aid of Casey or Porifiro, neither of whom she'd heard from since the day she fired them. Rance had thankfully not shorted out or otherwise malfunctioned since Senator John Hill bit Rance's replipenis, so there had been no serious heavy lifting to do. The only major project had been a build-it-yourself heated doghouse, acquired so Schmidt wouldn't suffer during the winter. It had taken Marcia a full day to put it together. Schmidt had since found little use for it.

There appeared to be one solution to the Rance/Schmidt problem. Since the two of them simply couldn't live in the same house, Marcia was planning to open premises for Rance, to which she would travel every day, like a real job. But that scenario was not possible for a year or two: it would take at least three million bucks to build and staff a state-of-the-art brothel that would feature, she imagined, not just Rance, but two new dolls, Danielle and Jesse, both of which were still in development at HoBots, but which should be available for purchase sometime later this year. Marcia, as wealthy as she was becoming, did not have *that* much money. So, for the time being, Rance would live in the boudoir, and Schmidt would live in the yard. Marcia had tried to spend a platonic night in the doghouse with Schmidt, but it had not gone well. There was just too much history.

At five to two, Marcia unbolted the door leading from her kitchen into the boudoir, where Rance was dozing lightly between the violet satin sheets.

"Rance."

"Mm? Is it time?"

"Few minutes, dear. Your date tonight is a new client. I think he's *really* new, like a virgin, at least that was the sense I got from him on the phone a few months ago."

"Goody!"

"He likes the lights off."

Marcia turned the dimmer to off, went back into the house, and bolted the door.

A noise at the money slot. A familiar and welcome noise, the brush of banknote paper against the machined steel of the sturdy drop box. Marcia collected and counted its contents: $750 in cash, and one of the many half-off coupons that during the slow month of May she'd foolishly handed out in front of the Yellow Rose, a manky strip joint on North Lamar.

She sat at her console, buzzed the man in, put on her headphones, and set the timer for one hour.

A loneliness like none she'd ever endured set upon her.

She took her headphones off, stood up, went into the bathroom, and sat on the edge of the tub. The loneliness followed her. She went into the garage and sat on a big coil of garden hose, and the loneliness found her there, too. In the utility room, leaning on the stacked washer/dryer, she held her breath and shut her eyes, but the loneliness found her yet again. A stalker in her own home, an ironic companion, a walking vacancy. It was Casey, or an anti-Casey, reminding her that he was no longer there.

When he quit, he'd left the house without shutting the door behind him. Marcia didn't get up to close it until dark. Autumn mosquitos had gotten inside, biting her ankles and shoulders all evening, while Hymie Jeffs and Rance were ensemble. She'd been too harsh. Casey was, on paper (and there was no such paper), her employee, but they'd worked as business partners until Porifiro came, when Marcia unconsciously reduced Casey to rank, a position that at first equaled, then subserved, Porifiro's. Of course Casey'd told Marcia to fuck herself. She'd been thoughtless, unkind, unfair.

They'd argued before. Once, while watching the Texas-OU game on TV at his house in Northwest Hills, they'd fought to an invective climax that forced a week's estrangement, only to make peace by virtue of a chance meeting at 7 a.m. in the automotive annex of Sears, where they both happened to be shopping for tires. Marcia and Casey later remarked that neither of them had any memory of what the fight was about.

Anti-Casey followed Marcia out of the utility room. She sat at her console, her new familiar on one shoulder. She opened up an Excel file. Then, a tiny squeak. Local; no farther than arm's length away. It was more of a *stk*. Then another, *stk, stuk schk*. Like a pixie-scale fishmonger slapping a mackerel against a cutting block. Marcia looked under the console: nothing. She checked the drawers: nothing. Yet it continued. Ah! Her computer. She turned the sound off. But still, *stck, tck, schck*.

She listened intently. Anti-Casey was still on her shoulder, cold, a vacuum, touching her head.

The headphones. Marcia snapped them on. The *stks* were now sickening hacks, guillotinings, battlefield misericords, swords falling through knees and ankles. She turned on the camera. A man in a beard was just leaving the boudoir. He slammed the door behind him. Marcia rushed to the boudoir door. Inside, Rance had been butchered. Jointed. Fluids and pieces of him befouled every surface. Marcia screamed. Rance was gone. Casey was gone. She was alone.

XXIV

December 2004

The late-afternoon traffic began to thicken. Rose and Justine became stuck about ten cars behind a pokey stoplight, the sort of overworked antiquation that might have once adequately managed one lane of traffic but was now in charge of four, each of whose many grumpy travelers needed to change into the lane farthest away.

"If I have the baby," said Justine, tucking her fingers between her belly and the Jeep's seat belt to keep them warm, "then I'm allowed to have you. If I don't, I don't get anybody. Right?"

Rose didn't answer. Instead, she said:

"I just don't understand why you don't want him. Her. I'd think you'd be happy to be healthfully pregnant after losing Valeria. What the hell, Justine?"

Ah. A fight was coming. A real one. Rose wouldn't make Justine choose. She'd stay with Justine forever, baby or no. She didn't feel like telling her that, though, not right now. She was furious with her girlfriend, and wanted her to drift in uncertain anxiety for a bit. At least for the ride home.

"Franklin forced himself on me, kind of," said Justine, "and I don't care to think of that every time I see the baby. I could never take care of it, anyway. I can't even take care of houseplants. A lucky bamboo died in my custody. A baby I made died."

"Don't punish the baby for what he did, Justine, Jesus."

To the left of Rose and Justine idled a Jeep CJ7 similar to Rose's. Piloting the Jeep was a college-age fellow whose affiliation could not be discerned from his dress but which one could be confident was Texas A&M, mainly because the Jeep's two backseat passengers were outfitted caps to cleats in Aggie maroons and whites and whose faces bore the ineducable ogle most Aggies seem to exhibit, ever-bewitched by the ever-changing mysteries of the great wide world.

All three Aggies found their arguing neighbors quite worth ogling.

"It's not just this baby, Rose, for your information," said Justine, ignoring their fellow travelers. "It's all babies. They all suffer. I don't want to bring a baby who, if it lives, will probably grow up depressed and bananas like me, or an awful liar like my mother, or a criminal like Franklin, or just broken and mean like a whole bunch of other people I can think of. I don't want to gamble that it'll be perfect and well adjusted like you."

"You're kidding. Right?"

"There's nothing wrong with you."

"Nice Jeep," called one of the stuck-in-traffic Aggie neighbors.

If both vehicles had been gilt sulkies drawn by winged narwhals, it might have been appropriate to recognize, with a nod or clubbish smile, the chance intersection of two rare roadsters paused in traffic on East First Street, but there were hundreds or thousands of these Jeeps in town, and Rose's wasn't even the same year. Still, Rose turned and gave the fellows a thumbs-up and sweet-by-any-standard grin. In the instant it took to turn from the Aggies back to Justine, Rose recomposed her expression into one more appropriate for a serious argument.

"Nothing wrong? Then what a great parent I'd make, right?"

"I don't want to argue in public."

"We're discussing, not arguing," said Rose, though she knew her tone was not discussive. "What if I do all the work? Diapers and formula-warming and all that other baby stuff."

"There's a little more to it than that, Rose."

"That's an '82, right?" shouted the neighboring Jeepmeister.

The light changed. The ranks shortened by two cars each. The Jeeps remained abreast.

"Eighty-four," said Rose, not bothering to grin this time.

"And what if it's born sick or gets hurt in delivery?" said Justine. "It'll change your life, an abnormal child."

"I did fine!" yelled Rose.

"Yeah, but what about your parents?"

"Yo, no offense," shouted one of the backseat Jeep neighbors, "but... are you a dude?"

Rose maintained a stock of retorts and counteractions for such challenges. The one this situation dictated was the opaque "If you guess right I'll help your mama make bitch pie," followed by an unassailable stare.

"Whooaaa," came the mocking three-Aggie carol.

"Leave them alone," Justine said, grabbing a handful of Rose's soccer shirt. The traffic light emancipated two more cars from each lane before turning red again. The Jeep driver took the opportunity to drive within an inch or two of Rose's Jeep.

"It's Pat."

"Fuck y'all."

"Leave us alone!" Justine shouted.

The jammed traffic, as if infected with the mounting antagonism, began to agitate. Rev, honk, inch, lurch, bumper-tap.

"That's definitely a chick," said a backseater, pointing at Justine, "so you must be a dude. Or a carpet muncher."

"I am both and I'm motherfucking proud of it, you corn-squeezing hayseed faggots!"

Another *Whoooaaaa*, this time inflected with a mixture of incredulity and look-who's-talking condescension. And a bit of *C'mon, let's see what you got, bitch*.

The light changed again. The neighboring Jeep angled into Rose, latching Jeep parts like kissing teenagers locking braces. The Aggie driver stomped on his brake, preventing Rose—and everyone behind them—from going anywhere. Rose opened the throttle—reverse then forward then reverse, burning rubber but unable to free herself from the other Jeep. Windows everywhere were coming down now, shouts and threats and what-the-fucks emerging from everyone.

"I'm gonna fuck you peasants!" shouted Rose.

"Ooohhh."

Rose put the Jeep in park. She vaulted her roll bar and landed in her narrow backseat. She came up with her Original Club Steering-Wheel Lock, scissor-jumped the roll bar back into her front seat, trampolined out onto her hood, and, in the same violent motion that carried her onto the other Jeep's hood, brought the lock down onto its windshield. Over and over. Before any of them thought to flee, Rose had richly frosted all three Aggies in broken glass and chrome flakes and rage.

"Ahh!" screamed Justine.

"Freeze!" shouted somebody. A thin, dramatically mustachioed man tightly vaginated in a way-too-small security guard's uniform was approaching Rose, gingerly planting one foot and then another on the car hoods, a serious-looking pistol trained with both hands on Rose's head. His sugarfoot stance, clearly perfected at a firing range, demanded obedience, and got it: Rose froze, her Club raised high.

"Bitch!" yelled the Aggies, who were evidently feeling safe enough, with the security guard running interference, to throw handfuls of glass at Rose.

"Put the weapon down. Now. Put the glass pebbles down. *Now.*"

Everyone obeyed. Rose looked back at her own Jeep. Justine was gone.

Rose, in the cell at the Travis County Correctional Complex, wondered if maybe, finally, she had exploded, burst in the faces of her bomb squad. She would have killed those fucking college kids if she hadn't been stopped. She would have pulped their soft Agricultural & Mechanical heads, sodomized all six of their tight Aggie holes with her Original Club.

"You know, I might not be cut from motherhood cloth, after all," Rose said to the tiny woman sitting next to her, whose weedy hair and blowzy, flaccid face suggested she might have a crystal-meth focus. "I just blew my chance, anyway."

"God loves a mother," said the woman. "You got a lot of glitter in your hair. It's pretty."

Rose ran her hands through her hair. They came away cloved with glass splinters and lightly running blood.

"Broken car glass doesn't look sharp, does it?" said Rose. "Just looks like green gravel you can play with. But it isn't."

"I just found out that the moon landing was fake," said Rose's companion. "That made me feel lonely inside, don't know why. Just ain't sure about anything now. You gonna make bail?"

"Yeah. Friend."

"That's sweet. A good friend. Good, good."

"He's not that sweet."

Wiping her hands on her shirt just dragged the little glass lances across her palms, cutting her more. Now blood and glass smirched her shirt, too.

The woman smiled. Her mouth was a sparse cemetery of jaggy tombstones.

"Reckon he'd bail me out, too?"

"I have a feeling he won't."

"Why didn't you call Justine?" said Matt. "Didn't you just move in together? Isn't she still living off you and a fat credit card?"

Rose and Matt sat on the hood of his Acura in the Crammed Shelf parking garage as Matt plucked glass out of her fingers and palms and brushed it out of her hair. The temperature had dropped thirty degrees in the last twenty-four hours, and atop the hood of the hot-running Acura was the warmest outdoor spot that either of them could think of for the job at hand. Matt didn't want bloody glass in his car.

"I did. She didn't answer. I felt like an idiot. I wasn't even going to ask for bond. I just wanted to beg forgiveness and make solemn pledges to be good and respect her wishes. Ow."

"Sorry. She never answers the phone, though, does she?"

"I know, but that time it felt like she was specifically not answering *my* call."

"Jesus, be still. Weren't you still on probation for that bartender?"

"'Were?' You make it sound like I'm in prison already, or dead."

"This is a big piece."

"Ow. Don't wiggle it. I'll vomit."

"I'm not wiggling."

"I have eight months left of probation."

The cold wind swirled trash around the empty garage. Rose considered her position, but could find no angle from which it appeared anything but impotent and defensive. The rage she'd so explosively imparted the Aggies had come from nowhere. Like a naval mine of the sort that could still occasionally be found floating in barnacled serenity, potent and ready, decades after the war it was fighting had ended.

She felt awful for fucking with those college kids, as much as they might've deserved what they got. She could've ignored them and just waited for the light. And Justine, poor Justine. What had she done to her? If she could just take it back.

It seemed unreal now. If not for the blood and courtroom paperwork and vituperation from Matt, she wouldn't have been sure it had happened at all.

"What's gonna happen?"

"I'm in some trouble."

"Jail?"

"Maybe—this is just the kind of thing probation officers like the least. Plus I never told him I was moving. You're supposed to inform them of every change of blah, blah. So, yeah, maybe, jail, maybe, yeah. Probably. I have to go back to court day after tomorrow."

Rose never cried, except at the movies, and at that TV ad for dish soap where they wash oil-spill oil off of a baby sandpiper. Just thinking about that one could break her up. But real-world human drama, even six-digit casualties of natural disasters or the worst of her own failed romances, couldn't do it.

Until now. Rose fell onto Matt's knobby shoulder and cried. Having virtually no experience with people beyond the exchange of tarot-card markers for backpacks at his job—no girlfriends, ever, homeschooled, and the only child in a motherless family—Matt was inexperienced with, possibly even ignorant of, such close contact with tears: with his body wholly clenched, he stiffly patted Rose on the back and repeated "There, there," over and over.

Eventually Rose stopped, more from discomfort than from depletion.

"Better? Finished?"

"Yeah."

"You're a mess. I've got some old napkins from Wendy's on the floor of the backseat, hold on, lemme find them. They're unused."

"What now, what now," said Rose, mostly to herself. "I don't know what to do."

"Want to abscond? I don't care about the bail. I'll help you."

"I have to talk to Appleshortner first. He's not such a bad guy."

"Call him from a prepaid cell so they can't trace it and bust you with a SWAT team."

"You grew up in front of a TV, huh."

"Yeah, so? It's coming in useful now, isn't it?"

"I need to talk to Justine."

"Maybe you're better off without her."

"You be quiet. You don't know what love is."

"*That* sounds like TV."

"Fuck you, Matt."

"If love is this, fuck love. Jail, blood, babies, snot? Who needs it?"

"Would you please get me the fucking napkins?"

Matt disappeared into the backseat of his Acura. The hood was cooling quickly. Rose shivered. Oh my, how she had blown it. More than the memories of collapsing auto glass, of eeking Aggies, of honk sonatas, of that blood-gelling "Freeze!," it was the atavistic fear and childish relent in her voice that had been Rose's loudest memory of yesterday. Rose didn't even know what had happened to Justine. Had she walked home? Was she hurt? Had she miscarried? Had she gone right back to the clinic? Back to New York? Maybe she was fine. Maybe she was more than fine, doing super, maybe she'd been looking for a way out of a one-sided relationship. Now without impediment, she could go to the abortion clinic, then have a chance at a relationship with someone else. Maybe she was already having an affair with someone whom Rose could never guess. The screwball neighbor with the bowl of suckers, some internet blowhard. Maybe even some *dude*.

"Couldn't find them," said Matt, "but here's a *Newsweek* from the trunk. Will that do?"

"Yeah. Sorry I cussed you out."

"It's okay. Me too. But I think you need to confront the truth that you are simply not a very good matchmaker. I can't even remember your last success."

"It would've been you and Evenie if you'd just admit that you love getting rimmed and throat-fucked and tied to workbenches by female Faroe Islanders. Drenching ejaculations are always preceded by agreeable stimulation. That's a success, in my book. It's up to the two of you to keep it hot and stay together. *My* job is done, and done well."

"Maybe you've simply been misinterpreting your signals. Maybe when you get one of your Bingos you should keep the two *apart,* at all costs. I was traumatized."

"No, you weren't. You just don't want anyone to know you have a non-het side. Maybe a bi-i-i-ig side."

"You think every heterosexual is covering up some bizarre sexuality."

Rose sighed. If she sighed too deeply she'd start bawling again, so she kept her breathing regulated and issued an order.

"Drive me through Wendy's."

Matt did. Then, her mouth crowded with fries and a Frostie, Rose directed him to the parking lot of Spinners, a Laundromat at the corner of Nitrate and Rug.

"Hey, you can see right inside," said Matt. "Dryer-watching is a well known digestive aid. And we don't even have to leave the car!"

"Turn around. If you look across the street, between those two duplexes and through the fork in that dead pecan tree, you can see my front door. I just want to see if she's okay without bugging her."

"Careful, or you'll wind up treading in a lake of restraining orders," said Matt. "Look, can I ask you something? Is it her you want? Or her baby?"

Rose did not respond.

"Wait, isn't that her?"

Through the trees, a block away, Justine was visible, struggling to unlock the door to their apartment. She was dressed in the same clothes she'd worn the day before: a white polyester maternity dress block-printed with little red songbirds and the notes they were singing. Over it she wore an inadequate blue windbreaker, an article Rose had only ever seen hanging in their tiny closet. During the very few cool days they'd experienced together, Justine had worn none other than Rose's gray fake-down vest. The windbreaker made her seem not only off-limits but somehow less pregnant.

"Jesus, Rose, don't cry again. I can't handle it."

"Go to Hyde Park."

"What? I've got shit to do, not the least of which is go home and change out of this snot- and grief-covered coat. I'll take you to get your Jeep out of impound and you can drive yourself to Hyde Park to carry out whatever loonball scheme you're hatching. What is it, anyway? Your scheme?"

"There might be a peace offering there. I have to catch it, though. Drive."
In the older residential parts of town like Hyde Park, alleys bisected every
block. In an alley between Avenues B and C, just beyond an old, neglected
cedar fence, Rose commanded Matt to stop.

"Why—"

"Quiet."

"—do potholes seem so much deeper the closer it gets to winter?"

"Wait for me. Are the back doors unlocked?"

"What? Why?"

"Just unlock them. I'll be right back. Leave the car on."

Rose backtracked toward the fence, crouched down, and began yanking
at the slats, one after another, until she found a loose one. She pushed it aside,
revealing a weedy, weather-bleached backyard dominated by a distressed
bird-mansion atop a tall, slightly leaning pole. Sotto voce, she called out:

"Dartmouth."

This was insane. Did Texas have a three-strikes law? Maybe she'd get
caught and go to prison for life, like people in California sometimes did if
they got caught three times for things like smoking dope or robbing parking
meters or lifting mascara from Vons.

"Dartmouth!" Rose called again, this time leaving off the sotto.

Rose could sense Matt's wincing disapproval, his unwillingness to abet,
his inclination to take off and leave her alone.

"Dartmouth!" she said, loudly, a real dog call. And lo, a real dog, a pug,
came around the side of the house. Dartmouth paused, espied his summoner,
barked wetly, and raced over to her, tinkling and drooling in volumes more
in accord with standard poodles or Shetlands. The little dog was creaky in his
gait and gray about the muzzle, which he worked hard to jam through the
opening in the fence. Rose reached in to help him, grabbing at a gather of
loose skin at his shoulder blades, waking the colony of little cuts on her hands.

"Ow, fuck."

"I'm calling the police right now," came a voice. "You let go of him.
Dartmouth, come here. I'm dialing right this instant. Dartmouth, come.
Nine... one..."

A late-middle-aged woman, one hand pressed into her lower back, the
other gripping a cordless phone, had appeared in the yard, wobbling rapidly
toward Dartmouth and Rose.

"He's not yours!" shouted Rose, "and I'm taking him to his rightful owner."

At the moment Dartmouth's loyalties were to Rose, and he was working hard, snurfling and sliming and whinnying for his freedom.

"That is my dog," said the woman. "I've had him for almost twenty years, and he's fragile and you let go this instant. The police are on their way."

"Good. This is my girlfriend's dog, lady, not yours. The police will arrest you, not me."

With a splintery thunk Dartmouth succeeded in forcing his head through the gap, but was stopped by the rest of his cobby, roast-like torso. The woman dropped her phone and grabbed hold of the animal around his middle. She pulled and dragged, glaring at her opponent.

Rose was arrested by the woman's big green eyes. As if it were Justine herself fighting for the animal.

"You're Livia, aren't you."

"Who the dickens are you?"

"This is your daughter's dog, not yours, and so you better let go. Livie, darling."

Dartmouth seemed not to mind being the means in a tug-of-war.

"You... who are you?"

"I'm Justine's tuck-in friend and this is her dog that she got for Christmas in 1987 and you better let go or you'll hurt him and you better believe they've got some serious animal-cruelty laws in Texas plus Justine will hate you more than she does now if that's even possible, *Livia*, so leggo of her baby."

And, surprise, she let go. Rose allowed herself to sit back in the alley weeds. The woman stared at Rose with a look she'd seen only once before: Olympe's expression, lit by the dashboard light of the Fiat they'd escaped Tegucigalpa in, somewhere near Coatzacoalcos. Dartmouth remained trapped between the slats, halfway to liberty, struggling and *nyrk*ing like Winnie-the-Pooh stuck in Rabbit's front door.

"She's here?"

"That is none of your business."

"Is she all right?"

"Never you mind."

"You tell me, she's my little girl."

"You call the police back and tell them to not come."

She picked up the cordless phone and showed the back of it to Rose.

"It doesn't have any batteries. No one's coming."

She had more than just epidote-green eyes in common with Justine—there was something peculiar to her movements, a cautiousness, a balancing, that she noticed in both women. And not just them; Rose had seen it in other women, too, certain women that she would later learn were

"Pregnant. You're... pregnant, aren't you?"

Dartmouth had reversed, abandoning his quest for freedom in favor of comfort. At long last, his head uncorked. He gave it a good, colloid-flinging shiver, and then ran off down the side yard.

Matt honked, rolled down his window, and shouted: "Rose! C'mon. We'll get fucking arrested."

"Rose. You're my little girl's... friend."

"You *are* pregnant. Aren't you in your fifties?"

"I am sixty-five, and I don't appreciate—"

"Justine told me you were..."

Rose paused. "You're... *Charlotte?*"

"I am she. Hasn't Justine ever shown you pictures?"

"And you're pregnant?"

"It is not unheard of at my age."

"I don't know, I think it's pretty fucking rare."

"Norris McWhirter has not come knocking. And I do not care for cuss words as ugly as that one."

"Rose, Jesus, come the fuck on."

"I want you to tell me if Justine is all right," said Charlotte. "I will not interfere with your lives. I just want to know whether she's well and happy. And tell her I'd like a phone call now and then. It's the same number. Dammit."

"I'm leaving!" shouted Matt. "Rose? Last chance. Look, I'm driving off... better hurry... right now."

Rose did not move. Matt, lathered up with impatience, screeched off, dropping tires into every pothole.

Charlotte and Rose stared at each other through the six-inch-wide breach.

"Can I come inside?" said Rose. "I have an idea."

"You certainly may not," said Charlotte. "You are a complete stranger, a felon, and a corrupting young person."

"I am your granddaughter's true love, I'm pretty sure, but she's upset with me and might have even might just broken up with me because I did something stupid, but I think together—you and me—we can get her back."

"There is," said Charlotte, her voice threatening to break, "*so much* you don't know."

"There is," said Rose, "a lot *you* don't know either, Charlotte Durant."

A few more moments of dewy, obstinate staring, and finally Charlotte said: "Can you drive?"

"Yeah, why, are you having contractions?"

"No, no. Are you cautious? Do you signal and practice courtesy and wave to your neighbors?"

"All but that last thing," said Rose, truthfully. She regarded herself as the most defensive and politest of all Austin's drivers. Yesterday notwithstanding.

"Why don't you come around and meet me in the driveway."

XXV

December 2004

Charlotte would never admit this to anyone, and in fact had grown up with self-preservative abilities sufficiently powerful where she could, if she chose, not admit it to herself, but the truth was that there had been more than a few people in her life whose deaths had come as bounties of relief, and, similarly, there still lived people whose deaths, should they come before her own, would bring carotic relief.

Among the dead was Amelia Mint. Fifth grade. A bully and teaser who circled in abusive squall around every aspect of Charlotte's school life for much of 1949, until late-onset chicken pox seized and quickly overtook the tormenter. It was the same day Charlotte first set eyes on the handsome sixth grader Lou Borger.

And there had been Ursula Calle, the polio-stricken bingo-hall shouter. The chronic pain from the disease and all its withering harrows led her to resign. Hers had been a slow, lonesome, van Goghian suicide, a pistol-shot to the intestines that took all of thirty-six hours to kill her. Charlotte was relieved Ursula was finally at peace, but, my goodness, why hadn't she shot herself in the head, the sensible target for a small-arms suicide?

Apart from banishing Charlotte's only-ever love, Mère had visited no memorable terrors on her daughter; it was simply the lifelong compound of Mère's seedling resentments, denials, tiny crimes, ugly triflings, prejudices, peeves, and cranks, all in the name of love, of course, that Charlotte had escaped on the day a blood clot climbed into her mother's brain.

Justine. The possibility that her granddaughter should live to learn the circumstances of her conception paralyzed Charlotte so completely that she had wondered if Justine might not be better off peacefully and pain-lessly dead. And if this bizarre Rose person—at this very moment sitting to Charlotte's left, in the driver's seat of Charlotte's 1979 Chrysler New Yorker Fifth Avenue, experimenting with the street-barge's various dials and toggles—was to be believed, Justine was not dead; she had been living in New York, where she'd always wanted, promised, and threatened to go.

But, according to this Rose, Justine was now home. In town. In Austin. In direct peril of an unconscionable truth. Charlotte put her hand to her breastbone, a gesture she usually accompanied with "*Oh me,*" but this time substituted with a brief, sharp inhale.

"Are you all right?" said Rose, evidently sensitized to proximate exis-tential panic. "Do you need an Alka-Seltzer? Or some Wal-phed? Oh god, it's not the baby?"

And the child, of course. Even though there was every desolating likeli-hood that the baby now so improbably alive inside Charlotte's World War II–era body (she pictured a gleeful Gerber baby slobbering in the bubble of a Vought Corsair) would not succeed in coming to be—Dr. Gonzales had been predictably specific about the fetus's chances—the splinter of possi-bility that the baby *would* make it was in many ways even more upsetting. What kind of mother could she be, after her failures with Livia? She was a failure even as a grandmother. This child's death would be, will be, a mercy.

Let us not forget Livia.

The moment Charlotte had discovered in Dot's diaries that Livia had slept with her own father, producing Justine, Charlotte did not cry, she did not go to sleep, she did not throw up, she did not call Dr. Gonzales for Valium, she did not place the diaries in the rusty wheelbarrow in the back-yard and burn them to white ash with her crème brûlée torch, she did not count days and calculate dates and estimate gestation periods, she did not recast the memories of the last thirty-five years in this new, merciless light, she did not decide that her newfound disgust for Livia outweighed her pity for her, she did not decide to banish Livia from her life; no, all of that came in the next few days. But the moment that Charlotte read Dot's entry of January 22, 1970, she leaned back against the hallway wall, lit a cigarette, took a single drag, dropped it into her beer, went downstairs, and called the downtown Marriott.

"Front desk, Nathan."

Charlotte had never been so relieved to hear a friendly voice. *Now* came the crying.

"Hello, hello?" said Nathan. "Miss? Hello?"

Charlotte could not speak. She could barely breathe for the storm of the cry. Then she threw up.

"Miss?" Incredibly, Nathan had stayed on the line. "Can I call an ambulance?"

"No," said Charlotte, with more strength and force than she thought she possessed. Far more than just tears and poisons were liberated by a good vomit-cry. They were pure deliverance. "I'm all right. I'd like a room for one, as soon as possible."

"Certainly. And how many nights will you be staying?"

"Until I finish these diaries."

"Pardon?"

"Never mind. Two nights, please."

"I have an excellent single overlooking the river."

"That's just fine."

"I will personally make sure," said Nathan, "that the grout is clean and the pillows fluffy."

Charlotte had spoken to Livia only once in the last six months. The conversation had been much like a death, a violent one, but Charlotte was not entirely sure which of the two of them had died.

But it was for the most recent demise—had it already been two months?— that Charlotte felt the greatest relief, and for that relief, the greatest guilt: Bull Wheeler. Her Westlake Hills friend, pinochle opponent, and, for several decades, her secret, part-time, and by far most capable lover. If she was to be cursed with an advanced-age pregnancy, she would rather have at fault none other than Big Bull.

Still, Bull had been growing antsy at the idea of a new child (he had already imparted six boys and triplet girls unto his wife, Nance), and had uttered into his and Charlotte's increasingly antagonistic discourse on the matter the possibility of public confession. Public meaning Nance. Public meaning Livia. Public meaning the counties of Travis and surrounding. Everyone knew Bull in one way or another. Charlotte felt foolish enough wandering around in Walgreens and H-E-B and Hobby Lobby as the oldest pregnant woman in Texas, and probably the oldest pregnant *single* woman in the world. Charlotte did not need any more exposure. She begged God for relief from Bull's threats to disclose, and, lo, God silenced Bull while the man was *in flagrante doggie-style*, in his marital bed, with his marital wife. Poor Nance. Lucky Nance. She would never know of her dead husband's inimitable feat of virility.

Unless Bull had kept some kind of damn diary. No, no. The idea of Big Bull Wheeler scribbling in a pink book protected by a tiny brass lock was laughable. And Charlotte laughed.

"What's funny?" said Rose, who was testing and retesting the emergency brake.

"Not a thing," said Charlotte. She studied Rose's slender, womanly wrists. They seemed at great risk of shattering behind the apparent power in her broad, veined forearms. "Are you satisfied with the brake's performance?"

"I don't know, I'd need a hill to park on. Where are we going, anyway?"

"I would like you to take me to an address in Tarrytown, Rose. The recent expiration of a local pizza baron promises a compelling estate sale, which, in forty-two minutes, is set to open its doors to the public."

"Okay, then."

"En route, I would like to hear your idea. But first, I hope you will be able to answer a few questions."

"Okay, then."

Charlotte paused, unsure where to begin her interrogation.

Rose seized the chance to ask a question of her own.

"Boy or girl?"

"Girl. There is little chance the child will survive."

There was a more-than-trivial chance Charlotte wouldn't survive the baby's birth, either. She wondered if she would experience an afterlife sentience tuned finely enough to feel the relief of her own death, or would she witness only the mass analgesia her death brought to others?

"That makes me sad."

Charlotte felt rotten enough wishing people dead, but somehow making this odd person Rose feel sad felt worse. She appeared capable of melancholies far steeper than any in Charlotte's experience.

"Now please back out of the driveway and go thataway," said Charlotte, as gently as she knew how.

"Did you pick out names anyway?" said Rose.

Charlotte had spent an hour or two browsing baby-names books at Babiverse, finally settling on Edith. She had never known anyone with that name, making it ideal by exclusion. Charlotte said it over and over in her head as she wandered around the three-acre superstore examining hemp baby blankets, electric playpens, steampunk breast pumps, and adorable onesies bearing shocking messages.

"I did."

"Would you tell me?"

"Does Justine know who her real mother is?"

Charlotte had merely been thinking this question, but somehow, without consent, it leaped from her mouth.

"She sure does: Livia," said Rose immediately, as if she knew the question was coming all along. "And she also knows Livia gave her up for adoption. Because she *cried* too much. And she knows that the adoptive parents returned her pretty much for the same reason. Overcrying. Like she was a pair of too-small cleats from Sears."

"There is more to it than that. Please turn here."

"And," said Rose, "she knows who her father is."

Of them all—dead and alive—Amelia Mint, Justine, Bull, Ursula, her own baby, and quite a few others—Lou Borger was the only one upon whom she sometimes wished harm and biles and agony. *Then* death. Other times Charlotte felt pity. But mostly she felt nothing; Lou was simply absent, unthought-of, a sorry oblivion.

"We looked him up on the internet," said Rose. "Ye Moppe Hedds records get a fortune on eBay. Jerry, Gary, Larry, Cherry, and Burt. You don't still have any, do you? 45s?"

Charlotte had always envied her granddaughter's paranormal capacity

for tears. Her own, whether of grief, sadness, joy, laughter, or relief, were—
the last six months notwithstanding—as scarce as moon rocks.

"Cherry—Livia—probably does. Ye honorary Moppe Hedd. But I do not."

"Why Cherry? That's Livia? Why not Mary, Sherry, Carrie, Kerry, Terri?"

"I've never known. Livia and I do not often discuss those years."

But they had certainly discussed Burt. On her last visit Livia had told her mother that he'd been sterile. It was not the fact but the tardiness of its delivery that been both the cause of the pursuant violence and the end of the visit.

"Let's go ask her."

"We are going to an estate sale."

"After?"

"Afterward, we are going to another estate sale. A lottery agent once jailed for fraud. Much is possible there. I hope you'll help me fan through all the books for hidden unredeemed tickets or hundred-dollar bills."

"After?"

"Livia and I do not speak."

"Why?"

Charlotte decided Rose was much like your ordinary rank-and-file four-year-old. Charlotte recollected that simple disregard effectively silenced most members of that complicated age group. Charlotte thus, silently, studied the sidewalk and its travelers as they sped by. Eventually, though, she felt the quiet in the car crawling on her neck, and so turned to Rose.

"I learned something about Livia that I did not like, to say the least. I have no interest in recognizing her as a daughter."

"Can you guys dialogue?"

"That word, as a verb, should be struck from the lexica."

"Well?"

"She has a perfectly attentive boyfriend to *dialogue* with."

"Does he know this terrible thing about Livia?"

"Archibold appears to know very little about the plane of reality."

"Archibold? His last name's not Bamberger, is it?"

"Why, yes, it is."

"I know him. He's been delivering magazines to Crammed Shelf for years. As long as I've been there. We're pretty good friends. He orders me special Latin American soccer magazines."

"Please go left at the guitar statue."

Rose was indeed a cautious driver. Gentle. Charlotte had seldom encountered a gentle driver, and she was happy to be in the reck of one for a change, now that Livia was no longer available. Charlotte had backed out of Livia's life, and Livia out of hers, repulsing magnets, south pole to south pole, with no meeting in any possible future. Asking a daughter if she slept with her dad is the sort of question Charlotte supposed only classical Greek dramatists knew how to handle. Charlotte knew no Greek theater, but surely, at the very least, some player would attack another, with a sword, a morningstar, a catapult, or, maybe, an open palm, slick from sweat, as Charlotte had finally struck Livia. Never had they had a violent exchange, and the strike stunned them both. Livia then left her mother's house and did not return.

"Please go right at the light."

Rose turned. The fairly steep hill was something of a project for the old Chrysler, which began to shimmy and decelerate.

"Please step on the gas pedal as hard as you can."

Rose did. The old yellow Chrysler stalled, just a couple of blocks from the estate sale.

"Here is your chance to test the emergency brake," said Charlotte.

Rose turned and stupefied Charlotte with the gentlest, most beatific smile the desolate woman had ever seen.

As the pair walked from Victorian birthing chairs to jars of wolverine urine, from rhinestone-peppered snoods to high-thread-count but unevenly yellowed Egyptian cotton sheets, from commemorative beer steins (Columbia Exposition) to glass-front displays of worthless bijouterie, from a miniature, operational guillotine (up near the cash register) to a charmless teddy bear featuring humanoid fingers, a hinged mouth, and a construction flaw to the crotch that left that area disfigured with a hideous camel toe, Charlotte grew disappointed with the estate sale at the same rate she grew interested in Rose's story of Justine.

"And she had an awful boyfriend who was in jail for five years," said Rose. "His nose hair grew a quarter inch a day. What's that?"

Charlotte held in both arms a long, semi-cylindrical object whose form suggested a taxidermied peccary, but was not.

"This is a sofa bolster," said Charlotte. "But it has lost its original weenie shape."

"Put that down," said Rose, pausing in her review of a chrome golfing panda. "You'll get bedbugs or bird mites. Or you'll upset the baby. They know when terrible things are afoot, you know, or when awful objects are nearby. Like that thing."

As if Rose had actually heard Charlotte say to herself, *Well, I won't be pregnant much longer, anyway*, Rose added: "By the way—what's your date?"

Charlotte held on to the bolster. "January 14."

Rose looked up and smiled. Except for tiny downturns at the corners, the smile was just as before: grand, arresting, divine. Charlotte could summon no mental rhetoric sufficient to describe its beauty, but she knew that Justine would always be safe if within the scope of it. Charlotte herself felt a rare comfort that a shadowed interior part of her wanted to call love.

Rose ran up to Charlotte and hugged her, the martyrized bolster between them. Rose's embrace was gentle and firm. This Rose hugs much like she drives. What else does she do like that? Maybe everything.

"This," Rose said, "makes my plan nearly perfect."

"This? Why?"

"No, not this, *this*: guess who else is pregnant. Guess who else is due on *the same day?*"

Charlotte squeezed her bolster companion. "Who?"

"Guess."

"Not..."

"Yes."

"I need to see her."

"I'm trying to convince her of that."

Charlotte sat down on a zebra-skin director's chair. Rose sat on the concrete floor next to her.

"Justine needs you," said Rose. "She loves you and has always felt horrible about sending you that note. She told me she tried to get it back before they delivered it."

"I wish she had," said Charlotte. She had not kept it. Charlotte remembered buying the felt pens and stationery for her in Sears. She'd never forget the vanilla light and smell of Clorox in the aisle. Charlotte never returned to that department store again.

"But she needs her mother, too. She can't have both unless you and Livia make up. Do you understand that?"

"I don't know if I can."

XXVI

October 2004

Livia stared at her computer in the Collections Department of Braun-schweiger's S&L, waiting for the auto-dialer to put her in touch with a debtor between three and six weeks late on an unsecured loan payment. Ah, there. Loan information and a name popped up on the screen.

"Yes, Mr. William Stone, please."

"This is."

"This is Mrs. Moppett, at Braunschweiger's, calling about the late payment on your loan. Have you been able to send in that $123.20 yet?"

"No, I, uh, don't have it."

"When do you think you will?"

"About two months?"

"Then you'll be behind three payments," said Livia, who recognized the timbre of the conversation as one where no silver would ever cross palms.

"Can you make a partial now? I can take a check over the phone."

"I don't have anything at all right now. I got fired. And I owe my dad a thousand bucks. When I get a new job, I'll need to pay him back first."

"Can you give me a promise of one payment, say, within two weeks?"

"I won't have it."

"If you get more than three months behind I'll have to send your account to a more vigorous collections department."

"Mrs. Moppett, I understand your position, but you must have better things to do."

She studied Mr. Stone's account. He was sixty-six. And forced to borrow money from his dad.

"I guess I do, Mr. Stone."

Livia hung up and called Charlotte. No answer.

She gathered up her purse and sweater and stopped by her boss's office.

"Art, I need a few hours off."

"Whuffuh?"

"None of your business."

Livia knocked. Livia had not been to her mother's since early summer, when they'd had a brief conversation through the closed door. Livia had hollered, "*Let me in, please!*" and Charlotte had said, almost merrily, "*Not now, busy!*" And it had been this way ever since they first separated, back in May, while stuck behind a construction project on Forty-Fifth on the way home from Dr. Gonzales's, where Charlotte, judging from her cuckoo behavior before and after, had obviously received an interesting medical opinion. Charlotte had bailed Livia's Nissan, walked home, and locked Livia out of her life. It was about the diaries, of course. And Charlotte's medical secret.

Livia knocked again.

"Who is it?" said Charlotte through the door.

"It's me, Mother." Livia took a step back. She thought of Mr. Stone. "Open up."

"Busy!"

"Open up or swear to god I'll break in through a window in the middle of the night and scare you into a coma."

The door opened.

Her mother did not look the same. Her hair had thinned, her cheeks flushed when she spoke, she wore atypically loose clothes, she had gained—

"Mother, you're larger. But you look skinnier."

"That, of course, doesn't make any sense. Any other insults to deliver before I send you away?"

Livia walked past her mother and sat on the old divan. Her mother remained standing by the open door, as if ready to flee. Or slam it so hard it set off car alarms.

"I want to know what's been going on."

"I just don't know what you mean," said Charlotte.

"Did you read something in those diaries?"

"What dia—"

"Stop. Something about me."

Charlotte shut the front door; the action was not too far from a slam. She went into the kitchen. Livia had plenty of time to glance around the room for the diaries—there were none to be seen—before her mother arrived with a glass bottle of Coke in one hand and a roll of zinc tablets in the other. By the slow, stiff, deliberate way she moved, Livia realized two things: (1) the diaries were no longer here—Charlotte would've been far more brisk in pace if she had been guarding them, and (2) there was something up—medically up—with her mother.

Charlotte sat down in the middle of the staircase, leaning back against the stairs.

"Mother, are you sick?"

"No."

"What is it, then?"

She sipped her Coke.

Livia realized that the house didn't smell like cigarettes.

"You quit smoking? And quit beer? Have you got cancer?"

"No."

Livia stood up."

"Tell me what the hell is going *on*!"

Charlotte stood up, too, turned to the side, and lifted the hem of her top.

"Oh my god," said Livia. "What who when wh—"

"Do not spread this around."

"Mother, this is—"

"There's little chance that it will live. I might not either. It will all be over in the next few months."

Livia and her mother both sat back down, Livia literally falling back on the divan, Charlotte lowering herself to the stair step as if she were a barrel of dynamite being lowered by a tower crane onto a piano.

"Who—"

"Not your business. The pregnancy discussion is over."

"But—"

"And to answer your other question, the diaries are gone."

Livia lay stomach-down on the couch and put her face in her hands.

"Did you read them?"

"I did," said Charlotte.

"And?"

"I noticed an entry in which it was reported that you had had relations with Lou."

Dizziness now, static in her head. Her hands smelled of the bank, of money.

"I—"

"You deceived and fucked your own father."

The disgusted accusation Livia expected, but the curled-lip sear with which her mother delivered its uglier verb, she had not. Livia looked up. Charlotte ate two zinc tablets. She stared at her daughter, and stood up as if to leave.

"I don't feel good," said Livia.

"I'll bet."

Livia took a step toward the door.

"Don't you dare leave now, Livia."

"It was an accident."

"Neither sex nor deception are accidents."

"I didn't know it was him."

"You had some free time between funerals so you thought you'd fuck your father."

The second use of the word shocked Livia less than it made her angry. She took a step toward her mother.

"*You* never never ever showed me a picture of him! I didn't know who he was—he was just a kind person on a night I needed one. One thing led to another."

"The new widow needed to fuck an older stranger."

"You ought not judge me when it comes to sexual caprice. *Mother*."

Charlotte stood, took three long strides, wound up like a sidearm relief pitcher, and struck Livia in the face, hard, with the heel of her open hand. Livia went down, hitting her head on a side table. She began to bleed from a gash in her hairline.

"Neither of us knew," she said, searching her head for the wound, now bleeding plentifully. "But here's something you don't know. Better wind up first, so you'll be ready to hit me again."

Charlotte did so.

"Burt," said Livia, "couldn't perform. Justine is Lou's daughter."

Charlotte let her raised hand fall to her side. She walked up the stairs and disappeared into the bathroom.

Livia wiped blood out of her eye, and left.

"Oh, what in the world has happened?" said Archibold as Livia came inside. Against her wound she held a folded paper floor mat of the sort auto mechanics put in a car to keep their work boots from soiling the carpet. "Let me see."

Archibold took her in for stitches. On the way there she told him the truth about everything, which she'd kept from him for a decade and more.

"Oh, my poor Livie," he said, touching her wrist. "Oh, poor everybody."

Livia took an indefinite leave from work. Archibold checked Livia into the psychiatric floor of St. David's. For three weeks she sat in a rough wooden chair large enough to accommodate her whole body if she brought her feet up and tucked them under her rear. No one bothered her. After the first week she was assigned a psychiatrist, Dr. Mazie Sloane, who insisted Livia try Lexapro and Trazodone as a course of treatment for what the doctor told her was major depression. Livia told her it was grief and sadness and shame, not depression, but the doctor insisted. Archibold visited every day. He urged Livia to try the meds, and she did, but instead of improving, she simply slept twice as much and suffered headaches that felt like a tiny strongman throwing safes against the inside walls of her skull. At the end of three weeks, Livia signed herself out, quit the meds, and went to bed. She promised Archibold she wouldn't hurt herself. She refused to see anyone except Archibold. Not many people wanted to see her.

On Christmas morning Livie got up and sat in front of the little Christmas tree Archibold had fashioned with a glue gun and a bunch of pecans. He had a spread of presents for her, but she had nothing for him. She began to tremble with the shame of not spending thirty minutes to go shopping.

"Settle yourself, Livie, I don't want any presents."

"I'm sor—"

"Do you know what I want you to do? What would be a nice present for me, and what will solve all of this?"

"What?"

"Forgive your mother."

"There's nothing to forgive. She didn't do anything wrong."

"Talk to her, allow her to forgive you."

"I tried. I'll never do it again."

"I want you to try something. Every time you wake up, be it from a nap or a night's sleep, I want you to get up, come and sit crosslegged on the living-room floor, close your eyes, and be your mother. Think like her. See what she sees. Allow yourself to imagine her imagination, and explore it. Find in her what she sees in you—what she used to see and what she sees now. You will come to be the mother that forgives her daughter, and to be the daughter that allows a bestowal of forgiveness."

"I…"

"Say 'Merry Christmas, darling, I'll do it.'"

"Okay."

"You don't have to do anything else. You don't have to call her, meet her, or attend family counseling. This exercise is for your mind and spirit only. And for me, I guess. I'll benefit by your returning grace."

One evening in January, Archibold arrived home with a copy of the Classifieds section of the *Statesman*. He said to Livia:

"There's gonna be an estate sale. It says it's gonna feature a bunch of 45s and LPs of Austin music from the sixties and seventies. I think we should go and see if we can't find a Ye Moppe Hedds record with your song on it."

"When?"

"This Sunday, the ninth."

XXVII

January 2005

Boy-o-*boy* did Murphy Lee Crockett wake up in a good mood.

After five humiliating failures, how delicious to arise in the morning—a nice, crisp one, too, judging by the window's pleasing frostwork—with the fresh, still-wet memory of a grisly, fully realized murder. No regrets, no empathy, no remorse. He was, officially, a Psychopathic Serial Murderer at the Beginning of His Lethal and To-Be-Legendary Career. And, not coincidentally, today was the first of the three-day True Crime Convention, the largest in the world. He would walk among the meek. He would visit the booths like the devil in disguise. This time next year, there would be a booth devoted to him.

Murphy attributed much of his past failure to hasty, insufficient preparation, overexcitement, shortsightedness, and shoddy ordnance. Conversely, his success last night he attributed to surgically precise planning, a cool head, and the feather-fine, ruby-hard edge of Zordmurk.

What a shame, though, that the fucking sword had broken while he'd been hacking away at that bitch. A fluke, surely, just an accident of contact physics, like how the laziest of knuckleballs sometimes disintegrate the toughest Rawlingses. Or else she had bones like... well, like Japanese steel. Whatever, she was history long before Zordmurk betrayed him by snapping off at the hilt.

He'd made his appointment months in advance, shortly after he'd received Zordmurk in the mail. His neighbor Porifiro had been bugging him about how he could set Murphy up with a girl who would break some off without any of that dating and courting nonsense. And she was very attractive, too. He showed Murphy a picture of his friend, who was indeed very attractive.

"You don't know her, man!" Murphy had said. "That's your cousin or something."

"Okay, never mind."

"Wait, lemme see." Murphy became aware of some changes in hormone levels in his body. She was very, very attractive.

"Okay."

"There's a detail that you should know."

"I knew it. She has AIDS. She's a man. She lives in Perth."

"No, no," said Porifiro. "She's a pro."

"A hooker? Jesus, Porifiro. Get out of my sight."

"Look, you're a friend, I'll throw in a hundred bucks."

"Yeah, right."

Porifiro dug deep in a pocket and came up with a bunch of wadded banknotes, which he made a production of smoothing out, squaring, and orienting, and finally handed Murphy five somewhat-humid twenties.

"It's expensive, man, a hundred bucks won't pay a tenth of what it costs for an hour with her."

"Are you serious?"

"But here," he said, going into another pocket and coming up with a ticket of some kind. "This is a half-off coupon."

"So it'll still cost me four hundred bucks?"

"More like $650. Best I can do, man."

"I do not trust you," said Murphy.

"Look, she hasn't had a good man, like you, in a long time, and she's my friend, so I've been trying to set her up with a good man, and you're the only one I know, Murphy Lee."

Murphy considered this. He'd always wanted to fuck a hooker.

"What's her name?"

"Marcia."

"You're kidding."

"What would I do that for? It's Marcia, Marcia Brodsky. You *know* her?"

Murphy could not believe his good fortune.

Porifiro began to giggle.

"What's that for?"

"I don't know, I giggle, that's why, look, here's the number. Don't talk except to answer her questions, then do what she tells you. You gonna have to wait a few months, probably—she's a busy woman. Do *not* mention my name. Confidentiality, you know."

Murphy called that night. What a thrill it was to hear her doomed voice on the phone!

"Right now I'm booked until February '05, Mr. Brady," Marcia said.

"Six months."

"Unless I have a cancellation. Would you like me to place you in the standby queue? You'll be number 154. Remember, it might be very short notice, possibly the same day you're called."

"Fine."

"Do you have a phone number for me?"

Murphy gave her the number to his recently purchased prepaid cell phone.

"Excellent! Can't wait to have you visit, Mr. Brady. I promise you a good time."

More hormones squirted around his body. If he wasn't afraid of AIDS and leaving evidence behind, he'd fuck her before he killed her.

His number came up almost a month early, January 13. Yesterday.

"Basic, right, Mr. Brady?" Marcia had said.

"Uh, I guess."

"You're aware of the particular nature of our services?"

"Yes."

"Good. Now, I'm going to give you an address. Just follow the path to the back door, place your fee in the slot provided. Your services today total

$750, half off the regular price. Cash only, all taxes included, no tipping necessary—then wait for me to buzz the door open. Oh, please ignore the dog—he's on a tether, and, anyway, he's all bark. Then go right to the door decorated with chili-pepper Christmas lights. Come right on in when you're ready. Oh, I can't remember—on or off?"

"Uh. Huh?"

"The lights? Would you like me to leave them on or off for you?"

He had not considered this. Would he be happy to merely hear screams, hacking thunks, whispery, flesh-dividing swipes, the splashes of arcing jets of pulmonary blood hitting the walls? Or see it all, too?

A flash of nausea decided for him.

"Off."

"By the way, how did you hear of me?"

"Uh, friend. He gave me the half-off ticket."

"Wonderful! I'll expect you at 2 a.m."

Murphy arrived on time. He pushed open the chili-pepper door, walked in, found Marcia sleeping under a sheet at the edge of the squash-court-sized bed, drew his sword, and began swinging, stabbing, slicing, hacking. Warm spatter found his face, his hands. To his pleasant surprise he found he was not at all nauseated. Murphy hacked and hacked in the dark, virgin silence.

The next morning, Murphy jumped out of futon, quickly dressed, jogged down to the corner, and bought the last copy of today's *Statesman* from a vending machine. His crime must be already famous: this box, concealed as it was by a dense copse of courier drop boxes, never sold out. On September 12, he had taken, for the price of a single issue, the whole stack of papers and sold them on eBay for a profit that made Murphy hope for more national tragedies.

Hmm, not on the front page. Or second or third. Murphy grew more and more disappointed as he walked home.

Murphy hated the *Austin American-Statesman*. They seemed to get off on ignoring Murphy Lee Crockett. Once, in order to send them an anonymous, untraceable note outlining his criminal intentions, Murphy had gone to the trouble of taking a bus all the way to fucking *Dallas*, trapped in a tedious, hot disguise (fake beard, Red Man cap with attached mullet wig, sunglasses), just so he could buy an overpriced money order from a Money Box in a crappy part of town, and drop by a Half Price Books to pick up a few stacks of second-hand magazines from whose articles he could, rubber-gloved, snip and paste to sheets of untraceable bond paper the letters necessary to spell out his dares and taunts, which, history would adjudge, would exceed the creativity, sociopathy, and emergency of the notorious missives of the Zodiac and BTK, and perhaps even the scrawled dares of... *the Ripper himself.* But no. The *Austin American-Statesman* had declined to publish or even acknowledge his note, no explanation given.

Plus, the incompetent daily ignored his actual murders, or, to be precise, his courageous attempted murders. What self-respecting paper finds attempted murder unnewsworthy? No one in the world realized a serial killer was out there practicing. Dummies. Only the *Chronicle* had noticed anything at all, and that particular incident—Murphy's thwarted halberd impalement of Peter Bradley, the marrow-boiling, chain-mailed bankruptcy attorney—had turned up in the highly disrespectful and unimportant column, "News of the Weird," whose editorial tone was one of luftmensch contempt.

Those days were over. Nevermore would the world overlook him. Even the limp *Statesman* couldn't ignore a sex murder in its own streets; a Shinogi-Zukuri-katana slaying of an elite, lovable, *white* prostitute ought be worth a column inch or so somewhere in the first twenty pages.

Yet no story appeared.

The only explanation was that the murder had been discovered too late to make press time. Or had yet to be discovered. He'd google the news now and then during the day today, and stay tuned to Fox. They'd be the quickest to pick up and nationalize the story of a cold yet impassioned edged-weapon murder of a sin-profiteer. Fox loved that stuff. And Murphy loved Fox.

At home Murphy turned on the TV, sliced a fat slab off of a fifteen-pound ham, built himself a monster ham-and–Kraft American Singles dagwood, and lay down on the futon to eat and fart and skim the rest of the paper. Vacuous comics, laughable arts section, stale news, and the intolerably meaningless metro happenings—today the *Statesman* brought to attention the Fourth Annual Shin-Splints Awareness Day Double Marathon, a 52.4-mile walk to raise awareness of the plight of those suffering from the affliction, a cause its participants might most sincerely beatify by limping the entire distance. Fourteen thousand faux gimps jamming traffic, ruining Murphy's day, taking up valuable broadcast, print, and internet news minutes that should be his.

Just to be thorough, Murphy browsed the obituaries. Nothing. He returned to the front page, which was dominated by another story about the fucking Reviewers.

A week ago, reported the *Statesman*, the band of moralists had invaded the large, supposedly impervious home of a megabudget film star of international adoration who happened to live here instead of Hollywood and who had recently been caught on video cheating on his wife, an infidelity that prompted his admission to a series of like affairs, mostly with youthful, surgically recrafted colleagues, devastating his wife and children, letting down his friends, irritating his agent, enraging his moneymen, titillating or appalling everyone else, and, evidently, inciting the Reviewers. The video that undid him, taken from the security camera monitoring an isolated ATM kiosk in downtown Bucharest and posted—briefly—on the website *ebaumsworld.com*, featured the star and a Tollywood substarlet in an obscene, full-face suckfest that passion quickly elevated to frantic, panty-stripping amplexus on the kiosk's brick floor. During the pleasantest stretch of their Dunhill-smoking postcoital nod, they were set upon and robbed of their clothes and valuables and Dunhills by a gang of boots 'n' bracers, a crime that gained the couple zero sympathy, and ultimately bought the pair bench warrants for sexual crimes from the judiciaries not only of Romania but of Andhra Pradesh, the starlet's home. After the star's wife, a self-help guru of great moral probity, moved herself and her belongings back home to her mother's in Jacksboro, the Reviewers broke into the now-bachelorized star's fortified mansion, and in a theretofore-unseen revue of comprehensiveness, disintegrated pretty much everything owned by the star, except a fine first-edition King James Bible, which they'd left open to Revelation.

That was a week ago. Today, the Reviewers were back.

Lone "Reviewer" Strikes Den of Iniquity
AUSTIN (AP)

by Binny Bake and Lofer Hagosiab
Austin American-Statesman Staff

In an act of vandalism the police are suggesting was committed by the gang of vandals known as the Reviewers, an Austin woman's home was invaded late Thursday night.

"Due to the nature of the act, the thing that got acted on, and the implement found at the scene," said Sgt. Towel, who is in charge of the investigation, "it is being thought by us the police that the perpetrator is a radical breakaway from the Reviewers, a loner with worse occurrences in his plans. Like murder."

The police are not naming the woman, as she might be a victim of a sexual crime.

"We are on the side of caution so we're keeping her name anonymous," said Sgt. Towel. "At the present moment in time we are focusing our ongoing investigation on finding a person of interest, who is identified only by the name 'Mr. Brady.'"

Murphy stopped chewing.

"But we believe this name to be an alias," added Sgt. Towel.

It is the policy of the *Austin American-Statesman* not to reveal the names of victims of sexual crimes, but we're going to do it anyway, because we found out who it was, and everybody else does it, anyway. It's Marcia Brodsky, of East Thirty-First Street. (Cont'd A5)

Murphy quickly turned to page A5. A5 discovered no continuation. Neither did A6 or A4 or A14 or C1 or D9 or *Parade* or the weather or the rest of the goddam paper. Murphy ticker-taped the entire issue and turned on *Fox News*, where the reporter Pamela DisGorges was speaking to the camera, a small white house in the background.

...erview Miss Brodsky this morning at the scene of last night's alleged attack.

The camera zoomed out, revealing a very attractive young woman standing next to Pamela and speaking into the microphone the reporter offered her. The wad of sandwich Murphy had been working on seemed to expand in his mouth.

MB: I can't believe this. I just can't believe this. I just cannot believe it. This is unbelievable. Oh god. Oh, I was afraid this would happen.

No way *could she be alive.*

PD: Miss Brodsky, the police seem to suspect a Reviewer is responsible for this. Do you agree?

MB: He seemed like such a nice man on the phone. I can't comprehend why he—anyone—would do such a thing. He didn't even, uh, experience Rance before he... slew...

Brodsky sneezed and began to weep, tears glistening in the morning sun.

PD: Are we to understand that it—

MB: Rance. *His* name was... Rance.

PD: ...that Rance was a doll?

The sandwich wad was now bullying its way down Murphy's esophagus.

MB: Rance was more a human being than Mr. Brady will ever be, more than you or I will ever be.

PD: Discounting the Reviewers, is there anyone else who might have targeted your business? Possibly a dissatisfied client?

MB: I. Have. No. Dissatisfied. Clients.

PD: Do you believe that perhaps the Reviewers targeted you because your home is not zoned for business?

MB: That's not immoral. Plus, I don't have to be zoned; I don't advertise on the property, so I'm totally law-abiding.

PD: Do you believe that perhaps the Reviewers targeted you because of your immoral status as a major-league abuser of unsecured credit?

MB: How do you know about that? I paid every single penny back and wrote apology notes to all the card-company presidents and I go to DA twice a week and just last night I dreamed that Daddy was proud of me and no longer spins in his grave. Rance was making us rich.

PD: Do you believe the Reviewers targeted you because of your immoral and illegal occupation as a madam?

MB: I'm not a madam. What I do isn't immoral or illegal.

PD: Selling sex? I believe it is both.

MB: I do not sell sex. I rent out self-pleasuring opportunities. Rance was simply a highly refined marital aid. If you went over to your friend's house and said to her, "Hey, Jenny, mind if I use your vibrator for a minute?" and you said, "Sure, just leave a dime on the bureau when you're done," that'd be just the same, right? And that's not illegal. As long as you pay tax on the dime. No one is being exploited. The only differences are that Rance simply has more settings than your basic off-the-rack vibrator, and more than a dime is being made per opportunity. And it's perfectly moral, too. You show me where in the Bible it says no self-pleasuring.

PD: Leviticus 25:5, "Do not reap what grows of itself or harvest the grapes of your untended vines."

MB: Oh. Well. Hm. That could be interpreted in a bunch of different ways, I guess.

PD: Please answer my original question. Do you believe the Reviewers are responsible for your predicament?

MB: Predicament? Go look inside. Rance is in pieces. His ichor is all over the walls. That's not a predicament, Little Miss Scoop Reporter, that's murder.

The air around Murphy grew hot and bright. The futon beneath him grew moist. It was the first time he'd ever wet the bed from pure rage. Murphy uttered a grand tantrum. He threw his television at his iMac, powdering the screens of both and setting off a small pyrotechnic show; he opened up and tipped over his refrigerator, scattering the contents; he tried to rend a paperback, but it remained unified, further infuriating him.

A soothing voice in his head:

Murphy Lee Crockett, you will bathe now. You will hone and strop your bayonet. You will dress in black. You will put on your fake beard and Oakleys and Red Man mullet cap. You will go out into the world. And you, Murphy Lee Crockett, will murder the first person you see.

XXVIII

January 2005

Okay, so Murphy Lee Crockett had not been able to kill the first person he saw. He'd come close, though, and there was still a chance: he had left the woman tied up in her own apartment. Very securely tied. Hog-tied. Murphy then decided he would drop by the big crime convention, where he would browse and mull while his victim suffered.

The big ad in the *Chronicle* a couple of days earlier had not mentioned that if one presented notarized proof of a felony arrest the box-office people would let you into the True Crime Convention for half price, or else Murphy would've brought the paperwork surrounding his conviction for the gasoline-filled-light-bulb bomb he'd detonated in a men's room when he was eleven. Though now that the whole matter had been expunged from the official juridical memory, he'd held on to the paperwork so that some future biographer might come across it in the official archives (to, of course, be acquired by Harvard following an ugly bidding war between all the Ivies, not to mention Oxford, John Rylands, and Bayerische Staatsbibliothek) and thus enrich the "Early Years" chapter of the biographer's official *Life* of the era's greatest taker of them.

"So I have to pay full price?" Murphy challenged the lady running the box office at the Palmer Auditorium. "Even though I'm a convicted felon with god knows how many other capital crimes in his past and future? Just because I forgot the proof? Just because I don't *look* evil?"

The lady, somehow moonfaced and gaunt at the same time, evidently considered the question rhetorical and so offered no response except to pop a fresh square of Nicorette and light a Misty 120. Someone farther back in line said, "Pick up the pace a little, buddy." That person added, "Or I'll kill ya," to the macabre delight of all those in the long line.

Murphy was a little tired of being everyone's mockingstock. After he'd cautiously snuck out of the woman's apartment after failing to kill her, he had gone home, taken off his disguise, and showered. He was planning to shave—the fake beard had been uncomfortable over his messy whiskers—but he was out of razors. He went next door to Porifiro's to borrow one. Porifiro had answered the door, Tom Mix in one hand, an electronic game of some kind or other. He immediately started to giggle. He did that every time he saw Murphy, lately.

"I heard," said Porifiro, "that you had your date, man."

"What?" he said, panicking. "How'd you know?"

"I didn't," he said, falling into a vortex of giggles. "I just said that to see if you *had* gone."

"Asshole. Well, yeah, I did have it, Marcia's a great piece of ass. What're you laughing at, you psycho?"

Porifiro fell to the floor and began to writhe in silent laughter. Tom Mix ran around the apartment, barking and barking. Porifiro eventually caught his breath.

"Brother, I used to work for that bitch, and I know the look on a man's face after an hour with that robot, and you've got that look, brother."

"You—"

"You look down between his legs and see that ole robot kielbasa, and you figure why not, right, no one'll know."

"I'll kill you."

"How's the old cornhole, Murphy Lee! All loose and stretchy? Wooo! You had that coming, you closet case. You really thought I'd set you up with a woman? Why would I do that? And no, you can't have a fucking safety razor."

Porifiro slammed the door. Murphy, unshorn, took a bus to the convention.

After Moonface informed him that there was no way he was gonna get any kind of discount, Murphy considered going back home for the paperwork, but on the way over, the bus had had to wait twenty minutes for a break in the stupid Fourth Annual Shin-Splints Awareness Day Double Marathon, which seemed to clog every single major thoroughfare and cross-street in the city with gimpy half-wits, most of whom carried a six-foot Styrofoam shin-on-a-stick which they waved and whipped and poked at the sky in order to draw attention to their cause. So Murphy handed Moonface two twenties that he desperately wished he'd soaked in blood before he came. These clowns would pony up a little respect if they thought he'd dredged money through blood freshly liberated from an unstoppable killer's most recent slaughter.

If. Maybe he'd change his middle name from Lee to If. He couldn't believe he'd been unable to kill that bitch. His second failure in two days. He hadn't even drawn blood, barely even touched her with Granddad's bayonet, one little poke to the back of her head. He'd probably scared her, at least, though he admitted she hadn't seemed all that terrified. She'd seemed almost like she'd been expecting someone to accost and threaten to kill her. She'd been more upset when he'd barfed while binding her up with packing tape.

He'd done a pretty good job of incapacitating her, though, so if he could just build up a little game face here at the convention, he'd go back and stick his bayonet in the crazy, disrespectful bitch's eyeball. He would not barf. He would not be seen. He would never be caught. He would begin plans for his second murder, his second for-real serial killing: Porifiro Mirrin. Murphy If Crockett.

Moonface slipped a ticket under the glass and a turnstile attendant rubber-stamped his hand with a radio-luminescent pigment. "Good morning," said the attendant, who bowed her head, and with a faultless curtsey and a wide sweep of arm welcomed him in as though it were a Roald Dahlian fantasy-land painted in hard-candy colors instead of the world's largest celebration of criminal wrongs. Roald Dahl himself, a Nazi sympathizer who as a child had accidentally sliced off his own nose and who liked to dispatch his fictional characters in merrily repugnant ways, would have been quite at home here, either as attendee, exhibitor, or subject. Murphy, who wanted more than anything to be a part of the world before him, gasped like a Little Leaguer in the Cooperstown foyer for the first time.

How many other uncaught killers were here, browsing the grisly booths? Would Murphy, by propinquity, recognize a brother? Would he, in turn, recognize Murphy? Would Murphy feel camaraderie, veneration, competition, love? Hatred? Would Murphy want to kill him?

He looked around at the crowds but saw no one with an aura that betrayed a past of ritual tort. In order to signal to any brothers (or sisters—loads of ladies in the profession), Murphy tried to flare his own serial-killer aura with a bearing-down and full-body clench, but this provoked only meteorism.

Oh *god*, how Murphy wished he'd finished off that bitch.

No matter. He would. Just be serene, patient. All the best criminals were. He unclenched, closed his eyes, waited until his breathing evened out, then opened them.

And before him was the convention's largest booth: Bolton's Second Amendment Freedom Hall, whose inventory was weaponry. It was divided into two parts: Background Check and No Background Check. The bulk of the latter were accoutrements (rope, plastic tarping, fake cop badges, caltrops, how-to books), and edged weapons, including bayonets—craftless repro bayonets, shoddy copies of his own McCoy. Murphy had decided on the ride over that bayonetting would be his signature method. With a runneled, edged weapon, there was plenty of room for creativity and experimentation and happy accidents. Dismembering, beheading, poking-themed torture, impalement, general chopping and slicing. But guns, bombs, crossbows, missile tubes, and other background-check crap requiring remote ignition or launching... all cowardly. Boring. Up-close killing, close enough that a murderer could smell the insides of his butchered victim, was for *men*.

Nevertheless, the tent excited Murphy, and served as the entryway for this black-and-red carnival of antisociety. And in an almost-divine perseveration of the metaphor, Murphy next happened upon a carnival-type ride: a life-size robotized diorama of the four presidential assassinations, in which one could participate either as assassin, with a genuine period arm (unloaded), or president, in authentic garb, at the moment of impact, with convincing squibs. And like a carnival, there were long boustrophedon lines populated with full-bladdered youths who should've gone before queueing up. Fuck that; Murphy didn't have all day. That bitch wouldn't stay hog-tied and mummy-wrapped in generic cheapo silver duct tape forever.

The next booth was bare except for a table neatly stacked with hundreds of copies of a LuLu-produced book entitled *Wherefore Scary Clowns?*, and a woman, probably the author, standing on a small blackout stage, reading from a copy of the book, which seemed to assert a theory as to why clowns and clown imagery figure so prominently in so many capital crimes. Murphy did not stay. There was so much to see.

Within an hour Murphy began to experience sensory fatigue. The booths began to run together: a Q&A forum with DNA-exonerated folks, a dealer in antiquarian crime books. (Among his stock was a little book from 1486, *De Venenis*, about poisons. Ten grand he wanted for it. What a dummy. Surely there were plenty of eely thieves roaming around here, looking for just such artifacts to pinch and fence on eBay.) There was a genuine gas chamber, in whose death chair one could sit while one's friend remotely gassed one. A faintly almondy perfume that was surely intended to mimic the odor of real sodium cyanide pervaded the entire auditorium. Nice touch.

There was a small but densely attended booth on money laundering and secret accounts, another on internet scams, and, of course, a vendor of prisoner art and writings, a robust commerce over which the state of Texas asserted notoriously gentle regulation. Only in Texas might artistically talented spree rapists make a buck representing their crimes in sculptures of chewed and molded bumf.

At the "Are You a Sociopath and If So How Bad" booth, manned by a Johns-Hopkins-trained Sikh psychopathologist, Murphy paused to study the line of men with flat affects as they patiently, calmly waited their turns. Murphy had already answered plenty of online questionnaires, and, with a sense of shame he ever struggled to own, knew already that he was not a socio-path, so he hurried on toward the end of the first row, where a PowerPoint presentation on the phenomenon of copycat crime and Young Werther's Syndrome was being given by a short man wearing a tight rugby shirt.

The next-to-last booth in the aisle was manned by the political arm of the Reviewers. They were protected by chicken wire, like an underappreci-ated band in a roadhouse. Maybe Murphy would come back and throw a beer bottle at them. And the last booth was a prison consultancy, Bottom Bunk, operated by a young woman whose tight pea-green latex catsuit stood in sensationally pornographic counterpoise to her lips, which were so red and moist it looked like she'd been eating pomegranates and sucking cock all morning. As Murphy passed by, he saw the lips say something about how her husband, the founder of the firm, wasn't able to make it today, because he was in prison doing research.

And at the back wall, behind a freestanding booth housing a wee but boom-box-voiced gasbag lecturing to an audience of none on international criminal judiciaries, was the snack bar. Murphy ordered a chocolate milk, and sat alone at one of the two round, sticky, cafeteria-type tables. He could barely think but for the booming, fanless lecturer.

never could reconcile that with the preindependence Malawian penal code

The chocolate milk snuck into the wrong tube, and Murphy choked.

"Okay, fellah?" said a man at the other table, also alone. A big man, seventy or so, dressed in a lumberjack's wool and old, cracked cowboy boots, the sole of one beginning to separate at the toe, giving it the aspect of a thirsty crocodile. He held on to a Styrofoam cup of black coffee with both hands as though it were part of the table and letting go meant falling to his death. One side of the man's face was still, as though from a stroke, but also flattened, as though his skull had just gone and jellied up one day and a child had come along and rolled it flat with her little Holly Homemaker rolling pin.

asserts that vigilantism was the only justice available to pre–civilized man or pre–customary law or pre–case law and that in fact vigilante justice would have been a laughable redundancy in the Bronze Age which satis

Murphy thought briefly about the man's question, investing it with larger meaning. *Am I okay?* Murphy was in fact quite dejected. He'd felt nearly euphoric when he arrived, but now he could only enumerate and dwell on his failures. He wasn't a sociopath, he loved his granny, he peed (*moistened*, at worst) his futon, he hadn't returned his faintly spoiled chocolate milk for something safe, like a beer, because he didn't want to be impolite. Murphy had never even really done any damage, except for his youthful arson. And the katana "murder" of a sex doll.

And this morning's home invasion and assault.

"I'm lousy, buddy, yourself?"

"Why, I'm just fine," said the man, who talked funny, probably an effect of his face injury or deformity or whatever that was. He sounded as though his gums were studded with rubber bullets instead of teeth. "Can I fetch you a napkin?"

Before Murphy could answer, the man was up and at the snack bar, plucking napkins out of a Lucite napkin box.

guidelines call for lashing to the suitably immobilized and spread-eagled accused's privates a pail into which the victims would place stones the very youngests' hands being guided by an adult relative until the accused's privates became

"What happened to you?" said the man, handing the napkins to Murphy, sitting back down, and again taking hold of his coffee-cup piton.

"Me? What happened to *you*?"

"Well, this was the result of a disagreement that ended in violence. It was well deserved, though."

"Yeah? Why?"

"I tried to take another man's blanket in the night. A cold night."

The animated half of the man's face blushed.

"Jeez, glad I asked," Murphy said, though he was curious, really. Were the men camping? Cell mates? Homos?

The blush dissipated. He politely regarded Murphy. Murphy didn't like this guy. He was too... *darling*, his granny would've said.

that is to say what future code will not care about the history of what is now becoming known as space law as inevitably astro-on-astro- or cosmo-on-cosmonaut rape or assault or casuistry will occur on international space stations

"And what brings you to the convention?"

"I'm here for research."

"That right?"

"I have this theory," said Murphy, "that there might be a killer at work, a serial killer, out in, ah, New Orleans, but the cops haven't figured out that the crimes are connected, even though the killer, I believe, has been sending taunting letters to the newspapers and the cops. I called them and offered my theory and filed reports and whatnot, but nobody seems to care."

The man nodded thoughtfully. "New Orleans is an ideal host for such a scenario."

"Really. Why?"

"Why, the police there have a reputation for discarding ethics in favor of convenience. Crimes thus proliferate in inverse proportion to the ethics discarded."

> would dispute the provisions in Sharia its capital sentence for apostasy but the sentence of earectomy in Hussein's body of torts—no pun intended—is performed under local anesthesia by a licensed physician as if the criminal were there for wart removal or

"Oh," said Murphy. "Yeah, I know all that, that's why I'm looking into the possibility myself. So that's why I'm here. I'm trying to get into the killer's mind. Trying to think like he thinks. He might even be here."

"That's exciting," said the man. Murphy observed him closely for shib-boleths of mockery, but found none.

"Yeah. Well. So, he killed six people so far. Almost seven. He's the real thing, and nobody cares."

"Hmm. Maybe the pattern is too subtle for the detectives?"

"You think I'm lying."

"Nosir, I do not."

The man had finished his coffee, and in the last thirty seconds seemed to have grown less interested in chatting, and looked like he was preparing to depart. Murphy realized he wanted the man's company. Needed.

"The fact is," Murphy said quickly, "the serial killer hasn't actually succeeded in totally killing his victims."

"I see. But the line, as I understand it, between killed and not totally killed is sharp and features no gray."

Again Murphy could not detect any sauce, though from the mouth of anyone else the statement would've been high-key sarcasm. This guy was either the driest or the most precisely earnest man he'd ever met.

"Fine. Okay, he hasn't killed anybody, though every attempt just barely fails. Just a one-in-a-billion streak of rotten luck. Tiny miscalculations resulting in the intended's survival."

"If I were an intended, I would consider my survival good luck."

That was a little judgmental. But also a slip on Murphy's part.

"Yeah, well, like I said, I'm deep inside his malformed mind, thinking like him. It's how the best minds at Quantico catch their killers, don't you know."

common to all lockups a slight physique or otherwise unable to defend oneself who is not already affiliated with a gang or harem is virtually guaranteed to be sexually assaulted badly enough to drive the person to request solitary confinement which among ordinary prisoners is the punition to be most avoided and if denied then the weakling will often commit suicide or more often try and fail at same rendering them even more victimizable

"What do his attempted murders have in common? Apart from their all being 'attempted'?"

"Can't tell you."

"All right, then."

"You seem awfully curious. Maybe it's you."

"No, not me," said the man, sincerely matter-of-fact.

"Well, that's good enough for me. You're officially off the suspect list."

"I only ask because I might be of some help here. Who's on your list?"

"You just want some credit when I catch him. Okay, tell me: how could you possibly help?"

"Well, I've known six serial killers in my day. Three were executed for their crimes, two others are on death row."

"Bull. S*hit*."

The man blushed again, purply darkening his earlier blush of embarrassment.

"Well, I…"

"What, you're a lawyer? You don't have a lawyerly look about you, no offense."

fied simply as actionable or not actionable which is of course comparable to the process of indictment but in Syria and surprisingly in the BeNeLux and Finland finds a state between the two as though a light switch position observably between on and off

"I was in the penitentiary for fourteen years. I met them there. One was a cell mate for a few months. It was his blanket I took, and paid for."

"Yeah? Who? I bet know who it is, I know my killers."

"Charles Bourque."

"No shit."

"No, none."

"Maybe you are my killer, then, in spite of your irrefutable alibi."

"No, I just got out, a week back, parole."

"You're kidding. Your first few days as a free man, you come *here*?"

"Well, I'm an element of one of the exhibits. A condition of parole."

"What was your—"

"I killed some people."

"Hm, plural, good. Murder? Manslaughter? Who? Why? Where? Are you sorry?"

> per saltum repudiated capital punishment observe drops in capital crimes until an instance so heinous that in effect vigilantism or let us say reverse vigilantism

"Also, abuse of a corpse."

Murphy paused. A curious sensation, starting at his feet, began to climb and constrict him like kudzu winding up a phone pole, a pokey but livid asphyxia that took Murphy a full ten seconds to identify as fear. Murphy wasn't on the internet messaging with some true-crime blowhard; this was a real guy, less than a body-length away, fresh out of prison for killing, *more* than killing, messing with their bodies after the fact, maybe screwing them, or chopping them up and arranging the pieces according to some horrific private symbology. Who knows what he's capable of, right now, in the True Crime Convention snack bar? Murphy, not for the first time, felt, in addition to punily frightened, holistically outclassed.

> mountebanks that diagnose with cardiomyologia long dead European nobles based purely on their portraits hanging in museums and more than a few revising all of Eur

"I mean," continued Murphy, "if you care to discuss it."

"It was a family."

"You... killed a whole *family*? Yours?"

The man did not answer. He did not seem to move. Presently, he said:

"I don't know if it'll be of any help, but one thing they all had in common was that they were all pretty likable, pretty friendly."

"What? Who? The family?"

"No, the serial killers I knew. In Angola. I'd say nice fellahs, if you didn't know any better. Even Raymond Herrmann. Looking back—"

"*Raymond Herrmann*!? Are you kidding? Jesus!"

"—he was a good friend to me."

hilariously considered by inmates at least the most honorable but if you consider the effect of a bullet to the body as not an invisible death ray like on the tamer television shows but as the strongest man in the world hitting you so hard with the end of a tack hammer that it tears your execution garment punches through your sternum and lodges in a ventricle cauterizing your flesh the round is so hot and I can assure you that based on interviews the

"What else?"

The man never let go of his coffee cup. He asked Murphy for details of the attempted murders, which Murphy gave, changing nothing but locations and dates and pronouns.

"So, whaddaya think? Any insights?"

"Well, yes," the man said after a moment. He looked right at Murphy, the first time he'd done so. The damage to the man's face was severe, the kind of wound once commonly seen among veterans of World War II. "What if..."

The scaling kudzu was now rib-cage-high.

"...your guy is..."

What must it feel like to get beaten up like that? To hear sharp pops and gristly crunches and tiny, high-pressure bursts, right inside your own head? The panic that comes with dislocation, the nausea that attends escaping blood, the helplessness of prostration, the illogic of sudden deformation, the time lost, death closer, sleep impossibly far away.

"...*not*..."

Jesus Christ, to get your eye squashed between collapsing maxillae? To get hit so hard your brain shakes loose and becomes moorless in your own skull? Do compressed eyes pop, as though gnocchi?

"…a serial killer?"

"Huh?"

"Maybe he's failing on purpose, subconsciously. He wants to kill, he thinks he does, but maybe he just doesn't have what it takes. That he's really a human, not a monster, that he just needs a little therapy or a good talking-to or a copy of *What Color Is Your Parachute.*"

"Respectfully, that's fucking stupid."

"Yessir, it could be. But it would explain why he hasn't killed anyone, and why you can't find him. You're hunting a killer, but there isn't one. You're just plain old barking up the wrong tree."

"Incorrect."

"That's not to say he, whatever he is, shouldn't be stopped. Maybe you ought to try the police again. I'll corroborate best I can, if you want me to."

"I imagine the police wouldn't listen to a word you had to say. After killing your whole family and all."

"It wasn't mine. My family is alive, as far as I know, but I surely died for them when I killed those other people."

you not the first Antarctic homicide to be swept under the permafrost so to speak for want of a sys

"Really. So you killed total strangers? I hate to judge, but that's fucking horrible." Murphy felt no shame in this statement. Murphy's program of murder was totally different than this monster's.

"It was. I was drunk and hit their car with mine. The Nguyens. Two little girls and their mother and grandparents."

"Ohh, *vehicular* homicide. I don't really count that. I take it all back. Not fucking horrible."

"Why?"

"Because it was an accident, right? Still, fourteen years is pretty light for five dead."

"And two dogs."

The man explained that his sentence for each death had been twenty-two years, but the judge who sentenced him ordered the terms to be parole-eligible and run in concurrence. The man had gotten a break for three reasons: the judge was rehabilitation-minded; the judge was a

Smirnoff man himself; and the judge all but announced that he felt that the Vietnamese were an ethnicity that in Louisiana should not carry as high a value as others—he had abstracted and simplified the family as "dead foreigners"—perforce, crimes against them were not to be reprimanded so harshly. They were recent émigrés, and since the man had killed everyone in the family, there were no relatives to speak for them, and very few friends.

"I can't believe you got parole."

"Well, I declined, but the parole board accused me of reverse false contrition and made me leave."

"You're kidding."

"Nosir."

"You wanted to stay? In prison? You're a weirdo, brother."

"Yessir."

"So why don't you do another crime and let yourself get caught and go back?"

The man said nothing. He withdrew into a brown study. His disposition seemed scolding or condescending or in some way asserting that Murphy was a simpleton, prompting Murphy to say:

"Or why don't you just kill yourself?"

"It is one of the conditions of my parole that I participate in a traveling anti-drinking-and-driving exhibit for one year."

"You're not going to kill yourself, so you can obey parole."

"Well," said the man, "yes."

"So do it after."

"The problem with suicide as an act of contrition," continued the man, "is that no one will see it as you did. It will be viewed as an act of cowardice, an escape from one's comeuppance. In fact, I think there is no way to both promise and commit true contrition. If a criminal wants to express genuine sorrow, and hurts himself, it will be seen as the criminal simply getting what he wants. The criminal, in order to be truly penitent, may not have what he wants, no matter how self-destructive or painful or steeped in real remorse."

"So I'm guessing you took Bourque's blanket so he would fuck you up."

The man, if nothing else, was practiced at saying nothing.

"What else did you do to yourself?"

After a moment the man told Murphy how it was possible to hone the edge of a plastic playing card, the durable kind they use in casinos, with a kind of sandpaper fashioned from salt and semen, achieving an edge sufficient to distaff and/or castrate without the mess and uncertainty associated with the normal prison method, which was a daylong commitment to a gradual choking-off of one's privates utilizing a garrote made from straws or some such.

generations removed can the real effect of execution be felt but like Schrödinger's cat will be both

"That's repugnant. Did you really cut them—*everything*—off? That's a lot of trouble to go through when you could've just cut your throat."

"Well, that wasn't the point."

"Your voice isn't high—sure you're not pulling my leg a little?"

"It doesn't change if castration is performed after puberty."

"You know what? You almost sound proud of yourself."

The man stood up. Murphy thought he was going to get beaten up. For one instant Murphy was entirely bound in fright kudzu. But the man said:

"Well, looks like it's time for me to go back to my booth."

"Wait, is that the one with the rusty mashed-up car, a couple down from the Black Widow booth?"

"Yes, but that's not rust. It's blood. That car was involved in another five-fatality drunk-driving crash, just a week ago. My obligation here is to talk about what I did, answer questions about the wreck, prison, and remorse, and let people see my face and my bobbed groin close up. Scared straight, et cetera. Good luck with your serial killer. If you really think there is one running around, I hope you seek assistance. This convention is a good place to find it."

"You're gonna drop your pants?"

"Yes."

"Wait, slow down. Where are you going after the convention? Staying in town?"

forgotten offhand but certainly Mexico and Uruguay were wont in drafting plead-the-belly laws which of course is an absurdity in Cathol

"I'm traveling with the convention, so next is Oklahoma City. I wouldn't stay in Austin anyway. I've got people here, and I know they'd be unhappy if they happened to run into me."

Murphy thought this a little saccharine, a little too poor-me. Maybe the man was right about his contrition paradox.

"Can I just ask you one more thing? Sir? Okay, here's a hypothetical situation: say my killer had a victim right now, all tied up, ready for dispatching, and say we were on the wall, you know, you and me, like flies, and we were watching him, how could we tell if he was a real serial killer or if he really wasn't, how could we tell? How would we know?"

The man stopped and looked down at Murphy.

He's on to me. Murphy imagined a massive SWAT/FBI/ATF/OSI raid, with tear gas and flamethrowers and bomb robots and stony Texas Rangers shod in boots made just for stomping on the fluffy heads of suspected serial killers.

continue to exercise even criminal prosecution as wholly unwrit as twelfth-century French customary law yet are quite enviably

"He would kill her."

This was a big man. Murphy looked up at his chin.

"But," continued the man, "I know he won't."

murder or not. Thank you.

XXIX

January 2005

Oh, shit, where did he come from? thought April.

In spite of the chill, April was standing on her balcony wearing only slippers and an (unlaundered) lilac bathrobe. She was watching a huge moco jumbie in the shape of a socked leg—how silly—walk down Airport Boulevard, part of some parade, when a man wearing a virtually spherical beard as dark as an attic approached, lightly startling her. He looked at first like the sort of man employed by pizza parlors and tree-trimming services to walk door-to-door deploying flyers.

"Hi," said April. "Look at all those crazy people in the street over there."

The man showed her a long, shiny metal thing, part of a car? Had she bumped into his car in the parking lot and not realized it? She was so ditzy lately! She was about to say sorry—she always apologized first, even if a situation didn't demand it—but before she could form the word, she realized that the metal thing was a long knife and that it was now poking the loose drum of skin under her chin and that it was guiding her back into her own apartment.

"Be quiet," said the man, shutting the door behind him. "Or I'll end this all right now. Now get on the floor. No, turn over onto your stomach." The man kicked away some of April's clothes and CDs and decapitated microphones and plastic toys to make a place for her to lie down. "Jesus, this place is disgusting."

"Yes, sorry."

"You," he said, "are gonna pay for my mistakes."

"You're punishing me? Why?"

"Shut up. Here."

A dull silvery object bounced next to her head and came to rest against her cheek. What was this? A toy? A ball?

"Wrap some around your mouth. All the way around your head and cover your mouth. Right. Around again. Again. Again. Again. Now around your eyes. Again. Again. Again. Again. Again. Fuck."

The roll of duct tape ran out, really upsetting the man. April heard him kick things around the room. She didn't care about the equipment—that stuff was largely invulnerable, even the mixing board, which she'd once dropped twenty feet off a stage—but don't you dare, sir, mess with the bassinet!

She was quite solidly disabled. She could neither see nor speak and could barely hear. Or breathe: if today's cedar-spore count had been any higher, she'd have been suffocating to death, so stuffed up did her sinuses get during that particular allergy season.

Surprise, the man sat on her bottom. She'd expected him to hike up her lilac robe—god, how she wished she'd washed it, she knew it probably smelled like a bean cassoulet—slice off her underwear, and get down to the heart of the... punishment, but nuh-uh, he took hold of both her wrists and bound them up with wire behind her, that's what it felt like, anyway, and tight, too, no slack like in thrillers where the victim eventually wriggles out. No, this hurt. He did the same to her feet, or started to, but paused, climbed off her, and made a horrible sound, a wet cataclysm.

Of all the world's nasty smells, that of fresh throw-up was to April the most familiar, given all the over-drunk boys she'd had in her apartment.

The man recovered and sat on her ass again, cowboy style. He started to cry, potent, coughy honks cut passim with brief roars of fury. It shook her whole body. What a strangely backward situation. She felt just fine—happy, even; she'd be a mother soon, just days at the most—it was the guy in charge who was a wreck.

The man, maybe also sensing the illogic of their intercourse, of her unvictimlike serenity, yelled, "What the fuck is wrong with you, you slutty blond bitch?" and slapped the back of her head. Then, *ow*, a sharp poke right at the base of her skull, forceful, then more so, until it broke the skin with a *pk* that seemed awfully loud in the close acoustics of her tape-wrapped head. That big knife. It crept in. It hurt. The tip scratched something deep in there, a tube or channel that felt important, neurophysiologically quick. April began to cry, squeezing out a few tears that collected in little pockets at the bridge of her nose where the stuck-down tape kept them from dripping down her cheeks.

All at once April felt terribly mortal. Afraid. What if this was more than just a routine rape? Torture? *Murder*? April began to pray to and bargain with and question whoever it was that designed and oversaw this whole mess.

The man dismounted, taking the sharp thing with him. He stopped crying.

A hard whack to the back of her legs. Instinctively she folded them up so her bound feet touched her bottom. The man immediately sat on her shins, pinning her legs in an uncomfortable jackknife position. He began to work on her ankles again, maybe undoing and retying them. He did the same with her bound hands. Then he wrapped the wire or whatever around her neck. This grandly panicked her. But he didn't tighten it, instead leaving it a slack loop. More fiddling. He stood. Ah. He'd hog-tied her. If she struggled at all, she'd tighten the wire around her neck and strangle herself.

It became quiet. Presently a breath of chilly air rolled over her, and she could hear, briefly, the din of the shin-splint awareness walk. Then it stopped. Had he left? Was he coming back? She tested her bonds; the slip-knot immediately and irreversibly tightened. She froze. She was taking no chances now. If she got free, she was going to go and get it. Today. Her surrogate wouldn't mind. She'd been cool all this time.

Please come back. Do your business, then let me go.

Even in her caution and patience, the wire gradually tightened around her neck, yank by infinitesimal yank. Okay, I've been punished enough, don't ya think? I said sorry, this is scary, let me go now, please, pretty please with sugar and so on, etc., goddammit. Please?

April stayed immobilized for what must have been hours. Never had she been so universally cramped and numb.

The breath of January air again, the drone of the shin-splint marathon. Who knew so many were afflicted? Those poor people.

He pulled on the wire, choking her, crimping her jugulars. This is it. I pay with my own life. This world is a godless and random place.

The pressure let up. It felt like he'd cut the wire around her neck. She relaxed. Her feet were still bound tightly to her hands behind her, but she could breathe now, relax her body.

"You owe your life to a broken-faced mass killer," the man said, and hit her on the back of the head again.

January drifted over her once again. This time he slammed the door. All quiet.

April began with violent full-body torques, sidling around her messy studio like a snake in the dunes. That her feet and hands were numb made it possible to wrench and yank and twist in ways that would've been unthinkable had her extremities been sensate. When the feeling returned, they'd surely have been damaged, maybe she'd lose one. Who cared. If she could reach she'd chew off a hand for liberty. Who knew how long that man would be gone.

It grew dark outside. She was exhausted. She fell asleep, waking every so often, screaming impotently into the silver tape, her nose stuffed up from allergies, feeling like she was going to asphyxiate.

It was light when she finally awoke. Rested, she redoubled her efforts. Soon she freed her numb hands. The feeling slowly returned and she was able to begin a delicate stage of her escape: peeling the packing tape from her face without tearing off her eyelids. Later, lids intact but lashes and brows all uprooted, she set to freeing her feet. By the time she pulled off the last ring of wire she was in tears from anxiety and urgency and fear that the man would return. She jumped up. She didn't change clothes. She'd get it and then drive to Seattle to begin their new lives.

XXX

Porifiro spent some of the money he'd made working for Marcia on a $135-per-hour psychologist named Sam Glazing Constantine whom he'd found after googling "closet me shrink." It had taken Porifiro ten fifty-minute sessions to finally mention to the doctor that there was a possibility that Porifiro might be slightly attracted to men. It took another five to fully admit that he was in truth unilaterally gay, and had known as much since he was fourteen years old, when he'd found himself accidentally poking the other kids on the wrestling team with the unretractable erection in his sweatpants. He had finally quit the team after being called out—*Pori's got a boner again!*—one too many times. He had since been covering this central Porifiro fact with the masculinity of baseball, lowrider trikes, weightlifting, girl-chasing, and homophobia. The last's most recent expression had been to Casey.

"I think I… well, I'm into him," said Porifiro in his sixteenth session.

"And that means…," said Dr. Constantine.

"Ah, man, you're gonna make me say it?"

"It will be another step toward self-acceptance."

"I like him."

"Love, you mean?"

"Yeah, I guess."

"You want to have sex with him?"

"Yeah, I do."

"In how bad a way?"

"The worst," said Porifiro, dropping to the floor and jamming his face into the carpet. "I've been into him since the day we met. But I was always mean to him, ratting him out for little things, poaching on his work, buddy-buddying up to Marcia and excluding him."

"That's for schoolchildren," said Constantine, scooting his wheeled, black-morocco chair up closer to Porifiro. "Go apologize and confess. That is my advice as a doctor."

"Shrinks aren't supposed to give advice," said Porifiro, lifting his head up, only to be met with the bottom of Constantine's chocolate loafer. "They're supposed to pretend to listen and make you analyze yourself."

"What've you got to lose? Maybe he likes you in return but was acting mean because you were hurting him."

"What if—"

"Our time is up."

Porifiro went home. He sat on his bed and played with his baseball cards. He put them away and played Simon for a while. Loneliness advanced. All three of his neighbors were gone.

Porifiro showered and shaved. He put on his best outfit, a pinstriped suit, light green shirt, and pink tie he'd worn to the prom senior year at Austin High. Then he drove his trike to Casey's.

"What do you want?" Casey said, standing in the door in a robe. He was unshaven and his beard was dotted with whiskers of red and gray, pleasantly contrasting his brown, side-parted hair. In one hand he held a short, broad glass filled with ice and and a translucent golden liquid of some kind. He took a big sip.

"Uh, I just came over to tell you I'm gonna apologize to Marcia and see if I can't get my job back. I've been feeling bad about it since it happened, and especially bad when I heard about Rance getting killed."

Casey stood for a long moment, looking at Porifiro through the screen.

"What're you dressed like that for? You look like a French gangster."

"Well, I wanted to apologize to you, too, for how mean I was all that time at Marcia's."

"That doesn't explain the suit."

"I thought I should look good for a double apology. You won't accept it?"

"No. I don't know. Maybe."

"Can I come in?"

"No."

"Then you come outside."

Casey *arrgh*ed, but stepped out onto the lawn anyway.

"My shrink said I got nothing to lose, so here goes."

Porifiro took two steps toward Casey and kissed him hard on the mouth. His whiskers were sharp, his lips tasted of whiskey. His body did not return the kiss.

"Whatcha think about that," said Porifiro, stepping back, utterly unmoored, statefallen, and as defenseless as he'd ever been. He wished Dr. Constantine was here, holding him up or carting him away.

Casey said nothing. He went back inside, letting the screen door fall hard behind him. Porifiro let his arms drop. He was going to stand here till he was arrested or struck by lightning.

After a moment, from inside the house:

"Are you coming or not?"

Porifiro went inside.

After a few hours of kissing, awkward confessions, and memorable sex—orgasms and gymnastic experiments and sex toys—the experienced man and the virginal one (if you don't count Rance) fell asleep in Casey's immodest, king-size bed. They woke up together in the early afternoon. Porifiro said, "Hey, why don't we both apologize to Marcia? We'll just drop by. Maybe it'll be just like it was before, us all working together, except now you and me'll be a couple."

"Are we?"

"You don't hate me anymore, do you?"

"No."

"So we're together. C'mon."

* * *

Marcia had not restarted her business, had not moved, had not been paid by the insurance company, had not cleaned or even gone into the boudoir. She played *Canfield* and *Alchemy* on her computer, she invited Schmidt back into the house, she avoided the phone, she lived in a faded pink nightie. The culprit had not been caught. And the sight of her two ex-employees standing on her doorstep did not improve her mood.

"Wasn't expecting to see you guys again."

"Hi."

"I kinda thought you might call me after the murder, but when you didn't…"

"We came to apologize," said Casey.

Porifiro added, "For being mean to you and for making you fire us, and not calling when they killed Rance."

"I don't know," she said, studying the two men, who were standing awfully close together for enemies. "Are you guys friends now?"

By way of an affirmative, they kissed: a sloppy, noisy, oral clash.

"Oh. My god. I knew it."

They sat around the kitchen table. Marcia made coffee. She was still not happy with the two men, but she was delighted that they were a couple. Maybe it had been Rance who was getting in their way.

"Are you gonna go back into business?" said Casey.

"I don't know. I might be burned out."

"C'mon," said Porifiro, smiling, his arm around Casey. "Think about the welfare of your employees. And I bet you got half a million for a new Rance."

"I don't want a new one. There will only ever be one Rance."

"He isn't fixable?"

"Are you kidding? They chopped him up. Into literally hundreds of little cubes and slivers and wedges. With a sword."

"A sword?" said Porifiro, sitting up straight.

"I thought he just got busted up," said Casey.

"Well, he didn't. He was the target of a gruesome edged-weapon murder."

"Any idea who did it?"

"Maybe a Reviewer. They didn't leave any fingerprints."

"You sure it was a sword?" said Porifiro.

"Yeah, the blade broke off. The cops took it."

"Marcia," said Porifiro, "how did the guy pay?"

"Cash and a half-off ticket."

"Oh no."

"What?"

"I gave a half-off ticket to a guy I hate and talked him into setting up a date, and I led him to believe he was gonna get with you, but, surprise, he was gonna find Rance. And look, the guy owns a big, sharp sword, I saw it when he bought it, and it was so sharp it gave him two horrible cuts. I thought it'd be funny, setting him up. But oh dear."

"But," said Casey, "the guy came here *armed.*"

"And... he thought he was going to be with—"

"He was after you, Marcia."

"Call the police!"

"He moved out of the Parallel Apartments the day after it happened."

"They'll find him."

"How will we prove it was him?"

"Still have the half-off ticket?"

"Yeah."

"Maybe there's a fingerprint on it."

XXXI

Justine's right ear ached and was all sweaty from talking on the phone for the past hour and a half. Her eyes stung from the droplets of sweat that had found their way to them from her forehead, her voice was hoarse and her mouth rubbery from screaming, her neck and shoulder cramped and shaky from squeezing the phone, her stomach and throat burning from the nausea caused by a particular bit of news, her legs numb from kneeling on the floor, folding laundry, six loads of it—every article in the apartment, including bedding and oven mitts and all the clothes Rose had left behind a month ago—because Justine had needed to at least be partly productive during the ninety-minute throe of shock, hate, rage, and shame that Rose's call—the first one Justine had answered since the Jeep episode—had prompted.

Earlier, Justine had had nothing to do but launder and despair and wait around for her water to break, but now she had to shower and scrub and put on clean clothes, because Rose would be here soon to pick her up and take her to St. David's, where her grandmother—grandmother!—was about to give birth to a baby girl named Edith—*Aunt* Edith—after which the new mother and the newborn, and Edith's fifty-four-years-older-sister, Livia, *Livia*, would be waiting for Rose to arrive with Justine. A genuine family reunion, orchestrated by Rose, would then take place, and, at the same time, the anticipation of Justine's own contribution would sweeten it all. An absurd and sudden explosion of family, each of them falling reborn from the sky, free of secrets, cleansed of venom and hatred, delivered from estrangement, shucked of lonesomeness and lies; each of them newly put forth in lively primaries; each an heiress, lost and now found, to herself; all soon to be crowded into Charlotte's hospital recovery room, Livia and her mother already having been reunited by Rose's brilliant subterfuge.

"How did you find them?" Justine had asked, between mournful yowls, about twenty-five minutes into the phone conversation. "My grandmother doesn't make *friends*."

"I'm very charming, that's how," Rose had said, pacing back and forth in Matt's apartment, where she'd spent the last month planning and executing the multiway match of her life. "First, I tried to steal Dartmouth for you, as a peace pipe, but Charlotte caught me and won the tug-of-war. She asked me to drive her someplace, an estate sale, and she told me what it was like—her confusion and guilt when you ran away, her relief at your phone call that night when you let her know you were alive, when you asked her to leave you alone, said that you'd be fine but weren't coming back, that it was Livia and Lou you hated, though you wouldn't tell her why."

"How about Livia?" said Justine, folding a sensationally stained dish towel.

"I know her only through Archibold Bamberger. Never met her."

"They're still together?" said Justine, not really caring. "Are they married?"

"Yep, nope. I happened to be friends with Archibold from work. I told him I knew that Livia and her mother were in a bad way. I told him about you, and that I needed his help to make the family right again. I have a lot at stake here, too, you know. All he had to do was persuade Livia to understand and forgive her mother, and I did the rest. He adores all three of you, loves you all, had been plain busted up over the mutual estrangement, so he immediately agreed. I told him that Livia wouldn't have to contact her mother at all; she just had to allow for the possibility of reunion, with Archibold as witness. After a couple of weeks, he succeeded. Then I set it up so your mom and Charlotte'd run into each other at a yard sale. It was easy and worked perfectly. There was crying and hugging, and even a polite argument over who had dibs on a broken hummingbird feeder."

"I hate you, Rose."

"I know, but listen, I have some things to tell you, things they know but never told you. Or each other, until recently. It will explain a lot. It's very Greek and tragic, so keep an open mind."

"I don't want to know!"

Rose began with the revelation in the diaries, and ended with the truth about Livia and Lou: the truth about Justine. For the first time in her life Justine was stumped of crying. But she didn't hang up. Justine found herself at a strange peace, as if she'd known all along. It was the only thing that made sense, an accidental incest. It explained why her mother didn't like her, why Charlotte hated Lou, why Lou ran off after Dot's death. So much more.

"Okay? Justine?"

"I don't know if I ever want to see you again. Or them."

"You really don't love me anymore?"

"No, I don't think I do. You're not the same."

"I did this all for you. This is what you came to Austin for, to find out what-the-fuck, right?"

"It's what *I* came back for. I didn't ask for any help. And I didn't ask for any horrible truths."

"You kinda did."

"You're making everything up, aren't you?" said Justine, though she knew everything Rose had uttered was the truth. "To get back at me for leaving you."

"No."

"Is there anything else?"

"That's it," said Rose, though Justine was sure it wasn't. They traded silences.

"What was that noise?" said Justine, finally, not wanting to hang up, but not wanting to talk, either.

"Matt, blending. What's that racket over there?"

"The shin-splint walkers."

"Oh. Yeah. They're out on our street, too. Big marathon."

Another long pause. Justine was cashed. She could no longer fold, think. But she was not uncomfortable. Just tranquil. Tranquilized. As long as none of the painful or embarrassing auguries of imminent childbirth woke her, she would sleep very well.

"Well," she said.

"Well."

"Bye."

"Wait," said Rose. "There is one more thing."

"I'm tired of bawling, I'm tired of feeling sick. I'm getting off the phone now."

"Charlotte's pregnant," said Rose, before Justine could hang up. "She's due today, just like you. What about that, huh? This is all destiny. There's supposed to be a reunion today. She's at the hospital now, on account of her age. Livia's there, too. And I'm going to come pick you up and take you there, and the Durants will be complete again. Then you can break up with me."

"B—"

"See you in a few."

Rose immediately hung up.

Justine, to her surprise, found herself in a state of faint, tearless hope. A wave of forgiveness followed, along with empathy, and understanding, all of these plaited neatly into a peace. She chose an outfit, turned on the shower, and refolded Rose's things while the water got hot. She thought deeply about makeup, about her brows, about two children the same age but two generations apart growing up together, about Rose's chest, about her grandmother's cigarettes, about her mother's hair, about Lou's cavernous hands, about what he must have felt—was he dead now?—about Dot, her delusions of healing, about the manifold imaginary deaths Justine used to make her mother suffer, about the fabric-like softness of the old ten-dollar bill Franklin had given her for sucking him off in a Port Authority shadow. Justine thought about the old alleyway Camaro and her little poem lip-glossed on the backseat—all she remembered was the last word, *pennysworth*; she thought about the fear in the eyes of Sherpa's raccoon, about the barn-sour tarantula in his driveway, about KVET and how little it had changed, about Betsey and her J-shaped scar—was she still alive, did Johnsonson go to New York to help her?

"Help!" cried somebody outside.

The somebody knocked at the door, loud even over the racket of the incessant parade. "Are you home? Plans have changed."

Justine paused in her deep review.

"It's me, April, your neighbor, open up Justine?"

Justine opened the door.

"God, April, what happened? Are you bleeding? What's that in your hair?"

April ran past Justine into the apartment.

"Hey," said Justine. "What—?"

"It's an emergency, I have to get it now, I can't wait, I'll explain everything later, but I was just attacked and I'm worried he'll come back, so after I leave, lock your door and call the police." April was in the kitchen yanking open all the drawers. "We need a good, sharp, clean knife, don't you have any? Even one?"

"April, who—"

"Are they in the dishwasher? Where's your dishwasher?"

"I don't have a dishwasher, and I don't keep sharp knives. April, who attacked you? Did he... violate you? Did you call the police? Jeez, the back of your neck. You're bleeding."

"Anything sharp at all?"

"I'm calling the police right now, where's my phone, I just had it, April sit down and relax, I have scissors somewhere, I'll help you cut that tape or whatever out of your hair."

"We need a knife!"

"Okay, okay, I have a box cutter in my purse, right there, on the counter."

"Oh, this is perfect."

"Don't cut yourself sticking the blade out."

"I won't. How much do I stick it out? Like an inch? I should know how thick it is, I read *What to Expect*, but..."

"Yeah, I guess an inch, doesn't really matter. Do you see my phone?"

"I love you so much, Justine, I know you did such a good job for me. Maybe we can do it again."

April bent to her knees, and with one quick, sure motion, lifted Justine's superhero shirt up to just below her breasts and slit open Justine's belly below the navel, a transverse incision ten inches long and an inch deep. As Justine stepped backward, uttering a distressed half gulp, half scream that April hadn't expected, the walls of the cut, at first tidily bloodless and striated, grew mucky with fatty blood. God, had she cut the *baby*? Justine landed almost silently on a dozen neat stacks of laundry, eyes open, hands reaching for nothing.

"Okay? Justine? Be still. I love you. 'Kay? This'll be over in a second. Thank you for carrying. Can you help me hold it open?"

The floor of the valley of the cut began to split, unzip, the internal pressure overruling the strength of the deepest layer of muscle and connective tissue, until a little shoulder appeared, then a head crowned, turning and lolling as if impatient and long-ready, scolding April for taking her sweet time to get here. Carefully April worked her hands between the lips of the cut. Justine's hands clawed and shook. It probably hurt as much as a real delivery, poor Justine, it would be over soon. April drew open the cut, curtains.

A girl!

She had cut the little thing, but not too bad, a little nick on the shoulder, it would be all right. Many years from now, Montserrat, tipsy from champagne, would show it off to friends and family at Christmas dinner... *Look what Mama did to me!*

April cut the umbilicus as close to her baby as she dared. Hm, that looked right. A perfect, perfect child. Montserrat, after the soprano, who was also perfect. Montserrat cried, loud and healthy, a proper natal screech. When the infant paused to take a breath, April heard the shower running, as if it was waiting for them. They went into the bathroom, and April tested the stream of water with her elbow. Oh, a bit too hot, let's turn it down a little, Montserrat, all right? April would never let this baby out of her arms, even if it meant never sleeping, never eating, never changing clothes again. April, nightie and all, stepped into the spray of water, holding Montserrat to her chest, and washed the fluids and membranes and sticky disorder of childbirth away.

PART THREE

XXXII

January 2005

Just a few hours after he left behind that bitchy neighbor tied up in her apartment, Murphy jammed all his belongings into his Chevette and drove to his granny's house on Chicon, where he was not completely surprised to find a coroner's van idling in the driveway, both back doors open, as if in wait to swallow another corpse. Inside the house the coroner and a couple of lackeys were all staring at clipboards and ignoring the evidently occupied black body bag on the living-room divan, the same piece of furniture she'd purchased new after Murphy had burned their first house down, in 1982. He'd lived here, in the house State Farm pretty much paid for, from ages nine to eighteen.

"Who are you?" said the coroner, a shortish, walleyed man with full, pink lips that Murphy imagined women would go out of their way to be kissed by but which reminded him of the animals inside conch shells.

"Is that my granny?"

"Who are you?"

"Murphy Lee Crockett."

"Let's find out."

Before Murphy could protest, a lackey reached down and unzipped the bag halfway down, revealing his granny's sunken face and cornucopian bosom.

"Yeah, that's my grandmother, Lydia Theuerdank Crockett."

"ID."

Murphy handed it to him. "What happened?"

"Looks like a stroke. Probably didn't suffer much."

The telephone rang. A lackey picked it up.

"What?" said the coroner.

"Boss, we got an emergency. Murder-suicide."

"Why's that an emergency? Everybody's dead."

"I don't know, they just said, 'Be there. Now.'"

"Well, let's go, then. Mr. Crockett, you won't mind if we leave your gra'mama till tomorrow morning?"

Murphy spent the next few hours unpacking his car and moving into his old bedroom at the back of the house, while Granny's body lay on the divan. He set up Granny's antique Dell desktop and searched the internet for information on Texas probate law, specifically how, and how quickly, he could claim his inheritance. It all came down to lawyers. Murphy, bitter and gleeful at once, went to bed. The sheets were exactly the same ones that had been on his bed when he moved out a decade and a half ago. They felt flaky and moist all at once, like a refrigerated croissant. Murphy finally fell asleep, just as a wisp of fetor began to circulate the house.

In the morning, after the coroner—who had clearly been up all night—came to collect Granny, Murphy began to go through the house. He started with drawers and cabinets and closets, moving on to the garage, shed, and attic, keeping anything that was simultaneously of potential value or use—spare change, combs, old lottery tickets, costume jewelry, tools, the lawnmower, all of her old books and mathematical journals, a stack of crumply 1930s one-dollar silver certificates that must've somehow survived the fire and that the internet informed him were worth only a few cents over face value, a mink-like coat, pain medication, fire extinguishers, a half dozen bluebonnet paintings, checkbooks, bank cards, a gold pen-and-pencil set—and through the *Chronicle* and Craigslist he scheduled an estate sale for February 17 at 8 a.m., where he planned to sell everything else, including linens, clothes, the carpet off the floor, silverware, and furniture, especially that carrion divan.

A month later, Murphy woke at 6 a.m. Sale day! He made coffee, checked to be sure everything had a price tag, drew a sign that read in black Magic Marker NO EARLY BIRDS!!, nailed it to a sharpened wooden stake, and, as he was sticking it in the front yard, found himself being arrested at gunpoint for destruction of private property. A sex doll.

"I can't believe that's all you're arresting me for," he said, through the steel mesh separating the front seat of the cruiser from the backseat, the cops from the robbers. "There's so much you'll never know."

"'Zat right," said the driver, Detective Irv Thwear. "Like what else."

"You think I'm stupid? I'm not gonna tell you."

"I think you're making up a criminal history for attention, a cry for help. Very common."

"No, it's true, I've done some things a lot awfuller than hacking up a sex robot—shit, that was nothing."

"Well I guess they'll all be your little secrets, then," said the partner, Detective Merry Gastélum. Both cops yawned.

"I'll tell you one thing I did," said Murphy.

"No, I don't wanna know," said one detective. "Me neither," said the other.

"I—"

"Shut up," said Thwear. "We know you're not a real criminal. Not a genuine psycho. Just a one-hit weirdo amateur, not capable of killing."

"But, guys, listen! I shot a lady in the ass with a poison dart!"

"Oh yeah? What was her name?" said Thwear.

"I'm not telling you."

"See, you're just making that shit up."

"No! I also shot a guy, kicked at a lady, poisoned at a guy, and stuck a guy with a halberd."

"So tell me names."

"Right."

"Don't worry, we can't prove anything, so, and you're already in trouble."

"And a really minor thing, I hog-tied a lady and stuck a bayonet like a half-inch into the back of her neck."

"Okay, pal, shut up."

"She—"

"Shut up, blowhard liar baby."

"I'm not falling for your reverse psychology."

"Whatever."

Murphy held his breath. He was starting to braise in his own sweaty desire to brag.

"I'm a serial killer."

Threar and Gastélum fell apart in laughter so disabling they had to pull over.

"Fuck y'all!"

"I cannot," said Gastélum, "*wait* to throw this guy outta my cruiser."

"Jan Bardee, Grady Gregg, Cynthia Braden, Bobby Brudi, Peter Bradley." Murphy leaned back, smiling like a clown.

"They're all dead?"

"Well. No."

"So you're a serial fuckup."

"They'd all be dead if not for tiny miscalculations."

"I know Gregg," said Thwear. "I wish you'd finished him off."

"So," said Gastélum, "if I'm not mistaken, you did have a little killing theme going."

"Yeah," said Murphy, impalsied with the ambrosial delight and relief of being understood for a change. "You're the first person to put it together."

"But," continued Gastélum, "the robot—Rance, he was called—doesn't fit with your pattern. Which leads me to speculate that Marcia Brodsky— who fits perfectly—was your intended victim. But it was too dark to see that it wasn't a real person you were fractioning."

"Goddam right! God, I love you."

"But who was the lady you stabbed in the head? Alice?"

"Oh, that would've been perfect! No, her name was April something. She just happened to be someone I ran into when I was in a bad mood. Totally random."

"'Zat right," said Gastélum. "Any chance her last name was Carole?"

"Yeah!"

"Hear that, Irv?"

"Yeah. Interesting. You oughta've killed her, Crockett."

"I *know*."

"She was arrested for murder a few days ago. She cut a baby from its mother's womb."

"Jesus, *she* did that? Even I'm not that horrible."

Thwear pulled over. He and Gastélum got out of the cruiser and opened a back door.

"Out."

"What for?"

"Now."

Murphy climbed out. Thwear turned him around, removed his cuffs, and spun Murphy back around to face the two detectives.

"You're letting me go?"

"Turn around again."

Murphy did. One of them recuffed him.

"Murphy Lee Crocket, you are under arrest for attempted murder. Seven counts."

"You told me…"

"We lied," they said.

XXXIII

February 2005

What had surprised and gratified April more than anything that first week was that she'd begun to produce milk. She had been nursing Montserrat because that was what *What to Expect the First Year* had said babies did, but, since Montserrat was the product of a generous surrogate rather than April's own imperfect, monstrous, unholy body, she had expected nothing from herself but aridity and nothing from the baby but squally disappointment. And that's exactly what she got for more than a week—the short, ugly stay at her ex-conquest Veniamin's house in Tulsa, which ended with April toppling his entertainment center on the Scrabble game-in-progress and Veniamin calling the police; April fleeing in her old Mazda with the baby before they arrived; the parade of truckers' motels on the way to Washington State; the night at her old high-school boyfriend George's house in Puyallup, when he remarked on the unexpected snugness of her vagina, he having presumed that the organ in its postnatal condition would be like fucking an empty coffee can—until one afternoon, in her car, on the ferry to Bainbridge Island off Seattle, Montserrat, for the first time, began nursing in what seemed to be profound contentment. April gently disengaged, squeezed her nipple, and watched the extraordinary liquid roll over her knuckles. April began to cry with such ululating violence that a man in a pickup truck next to her got out and tapped on her windshield, *Are you all right, Miss?* and she, nodding, tearful: *Yes! Yes! Yes!*

What had also surprised her was that it all ended, and how. April had been a mother only a month.

Montserrat soon stopped nursing. She began to lose weight, she stopped crying, she never slept, her pallor-dimmed face became almost immotile. They finally left the poisonous Northwest and arrived in Detroit, where the first thing April did was go to an upscale healthful grocery store. April tucked a tightly bundled Montserrat into a corner of the grocery cart and surrounded her with produce—fresh collards, a tree of broccoli, jungle-green kale, little red new potatoes, a huge clove of garlic, a melon. They strolled past shelves of formula and jars of organic whirled peas and tubes of herbal cradle-cap remedies, finally pausing at a small display of baby blankets, foot-and-a-half squares of pastel merino, their edges foliated with multitudes of nylon tags of all sizes, how charming, a baby loves the tag on its blanket! And, oh, it was only a step April took, it was only a single step away from her baby, when a man she'd seen in the parking lot snuck up and plucked Montserrat out of the cart and ran, and a half dozen people all at once crowded the otherwise-empty aisle, all ordinary-looking citizens except for the big black pistols they pointed at April and their deep, vicious voices yelling, *"Down, down on the ground..."* How hard and cold the store's lino-leum floor felt against her mouth, how filthy the cracks in the floor looked close up, how it tasted of salty tomatoes and pencil shavings, and, later, how dear and welcome that linoleum seemed compared to the black and airless interior of the police car; compared to the penetrating fluorescents in the ceiling of the interrogation room; compared to the wine-and-spoiled-cream smell of the bunk in her cell; compared to the gingivitis breath of the man who informed her that Montserrat had been dead for at least two days before April was captured; compared to the weightlessness of her empty arms and the knowledge that they would remain so until they put her to death. They would not, though. April would go to bed tonight, she would wait until the guard did his rounds, she would tie one end of the ripped-out seam of a pillowcase around a bedpost and the other end around her neck, and she would turn to one side, then to her stomach, and to her other side and back to her back; the motion of an alligator tearing prey, but silent, and slow, around ten times, then twenty, then twenty-one, twenty-two twenty-three twenty-four

XXXIV

January 2005

After hanging up with Justine, Rose ran around Matt's apartment looking for the keys to her Jeep. She hadn't seen her girlfriend in a month, and Rose's plan to bring her back together with her family was being foiled by missing keys. She jumped onto Matt's couch and jammed her hands down between the cushions.

"Aagh! Where!"

"Chill, Rose, Jesus," said Matt. "There's no hurry *now*. Right? You two made up, you've matchmade a whole family, so settle the fuck down."

"Aagh! Charlotte's due *any minute*! And maybe Justine, too!"

"Did you check the front door?"

Rose paused. She ran to the door. There they were, with her copy of Matt's key still in the lock. She yanked them out, and, without even shutting his front door, she ran outside.

"Put on a coat!" Matt shouted after her.

Rose drove off, clipping a curb with a rear tire.

Rose hoped that when she got there Justine would be having her first contractions. Oh, how exquisite it would be if Rose could race her to St. David's, where she and her grandmother could have their babies at the same time.

Oh, shit, shouldn't have run that red light. It had *just* turned, though. Rose liked to think of it as an orange light.

What had changed in the past month? Had Justine toppled all of her trophies, tossed Rose's frozen chicken tikka masala dinners, thrown out and replaced the futon mattress, plucked Rose's hairs out of the household hairbrush, subtracted from her psyche everything Rose? Had she cut herself; did she have a special internet friend, a pharmacy job, a fresh life?

At the corner of South First and Oltorf was another orange light. Rose snuck through it. So did a city cop, who pulled her over with all the fanfare and fireworks a cop car could produce.

"Sir!" said Rose, as the pigeon-footed cop walked slowly up to the window.

"Licenseregistrationproofofinsurance."

"Sir," said Rose, emptying into the passenger seat the bowling bag she used for glove-compartment overflow. "I have to be somewhere, it's extremely important, can we postpone this? What if I just drive over to the station later and we can finish there? Just an hour or two, promise."

"Lcnsregstrnprfinsrnce."

"Please? I'd be so grateful, sir!"

The cop spoke into his radio. "Requesting backup."

Rose handed all her car-related documents over. Her registration had expired, her car needed inspecting, and she'd been meaning, *so meaning*, to get with Geico. At least a three-hundred dollar ticket. But of course that wasn't what worried her.

The cop went back to his cruiser and sat on the edge of the driver's seat, legs stretched out, his boot heels scraping the asphalt. Backup arrived. Both cops came up to the car, one on either side.

"You shoulda called your PO when you moved, uh, Miss Balaguer."

"I did, sir!" But she hadn't. She'd been planning to call the same day she was going to bring all her tardy automotive paperwork up-to-date.

"Sure you did."

"Sir, it's a matter of life and death! I'll turn myself in once I'm all finished! Pleeeeeeze?"

"You better call the richest person you know, because your bail's gonna be sky-high. Why don't you step out of the car."

Instead, Rose deftly slipped the Jeep into gear and drove away. In her rearview the two cops were still standing there. Then they jumped into their cars and came after her.

Rose flew. She darted around Sunday drivers, she swerved down side streets, she sped down one-ways, she bullied her way through intersections, she nearly clipped a man on a ten-speed, she did clip a vast Ford F-350, she entered and exited the freeway, she drove through alleys, she nosed pedestrians out of the way. There were so many of them, pedestrians, too many, a parade's worth, yes, that's a *parade*, jammed with limping clods, so many that she could not elbow her way through them. She was forced to stop completely, surrounded by shin-splint sufferers. Before she could even climb out of her Jeep, two pistols were pointed right at her head.

The back of the cruiser seemed not to have a heating vent. The cold of the black vinyl seat ate right through her corduroys and nipped at her thighs. Would her tears freeze on her cheeks?

Rose leaned her forehead against the Plexiglas dividing the front seat from the back. The last time she was arrested, she'd been able to work her handcuffs so that they slid under her bottom and wound up in front, but these were too tight. What could she do if she escaped, anyway? Jog to the hospital? She was too far away.

She was going to miss everything.

Late in the evening Rose paid her cellie, DeeDee MacHugh, five bucks cash to borrow her smuggled-in Blackberry.

"Three minutes," said DeeDee, handing Rose the phone. "Ready? Go!"

Rose dialed Livia.

Livia told her everything.

Rose spent the following month in a cell with DeeDee, unable to rise from her bunk, until Livia bailed her out on the last day of a violent storm.

XXXV

February 2005

From the northwest a cold front arrived, bearing temperatures too frigid
and ice too sharp for central Texas—for its people, its mood, its traffic, its
spirit—and from the south another front arrived, a hot, rolling auster of
smoke and ash from burning Mexican forestland.

The two vast weathers collided at noon in an eight-hundred-mile, east–
west line at whose midpoint lay the unprepared city of Austin, where the
climatic meeting at first produced violent gusts of wind, then brief, gray
tornadoes, then single-digit temperatures, then, for two full days, an ice
storm that left an inch-thick membrane of opaque, ash-invested ice on trees
and buildings and cars and streets and the homeless. The city's residents
woke the first morning to discover that a feathery layer of fine, grayish soot
had covered every surface inside their homes except for the clean white areas
on the pillows where they'd laid their heads. Shuddering coughs, exploded
pipes, downed power lines, breathing through T-shirts, emergency-vehicle
sirens caroling all day and night, stalled and wrecked cars and killed trees
blocking the treacherous roads, whole families sleeping on mattresses in

kitchens where their ovens, doors wide open, efficiently warmed them all, but sometimes also, through faults in the appliances' air-fuel mixtures, imperfectly combusted the natural gas, asphyxiating them. Dozens died this way, and many others died in wrecks and collapses, from exposure, falls, plummeting icicles, and the failure of machines. But most were going to survive the frigid black interruption and return to their lives, running pharmacies, collecting debts, delivering deliveries, cashiering at bookstores, doing time, avoiding punishment, burbling like babies do, idling in wealth, chroming tricycles, outrunning loneliness, reporting weekly to parole officers, moving from one home to another, conspiring with police to lie to the world to save the soul, and possibly the life, of one woman who against the longest odds in medicine had persisted in living, under powerful sedation, in a hospital whose generator had not choked and died on the nearly unbreathable air of a smoke-and-ice storm stalled over her city.

When Justine finally awoke, on the last morning of the unique storm, after a month's profound, drug-induced unconsciousness, she screamed for Rose, for her mother, for Dot, for Charlotte, for her baby, but only a nurse came, who adjusted her a bit, spun dials and punched buttons on the many devices and consoles and portable computers that filled the hospital room at St. David's, and who ignored Justine's questions, instead calling for a doctor, a thin woman wearing rubber gloves and an ID badge—Dr. Leona Kraus—whose clothes hung from her like wash on a line.

"Well, hello, Justine. You gave us quite a fright for a while."

"What...?" she said, eyes barely open, mouth dry as the Sonoran.

"You're extremely lucky. There are only a few documented cases of..."

Dr. Kraus had been instructed by the FBI not to inform Justine of anything that had happened since her assault, though she could talk about its medical consequences. The doctor had readily agreed with the FBI, because she thought the shock of so much bad news might actually kill her patient. Dr. Kraus had seen such things before. It was why she'd decided to go along with Justine's mother's plan.

"What do you remember?"

"I'm thirsty."

Dr. Kraus left the room and came back with a bottle of warm Poland Spring. She opened it for her. The doctor, who had once been attacked herself, empathized with Justine, and the anxiety of the memory of her experience caused her hand to shake as she gave her patient the bottle. Justine took it with both hands, which were also trembling. Dr. Kraus, when under stress, would often conjure sudden morbid scenarios in which she was forced by an unknown god to choose from two sufferances. Today she found herself struggling with whether she would rather be raped again by a man they'd never catch or endure what Justine had.

"You were attacked. Do you remember that?"

The doctor could not decide. Her rape, a violent assault inside a walled cemetery in New Orleans by a man she never saw who smelled of roasted meat and rubber and whose footsteps when running away reminded her of centaurs, had been thirty years before, and was still the standard to which she compared all suffering.

"Somebody cut you very badly."

Dr. Kraus clenched her thighs and drove her legs as close to each other as she could.

Justine, with no little effort, lifted her arms and touched her belly. Under the blankets and sheet and thin hospital gown Justine could feel a long... what? A discontinuity. With the little strength that remained in her atrophying muscles, she threw back the covers and hiked up her gown. Two crowded lines of small white comma-like scars ran on either side of a raised, foot-long scar across her sunken abdomen. The configuration reminded Justine of a zipper. She touched it.

"Where's my baby?"

The bathroom door was open. Dr. Kraus caught a reflection of herself in the mirror. Oh, that's what she looked like when at the mercy of her PTSD's cunning trials: a smiling crone. She wondered what Justine would see when she looked into the mirrors of her post-trauma life.

"I'm going to raise your backrest."

When her upper half had been raised high enough to see under the closed door the shadows of people walking by, Justine said, "I think I remember... I was waiting to see my grandmother."

"I see."

"And mother and my, uh, Rose. But my neighbor came over first and cut my stomach."

Sweat leached through Dr. Kraus's bra and was now appearing in patches on her blue blouse. She would have to decide soon.

"It felt like she was drawing a line on there but the point accidentally slipped in. Oh, I remember, it was my box cutter. Did she hurt my baby?"

"I don't know."

Justine began to cry, but, dehydrated as she was, she produced no tears, only sobs, violent ones, like temblors sine-waving her body.

This alarmed Dr. Kraus—Justine was hardly out of the woods, and any trauma, physical or mental, was liable to be dangerous. The doctor immediately produced a sedative and injected it into Justine's PICC line. Dr. Kraus decided at that moment that she would rather endure the rape again than be eviscerated and rendered childless. The god in her head who'd forced her to choose withdrew. The doctor relaxed. When she got home, she would begin taking a higher dose of ziprasidone.

"I'm afraid," said the doctor, when Justine had worn herself out, "that I don't know much except that I performed three surgeries on you, and you came close to death more than once. But you're going to be fine. We're in the middle of a storm right now, and travel is precarious, but your family will be here as soon as they can. They'll answer your questions."

Justine could not bring herself to form the words *what family.* The doctor dabbed at the sweat on Justine's face and arms. She sat with her for a while. Justine fell asleep, dreaming of Halloween pumpkins and yawning animals.

Justine did not notice that Livia had come in till she was sitting next to her bed, holding her daughter's hand. Livia wore a parka and hiking boots. Clots of ice hung in her black hair. She wore her makeup just as she had when Justine was young. The shades of muted color seemed no longer to accent her features but to smother the evidence of their decline. Particularly her shadow and mascara. Looking into her eyes way back when was… well, had Justine ever really looked into her mother's eyes? And now, was she really, genuinely looking? If so, what for? Her baby? Did Livia know what had happened? Instead of asking, Justine blurred her vision so her mother looked as she always did in Justine's memory, a nulliform wash of grays, moving like a cloud of swifts.

"It's me," said her mother. "Just me."

Livia had spent three weeks in this same hospital, after the final pop of the guilt of a lifetime of lies. She was no longer afraid of the truths emergent, no longer afraid of her daughter and what she knew. In that vast bed, among its attendance of monitors and pumps and tubes, her daughter looked like a broken doll. *This is my fault.*

"Tell me," said Justine, already certain that her child was dead, "what happened to my baby."

With her fingers Livia combed melting ice out of her hair. She fought an urge to eat it, the slick, grayish lumps, how good it would feel on her throat, so dry now from the zero-humidity hospital atmosphere.

"I've got something to tell you first."

Justine looked around the room. The doctor was gone. The TV was on, a dance contest of some sort.

"It's Charlotte," said Livia.

Whenever she spoke that name aloud Livia would gradually notice in a corner of her field of vision a figure: her mother, a mere punch of black, a featureless silhouette, a smear of oblivion, standing open-armed, as if wait ing for an explanation of her death and why it occurred at a moment when living was worth the fighting for. "She passed away, during childbirth. Her baby didn't make it either."

"Edith?"

"Edith. They died on January 17. A month ago. The same day you were..."

Justine turned away. She did not wish to look at her mother's age-hatched face, her graying hair, her dispersing sexiness; she did not want to watch as she shook beneath the weight of her duty to her daughter, or redden at the guilt of her relief that the bearing was now done. Justine was ashamed to feel a tiny bit of relief that there would be no Edith for her to covet, and a grander relief that she would not have to confront Charlotte at all.

"Justine?"

Charlotte had not survived, this was true.

But Livia had lied about Edith. Edith was alive and healthy. Upon Charlotte's death, Livia became guardian.

Yesterday morning, at home, while Livia was holding Edith in her lap, looking for evidence in the baby's rather stern face that the two of them were related, the telephone rang with the news from the FBI that the woman who'd stolen Justine's baby had been caught.

"What about the baby?" Livia said to the FBI agent, calmly; she knew the answer. Everybody did.

A moment of static, then:

"I'm sorry to report that the child has passed away."

Outside, the storm threw ice at the windows.

"I'm sorry," the agent repeated.

Edith began to cry. Archibold came into the room and took Edith out of Livia's lap. Livia looked down at her thighs where Edith had been lying. Her jeans were still warm. She leaned forward until she could see her sneakers. If Justine survived, these shoes would take Livia to see her daughter, and Livia would have to tell her that Edith was alive, but that Babette was dead; that Livia got to be a mother again, and Justine didn't.

"I wish it was me," said Livia.

"Pardon?" said the FBI agent.

"What?" said Archibold.

"Are you all right?" both of them said at once.

"I don't know."

"I must report also that the kidnapper is dead, too," said the agent.

"Thank you."

"We won't release anything to the press until you have notified your loved ones."

Livia hung up. She stood. A tendril of cold wind found its way into the ill-insulated old house, chilling Livia's bare ankles and gently stirring the leaves of the old dieffenbachia in the corner before finally falling to the floor, motionless.

"Who was it?" said Archibold, but Livia didn't hear. She left the room, went through the kitchen to the back door, and walked out into the storm, coatless, sockless, alone.

The snow, a few inches deep, eddied and drifted in the buffets of wind. A great *cligk-cacagt* could be heard now and then as a tree limb conceded to the weight of its coats of ice. Livia walked down the alley, block after block, anesthetic to the cold, until she was stopped by a massive felled sycamore blocking the way. She sat in the snow.

A notion struck her hard, a swift wherret to the side of her head. She realized how cold it was, how cold *she* was. She had left her sister and her husband alone. She began to make her way back, tearing at the new notion, testing its solidity and mettle. Yes, it might work.

At home, Archibold placed Livia in a hot bath. She shivered alarmingly.

He massaged her toes and feet. Edith lay on the bathroom floor, grasping, kicking, throwing her tiny fists around.

"I didn't even know you'd left," he said. "What happened?"

Livia told him the FBI agent's news. She also mentioned the idea that had struck her as she'd sat by the sycamore.

"That will never work," he said, sitting back against the sink.

"I don't think there's any choice. You've heard Dr. Kraus talk about the dangers of mental trauma after serious physical trauma."

"Justine just learned the truth about herself, her birth, her real father, and now you want to wipe all that away with a *bigger* lie?"

Archibold allowed Edith to squeeze his pinkie. How powerful this little thing was.

"The truth'll kill her, Arch."

"Ouch, leggo!" said Archibold, pretending to draw his pinkie away from Edith, who squealed in delight. "Hey, leggo, you!"

"I can't take care of her. I have a child, but I don't want one, and Justine and Rose, who want one, have nothing. Theirs was murdered. It seems obvious to me that Edith should be theirs."

"Yes, but why the big deception dance?"

"I know Justine will be happier if she thinks her own baby survived. She has no real connection to Edith. An obscure infant aunt."

"She'll find out someday," said Archibold, his voice rising. "Then she'll be devastated. She'll have been deceived again. And I can't even imagine how Edith would take that news when she grows up."

Edith let Archibold's pinkie go and began to cry.

"Bring me the phone," said Livia. "I'm going to call the doctor and the FBI agent. This will work."

"One secret, many mouths."

Archibold picked up Edith and left the bathroom. Livia, finally warm, closed her eyes and slid down till the water covered her face.

Only Dr. Kraus, Livia, Archibold, and the FBI would ever have to know.

After a full two minutes underwater, Livia realized that Archibold was not going to bring her the phone. She climbed out, put on her terry-cloth robe without drying off, and called Dr. Kraus. Livia explained her plan. She asked the doctor how hard it would be to fake a birth certificate. The doctor said she could do it.

Later, Livia told Archibold that Edith was going to become Babette. Even Rose wouldn't know. Livia would tell her Edith had been given up for adoption.

"They'll find out," whispered Archibold, sitting by Edith's crib, watching her sleep.

Justine, covered in sweat, tried to push a lock of hair off her forehead, but it resisted. Her mother reached over to help but Justine batted her hand away. She decided she would not ask again what had happened to her baby. It was quite obvious, anyway. She didn't want to know the details. Poor Rose surely did not take this news well.

"Rose will be here soon," said Livia.

"I don't care."

"But I think you will."

"What's that mean?"

"Don't you love Rose?"

Dr. Kraus came into the room. She turned off the TV. She asked Justine if she felt like eating. Justine did not feel like eating. She felt like nothing: a wet, aching zero.

Livia looked away as the doctor lifted up Justine's paper gown. The scar was surrounded on all sides by livid stretch marks. Livia's own belly was furrowed with them, reptile and angry, and when she was younger, every time she'd been with a lover who pretended to ignore them, or, worse, paid them fetishistic attention, her resentment of Justine grew that much blacker. Now, though, at the sight of her daughter's scars, a patchy scape broken up only by a violet rope of tissue, she felt no schadenfreude. Now she only wished her own scars were worse, that her own belly had been lacerated, raped by a thief's hands, and emptied of a daughter.

Dr. Kraus watched the two women. Justine lay on her bed with great propriety, as if it were a rampart over a borderless demesne she governed with an authority granted of her infirmity. Justine was in truth helpless, highly mortal, and as brittly vulnerable as a lacewing, but her essence seemed powerful. Livia, though, appeared uncomfortable, off-balance, and little; a floundering tourist in a very large country. Dr. Kraus wondered whether she was doing the right thing. She told herself yes; it was best for her patient.

Livia fidgeted. She was growing hot beneath her sweater and coat. Where the hell was Rose? She was only a day out of jail, and only freshly informed that Justine was awake, and of the existence of Babette.

Livia called Rose.

"Where are you?"

"I'm right here."

Rose, brushed with snow, holding a well-bundled object in her arms, entered.

"Justine," she said, "meet Babette, our daughter."

Livia watched her lie hang in the room, a black gossamer catafalque.

XXXVI

August 2009

Babette was mad at her mother. It seemed like whenever Babette found something she loved, Mommy took it away. Babette had found a salamander under a half-buried brick in the alley, where she wasn't supposed to go. He was dark gray and decorated with yellow dots, one of which was shaped like a heart. She'd brought him inside to show her mother, but she simply took him away, saying salamanders had poisonous skin secretions.

"Then why can you hold him?" shouted Babette, glad she hadn't licked the salamander. Babette liked to taste things. Dirt, the outsides of cans, hubcaps, the wrong end of the toothbrush, her mother's hair while she was sleeping.

"I'm an adult."

"Rose never takes my stuff away!"

Babette liked Rose more than her main mother. Maybe it was supposed to be like that. Babette did love them the same, though. Well, maybe Rose just a tiny bit more.

Her mother put Mander in a shoebox on top of the refrigerator with some lettuce and a pickle-jar lid filled with water.

Babette decided to take something of her mother's as payback. She began to go through the lower drawers of her mother's dresser. She had to drag a folding chair in from the den to get to the top one. Inside were lots of panties, a roll of dimes, a chipped arrowhead, two fifty-dollar bills, a key ring with like a thousand keys on it, and... what was this?

It was a flat-bottomed wooden egg with a doll painted on it. Babette wondered if the doll was for her, a present, even though Babette's birthday was months away.

In general, Babette didn't care for dolls. She liked nature. She was happiest when in the yard rolling doodlebugs around and breaking sticks and examining dandelions and licking trees and watching birds. Especially birds. Man and lady cardinals playing in the sycamores, bluejays as big as chickens harassing the neighborhood cats, cooing doves, and, every now and then, owls. They would sometimes take a seat at the very top of a phone pole in the alley, where they would watch the world. But Babette's favorites were the parrots. She had her own. Green, a petit Quaker parrot, wasn't really hers, but he had made his home in her mother's big giant Château Frontenac birdhouse on the pole in the backyard. Green was a collector. He would snatch pennies and barrettes and pecans and bottle caps and take them to his nest. Green hadn't been coming out as much lately. Mommy said it was because it was summer and he was hot and tired, and Rose said it was because he was on a trip to visit friends in Sweetwater.

Green and all the other wild things in the backyard were far preferable to dress-up and tennis and Binni Ballerina and Moon Sand Adventure Island and electric guitars and dune buggies and bubbles and all the other stuff she had in the house. Borrrr*ing*. Especially dolls.

But this one, the doll in the top dresser drawer, was special. For one, it was purloined. For two, Babette had dropped it when taking it out of Rose's drawer, and it had broken in half, where inside was another doll—exactly the same, except a little smaller. Babette picked it up and shook it. There was stuff inside! More dolls? She dropped it again. It didn't break, but instead rolled under the bed, right to the middle. Babette crawled under. It was nice here. She shook her new doll again. It was hard to see in the dark, but she could feel a little groove in the doll, right in the middle. It ran all the way around like a belt. Babette got her little fingernails into the groove and, with a grimacy effort, pulled it apart. Another doll!

Babette spent the next day opening doll after doll with whatever got the job done: a nail file, toenail clippers, the key to her toy cash register, a quarter, a kick down the hallway. The smaller the dolls got, the harder they were to open. Now she had nine, each of which she'd reassembled and lined up on the picnic table in the backyard.

The smallest one was no larger than a Jelly Belly. Was there another one inside? She tried everything she could think of to open it. She hit it with a hammer, but she kept missing, making little white marks on the concrete walkway. She stomped on it in her Baby Britches cowboy boots, she threw it against the house, she mashed it in the utility-room door, she dropped *Gone with the Wind* on it. She even stuck it under the car tire in the driveway, but no one seemed to need to go anywhere.

"Mommy, why don't you go to the store."

"Why, what do you need, darling?"

"Um... some... beans."

"You just want me to leave the house so you can get the salamander down."

Babette had not thought of that. Maybe she could have both Mander and the littlest doll!

"I really need some beans."

"Go play."

Babette stomped off. She retrieved her doll from the driveway. She reintegrated the other dolls as best she could and replaced them in her mother's top drawer, keeping the little one in a black purse with a silver chain strap that Rose's friend Matt had given her. For the rest of the day Babette schemed on how to crack open the little doll.

That night, after Justine went to bed and Rose was lying under a blanket on the divan playing chess on her laptop, Babette came out of her room.

"Rose, can you help me open this?" she said, handing her other mother the tiny doll.

"Where'd you get this?" said Rose, leaning over to examine it under the lamp. Much of the paint had been worn away from Babette's labors.

"From... Green. It fell out of his nest."

"That right."

"Yep. There's something inside, I bet."

"This," said Rose, standing up, seeming as tall as the ceiling and dark as a storm, "is your mother's. It's the smallest one. There's nothing inside. I want you to go put it back in the other dolls and go to bed."

"But there *is* something inside!"

"Shake it. Doesn't make any noise. Empty. See? Let me put you to bed. Want a juice box?"

Babette lay in bed with her purse and the little doll inside. She sucked on her juice box. She took the doll out. She tried to bite it. She bit as hard as she could. It tasted salty and dry, like the dirt in the backyard. She rolled it around on her tongue, tasting the alley, Mander and his brick, Green and his nest, Dartmouth's gravestone, the bitter tulip petals, the raspy wooden fence, the flaking paint on the picnic table, the handle of the screen door, the cool, weedy dirt in the cracks in the walk.

Babette spit the doll out into her hands, dried it on the sheet, picked off the last flecks of green and red paint, popped it back into her mouth, and, with the last sip in her cran-raspberry juice box, Babette Balaguer Moppett swallowed the littlest doll whole.

This book would have foundered long ago without the encouragement, heed, and counsel of the following: Rebecca Beegle, Robert and Cathy Cotter, Karen and Joe Etherton, Melissa and Brian Dempsey, Maria La Ganga and Keith Harmon, Bug and Betty Cotton, Ron DeGroot and Mary Jo Pehl, Carly Nelson, Adam Krefman, Adam Eaglin, Andi Winnette, Jude Spaith, Wayne Alan Brenner, Nancy Gore, Jackie Kelly, Kim Kronzer, Gaylon Greer, Diane Owens Prettyman, Pansy Flick, Delaine Mueller, and so many others I have surely and inexcusably failed to mention. My profound thanks to all.

Bill Cotter lives in Austin with the performance artist Annie La Ganga.